*Praise for Caprice Crane's novels*

**FAMILY AFFAIR**

"Perceptive, touching, and always hilarious, this is Caprice Crane's best work yet. It's an irresistible story with equal parts humor and heart."

—Emily Giffin, *New York Times* bestselling author of *Love the One You're With*

"The phrase 'You don't marry the man; you marry his family' has never rung so true. *Family Affair* is so full of heart and humor, you'll want to squeeze into the family station wagon and sit shotgun for the ride."

—Stephanie Klein, *New York Times* bestselling author of *Straight Up and Dirty* and *Moose*

"With a finely tuned ear for dialogue and a biting sense of humor, *Family Affair* is another winner. Crane is masterful at creating lovably flawed characters and placing them in hilariously relatable predicaments. I simply adored this book because no one does fiction funnier than Caprice Crane."

—Jen Lancaster, *New York Times* bestselling author of *Pretty in Plaid*

"An unflinchingly honest, fiercely funny, unexpectedly tender story of a marriage between two very appealing people you'll root for every step of the way."

—Melissa Senate, author of *The Secret of Joy*

"Hilarious and sharp, with perfect emotional pitch, *Family Affair* provides everything Caprice Crane fans have come to expect—freshness, truth, and fun."

—Lani Diane Rich, author of *Wish You Were Here*

"This is a clever and unique take on the romantic comedy—witty, touching, and often laugh-out-loud funny. I loved it."

—Alison Pace, author of *City Dog*

**FORGET ABOUT IT**

"So funny and wise, I forgot about my own problems while reading it."

—Valerie Frankel, author of *Thin Is the New Happy*

"So clever I wish *I* had amnesia so I could read it again for the first time."

—Jen Lancaster

"Another triumph for the author . . . Jordan's transformation from subservient to assertive is incredibly fun and empowering."

—*Romantic Times*

"Savage wit and breathtaking tenderness . . . Caprice Crane has romantic comedy in her DNA."

—Jeff Arch, Oscar-nominated screenwriter of *Sleepless in Seattle*

"Hilarious . . . delightful from start to finish."

—Stacey Ballis, author of *The Spinster Sisters*

**STUPID AND CONTAGIOUS**

"Definitely not your mother's chick lit . . . filled with one hilarious and clever surprise after the next."

—*Romantic Times*

"With this winning romantic comedy, former MTV head writer Crane delivers a first novel reminiscent of Laura Zigman's bestselling *Animal Husbandry*. Crane makes light comedy, usually so difficult to create and sustain, look effortless."

—*Booklist*

"Crane's . . . style of writing is both endearing and hysterically funny."

—*Star Magazine*

"A truly exceptional book—funny, twisted, clever, mean, and always brilliant."

—Anna Maxted, author of *A Tale of Two Sisters*

"So much fun . . . snappy dialogue . . . Crane's giddy, playful prose feels fresh."

—*Publishers Weekly*

"Heaven Albright, the irrepressible and sexy heroine, is bursting with humor that is smart and infectious."

—Brian Doyle-Murray, co-writer of *Caddyshack*

"*Stupid and Contagious* is anything but stupid and is completely contagious. Infectious, riotous, and hip beyond belief, it's a great read."

—Isabel Rose, author of *The J.A.P. Chronicles*

"A witty romantic comedy debut."

—*Kirkus Reviews*

"Smart and feisty! Milk-snorting funny and playfully intriguing! Love it!"

—Karen Salmansohn, author of *The Bounce Back Book*

"Insanely funny and outrageous, *Stupid and Contagious* effortlessly captures the glorious awkwardness of becoming who you are, finding that special someone who drives you crazy, and ultimately following your dreams wherever they may take you."

—Erica Kennedy, author of *Bling*

"Caprice Crane's writing is so cool, I feel like the geek girl stalking her locker, trying to slide a mix CD through the slats before she spots me. *Stupid and Contagious* is hilarious and insightful. A book with its own soundtrack, this is one not to miss."

—Pamela Ribon, author of *Why Moms Are Weird*

"Caprice Crane brings her respect for music and all of its universal sentiment into her stylish, page-turning, sharp-tongued debut novel."

—Liza Palmer, author of *Seeing Me Naked*

"Caprice Crane rocks! This is the best book I've read in a long, long time. Sharp, original, and wickedly funny, this is a must-read. I absolutely loved it."

—Johanna Edwards, bestselling author of *How to Be Cool*

ALSO BY CAPRICE CRANE

*Stupid and Contagious*

*Forget About It*

*family affair*

# *family affair*

A NOVEL

Caprice Crane

BANTAM BOOKS
NEW YORK

A Bantam Books Trade Paperback Original



Published in the United States by Bantam Books, an imprint of The Random House Publishing Group, a division of Random House, Inc., New York.



Library of Congress Cataloging-in-Publication Data
Crane, Caprice.
Family affair : a novel / Caprice Crane.
p. cm.
ISBN 978-0-553-38623-3
eBook ISBN 978-0-553-90694-3
1. Married people—Fiction. 2. Marital conflict—Fiction.
3. Extended families—Fiction. 4. Family—Fiction. I. Title.
PS3603.R379F36 2009
813'.6—dc22 2009020741

Printed in the United States of America

www.bantamdell.com

2 4 6 8 9 7 5 3 1

Book designed by Caroline Cunningham

For my fabulous grandmother Betty Yaeger, whose antics are only forgiven because she firmly believes she's the queen of England—or some facsimile thereof. The woman who at ninety-three years old said to my mother the night before her most recent birthday, "Why is everybody celebrating you? *I'm* the one who went through all the suffering and the labor." A truly magnificent one-of-a-kind being, whom I adore despite—and *because of*—all she is. This one's for you, Grandma.

*"Blood's thicker than mud.*

*It's a family affair. . . ."*

—SLY AND THE FAMILY STONE

# *acknowledgments*

First, and always, I thank my mom, Tina Louise, whom I love, cherish, and adore more than could ever be expressed right here. You are my heart.

Thanks to the rest of my tiny family, which actually leaves only my grandmother and my stepmom, Ginger Crane. I love you. This year was a hard one. (R.I.P., Dad. "Go placidly amid the noise and haste. . . .")

Well, and my dog, Max, my baby shih tzu, who is not so much a baby anymore but I keep lying to myself to keep him young. Max is the most handsome boy with the most stunning underbite that has ever graced a face.

Thanks to Sarah Self at Gersh, my awesome agent, who dubbed this "The Year of the Crane." (Hopefully, I'll get more than *one*, but I'll take what I can get.) Thanks to Jenny Bent, for guiding me to Bantam/Random House, and to my amazing editor, Danielle Perez, for welcoming me to my new publishing home. And to all the other wonderful people at Bantam/Random House who are working so hard on my behalf.

Huge thanks to two friends who read and reread this book tirelessly: David Vanker, for helping me see the forest through the trees and always reminding me of Thomas Mann's quote "Only the exhaustive is truly interesting." And to Chris Keeslar, whose magic extends far beyond his World of Warcraft game console.

And of course a giant thank-you to the rest of my dearest friends, who really are my family when it comes down to it: Rick Biolsi, Adam Carl, Denise Diforio, Glen E. Friedman, Dave Fruehe, Gilly Garrett, the Goodmans, the Gores, Jeff Judah, Devon Kellgren, Jacqueline Lord, Nez Mandel, the McNowns, Missy Peregrym, the Pruetts, Simone Reyes, Gabe Sachs, Jeff Schneider, Allison Schroeder, Michelle Sterne, Joe Vernon, Amanda Voelker, Kim Whalen, Scotty Wood, and Harley Zinker.

Last but certainly not least, the extraordinary Armstrong family: Jeremy, Nancy, Gordon, and the rest of the ever-growing clan. The partial inspiration for this book. Had Jer and I not broken up in high school . . . this could have been us. We certainly caused enough trouble.

*family affair*

# *layla*

Eric Clapton stole Pattie Boyd from George Harrison. This is common knowledge by now. What's less well known is that Eric Clapton stole my father from my mother. Our nuclear family was another casualty of the undying allure of sex, drugs, and platinum-selling vinyl. I used to wonder what would steal my own marital happiness.

Being named after a Clapton song is a mixed blessing. There's the instant recognition factor, sure, but it also provides every would-be suitor a ready-made pickup line: "Layla—like the song? Were your parents listening to that song when your mom got knocked up?"

"No," I always reply, "but wouldn't it be cool if my name were Bruiser, 'cause then our names would rhyme!"

In seventh grade, Garret Paulson ventured a little lyrical perversion and taunted me with "Layla, you've got me on my knees; Layla, I'm begging, darlin', please." I got the last laugh, or rather, twenty or so seventh-graders at Presley Middle School did, when I swung my field-hockey stick into his groin. Talk about being on your knees . . . Live and learn, I guess.

The name choice was my father's doing. "Layla" was his favorite song, and my mom didn't argue—she liked the idea of me not having a popular name. Hers is Sue, and she was surrounded by Sues all her life, constantly answering when she wasn't called and feeling like just one among many. From the start, she wanted me to stand out—thought it was my destiny—so she went along with Layla. And dressed me in a tie-dyed Onesie.

After all the years of having my name, for some reason I still get a kick out of hearing it—almost every time. The exception is the case of its being barked at me as if I wasn't only nine feet away from the person shouting it. This time, it's Brett, my husband.

"Layla!" he yells, again.

I'll tell you why I haven't answered: because I know the acoustics of this house. I know when someone can hear you and when they can't. I know because I live here. And because I'm not an idiot. Yet he thinks that when I call his name and he's in the very next room—looking at a game on the TV or screwing around on his computer or whatever the case may be—I don't know he can totally hear me. He'll ignore me and then act all innocent. It insults my intelligence at its very core.

So I'm returning the favor. He knows damn well I can hear him. Just like he heard me this morning when I was trying to get his attention. Of course, his boy Troy Aikman was talking on the TV at the time, and I knew he'd want to watch.

My ignoring him seems petty, I realize, but he's driven me to it. We weren't always like this—just lately. And I know I'm the one who sounds like the jerk in this situation, but I'm only reacting to the way he's been treating me. Which doesn't make it better, I suppose, but it at least puts things into context.

"Could you not hear me?" Brett asks, as he storms around our place looking for something.

"What?" I say. "Did you say something?"

"I was calling you from the other room."

"Oh, I'm sorry," I reply, genuine as can be. "I didn't hear you." *Just like you never seem to hear me anymore unless it's convenient.*

"Have you seen my keys?" he asks.

"I think so. In the kitchen. Or maybe on top of the hamper. Yeah, the hamper. Definitely on top of the hamper."

He walks toward the bathroom without uttering anything resembling a thank-you, and I hear the keys jingle as he grabs them. Then I hear the front door open.

"See you at the game?" he calls out.

"Um . . ." For a split second I debate whether or not I should go. Then I consider the fact that I've been rather lax in my game attendance of late. And I also remember that at least I'll have Brooke, my best friend from grade school, there to keep me company. "You bet."

• • •

Brooke and I sit together at the fifty-yard line, and I chomp on stale popcorn as she rates the asses of the guys on the opposing team.

"I'm gonna give him a seven," she says. "I think it's hairy."

"Gross. Why would you think that?"

"Because he's already going bald, and hair tends to migrate. When they don't have hair on their head, they seem to have it everywhere they don't want it."

"Okay," I say. "Which begs the question, why, if it's hairy, does he still get a seven? That's a fairly decent score."

"I take it back. Make it a five." Then she points to another guy. "He gets a two. Too big. The bigger the butt, the more chances of skid marks. I've found they don't wipe well when they have big butts. Too much land to cover."

"I'm kind of horrified right now."

"Try doing the laundry. *That's* what's horrifying."

"Whose imaginary big-butted laundry are you doing?" I ask, because Brooke hasn't been in a relationship for at least a year.

"Nobody's. By choice."

"Nice work if you can get it," I say, as I watch Brett run along the sideline, his shock of dark hair flopping every which way. At six-two, one hundred ninety pounds, with shoulders out to here and a body in perfect fighting condition, you'd think he might be running onto the field himself to take the next handoff. And I know that nearly every female in the stadium is wondering what he looks like in those spandex shorts and compression shirts they wear at practice—I've heard them talking in the ladies' room.

"How's the coach lately?"

"He's good," I say, as I shove a handful of popcorn into my mouth.

"Has he even once looked up to see you in the stands?"

"He's trying to win a game, Brooke," I defend. "He knows I'm here."

"He used to always look up. That's all I'm saying."

"Well, thank you for pointing that out to me," I answer, as if I hadn't noticed. I sure as hell had noticed. I don't know if he appreciates my even coming to the games anymore. Hence my aforementioned recent lack of attendance.

I've done my damnedest to be a good wife—to always be supportive and make sure he knows, every day, how much I love him. I've spent many a day and night standing on the sidelines, wearing a hat with a large plastic beak jutting out the front, screeching and waving as I watch the team for which he's defensive coordinator. As I watched them lose. And lose. And lose. Never mind that I don't even really like football—I love Brett. And he loves football. He always has. I learned the basics so I could at least follow along, even though he'd still say I need Football 101. I was there cheering him on through every down of what was originally a miserable college coaching career. To me it was a failure only in name, because I was as proud of him as I would be if he'd never lost a game, even though the University of California at Culver City (UCCC) Condors were on their way to setting a new collegiate Division III record in losses that year. To his credit, even though the team had one of the lowest winning percentages ever, they had the highest graduation rate in the conference. At Brett's insistence, he and the head coach, Frank Wells, had been stressing both unity *and* academics—the whole package. The school paper suggested changing the name from the Condors to the Scoreless Scholars. No one on the team thought it was funny in the least. In fact, the entire offensive line was going to trash the paper's offices, but they all had computer lab that day.

How bad were they at that point? They'd lost their previous twenty-five games going back two and a half years, starting before Brett and Coach Wells took over. Brooke even had a running bet with me that if they ever won, she'd give me five hundred dollars. Brooke, who was working on an assistant's salary and could barely swing her rent each month, was *that* sure of their suckiness. I didn't make her pay when they finally did win—but I probably should have.

In one particularly painful game, the team gave up forty-two points—in the first quarter. Another time, they lost to a team whose bus had broken down, leaving a good half of their players stranded two hours away while the other half put together a forty-nine–zip shutout victory. I cheered for Brett's guys throughout, and meant it. I loved being there for him, even when things looked their roughest. Maybe even especially then.

During that season, due to an early injury sidelining their field-goal kicker, Brett played a hunch and recruited the drum major from the marching band to take his place. When *that* guy twisted a knee, Brett and Coach Wells simply started going for it on every fourth down, whether they were on the five or the fifty, and whether they had one yard or thirty to go. The crowd loved it. Unfortunately, so did the other teams' opposing defense. And the school paper. But that was Brett's style, which he encouraged in Coach Wells: He was willing to take a risk and live with the consequences, no matter the opposition. That was something that only made me love him more.

Which reminds me of one particular game—the one that changed our lives, actually. With thirty seconds left, they were down by just five points and the Condors had the ball on the other guys' seven-yard line. In two and a half years the team had never been so close late in the game. You wouldn't know it to see the stadium seats filled with a thousand Condor faithful, enticed by the recent zany play. So what if the other ten thousand seats were empty? I alone screamed loud enough for at least a couple thousand people.

Oh, how I remember. It was a critical moment, and he clearly had something he was talking himself into, but what did Brett do? He first glanced up to search the crowd for me. My heart raced, and I met his gaze and waved like a lunatic, so proud, so in love. I could see it in his expression—he was planning something crazy. And that's what I loved about him: his craziness. You need that touch of insanity to have the kind of chemistry we had. And win or lose, I knew we'd roll with the punches, as we'd done since the day we met in high school. The sex was better when we won, to be honest, but either way it was pretty damn good. A girl only needs to be taken on the kitchen floor, then the living-room sofa, then the dining-room table so many times. Sometimes a bed does the trick just as well.

But back to Brett's play calling. On the key play of the key game of his early coaching career, Brett managed to talk Coach Wells into calling a triple reverse to the fullback, or something like that, something he'd been drawing up for about a month, involving three lateral passes that would leave this particular opponent's defensive line stymied, running from side to side and gasping for air. The play was executed brilliantly—well, except for the fullback fumbling the ball out of bounds right before the goal line. The Condors lost, but the loss didn't mean much. A lot of fans went away disappointed but not surprised, and it gave the team a chance to rally behind the hapless fullback, something that doesn't happen enough in team sports. Somehow the close loss also gave them a vitality they hadn't known beforehand. It was as if they gelled suddenly, and achieved the chemistry Brett and Coach Wells had been trying to foster all along.

Yep, it worked. Some of the players changed, the fullback went on to be drafted (a real shock, considering the UCCC program!), and Brett and Coach Wells haven't lost a game in the two years since. And things are . . . different. Without suggesting that losing is better than winning, I *did* see *Rock 'n' Roll High School,* after all, so I know damn well that winning is better than losing. I can tell you that in an odd way, going to the games isn't as fun as it used to be. Maybe it's because it seemed like Brett needed me when they were losing. Like he and I were more of a team.

Of course, I'd known the losing wouldn't continue indefinitely. I'd known Brett would find his mojo, and he and Coach Wells would lead the Condors to wins, because that's who he's always been: a winner. Helping take UCCC to the top was—insert Darth Vader voice here—Brett's destiny.

"They're clearly winning again," Brooke says, pointing to the scoreboard, which has the Condors at thirty-seven to eight. "Do we have to stay?"

I stare at the field and try to will Brett to look up at me. He hasn't even glanced my way the whole game, and I don't think he'd notice if we took off. I missed a couple games already this year—first time ever—and he didn't complain. And I saw *most* of this one. I know they're winning, too. I stare so hard that if I have any magical powers the strength of my gaze will surely bore a hole into the back of his head. Which remains facing the same direction, proving definitively that I am not a witch. Nope, he's not turning to look back at me.

"Fine," I acquiesce. "Let's bail."

"Where should we go?" Brooke asks. "That hot dog didn't quite do it for me."

"Swingers?" I offer, thinking that I wouldn't mind one of their brownie sundaes.

"Oh my God!" Brooke screams. "I totally had a dream about that dessert last night. I swear!"

"Then it's clearly our destiny," I say, as we head to my car.

Darth voice aside, I'm big on destiny—of course, by that I mean the destiny we make ourselves, give or take. I think we all end up where we're pointed. My mom used to say, "If you don't want to end up in a bad place, don't head out in that direction. If you don't like where you are, leave." Of course, she probably never should have said that last bit in front of my dad. He took it a little too seriously.

My father's love of music, and his unrelenting drive to become the next Clapton—or Jimmy Page or Jimi Hendrix—drove him to change his last name from Brennan to Foxx when I was two years old. (Two x's and one syllable would decidedly bring him fame and fortune: Changing your name to Foxx or Gunn or Starr was all the rage at the time.) It also drove him to walk out on my mom and me, never once looking back, to pursue his dream on the road with his heavy-metal band, Afterbirth. An ironically named venture: It seemed Dad wasn't particularly compelled to stick around and see how things turned out after *my* birth.

Actually, I'm being too hard on him. My dad was a great provider—of names, neuroses, and abandonment issues. And luckily it all turned out just fine. I was raised by my mom, who worked double shifts to support me. This left her with little time for dating, remarrying, or giving me any siblings, but that was fine, too. I mean, sure, it would have been nice to have a sister or brother, but my mom and I developed a closeness I don't think we'd have were circumstances different. As it was, Mom and I formed a team, and I loved it being us against the world, even if the world didn't know we were fighting. I'd once kind of hoped Brett and I would make a similar team, and he'd lead us to the Super Bowl of life, to steal one of his—or his pal Coach Wells's—football analogies. Seems unlikely these days.

When I was about seven, I once thought I recognized my dad at the arcade on the Santa Monica Pier. I knew him from his skinny ankles. I didn't remember much of the man, but his tapered jeans made his ankles stand out from the rest of his well-built form. He was playing Skee-Ball, that endlessly frustrating game where you roll a wooden ball down a lane, up a little ramp, and into a bull's-eye with holes in it, the smallest and innermost circle yielding the most points. I remember the episode vividly because of what he bore on his shoulders: a little girl who should have been me. The girl looked nothing like him and probably belonged to his date, a lanky blonde with smoky eyes and a throaty laugh she emitted every time her spawn nearly fell from her perch.

I tugged at my mom's sleeve and pointed at the happy threesome. "Is that my dad over there?" I asked.

"No, sweetie," she said. "Of *course* that's not your father." But she spat at him on our way out. So add hallucinations to the list of gifts from Dear Old Dad.

Brooke and I get to Swingers and order one brownie sundae to share and two cups of coffee. I find that I'm eating the majority of our dessert, even though she was the one supposedly dreaming about it.

"I have to watch my girlish figure," she says. "How else will I trick some poor schmuck into marrying me?"

"Love?" I offer.

"Yeah, how's that workin' out for ya?" she counters, with no small amount of snark.

"Very well," I lie. Well, not lie, but I do admit that things have felt a little bit off lately. I can only attribute it to the fact that we're nearing the middle of the season and Brett gets stressed out every year around this time, and it worsens as it goes along. Which I understand.

The waitress comes by and warms up our coffees. I think Brooke and I both notice that she wears a name tag that says *America,* but Brooke lacks the filter not to comment.

"America?" Brooke says. "Is that your name? I had a maid named America when I was little!"

"Brooke!" I say as I sink in my seat and smile apologetically at the waitress, who is glaring at us. She stalks off.

"What? I like the name. I was complimenting her."

"I don't think that falls under the compliment department," I say.

Brooke feels bad, I can tell. "I *loved* America, if it's any consolation," she says. "Or maybe I just loved having a maid. That was awesome. That was when my mom was married to Lance and we lived on Roxbury Drive. Those were the days. He was so freakin' rich. Too bad he turned out to be gay. Man, I loved having a maid. Oh, America, were you only around today."

"Let's just move on," I say, looking around to make sure our waitress isn't within earshot, uncomfortable at the mention of her name again.

People who are mean to waitstaff in restaurants are a major pet peeve of mine. I know Brooke really didn't mean anything bad by it, but she can be a little clueless at times. On the other hand, at least she didn't mention the waitress's horse with no name. It's just a hot button for me, since I spent so much time in restaurants growing up.

My mom worked at Carlo's Pizza and Trattoria, which was more pizzeria than trattoria, what with the paper plates translucent from grease, orders hollered over constant chatter, and shabbily dressed clientele, but Carlo, the owner, thought using the word classed up the joint. In retrospect, I'm pretty sure he wasn't even Italian.

My mom worked there since I was about twelve years old. I did most of my homework assignments, ate most of my meals, and gained most of my freshman fifteen (which I've heard wasn't supposed to happen until I was a *college* freshman) at Carlo's. I also took AP Human Nature there, which came in the form of being delivery girl for two years, once I got my license. And a hostess prior to that blessed day. I learned that people will try to get away with just about anything—and will succeed as much and for as long as you let them. People push until you push back, and nobody illustrated this better than the customers.

I won't bore you with the details, because they're mostly unimportant, but let's just say that "Keep the change" can be very misleading. You don't know embarrassment until you've started to walk away with two dollars and eighty-seven cents only to have some guy yell after you, "Hey, where do you think you're going? I said keep the *change*." Or the other variation is the bill coming to nineteen dollars and thirty-nine cents and the customer handing you a twenty-dollar bill, saying, "Don't worry about the change." Okay: a) What makes you think I'm going to worry about sixty-one cents? And b) I *am* worried if that's my tip. I want to go see a movie, not buy a stamp.

For all the obnoxious customers, and after all the days I complained to my mom until I was blue in the face, I'd do it all over again, times a thousand, if I could just laugh with my mom again. We often ended up laughing about all my complaints regarding the job. Her eyes crinkled when she cracked up, and she'd shake her head back and forth as if to force away the humor because she was embarrassed by her laugh. It was a magnificent laugh.

My mom—my beautiful, overworked mother—died of breast cancer when I was in the tenth grade. I'd thought my life was over, too. If it wasn't for Brett and his family, it might have been. Brett and I had been dating for about eight months when my mom was diagnosed—he was one of the few guys who didn't open with a Clapton joke; his own music knowledge wouldn't allow for such a "gimme"—and for a year and three months when she was dying. The Fosters took me in like I was part of their family. I moved in for a week when she first passed away because I didn't want to be alone, and I never quite got around to moving back out. We never made anything official, seeing as they kept expecting my absentee dad to report back in, but after a while it was like I'd been born one of them. We were a new team. All of us. I loved it.

So, yes, I've lived with my then boyfriend/now husband since high school. Which makes me either very cool or very Appalachian, but in any event, Brett and I dated through high school, then went to the same college, and we got married right after graduation. His mom, Ginny, is awesome. I couldn't ask for a better surrogate. His sister, Trish, was my maid of honor, and his dad, Bill, walked me down the aisle. Trish and I started our own pet photography business—by which I mean we take pictures of animals, not that I have numerous photography businesses and this is my favorite—in which I'm the photographer/product developer/customer-service person, and she's the marketing/accounting/everything-else person. It's another team that means a lot to me.

I'd always known I wanted to work with animals, but I had no idea I'd end up a pet photographer. My first attempt to break in to the animal business was at Miller Animal Hospital. I'd decided I wanted to become a veterinarian but wanted to test the waters before I went to school for it. I got a job as an assistant veterinary technician, but the only opening they could offer was the graveyard shift—which I enthusiastically accepted, hoping to distinguish myself as an eager-and-willing future vet.

My first night's excitement was a phone call that came in at one a.m. from a panicked woman having a crisis because her dog refused to look at her. She kept calling the dog, "Edgar! Edgar!" but it came out more like "Ed-gah!" because she had the not-so-subtle remnants of a New York accent. "See? He won't look at me!" Obviously I couldn't *see,* since I was on the phone with her.

"Have you done something to betray his trust?" I asked. "My old dog wanted nothing to do with me when I switched his regular dog food to that stuff in the blue bag."

"I didn't change his food!" she said. And then she yelled again, "Edgar!"

"Do you happen to have a hat made out of ham? I'll bet that would get his attention."

She had no ham hat, and wasn't enjoying my hypothesizing. I didn't know what else to do, so I said she could just bring him in. I knew there wasn't anything wrong with the dog. I knew that like I knew that Matthew McConaughey would appear shirtless in the next week's *Us Weekly*—and like I now know that husbands, like dogs, sometimes won't look at you—but I was bored, and this was going to be my first client. Plus, as far as I was concerned, any and all canines were welcome to visit me anytime.

The woman arrived about twenty-five minutes later with a shower cap on her head and the remnants of cold cream along her hairline. She thrust Edgar, a shar-pei–terrier mix, onto the front desk. Of course no dog likes to balance precariously on a ledge five feet off the ground, so he looked like a quivering Don Knotts. True to the shar-pei half of his heritage, his face had a landslide of doggie skin that weighed so heavily on his eyes it's a wonder he could look at anything at all. Of course, this also made him look like he could have been hatched from the woman, who had a similar landslide of skin overtaking her face. I won't mention her lipstick, which looked like it had been drawn on with oversized clown makeup.

"Edgar!" she shouted at him. "Edgar!" No response.

So I gave it a try. "Edgar?" I gently called. No response. Then I got the idea to change my pronunciation: "Ed-gah?"

And that actually did it. He *looked* at me. Thus making it clear that eye contact wasn't the problem and that he wasn't going deaf.

"Ma'am," I said. "I think . . . I mean, I'm pretty sure he just looked at me . . . so I think he's okay. At least, as far as eye contact goes."

"Why won't he look at *me,* then?" she asked.

I didn't have an answer. Except that maybe her high-pitched Brooklynese was unsettling even to him, and he didn't want to encourage her speaking any more than necessary. I was smart enough not to propose this. Brooke probably would have.

"I wouldn't worry about it," I said, even though clearly she was worried since she'd brought poor Edgar in—which I suppose was technically my fault.

"Me and you," she said to the mutt—which ironically came out sounding like "Mean you"—"we never had problems communicatin' before. Why won't you look at me?"

I never got a chance to hear his response, if Edgar was going to give one. (I wonder sometimes if it would help me with Brett now.) Dr. Eisen, the on-call vet, walked in at that point from his napping post in the back and asked what was going on. His eyes were bloodshot from resting on his arm instead of a pillow, and he had a crease in his cheek from his shirt.

When the woman explained her crisis and his eyes turned to me—eyes that said, *Really? You actually told this woman to leave her home at one a.m. and come here because her dog wouldn't look at her?*—I had no excuse. Edgar got his complimentary dog biscuit and they left the office, and Dr. Eisen explained in a borderline-hostile tone that we were open after-hours only for emergencies, and that if we let every crazy person bring their pets in at all hours, we'd be jeopardizing the lives of the pets that needed real emergency attention. Then he went back to sleep.

Not twenty minutes later there was an actual emergency, and it proved to be more than I could bear. A woman stormed through the front doors and fell to the floor with her yellow Lab in her arms. He'd been hit by a car, was bleeding from several spots, and his breathing was shallow. The woman was in tears, and I'd like to say I comforted her, but I had no experience in such matters and instead fell to the floor with her and her dog, and started to cry as well. Wail, in fact. I sobbed with the woman as if the dog was *our* pet. Of course, I'd yelled for Dr. Eisen first, and when he rushed out to bring the dog to an exam room, I could tell by his look of disdain that I was going to get another talking-to.

"Layla, please follow me," he said sternly.

I got up, brushed off my pants, and trailed him to the back. I held the dog and petted his head as Dr. Eisen cleaned and stitched the wounds, my face drenched in tears and my chest heaving from heavy sobs. Every time I regained my composure, the dog would look at me with his large brown eye—the only one that was visible as he lay on his side—and I would lose it all over again.

Once the dog was sedated and resting comfortably, Dr. Eisen sat me down.

"Layla," he said, and then took a breath—that breath you always know is going to be followed with bad news. "I appreciate your enthusiasm for this job and your love of animals, but judging from tonight, I don't think this is the right field for you."

"But—"

I started to defend myself, but he cut me off instantly. "There will be far worse cases, much more blood. Some animals—many—won't make it, and you need to be tough."

"I *am* tough," I said, as I reached my tongue up and toward the right to catch another salty tear.

But that was it. I was fired. After one night on the job. Not even after a night—after four hours. Veterinary school would not be in my future. Which was fine, I suppose. One unresponsive Edgar and an overly empathic response to a wounded Lab's owner saved me the additional four-year school commitment after the standard undergrad time. And after messing around taking pictures at a dog park one day, I realized that I was actually better at something *else* involving pets. And now I'm in the right place—at least, regarding my job. Sometimes it's good not to get what you want.

Also, I like that the animals don't tend to die on you from getting their pictures taken. Sorry—their "portraits." We're trying to go upscale.

"You know all this talk about SUVs and how bad they are for the environment?" Brooke says, as she swipes the last bite of our sundae. "Do you know there's a huge tax break if you buy one that's over a certain weight and you claim it as a business-only vehicle?"

"If you're a farmer," I say.

"I'm serious. They're called *light trucks*. They're classified as a work truck. And you can essentially write the whole thing off on your taxes. So basically you can get a free Hummer!"

"You just wanted to say 'free Hummer.' "

"No, I'm seriously gonna get one."

"Not to be a stickler for details," I say, "but you don't even have a job. I'm pretty sure you need a business, or at least a job, anyway, to be able to write things off."

"Yeah, I'm working on that. It's not easy. People aren't hiring brilliant, charismatic what-have-yous."

" 'What-have-yous'?" I question. "Is that how you're marketing yourself these days?"

"Not all of us know what we want to do from the age of two, Layla. Not all of us are still living our high-school glory days."

I always know Brooke's annoyed with me when she says my name. Any other time she'll call me "Lay" or "bee-yotch" or "dude." "Layla" means business. I also know because now she's taking potshots at my marriage to Brett.

As I figured out my career path, Brett wasn't too far behind. There was only so long he could hang out and watch Trish and me play with animals—and only so long we would put up with him distracting our subjects with a pepperoni Hot Pocket just seconds before we got the perfect shot. Following his dream, albeit humbly at first, Brett went back to Hamilton High, our former high school, and got a job assistant-coaching with his old mentor. Frank Wells suggested that he'd now stick to offense, his true passion, and he'd name Brett defensive coordinator as well as JV coach. Brett accepted. And after a beginning rough patch of their combined approach, there was a fairy-tale quality to their success. Together they brought the team to the state championships three years in a row. Then they both moved up to coaching at UCCC, which was—unsurprisingly, given the record I mentioned earlier—looking to head in a new direction.

You know how that turned out. Winners.

Brett. As you now see, he's a great defensive coordinator and coach. If not a father, he's at least a wise older brother to most of the team. Of course, what most sets Brett apart—and also some would say is his greatest flaw, given the craziness of his visions—is that he's always thinking big picture. Always. That's why he pushes his boys at academics as well as athletics: He knows there's always a place for both, and that in the best of all worlds, the two complement each other. He dreams bigger than blocking drills and impromptu Gatorade showers.

It's always been that way with him. He's always been a mixture of goofball and prodigy. Through high school, he was star of the football team—and when I say star, I mean he was Sol itself, with everything else revolving around him. He was certainly the most highly recruited player in our high school's history. You know, he was the kind of kid you read about in the newspaper, whose parents are sitting down for meatloaf with a new college recruiter virtually every night and fending off midnight phone calls from those without the good fortune to find a seat at the dinner table. But he was also secretly editor-in-chief of a weekly pro-football scouting report that he self-published and distributed from his parents' basement until the NFL sent him a cease-and-desist order; some of his insights were so dead-on they suspected him of having informers in every locker room in the league. They didn't get that Brett's not the kind of guy who needs informers.

In college, he might have been on a path to playing in the pros but was spared a likely future collecting Super Bowl rings, knee scars, and fortunes in endorsements by a complete tear of his Achilles tendon. I think that, for the rest of his life, somewhere inside he'll be running down an imaginary sideline, waiting for a perfect spiral that he'll catch and carry into life's end zone for the game-winning touchdown.

He certainly tried after the injury. A perfect example of his big-picture thinking getting him in trouble was the illegal protein-bar concession he ran out of the campus rec center. Fosterbars, he called them. He researched healthy ingredients and with some other kids created a snack that everybody, quite literally, ate up. It was extremely successful. At least it sold well in the area until the school's athletic director somehow ended up with a tainted bar and shut the operation down. Brett was a victim of his own grand schemes in that case. He tripped himself up by attempting to meet soaring demand with materials sourced from a questionable vendor selling product out of an unmarked semi. Turns out it was expired government-surplus granola. He should have known better. Who in the government eats granola?

But that debacle's all in the past. Now he's on top of his game. He coaches like a whirling dervish, a latter-day Knute Rockne with enough Joe Paterno to be a player favorite, and he also indulges his entrepreneurial side. He's playing around on Craigslist, trying to get some designers to help him. Or at least he's been talking about it. He believes the next big thing will be his value-priced athletic underwear, coming soon to a big-box retailer near you—the first truly affordable Under Armour competitor.

Yup, he'll likely be successful. He's successful in whatever he does. Great guy, fun-loving, good at everything—you can see why I wanted to "team up" with him and his family. And you probably still don't really see why I'm annoyed with him.

At least Brooke gets it. Sometimes she gets it a little too well. She points things out that I'm trying to let slide. And I know she's just looking out for me. But in case I don't, she reminds me that she loves me when she hugs me good night. And then she flips me off.

# *brett*

I'm not saying she should go back to wearing the hat with the beak jutting out the front of it. Frankly, that thing was always a little much. But when your wife is sneaking out of games and thinking you're not gonna notice? That's like me not noticing when Layla claims that she's twenty-seven. How 'bout we make that twenty-nine? We're both teetering on the edge of the big three-oh, and hiding from it won't help. I don't know what it is about chicks and their age, but none of them ever want to give you a straight answer.

Tell you what: Take the current year, subtract the year you were born, and there's your age. There's no three-year curve, there's no two years off for good behavior, and unlike most other situations, your boobs don't count for anything.

How is it that every girl I went to school with is now two years younger than me? You want honesty in every relationship, and the first thing you do is lie about your age? Is it a mortality thing? Do you think the Grim Reaper isn't going to double-check? You lying about your age is the same as us lying about our income or penis size: Eventually the truth is gonna come out. Not that I lie about that kind of stuff.

But I do lie—I mean, you have to lie if you want to stay happily married. People who say you need one hundred percent honesty have never been in a lasting relationship—and by "lasting," I mean the kind where both people are actually speaking to each other after the first three months. It's immature and frankly insulting when people peacock with that moral "I never lie" high ground. And I'm not just talking about the standard "No, you don't look fat in that," "No, your friend is not hot," and "Yes, I will always be attracted to you, even when you have three hairs growing out of your chin and tuck your boobs into your pants." That stuff's a given. I'm saying you have to lie through your fucking teeth if you want to avoid a life of pure hell. Especially when your family is involved. And Layla? She's a *lot* more family than your average wife. She's probably more family than anybody's wife in the history of marriage.

Layla is to my mom what my lesbian sister, Trish, can never be: girly, giggly, and, most important, in need of a mother. Trish and my mom have a fine relationship, but it just isn't the quintessential mother-daughter bond that Layla and my mom share.

And Layla is to my dad what every corny, bad-joke-telling average Joe needs: an audience. And not an audience that will consistently groan and roll its eyes as blood relatives tend to do. Layla really thinks my dad's lame jokes are charming, and she'll genuinely laugh at them every time. Sometimes she'll even request that he tell one again, which he sets on like a dog with an errant chunk of sirloin.

My little brother, Scott? He worships her. He didn't look up to me the way little brothers look up to their football-star big bros for advice on dating or school or CD collections; he thought that Layla was a goddess, and he couldn't believe she'd settle for a mere mortal like me. Of course, he's still living at home, playing World of Warcraft online and drawing half-naked demonesses with her face—for his classes at Medina Art College, he swears. God love him. I guess I do, too, the little perv.

I may sound like an asshole just point-blanking this stuff, and yeah, I've certainly made more than my fair share of mistakes, but isn't that how we're supposed to grow? By learning from our fuckups? Character is defined by the choices we make under pressure. And lately the soundtrack in my head has Bowie's and Queen's song of the same name on a constant rotation.

I don't need silk underwear—I mean for *her* to wear, not me, and frankly neither arrangement has even come up for discussion. But there's some abstract notion floating around my pesky little brain that tells me Layla's nighttime uniform of my old boxers and a stained T-shirt isn't meant to turn me on. I'm not sure when exactly the switch flipped and she went from buying those sexy matching bras and underwear to this. And of course she doesn't have to put on some barely there number and do a dance for me every night before bed. But there was a time when she *did*. So how am I supposed to not notice when it stops?

It's not just the lack of frilly things—honestly, I don't care. If I had to pinpoint the one factor that's been making me crazy lately, it's the way she is around my family. Or rather, the fact that she's always with at least one of them at any given time. I know it's partially my fault. I always encouraged her to spend time with them. But there's a difference between spending time and becoming one with. I guess Layla never got the memo.

I mean, aren't you supposed to hate your mother-in-law? This isn't natural. Isn't it against the laws of physics somehow? When I was growing up I got in a fight with my little brother every day. She's never gotten in a fight with him. Not even once. Well, *once* she got in a fight with him: He was mad because she got a better present for my dad for Father's Day. And seriously, while we're on the subject, how did she know my dad would love that electric tie rack? He watched that thing spin for hours, like it was a mobile and he was an infant.

It didn't used to be like this. I didn't used to resent her. In fact, I used to feel invincible around her. My football team was a disaster a couple years ago—losing nonstop, which was a real blow after Coach Wells and I came from winning with our high-school program—but somehow she made me feel triumphant. You might think it odd that the miracle we were waiting for was a close loss on a crazy play I dreamed up, but when you're a small school with a program that can't use scholarships as bait (damn Division III rules!) and you don't have one recruit who'd be even third string on many of our competitors' teams . . . well, you take what you can get.

Some had been saying, "Yeah, every time the Condors get this close, they find some new way to snatch defeat from the jaws of victory." Not Layla. She had me feeling like anything was possible. She'd be there, directly behind me on the sidelines, wearing that red-and-mustard jersey that always stood out in a sea of green and gray. And a hat with a beak on it. She has a heart big enough to make everyone around her wish they were her. And a body that makes just about every one of my college boys wish they were me.

All around her, always, like a personal choir, are four people who think the sun shines out of her—well, who love her sometimes, it seems, almost more than I do: Mom, Dad, my sister, and my brother. Layla would get them to come to my games even though our record losing streak wouldn't exactly have them racing to the car. She's the type who's so purely good you almost resent it because you look so crummy by comparison.

I remember once, after a particularly hard loss—another game when we'd got sort of close to winning—she gathered a selection of our most die-hard fans and had them waiting right outside the locker room to give the team an ovation as they filed gloomily past. As they got onto the bus, I could swear every man on that team held his head a little higher.

When my grandmother was dying, Layla was the one who sat in silence with an understanding smile on her face as Mimi cussed out the shit-brain Democrats, the dirty Europeans, and the nurse she thought had stolen her favorite wig. After six months of that, everybody else in the family gave up. Layla kept on for another year. That's right: a year. Twelve months. You try it.

Once, she got it in her head that the team needed a different kind of talking to, and she organized a sit-down with them. She'd listened to what I was trying to do, and she told them they weren't playing like a team—and that they needed to air their grievances so they could move past them. I was about to laugh my ass off, imagining football players ready to "share their feelings," when suddenly I heard some freshman guys saying they were pissed that they never got to play, other freshmen complaining about the pranks, seniors mad at certain guys who were only out for themselves . . . and lo and behold, the players actually started communicating. After that they all came together behind John Simms, our fullback, after that one goal-line fumble—well, I'm not certain that one powwow wasn't what turned the team around.

Yes, she was always there, behind me, backing me up. And I have to say it helped knowing that in the end, win or lose, I got to go home to the sweetest, kindest, craziest, hottest woman in the entire crowd. Sounds corny, I know, but seriously, how lucky was I that she happened to be my wife?

I met Layla in high school. She was pals with my friend Doug. She had dark, wavy hair and this arch of freckles across the bridge of her nose, which I thought were adorable and which she hated—the freckles, not the adoration. Her eyes had little flecks of gold that matched her hair when the sun hit it. And her smile? It's like she's in on some secret and you're desperate to find out what it is. I fell for her instantly, which was romantic to Layla but not nearly as endearing to Claudine DeMarco, my girlfriend at the time.

I wasn't going to cheat, and I wasn't going to lie (teaching me early on what a mistake that is, as you'll see), so I sat Claudine down after fifth period and broke up with her. She screamed bloody murder for a minimum of a half hour. I was very late to geometry. I sat and listened—it was the least I could do—as she wailed and sobbed and wiped her runny nose on her sleeve and yelled at me some more. Tears spilled down her mascara-streaked cheeks, and she kept at it until her eyes were slits and her voice sounded like she inspired the word "hoarse." It was madness. Finally, it stopped. She blew her nose, regained her composure, and looked seriously at me for a moment. Then she shrugged her left shoulder and calmly tossed out, "I guess I should have given you oral, huh?"

I was ridiculously proud of myself for somehow managing not to reply with "Hell, yeah." But the truth is, that breakup had nothing to do with the lack of oral. It was the lack of something else. Something I didn't even know existed in the world until I met Layla.

But, yeah, oral would have been cool.

We started out as a group: me; my buddy Doug (who was always too much of a clown to have a girlfriend back then—now he's in IT, which I always joke is equally attractive to women, though he just got married); Steve; Steve's girlfriend, Michelle; and Layla. The five of us would hang out during lunch and every day after school. Weekends were ours to tear up the town—which mostly meant Doug, Steve, and me playing video games, Layla and Michelle making fun of us, and then all of us dropping by the multiplex to see whatever new movies had been released. Eventually, Steve and Michelle broke up, Doug moved away, and our party of five became a table for two.

Layla was the first person ever able to make me behave. And I don't mean by scolding me or laying down any kind of law. She was the first person who inspired me to not be a dick. I actually cared what she thought of me, and wanted to do things that would make sure she *kept* liking me.

Apparently, it worked, because we got married about five minutes after we finished college. I'm not sure it was the wisest move, since neither of us had ever been with anyone else, but at least I knew I'd never suffer by comparison. It just seemed like the natural thing to do. It's never been a secret that I'm not the poster child for impulse control. So, sure, we may have been a little young and may not have put in the right amount of forethought, but luckily for me it worked out. I took no small amount of ribbing from my buddies over getting hitched so soon and so young, but I knew that there wasn't a single guy among them who hadn't been secretly in love with Layla since she burst onto our scene, so I took every crack with a grain of salt.

I knew I loved her the first time she called me an asshole. Romantic, huh? Sad but true. She was the only person to call me on my shit, and she wasn't bitchy or controlling. Just honest. And usually right—though I rarely admitted it.

I like to say I grew up with Layla, but I bet Layla would insist she's still waiting for me to grow up.

All of our friends started to get married about five or six years after Layla and I did, and about twelve years after we started dating. But there was something intrinsically different about those relationships. Maybe because they hadn't been there for every first, good or bad. Maybe because they were based on a more adult foundation. Either way, watching my buddies and their wives, I couldn't help but wonder if there was something missing from my own marriage. I've been thinking about that a lot lately.

Don't get me wrong—I love her. I know she's the best thing I ever found. She's solid. She's every guy's perfect girl. She's definitely, one hundred percent without a doubt the girl I'm supposed to spend the rest of my life with.

I think.

She really should have stayed for the whole game.

# *layla*

Brett comes home and the roles are once again reversed. This time he's ignoring me. Although not in the usual way. He's not playing deaf—he's pissed. He stalks around the apartment and everything he does is punctuated with a loud bang. He tosses off his shoes—*bang*. He hangs his jacket up and slams the closet door. He goes into the bathroom and slams that one, too.

"Great game," I say, when he finally comes out.

"Yeah? What was the final score?"

"Thirty-seven to fifteen?" I say, my pitch just slightly raised, which might suggest I wasn't positive, but I did check before I got home. Still, the way he hurled the question at me, I feel panicky and wonder if there was an extra field goal or something.

"You don't have to come to the games if you don't want to," he says.

Instantly I feel like crap. I *do* want to go to the games. I want to support him, at least. I've always supported him. It just didn't feel like he cared either way anymore. But apparently he does.

"I'm so sorry, babe," I say, and mean it with all my heart. "Brooke was itching to take off and I didn't think you'd notice and I haven't seen her in a while and we wanted to catch up and—"

"It's okay," he says, taking in how awful I feel. "It just bummed me out."

"I'm sorry," I reply, and then smile as I walk to him. "How can I possibly make it up to you?"

He meets me halfway, and I know I'm forgiven. Sure, we may have hit a rocky patch lately, but when we do connect—when we're on the same page—it's paradise. We both know that.

I knew I loved Brett the first time he took me to my dad's grave. I didn't know where we were going when he kidnapped me after school that rainy Friday, and I wasn't in the mood to go anywhere, let alone somewhere against my will and with no clue as to where we'd end up. We were too young for him to be proposing but not too young for him to try his hand at romance in an outdoor, public (albeit remote) place. This was before my mom passed away, so when we got to the graveyard I was certain he'd taken his quest to obtain my virginity to a whole new level.

"A graveyard? Seriously?" I spouted, hand on one hip, mouth pursed in a smirk, one eyebrow cocked.

Brett reached his hand out and softly touched my sure-of-itself eyebrow with a finger, guiding it back down to its natural position. "Yes, a graveyard," he said, and he kicked dirt from the front of a worn-away headstone.

"Not on your twisted life, pal," I said, but before I could get the words out I noticed something in his face. He was serious, and we weren't there to have sex. He held his hand out for me to take, which I did.

Brett inhaled a deep breath and then nodded toward the headstone. "Layla, I'd like you to meet the deceased Nick Brennan. Er, Foxx."

I stood there for a moment in shock. The back of my throat started to feel like it was coated with a layer of cotton candy. I swallowed a few times to make it go away, but each time it became more difficult. Had my father died? Nobody had told me? It would be fitting, since he'd left me out of the loop on everything else that had happened since 1988 when I'd last seen him.

"I don't understand," I said, as I started to tremble.

"No, no . . ." Brett rushed reassuringly, taking me in his arms and holding me close. "He's not *really* dead."

My wayward eyebrow poked back up. "Brett, what in the name of . . . ?"

"Your dad's a shit. I say we bury him."

Nine words. Uttered as though he were telling me what time it was. That's all he said. But what I heard was this:

"That poor excuse for a father has caused you so much pain, it's criminal—whether you want to admit it or not. I know you go to the mailbox every time your birthday nears, or during Christmas or Easter or any other time a father should acknowledge his only daughter, and I watch you flip the mailbox open and shut it just as fast. You always get this little smile when it's empty. Every time, you shrug and get this smile on your face that I imagine is you saying, *Oh, well . . . maybe next year,* but that smile breaks my fucking heart. Because I know what's underneath. And I wish I could make a card appear in the mailbox, or a heart appear where that gaping hole is in your father's chest. But I can't . . . and it doesn't. So I say we *bury* the fucker. I say we pronounce him dead, and from this day forward he is. A dead father has got to be less painful than one who's alive and doesn't appreciate or even recognize that he has a daughter."

They say women develop faster than men. So do our interpersonal skills. Mostly. So you might guess I was reading into it. But I don't think so. Those nine words meant the world to me.

I wept. It was the kindest thing anyone had ever done for me. I wept over the loss of my father—probably for the first time—and I simultaneously shed happy tears over finding someone who cared enough about me to do such a thing. Brett had found a headstone that was so weatherworn it had no legible name, and he'd claimed it for me, for my life ahead. He encouraged me to talk to my father—or to the stone, at least—and to tell him how I felt. Then, once every year on the same day, he promised to bring me back to visit and "catch my father up" on what he'd missed.

Brett was a winner. He was the real deal. And it was that first visit to my father's "grave" when the little cartoon birds swooped off the Disney celluloid, singing, chirping, and stitching my damaged heart back together with multicolored ribbons borne in their beaks. I never looked at another boy through high school.

After that, it was off to college together—to a school I wouldn't even have put on my list had it not been his first choice (I figured I'd go to veterinary school right after, so where I did my undergrad wasn't really all that important)—and a lifelong commitment to the eternal goof that he would quickly become (still somehow managing to be a successful goof). I haven't ever regretted it, really, though he's given me reasons to a few times.

I'll never forget his twenty-first birthday. He drank too much—and by "too much," I mean it was a miracle he wasn't hospitalized with alcohol poisoning in addition to severe lacerations. He'd attempted to open a beer bottle with his eye socket: a neat bar trick, except in this case the bottle cap proved more resilient than the skin protecting his orbital bone. Particularly funny, though he'd never admit it, the cap had been a twist-off. In fact, the entire incident was transformed in the retelling into a bar fight. No word as to whether the bottle also sought first aid.

The kicker was that Brett's two roommates heard me screaming, thought we were arguing, didn't want to get involved, and stayed out the whole night at a friend's. Brett and I stumbled back into his place at about seven forty-five a.m., while Matt and Corey, aka Tweedledumb and Tweedledumber, staggered in at eight. I was starving after staying up the whole night in the ER, so before I'd even changed my blood-splattered shirt I made myself a bowl of cereal and wound up dozing off, still seated upright with the spoon in my hand. When Matt walked into the kitchen and saw me—eyes closed, blood everywhere—he assumed that Brett had *stabbed* me, and immediately started hatching an escape plan. He sprinted out the front door, stole a ladder from the next house over, and climbed up to Brett's bedroom window, shouting at the top of his lungs for Brett to "Grab the necessities and get the fuck out before someone calls the fuzz!"

Without addressing what he apparently thought of me, leaving me for dead as he did, Matt's use of the word "fuzz" should tell you just all you need to know about Brett's choice of friends. I woke up to the commotion, went to see what was going on, and saw Brett—half out the window, panicked, not even knowing *why*—with Matt screaming for him to hurry because I was awake (and apparently alive), and Corey blurting something about having a cousin in Mexico.

Yes, I married him nonetheless. We don't talk to Matt much anymore, though.

## *trish*

They say you should never be in business with family—too close, too much history, too much potential for bloodshed. "They" never met Layla. True, we've had our shouting matches, but invariably it ends with me crying and apologizing, admitting I was wrong. It takes a very special person to get Trish Foster to admit she's wrong—let alone to admit she's ever cried.

Layla's my sister-in-law. And my business partner. She came into our lives through Brett, but ask most Fosters and they'll tell you that if she hadn't, we'd have gone out and tracked her down. She's that much a part of our tapestry.

For as long as I've known Layla, she's always had a camera with her, sometimes to my annoyance. But that kind of tenacity pays off. She's a phenomenal photographer, which anyone can see from her pictures. So my decision to join forces with her was a no-brainer. Her love of capturing memories through eternal images is matched only by her love of animals. She's great with them—much better than I am. Not that I'm not a total animal lover, because I am (I'm the overly proud mother of a two-year-old dachshund), but she's the one who wanted to be a vet, spent six years volunteering at the ASPCA, and went through a bit of formal training. Okay, apparently it was just one night, and she's no Cesar Millan, but she knows her way around a mutt. Just don't let the mutt get hurt. She tends to be a little too empathetic.

Funny, then, that I'm the one playing with the dogs. I'm what you'd call a dog wrangler—or an animal wrangler, really. I'm the one making funny faces and strange noises, and often dangling a piece of meat over Layla's head to get the beast's attention. She never knows what I'm doing, because her face is attached to the camera, but I'm sure she can feel me moving all around her (and smell the piece of Swiss cheese perched beside her left ear) and one of these days I'm going to get someone to photograph us while we're photographing the pets, because I have a feeling it's quite a sight.

Speaking of sights, Layla's on the phone right now, and she's got this crazed expression that I'm not sure how to read exactly. The only other times I've seen it is when she's telling a joke and waiting for the right moment to deliver the punch line, or when she's messing with a telemarketer. She does that last thing quite a bit, actually. She likes to ask them to wait and then puts the phone in a drawer and walks away. Or if it's a woman, she'll make her voice all husky and ask, "So, what are you wearing?" When they get all bent out of shape and tell her she's being inappropriate, she'll say, "*You* called me. The only people who call me *want* to talk dirty."

I love that girl.

# *layla*

Wow. I was thinking about Brett's game that I have to go to tonight, not wanting to repeat last week's debacle, when the call came. Now I'm standing here, stunned and grinning, still clutching the phone after the guy has hung up. Trish swipes the phone from my hand and cradles it to her ear.

"Hello? Is anyone there?" she asks the dead air, and then hangs up and turns to me. "What was that? Why are you standing there with that creepy smile on your face?"

"Not creepy," I say.

"*So* creepy. You either won the lottery, which you don't play, or you just found out your house burned down and you're in some sort of demented denial."

"Neither," I tell her happily, though her lottery guess is the closer of the two. I'm also thinking this *is* good news, because it hasn't even sunk in yet and my face is already advertising. "Are you sitting down?" I ask her, even though she's standing one foot in front of me.

Trish gets that look she always has when I'm not getting to the point—or, rather, when I'm dragging something out because I just might have really freakin' amazingly good news and can't verbalize it. "What *is* it?" she demands.

"That was PETCO," I say, trying to contain my grin enough to produce the rest of the sentence.

"No!" she says.

"Yes," I say.

"Really?" she says.

"Really," I say.

"And?"

But then the buzzer rings, cutting me off, and in walks an incredibly tall, undernourished man, probably around fifty, his almost equally tall and pencil-like wife, and six greyhounds.

"Hi," Trish says, as she ushers in the couple and their similarly starved brood. I can't decide who's leaner. I know greyhounds are lithe and lean to begin with, but this family is like a mob of animated stick figures.

"Thank you for seeing us on such short notice," the woman says. "We just left the animal communicator, and we called seven other pet photographers before we finally got you."

"Well, it's no problem *squeezing all of you in,*" Trish quips, and I shoot her a look that I hope says, *These are not the things we say to people, Trish. These are the things we say about people once they've left the room.* Geesh, is she going for the Brooke award?

"Perseverance," I speak up, trying to deflect from her comment. "If at first you don't succeed, try and try . . . the Yellow Pages. And other sayings of the like. Does anyone use the Yellow Pages anymore?"

"We normally like to meet with the pets and people a week before the photo shoot, so we can get a feel for the animals—their personalities, and also their relationships with their owners," Trish inserts. "This type of same-day deal isn't our norm." She wasn't so pleased when I okayed the shoot a half hour earlier, but the couple sounded so desperate that I didn't want to let them down. Now, with her curiosity boiling out about PETCO, she is *en fuego*.

"Anyway," I deflect again, "who do we have here?"

The man clears his throat. "This is Lucinda. That's Cally. Hermes. Rocco. Dante. And that's Wilhelmina."

"Are they allowed treats?" I ask, reaching for the cookie jar.

"No!" both the man and woman shout simultaneously, with a conjoined look that's like a hot curling iron held at my throat. I immediately withdraw.

"As I was saying," the woman huffs. She pats Hermes. At least I think it's Hermes, but they all moved, so it could be Wilhelmina. "The animal communicator told us that our babies feel left out. *Very* left out. They want to be on holiday cards. They feel that as family members it is a slap in the snoot for them to not be included in our annual photo session."

"So wait," Trish interjects. "You take pictures of you and your children each year? And make those into cards?"

"These *are* our children," corrects the woman, as she gestures toward the dogs.

"Of course they are," I say.

"Okay. Wait, wait. So, you guys take pictures of just the *two* of you? And you send those out every year as holiday cards?"

"That's what they said, Trish," I remark a little more aggressively before turning back to the couple. "I totally understand how they feel. And we will rectify that immediately. This year, these gorgeous creatures will be opening at a mailbox near you! Right, Lucinda?"

"That's Dante," says the father. *Dammit, the dogs moved again.*

"Could you excuse us for a minute?" Trish asks the Skinnys, and before she even gets a response, she drags me into the next room—which is perfectly fine with me, as my brain is itching because I'm so desperate to tell her the incredible news.

"Spill!" she demands.

"They want to franchise TLC Paw Prints booths across the country, starting with a five-store pilot!" I squeal. "We have to get them a prototype."

"Shut the fuck up," Trish says.

"What, I'm going to joke about something like that?"

"Shut the fuck *up,*" she says again, and then again, though it's clear she doesn't want me to shut up at all. She starts to beg for every detail, right down to how they said the word *pilot*.

TLC stands for Trish and Layla's Canine Photography, and even though we've branched out to cats and bunnies and the occasional ferret, we are predominantly dog photographers. Plus, tender loving care is exactly what we deliver while readying Sparky for his close-up. We'd been pitching PETCO to let us set up a Paw Prints photo booth—one single booth—in one of their stores to see how it would go over, and unbeknownst to us, they'd done some test-market research that went over like gangbusters. Now they wanted to try out the concept regionally, and possibly franchise hundreds of them. Using *our* name. All we have to do is get together a prototype and some loans to cover start-up expenses.

"Holy fuckin' shit," Trish says, as she backs up from me, shaking her head in disbelief. "We're huge."

"Easy there, big fella," I urge. "We're not huge. We have an amazing business opportunity being presented to us. But one step at a time."

"Layla?" Trish says, in a tone that means I'm about to be reprimanded. "This is one of those times we've talked about. Where you celebrate in the moment. This is a victory. This is not something to be cautious about, this is not something to decide later if you are happy about, and this is not something that is going to be taken away from you. This is an amazing moment. Now start jumping up and down and fucking act like you just franchised your business across the fucking country, because you *did*."

"Oh my God!" I scream as it really sinks in, and we jump up

and down together. But then the dogs start barking—all except Rocco, for some reason (I can tell Rocco from the rest because of his lazy eye)—and I have to go back out and calm the Skinnys down. It occurs to me while watching them that they could easily be the kind of people who can eat anything they want, as much of it as they want, and then burn it all off in fifteen minutes just by being so uptight.

But what am I doing being catty? I'm more of a *dog* person—one who will soon have photo booths across the country! It's nice to have something you've worked so hard to achieve come to fruition. I should be happy in the moment—and just be glad I got where I was pointed.

# *brett*

Trouble in paradise. Particularly today.

A wandering eye has never been my problem. My eye doesn't wander, really; it stays put in my skull. Which is not to say that into my field of vision does not occasionally cross an obstruction—something or someone it's nearly impossible to see through, around, or beyond. So I look. But only accidentally.

There's a new SID (sports information director) at UCCC. She's basically the PR point person. Forget the fact that she's in my direct line of vision, there's *worse* news: She has particularly perky tits. And she's on my practice field. That means forty-five boners just popped, and I have to reprimand my football team for ogling these breasts, which are pointing and waving at us, *Hey! Over here! Ogle me!* Well, maybe not the "ogle me" part, but definitely the "Hey! Over here!" part.

I knew there was potential trouble when I first found out that Hot Girl was not, in fact, just some random chick, but instead the newest member of our staff. Yes, Hot Girl was actually Hot SID, which sounds just a bit too close to STD for my taste, which is maybe for the best. I ignored her in the cafeteria the first time I saw her, because I find it's better to avoid cleavage that doesn't belong to my wife.

Her name is Heather. Of course it is. I find that name's the perfect blend of nice suburban girl with "She can do *what* with her *what*?" This girl is way too pretty, and certainly a liability around the football field. You try to preempt staring under these circumstances, to perfect the casual glance that takes her in but doesn't linger too long, as if she's just another streetlamp, but in fact she's a ten-car pileup headed by a rolled-over semi loaded with melons. And the doors have popped open. And they're spilling all over the road.

"No gawking," I hypocritically bark at my guys. "Anyone looks anywhere but at the ass of the guy in front of him, you'll drop and give me fifty. And I'm not talking pesos."

They laugh. I've yet to inspire the fear in these guys that Coach Wells implanted in our team from day one. Maybe that's because he's older and I'm just an assistant. Maybe it's the "ass of the guy in front of him" remark, because a twenty-year-old male football player would rather be kicked in the crotch than be suspected of being gay at practice—even the two or three who I am certain *are* gay. Maybe because they know my bark doesn't match my bite.

Frank Wells—I still call him Coach—and I are pretty tight. Maybe even tighter than my dad and me. We just get each other, and he's easy to talk to. Granted, he's always using football analogies to make his points, but there's something comforting in that. People give him shit for it all the time, but I kind of like it—you really gotta be creative to pull off some of the analogies he does. That's something I'd like to be able to do: Layla'd show me one of her dog pictures, mention a problem she had, and I'd be able to bring it back to football and say something wise. And motivating.

"Okay, ladies, conditioning," I shout at the team. "Touch the line!" Groans come from a couple of players as the team forms two lines on opposite sides of the field, five yards apart. "And go!"

The first two players start running across the field sideways until they reach the end, where they have to touch the line. I stand at the line to make sure they touch it. If one guy misses, they all have to start over. These drills are called gassers. We do conditioning at the end of practice, when they're already empty, and they run another two hundred yards, stopping and starting until they practically fall over. It's torture, but anything that doesn't kill you, I remind them, probably needs to be done twice tomorrow.

"Don't cross your feet, guys. Technique!" reminds Coach Wells. One of Wells's favorite maxims is this: "Practicing technique is kinda like brushing your teeth. You don't do it for a couple days, everybody knows." The guys poke fun at Wells for all of his sayings—behind his back, of course—and I guess we did, too, in my day, but as I said, now there's a certain charm to them. I'd be lucky to be half that smooth.

• • •

I get to the cafeteria and there's Murphy's Law—or the corollary to Murphy's Law, anyway, the law that states that if there is one person on the entire campus whose name is spelled C-E-R-T-A-I-N T-R-O-U-B-L-E, that is the person you will run into in the cafeteria. So there is Heather, by herself, carrying a tray. She looks in my direction, and I send up a prayer to the Big Guy *not* to unite Hot PR Girl's (what I imagine to be) very toned ass with a seat at my empty table. That is a world of trouble that I do not want to get into. It's bad enough that my wife spends all of her time lately with every member of my family except me. It's always something. She's not coming to a team party because she's baking with my mom, some delectable treat that I won't even get to sample. Or she's building a ship in a bottle with my dad, because nobody does that anymore and they thought it would be fun. Or we're not spending my day off together because she's taking my brother,

Scott, to Century City to help him pick out some new date clothes. Does Scott actually *have* a date? No. But they're thinking that if he gets one he should have the clothes.

Occasionally, her friend Brooke pops into the act. But not too often.

It's hard to get mad at her, because Layla's so freakin' genuine about it. She just loves my family, and they're totally crazy about her. It's almost like there's something *too* right about it. I rarely complain. I've just sort of accepted it. But you know what? It's lonely. It seems like I'm always the last choice if it's between me and them.

But back to Heather, who is the last thing (okay, the last two things) I need to be all up in my face. So of course she walks right over, and in my head she asks, eyebrow raised, head cocked to the right, "Mind if I join you?" Then the fantasy nibbles on its bottom lip while it awaits my answer. The ghost girl knows the seat's not taken. She's playing it cool.

The real girl isn't playing at all. She's walking right by, looking around awkwardly like the new kid—which she is, come to think of it. So chivalry, or a reasonable facsimile, takes over.

"You can sit here," I say. "I mean, this is a seat that's open, here."

"Oh. Okay." And she smiles and sits.

"I'm married," I practically shout, as I hold up my ring finger for proof. "See?" That's the kind of thing you do when you go temporarily idiotic. "Not that you asked."

"Got it." She laughs. "Seat's not taken . . . you are. And how did you know I was just going to proposition you? Was it the Eau de Desperation that I spritzed on this morning?"

"I'm sorry. That was really schoolboy of me. You just wanted a place to sit and eat your gourmet lunch."

"Apology accepted," she says, with an easy smile. "Your wife would be proud."

I gulp. "It wasn't about you—it was totally me. I was reminding myself. Just shouldn't have done it out loud." A for effort. F for tact.

She gets an A for tact and gently changes the subject. "I thought I'd never make it out of that cafeteria line."

"You'll learn. The way things are going, they're talking seriously about some sort of reservation system." Which is true. UCCC has an up-and-coming football team and great academics, but a greater feather in its cap is its cafeteria, which would blow away any food critic who knew it was here. We have a five-star culinary arts department, and the chefs-to-be run the cafeteria as part of their training. It's pretty genius.

"First meal here?" I ask, as I inspect her tray. "You'll be okay with that. Just stay away from those garlic mashed potatoes." I point to her tray.

"Yeah, my last school cafeteria had the culinary expertise of a school cafeteria. I was hoping for an upgrade." She looks at my plate and sees I also have the potatoes. "But . . . ?"

"No, no. You misunderstand. They are *insane*. I dream about them. I'm not kidding. They roast the garlic to perfection first, and there must be some secret ingredient because they're seriously like crack. One bite and the monkey will be on your back."

She looks at me like she's not sure I'm telling the truth. Then she takes a bite. She tries to affect a "no big deal" look, but five seconds later she takes a second bite. And then a third. "Oh my God, you're *not* kidding. I want to eat these every day for the rest of my life." She closes her eyes and moans as she savors another bite, and I force myself to look away and remind myself that we're talking about a starchy tuberous crop, because the eyes closed/moan combo is a bit too much to handle.

"Okay, Meg Ryan," I say. "I told ya. I don't kid about carbs." Suddenly I sound like a bumper sticker promoting the Atkins diet.

"Oh, so you were worrying about my weight," she asks, mock-offended, but then drops the act when she gets distracted by three guys in business attire. "Who are *they*?"

"Ah, the suits. There's a law firm a couple blocks away. They got hip to how good the food is here, and they sneak in every so often."

"Nuh-uh," she says in disbelief.

"You don't believe me? Then explain *that*," I say, as I nod toward a far corner of the cafeteria, where about seven octogenarians sit and laugh as they dine.

"I . . . wish I could."

"Senior center. Two blocks away. They're first in line on days we have quiche. I think they assume there's some sort of early-bird special because they're so used to it out in the real world. Of course, maybe they've been here often enough to know that all the good stuff is picked over by the time the later afternoon rolls around."

She laughs out loud and smiles as she extends her hand across the table. "By the way, I'm Heather."

"Brett," I say. "I'm the defensive coordinator for the football team. We do okay, as you probably know. But really what I am is kind of an investor. Well, an inventor. Well, I wanna invest in this thing I'm inventing." *Duh.*

"What is it?" she asks.

"Oh, it's just this . . . athletic apparel . . . thing." I suddenly feel foolish talking about an idea that isn't that far along yet, and we settle into an awkward silence, each of us eyeing the other, eating our meals, and wondering if we're going to have sex. *Hold it—where'd* that *come from?* I haven't actually thought about having sex with anyone besides Layla since . . . ever. I mean, we *all* have fantasies. But this is a real girl. Sitting across from me at a table. With one dimple to the left of her mouth and her hair tied back in a ponytail, unsuccessfully trying to make herself less sexy. This is starting to suck.

"So what exactly do you do?" I ask, even though I know. I have to break the increasingly awkward silence.

"I'm the new SID. I'm replacing Mike Stiller."

"He was a good friend of mine," I say. And then add, "Duh-nuh-duh!" à la the part after "Jeremiah was a bullfrog."

She looks at me with a furrowed brow, and then looks away quickly. I do it again because I'm not content to let go of my song reference as a joke. "Duh-nuh-duh!"

"Do you have some form of Tourette's?" she asks sweetly. I mean, as sweetly as you can sound when you're asking someone if they're *challenged*.

"That was 'Joy to the World,' " I say. She just looks at me blankly. I now go so far as to start from the beginning. " 'Jeremiah was a bullfrog'? 'Was a good friend of mine'?"

She stands up with her tray. "I'm sure he was. Nice meeting you."

"It was a song," I add, even though she's already out of earshot. *Is she too young to know it?*

I turn around and want to punch my own face in. Not just for coming off like an idiot but for bringing up my idea while I did so. I always do that. Whenever I'm nervous or surprised by something, my brain panics and expels the first thought that comes to mind. Which these days is almost always—you guessed it—Wonder Armour. *Bleh.*

• • •

I sit at the bar with Doug (yeah, my pal from high school moved back to the Los Angeles area around the time I started working at UCCC, and we picked up right where we left off) and our friend Jared. I'm recounting my unfortunate first encounter with Hot PR Girl, which I regret immediately because I'm suddenly suffering an unbearable Crime Against Music in the form of Doug singing Van Halen's "Hot for Teacher."

"I got it bad, sooooo bad . . ." squawks Doug.

"It's *bad,* all right," I answer, referring to his singing. "And she's not a teacher."

"So how's Layla?" Jared asks. "She's really solid, dude."

"You calling my wife fat?" I joke.

I know what he means, though. We all hung out a couple of times, the four of us, when Doug first moved back to town, and Jared hasn't shut up about Layla since. Everybody loves her. But Jared's got other reasons for singing her praises. He's the recent recipient of a Dear John letter that wasn't intended for him to find. He was trying to hide an engagement ring he bought for his girlfriend, and when he went into the sock drawer, he happened upon the note. When he called her on it, she said she wrote it "ages ago" and swears that she's happy—but he can't shake it from his head, and now he's afraid that she's gonna dump him any second.

"That damn sock drawer," Jared says morosely, as he takes a swig of his beer.

"That's a great band name," I say. We come up with band names constantly—never mind that none of us is in a band.

"Or at least an album title," Doug adds.

"You ever think about the fact that your wife is the last woman you are ever going to be with?" I ask in Doug's direction. We had a running joke that he'd never get married—that every IT guy's true love is Diet Coke, since that's the only thing most take to bed—but he managed to find the right girl regardless.

Jared feels the need to interject. "No, because I don't have a wife. I could have had a fiancée, but that damn—"

"Sock drawer," Doug and I say in unison.

"I was talking mostly to Doug, bro," I add.

"Yeah, man. Layla's the last person you are ever going to be with. But you got married like twenty years ago."

"Six," I correct.

"This is the kind of stuff you should have thought about, oh, I don't know, *before* you got married."

"Yeah, man," Jared adds. "And Layla's awesome. What more could you want?"

"I don't know. Nothing. You're right. Layla's the best," I say.

"Trust me," Jared replies. "There's nothing more."

"Then that's pretty fuckin' sad."

"Who pissed in *your* cornflakes this morning?" Doug mutters. "All this 'cause you got some wood over a chick?"

"First of all, I didn't get wood," I correct. "And second of all, nothing. It's cool. I'm just contemplative tonight. Is that all right? Can we be grown-ups for one night? Is that allowed?"

"We've *been* grown-ups, dude," Jared says. "Sounds like you're just getting the memo and may not like the responsibility that comes with it."

"Fuck you, dude," I say, only I realize he might be right, and that fuckin' stings.

Luckily, I need to head back to school to do some prep work before our game against NWMSU. Otherwise, I'd have to hear more of this garbage. So I leave the guys to finish their happy hour, which will probably extend until the game, when they always show up to support the team by being slobs and yelling shit.

It's not that I don't love my wife. I do. I love the hell out of her. But there's a fundamental difference between loving your wife and loving being married. One has nothing to do with the other, I'm beginning to realize. Especially when it doesn't feel like we're connecting the way we used to. She did leave the game last week.

Am I going to find a note in the sock drawer one of these days?

# *layla*

Ginny shows up at our office—which is more pet playground than workplace, especially now that Lou, Trish's dog, is back from the groomer—but that's never seemed to matter. Ginny gets us. She always has.

"We don't photograph *people,*" Trish teases. "Sorry." She pretends to shut the door in her mother's face.

"Don't think we've met," Ginny says, holding her own. "I'm here to see my daughter: *Layla.*"

"Ouch," Trish says, and she takes a few steps back, pretending she's been stabbed. "Careful there, Mom. Any more of this emotional abuse and I could turn into a lesbian."

I push Trish out of the way and embrace Ginny. "Can you believe it? You were my first call!"

"Of course I can," Ginny says. "I'm so proud of my girls." She pulls Trish into a three-way hug. She's so amazing. We're lucky to have her.

"So, did you just come to celebrate in person?" I ask.

"No, honey, we had dinner plans, you and I. Remember? Now we have a great reason to celebrate."

*Crap.* I'm surprised I've forgotten. "Shoot. Did we? I thought we said tomorrow, but my days all blend lately and here you are, so . . . great!" I smile as I rack my brain to remember if we'd actually said today. I'm still foggy with thoughts of PETCO and the loans we'll have to apply for. "Trish? You in?"

"A celebration dinner?" Trish raises her eyebrows. "Mom paying? Hells yeah!" At this point Trish's dog gets jealous and starts scratching his tiny little dachshund paws against her leg, so she picks him up and pulls him into the group.

"Did you call Brett?" Trish asks me. And there must be something in their psychic sibling connection, because as soon as the words leave her lips my cell phone rings, which snaps me out of the contemplative trance I'd slipped into as I watched Trish's dachshund try unsuccessfully to scale her leg. They're funny little beings, dachshunds. They seem to go from being puppies to tripping over their ears and dragging their chests on the ground. I like to assume they're happy, but a lifetime of scraping your boobs across the pavement just doesn't seem ideal. Then again, snails don't mind.

Brett's call is still ringing on my phone. I press send. "Hello, husband."

"Hello, wife. Are you coming to the game?"

*Crap again.* I hear the excitement in his voice, but I'm pretty sure he'll let me off the hook this time. I really was planning to go with him, but now with Ginny here, and Trish and I celebrating the likely PETCO deal . . .

"I'm sorry, babe. Something came up. Maybe I can come late. I told your mom I'd go to dinner with her, and she's *here,* and Trish and I—"

"Huh," he interrupts. Apparently, he's angrier than I'd anticipated. He didn't give me a chance to explain my wonderful news, and he retreats into monosyllabic answers when he's pissed off but doesn't want to get into it.

"I'm sorry," I say. "I totally forgot. You see, Trish and I—"

"No big deal. It'll make it that much more special if you ever *do* show up and stay for a whole game again."

"I have great news—" I try one last time.

"Great," he snaps. "Tell me when I get home." He hangs up.

"He hung up," I say to Trish and Ginny.

"Oh, sweetheart, we can do a rain check," says Ginny. "Why don't you go to the game?"

"No," I say, slamming the phone closed as though there was someone on the other end to hear it. "We're celebrating."

*He's not even curious? How many times do I say I have great news? Probably never. And did he really just hang up on me?*

The second we get to the restaurant I start feeling terrible. I fumed for the whole car ride, but as soon as I get outside my own head I feel like the worst wife ever. It's true, last week I left early and I've missed a few other games this year, but how many seasons of how many teams have I been there for? Considering that, I've been pretty dutiful. Still, this is Brett's job, and I'm being totally unsupportive. I make a vow to myself to dig up my beak hat and get my ass into those bleachers for the next game no matter what, and quickly dial his cell-phone number to apologize.

"This is Brett. Leave a message."

*He's screening me? So much for my rescue mission.*

When I hang up the phone, Trish is giving me the look. "What?" I say defensively.

"You *know* what," she says. "We're celebrating. Stop obsessing. His team will win or lose and he'll come home and you'll be in bed, eating cereal, wearing his boxers and his *I Fucked Paris Hilton* T-shirt."

"No, he *doesn't* have a shirt that says that," Ginny says. Trish and I both look at her, two looks that both say: *Have you met your son?*

"Brett's been acting really weird lately," I say. At which point the look is now directed at me: *Have you met your husband?* So I add, "I mean, more than usual. He's all sensitive and edgy.

Honestly, since when does he care if I go to his games? I mean, I understand that I should be there, but it's unlike him to get all upset about it."

"He's Brett," Trish offers.

"Yeah, but he's also doing that sleep thing."

Ginny puts her fork down and does a trademark Ginny reveal: the leg cross-uncross, which tells you she's just become uncomfortable times two. "He's sleep-coaching?"

"Yeah," I say.

Brett coaches an imaginary team in his sleep when he's worried about something or about to make a change. It's sleepwalking but with an extra movement or two, so it's harmless if a little weird—though he's woken me up once or twice with shouts for tighter pass coverage. He does this especially toward the end of football season, when the important games come around. He crouched by make-believe sidelines for weeks before we bought our house, and from what I understand he nearly wore a path in the carpet at his parents' place, flailing his arms and celebrating fantasy touchdowns, before he proposed to me. *But what's he nervous about now? What momentous occasion could be on the horizon?*

"Do you think . . . No, I shouldn't say," Ginny says.

"Spill it," I growl.

"I know what she's thinking," Trish says. "And you know, she could be right. . . ."

"Can we cut the cryptic crap and let Layla in on the lightbulb?" I say to the pair, who seem to have discovered a new continent they don't want anyone to know about.

"She's talking in third person," Trish says to Ginny. "Nice alliteration, though. Tell her, Mom."

Ginny inches her chair toward mine, and I start to get nervous. She takes my hand in hers and smiles at me, which only magnifies the tension. "Honey?" she says.

"Yeah?" I reply, eyebrows raised. And then she inches closer and hugs me.

"Oh my God, Mom, can you *be* more annoying?" Trish spouts. Then she turns to me and suggests, "Brett wants to have a baby."

*He does?*

"He does? Did he tell you that?" I ask, as I try to process what they're saying—and yes, it does kind of make sense. Before he proposed to me he *was* extra-sensitive and almost snappy, though not in a mean way, just tense. The fact that he's become an almost unbearable ass now could simply be a reprise of that otherwise joyous time. After all, a baby's a new beginning.

"I think so, sweetheart," Ginny says. "He's probably thinking about starting a family of your own, and he's gathering the courage to bring it up."

"Wow," I say.

"I'm gonna be an aunt!" Trish cheers.

"Easy there, Tee," I say. "Let's not put the crib before the epidural."

"No wallpaper borders," Trish remarks darkly. "We can stencil, maybe."

"Oh!" Ginny squeals, eyes watery. "You and Brett will have the most beautiful children."

"Children," she said. Plural. Little baby Fosters. Little Bretts and Laylas. The more I think about it, the more I like it. It's weird, I never was one of those girls who thought about her biological clock; in fact, maybe mine's broken since I am . . . nearing thirty, but my alarm hasn't rung. Yet now that they bring it up, it feels right. Coming from such a small family—if I can even call our party of two that—I always knew I'd want to marry into a big family and probably have kids, but I never knew it would happen. I just got lucky with the Fosters. And making a baby with Brett would be the first real blood tie I had to my last name.

As if on cue, the moment I really start to settle into the glorious thought of Brett and me and baby makes three, an infant at the next table starts wailing.

# brett

Two things I hate: people who don't just come out and say what they mean, and strawberry anything. And also when something that's supposed to be simple and a break from the grind becomes a clusterfuck. So that's three.

Each year brings the Foster Family Autumn Barbecue—some say Famous, but I've taken to saying Notorious—and Layla's famous (I say notorious) strawberry-rhubarb pie, made with strawberries and rhubarb that she grows in a scrubby patch of dirt in our backyard. It was charming for a while, her playing Young MacDonald in the back forty square feet, but like all things charming, it eventually started to irritate the shit out of me. I don't want to sound like an asshole; it's not the idea of growing things in the backyard that gets me. It's the sanctimony, the "look at me." And then she puts strawberries in everything. Strawberry shortcake, strawberry cheesecake, strawberries and cream. I swear, one cold night we had strawberry stew. I know everybody else in my family loves the stuff and eats it up, but what about me? I've given up saying anything, because it does no good. I just live with it.

The family barbecue is something of a legend around town. Mostly because there are only nine Fosters—my mom and dad,

Scott, Trish, and me; Layla (Foster in name only); and then my dad's brother, Nate, his wife, Allison, and their daughter, Lucy—yet our little event has over the years morphed into a block party for practically all of Los Angeles.

Nate and Allison are crunchy granola folks. Allison refused to go to a hospital when Lucy was being born and gave birth underwater with a midwife and a lot of bad music playing. They believe in holistic medicine only, which essentially means *no* medicine. Lucy wasn't even vaccinated, and she's never had a shot in her life. I guess if she's healthy, that's all that matters, and she is. I call it dumb luck. Just not to their faces.

Now, I'm not one to judge—or, rather, I try to keep my observations mostly to myself—but they don't feed the girl breakfast. They give her chicken noodle soup or purees of vegetables and brown rice in the morning. That's *not* breakfast. I mean, that's just un-American. As a favorite uncle, I find it my duty to corrupt her whenever possible. Therefore, the barbecue is one of her favorite days of the year.

But we're not why it's legendary. Rather, it's because the entire neighborhood and several crashers from adjacent neighborhoods come every year, resulting in the transformation of Riverside Park into the Foster "Extended Family" Zoo. It's become not just a family tradition but a local convention, so busy that food trucks and vendors show up like clockwork and generally make a killing.

Layla and I roll up to Riverside Park at eleven-thirty a.m., and it's already packed. She's telling me again about this great deal for her and my sister, something about PETCO maybe franchising her photo-booth rights, but it doesn't sound like it's set in stone yet. I nod, thinking I'll believe it when I see it. I'm still thinking about my team's last game and how they're not doing as well this year as last.

I bust out my mitt and head over to the baseball diamond as Layla heads toward my dad's annual poker game. Layla's been a part of that game since we were juniors in high school, and she and my dad's friends take their card playing *very* seriously. As seriously as anyone can take a poker game where there're potato-salad droppings on the table.

Layla says that they all have certain tells and she knows when someone's bluffing nine times out of ten. She says my dad purses his lips and flares his nostrils and tries to look worried when he has a good hand. When he has a bad hand he massages his earlobe and smiles. Get it? He does the *opposite*. She says that Crazy John DeMarco will hum Sinatra when he has shit for a hand to bluff happiness, and if he's quiet he may actually have something. Elvis Presley songs can go either way. Rick Bennett keeps looking at his cards if they're bad, and looks around the table if they're good. And so on. I think she's full of crap—but then again, there's a reason I'm not part of the game, which involves a serious losing streak that began as soon as I started playing and ended when I retired. I prefer my sports to require the movement of all four limbs, anyway. I don't even consider poker a sport, honestly, though the poker activists insist that it is. And with all the money it's generating these days—as was the case with the British Empire, the sun never sets on Texas Hold 'Em—I guess they can call it whatever the hell they want.

"Your wife is taking Dad *downtown,*" Scott says when I return from the baseball game, with a head nod to signal that he's impressed. As if that would be a shock. As I said, Layla is Scotty's dream girl. Unfortunately, she's also his sister-in-law, so *that* ain't gonna happen. It's sweet, though. Sometimes when I see the way he looks at her, it reminds me of what I have. He's measured every girl he's ever dated against the Layla stick, and sadly, few measure up for more than a couple months.

"I know, little bro. She's the wind beneath your wings."

Scott takes my cue and starts to sing the tired Bette Midler classic. " 'Did you ever know that you're my'—hey! How awesome would that be for a gyro commercial?" he asks, all excited.

"Like the Greek sandwich?" I question. "Did you ever know that you're my *gyro*?"

"It's genius."

"Yeah," I say. "Except *not*."

"Put down the Hateorade, dude. That is gold!"

"They don't make commercials for gyros."

"Because they don't know me," Scott says. "Maybe that's my new career."

"Writing commercials for products that don't advertise?"

"Milk advertises!" he says. "It's not a brand of milk. Just milk. And cheese does. In fact, so does soup. 'Soup is good food'?"

"That's Campbell's," I correct.

"Milk still does," Scott points out, with a little less oomph than before. Then he mutters, "And so does cheese."

I'm already over the picnic. I'm ready to go home and have a nice quiet day with my wife. Maybe we can get over the tension that's been dogging us lately with some time on the couch. And on the kitchen table. And on the rug. It's hard not to get bored having sex with the same person year after year, but I will say this: Layla rocks the bedroom when she wants to. She and I always had sparks. Which is probably why I get so frustrated with the way things are now. Because they were so mind-blowing once upon a time and they've really faded.

But when I glance over at Layla and catch her laughing—no doubt at one of my dad's stupid jokes (the newest one's about a beer, a mop, and a skeleton who can't hold his liquor)—I know I'll be stuck here all day. She's got Lucy on her lap, and she's throwing a disgusting mud-and-saliva soaked tennis ball for Sammy Davis Junior, my parents' black Lab-terrier mix. She looks over to Scott and me and smiles.

*Great.* I guess we're skipping the table and the rug tonight. What a surprise. She's going to want to stick around for the long haul.

# *scott*

Layla is a goddess. Her hair—Jesus, it's like you expect it to be fake. It's sumptuous, like on a Botticelli or a Titian. But if you pull it, it's real. Because I have. And her little fingertips? They have no creases. Like she's carved from stone. But they're not cold or stiff or anything. Pygmalion made her; then she kicked him in the nuts, ran away, and developed a personality.

Layla is a *goddess*. I've spent more hours sketching her face than any art project I ever had in school. How the fuck did my dumbshit brother get so lucky?

I don't know which I hate more: the fact that I didn't get her or the fact that he did.

At least she and Brett stuck around for the whole barbecue. I could tell he was anxious to take off.

# *layla*

I'm feeling thoroughly maternal. I'm hyperaware of my ovaries. It's unreal. I guess that's the power of suggestion. So because I want to try harder, because I want to surprise Brett with unwarranted sweetness, and because it's Wednesday, I decide to bake brownies and bring them to his team at school. I've perfected the brownie. If I wasn't about to get rich off our pet photo booths, I would totally be the next Mrs. Fields.

Brooke stops by on her way to her job interview and relentlessly makes fun of me for baking.

"You are so lame," she says.

"Stop sweet-talking me like I'm your boss," I tease. "How many jobs have you lost in the last two years?" Brooke, for some strange reason, keeps taking jobs as a personal assistant, yet she has the worst attitude and personal skills of anyone I've ever known. She doesn't quite match the whole phone-answering, errand-running job description, so she's constantly getting fired.

"What I was going to say, if you hadn't so rudely cut me off, is that you are so lame if you don't let me have one of those brownies."

I fill Brooke in on the latest news, particularly the possible

PETCO deal, the forms Trish and I filled out to apply for loans, and Brett maybe wanting a child. She goes off on another rant.

"Jesus, really? You, too? You're already Miss Married. Can *one* of my friends not get pregnant and move to New Jersey?"

"First of all," I say, "I'm not pregnant. The idea is that we will potentially discuss it and maybe start trying. And second . . . New Jersey? Why the hell would I move to New Jersey?"

"I don't know," she says, with a wave of her hand. "My friend Lily did that. I never saw her again."

"I couldn't care less about Lily, or Rosemary, or the Jack of Hearts," I say.

Brooke just looks at me, confused.

"Do you not own *Blood on the Tracks*?" I ask. "Never mind. I promise you I will never move to Jersey," I solemnly swear. "I think only New Yorkers do that, anyway."

"Thank you. May I please have a brownie?"

"You may. But take it to go; I gotta hit the road. Good luck on your interview. Try not to tell them you got fired last time for calling the boss's wife a fat cow."

Brooke shrugs. "She was."

• • •

I show up like Susie Homemaker with my basket of goodies at the end of Brett's practice, and as I scan the sea of would-be brownie munchers (way to turn something completely innocent and make it sound eight kinds of *wrong*), I hope I made enough. I do the math in my head: I made three pans and cut three rows in each, divided those into six sections, which made eighteen per pan times three is fifty-four brownies, minus the three I put aside for Brett and the one that Brooke snatched, equals a total of fifty. I think Brett usually has around forty-five guys, so provided the team hasn't grown, I'm good.

As I walk onto the field, secure in my math and brownie-to-player ratio, I notice a female form in front of me. Granted, college girls do not look like college girls anymore—at least they don't look like we did when *I* was in college—but there is a seriously stacked girl out there.

My approach goes unnoticed by Brett, but one of his dutiful players tips him off.

"Coach," he says, and when Brett looks up, the kid nods in my direction.

"Hey, you," he says, as he gives me a one-armed hug. "Come to photograph a different breed of animal?"

"Yes," I say, as I pull back the plastic wrap atop my basket. "The eating habits of the UCCC Condors. I know they're carnivores, but I come in peace to tempt them with chocolate." Then I lean in and talk out of the corner of my mouth. "There are three more for you at home."

"Well, I have to say this is . . . unexpected. Definitely." Brett half smiles and gives me a look, and then he takes the basket and holds it up to the team. "My lovely and loving wife has brought me treats. Her world-renowned death-by-chocolate brownies. I know you girls are all trying to watch your figures, but if any of you step up and actually show me the hustle"—and here he jams an entire brownie into his mouth, then speaks with his throat full and teeth streaked with chocolate—"I mi' be willug to share nem."

Ah, the practice isn't quite over. The team gets back into formation and Brett turns to face me again. I'm wondering when he's going to introduce me to his *friend,* the chick standing next to him. I notice that I'm clenching my jaw in a forced smile as I look in her direction, wondering who she is. Brett notices, too.

"Sorry. This is Heather," he finally says, as he gestures to the undeniably gorgeous woman. "Heather, this is Layla. My wife."

"I'm his wife," I repeat. "The old ball and chain," I add pathetically, not really knowing why I suddenly feel the need to do so.

"Great to meet you," she says, reaching for my hand and flashing her veneers. "I've heard *so* much about you."

She has? Because I've heard nothing about her. Not a word. Not a lone syllable even.

"Yeah, you, too," I say, as I smile.

"Really?" she asks.

*No.* "I think so . . ." I say as I look to Brett. "Have I?"

"Heather's our new PR guru," he jumps in.

"Teaching them to meditate?" I ask, almost prickly and unlike myself.

"Ha, no," Heather says. "Everything but." This gets a bunch of snickers from the perverted young minds within earshot.

"Okay, then, I'm going to take off," I say, with a quick kiss on the cheek to Brett and a smile and nod at Heather. "Nice to meet you!" I practically shout, instantly aware of the exclamation-point enthusiasm I've used to drive the point home, all out of proportion to the moment.

"You, too," she says.

"Thanks so much for the booty, baby."

As I walk away, I wonder so hard that I feel like my brain should be oozing out of my head: Why the hell didn't she excuse herself when I showed up? Why do I feel like the interloper, the one interrupting a moment? A moment that they are going to get back to as soon as I'm out of their sight. Doesn't she have somewhere to be? Shouldn't she take a hint? I'm not a jealous wife. I've never been the jealous wife. But I've never walked into a situation like this. And I know he was at work and I was just there dropping off the brownies, but couldn't he steal away for a moment to properly thank me? And why does the new PR woman need to be at football practice? Let the team drop and give him twenty and let her drop back down to hell.

# *brett*

When you come to a point in a movie where you know something bad is about to happen to your favorite character, you want to tell him. You want to yell at him and say, "Dude, can't you hear the ominous soundtrack? You know that guy who you think is your friend, the one you fought with in the war? Well, he just called the bad guy and double-crossed you, and you're about to take a bullet. Just thought you'd like to know." So when you come to a point in life where you know something bad is about to happen to a favorite character, and this time it matters because it's real, you warn him, right? In my case, wrong. Nobody says a thing. I must not be anyone's favorite character.

So that's how shit like this happens. I stay out with the guys later than I probably should. I tried to tear myself away, but there was something happening that I hadn't experienced in a long time: fun.

I miss going out and staying out. And I miss being excited about who I'm coming home to. Lately I've been so annoyed. . . . I got married too young. I never thought that before, but clearly I did. *We* did. It's not her fault or mine, really. I love Layla. Even when I compare her to Heather—who's talking to me again, at least in a work capacity, kindly forgetting the whole "Jeremiah was a Bullfrog" incident—she comes up looking pretty good. But when I hear Doug talk about things he's doing with his new wife and how excited he is about everything, it just makes me feel like Layla and I are missing something. And when I hear my single friends talk about how blissful and uncomplicated their lives are, I can't help but feel a little bit jealous.

So I mention this to my friends, because we're friends, and that's what friends do: They bitch about shit. Their wives, their jobs, their performance anxiety. Well, no one ever mentions their performance anxiety.

But to add insult to misery, Doug slips about something so monumental—such a colossally freakin' big deal—that I do an actual spit-take. Which is less outward-spitting and more choking on my beer as it goes down my windpipe.

"*What did you say?*" I ask, once I regain my composure, because what he said doesn't make sense.

"I said, if I'd known you were gonna be so ungrateful, I'd have held on to Layla when I had her."

"Held on to her? In your *dreams* you had her."

"Well," he says, a little defensively, "I suppose that one time in my parents' basement doesn't qualify as a dream. . . ."

My face feels like it just got set on fire and then put out with a rake. And my expression must read something similar, because Doug immediately stiffens.

"Look, I don't mean anything by it," Doug adds. "Layla's great. And you have her, so what the hell are we talking about?"

"Nothing, we're not talking about a damn thing."

Which still probably sounded a little angry. It would appear that my friend Doug is trying to tell me he was with Layla before I was—and I don't buy it, since I know that Layla and I lost our virginity to each other. But on the off chance that the world is coming to an end and he actually did sleep with Layla before I did, I don't want him knowing I've been oblivious to it all these years.

I get home and Layla is in our bed, wearing a lace getup, high heels, and a come-hither smile. . . . And if you believe that, you're not paying attention. The reality is this: I get home and Layla is in our bed, wearing her ratty ten-*plus*-year-old *Yo quiero Taco Bell* Chihuahua T-shirt (which I once tried to throw away and she fished out of the trash), eating dry Cap'n Crunch straight from the box, and scowling at me.

"Major pileup on the freeway?" she says, and then shifts her eyes back to the TV. "Or just in the part of your brain that knows how to tell time?" She's watching one of those cop shows. *Law & Order SVU Need 2 Get a Life.*

"I don't know," I answer, and look at my watch. "Is it that time when you give me a bunch of shit for staying out too late—which, by the way, is *so* welcoming. I can't imagine why I didn't race home earlier."

"Had you raced home earlier, I wouldn't be giving you shit. This is my point."

"Oh, is that your point? You're just so subtle I was having a hard time reading between the lines."

"Nice," she says. "Sarcasm is definitely going to help."

"Tell me what *will* help and I'll do it."

"Okay," she says, and places the cereal box down on the bed to free her hands. "One, don't stay out so late and not even bother to call. Two, don't come home drunk every time you do stay out so late."

"So wait. I *can* stay out late as long as I don't come home drunk?"

She ignores me, resumes her tally, and ticks off her third finger. "Three, act like a grown-up. You spend so much time around college kids, I think sometimes you forget you're not one of them. You're irresponsible."

"Okay, so we're done with the things I need to do, and now we're just calling names?"

"I'm not calling you names, I'm saying you need to grow up."

My head just about explodes. *I* need to grow up? When she's been quietly backing out of the relationship for the past few weeks, or at least not caring about what makes me happy anymore, and spending all her time with my family and her friends? When she quite possibly has been lying to me for *years* about us sharing the most special moment of our young courtship? *Shit.*

She's right. I do need to grow up. We both do. And I think that may be the real problem. I think I *am* growing up, and growing *out* of this relationship. I went from being totally convinced that there was nothing better out there, to being mostly convinced, to being kinda convinced. Now I'm starting to be convinced that she's *not* the one. But now is not the time or place for this conversation. Not with the booze I drank burning in my brain.

"You're right," I say.

She's stunned. "I am?"

"Yeah." I nod. "You're right, and I'm sorry."

She softens immediately. "It's okay."

"No, it's not. I really am sorry. And I think we should talk about this, about us, about a lot of things, but not right now. It's too late and I'm too intoxicated. But tomorrow? Dinner?"

"Yes. Yes, please. That sounds perfect."

"Can I sleep in these clothes and start growing up tomorrow?" I ask.

"No," she says, with a wicked smile. "But I'll help you out of them."

This is a surprise. I miss her being like this. If things were always this way . . .

Even though I'm conflicted about us and where we're going and what our future holds, if that smile is any indication of things to come, I'm not saying no.

# *layla*

There are two ways to describe my clothes after a day of work: stretched out and/or hairy. My jeans fit every morning when I put them on, but by lunchtime they are always stretched out and look like I've been dragged behind a horse. Why? Because I spend the majority of my working day on the ground. I sit on the floor, because when I'm shooting I like to be at the dogs' height. It makes them feel comfortable, and I think it helps us develop a good rapport. But the rapport you need with a high-strung, short-haired pointer who would rather lick your face and nuzzle your crotch than sit for a photo, and with a decidedly low-key, brush-cut husband who, come to think of it, would also rather face-lick and crotch-nuzzle than sit for a photo, are two very different things.

Brett's been tough to read lately. And this whole situation is new: He was weirder than I've ever seen him last night, though it all ended well. There was an intensity to his lovemaking, something almost desperate. I tell myself not to read too much into it. I've been proposed to, but I've still not heard that most delightful and dangerous proposal that two people float at each other when they've decided they're ready to become more than two. Maybe others feel guided by an unseen biological hand. Maybe they have love to spare and want to shine the excess on a new life. Maybe they get the feeling that something more between them is needed. In the case of Brett and me, it's hard to say what's prompted it.

TLC has three shoots today, and then I have my dinner with Brett. Trish is convinced he's going to talk about us starting a family. I brought a change of clothes so, in that miraculous moment, I'm not covered in fur.

Shoot number one is of Rex, a skittish Siamese cat we met a few days ago at his consultation. When Rex and his mom arrive, Trish takes Lou and locks him in our office, so Rex doesn't have a conniption.

"Sorry, Lou," Trish says, as she shuts the door. "It's a cat. You know how *they* are."

"Can we not disparage the cat population?" I quietly admonish, since Rex's cat-loving owner is a mere twelve feet away.

"Hello," Trish says warmly to the woman to whom the cat is stuck. Literally. The cat has clawed into the woman's sweatshirt and will not let go.

"*Hmm,*" I muse. "Do you want to be in the photo, too?"

"No," the woman says. "He'll warm up."

What happens next happens so fast I'm not even sure how to describe it. I *think* the woman plucked the paws from her shirt and put the cat down, but the cat may have released its own grip and flown off. Either way, in a Tasmanian-devilish blur, the cat moves past us and out of sight.

We spend the next two hours (our studio is *not* that big, mind you) searching for Rex, calling for Rex, crying for Rex, and assuring Rex's mother that he has not left the building, as there is no other way out.

But then she hears movement in the back office and insists Rex is there.

"No, that's Lou, my dog," Trish says.

"You have a dog? There's a *dog* here?" she screeches.

"It's just a dachshund," I say. "They're small. Low to the ground. Zero jumping ability. Very nonthreatening."

"Rex!" the woman shrieks, and flings the door to our office open. Lou cocks his head and looks up at the screaming woman. "What did you do to my Rex?"

"He didn't touch Rex," Trish says calmly.

"It's been two hours," she screeches. "He could have devoured him in that time. Call nine-one-one!"

"What? Why?" Trish asks.

"Before he starts to digest! They need to pump his stomach!"

"Really?" Trish deadpans. "So in addition to you believing that my dog—who happens to actually be *smaller* than your cat—*ate* your cat, you also believe that he's swallowed the cat whole."

Trish is losing her patience. Part of working well together is being intuitive—knowing when your partner is sixteen seconds away from choking a customer. I see the look in Trish's eyes, and I rush to stand as a buffer between the two. The woman is hurling accusations at Lou, Trish's baby. And them's fightin' words.

"The door was closed," I offer. "There's no way Lou even saw Rex."

But Lou does smell him. Lou scurries over to the kitchen and starts standing on his hind paws and scratching at the oven, wagging his tail.

"What is it, boy?" Trish says.

We follow Lou and open the oven. Thankfully, Rex isn't in there, but Lou is insistent. We stare at the oven, at the microwave, at the cabinets . . . nothing. And yet Lou is now trying to jump on top of the oven, bless his tiny little legs.

"What's he saying?" the woman asks, as if we speak dog. I mean, if anyone speaks dog, it's us, but she's looking at us like we have a dog-to-English dictionary.

"He may smell Rex," I offer.

"He's certainly not lethargic, what with having eaten your whole cat and all. Look at all that energy," Trish muses.

And then I see a tail. At least the hint of a tail. It's behind the microwave in a cavity that's barely within reach. A spot that only a frightened cat would seek out as a hiding place.

"Okay, crisis over." I exhale. "I've found Rex's tail. And I'm certain that Rex is attached."

"Rex!" the woman coos, and reaches up to coax him from the cavity into which he's wedged. As soon as she has him safely in her arms, she whirls back on us. "This is an unsafe setting, and I am not letting you photograph my Rex. Today or ever."

"We're crushed," Trish says, and I don't do anything to contradict her.

"You should note on your website that this isn't a cat-friendly environment, so that other cat owners won't make the mistake of coming here."

"We'll get right on that," I say, as I usher her to the door.

"I know lots of cat owners," she threatens.

"Bye-bye," I say, almost singsongy.

She leaves, and Trish and I have a laugh. Trish has always said we shouldn't shoot cats unless it's with a gun, but there's a hint of truth in every joke, and today didn't do much for the cause.

Our second customer is a celebutante (whose name will go unmentioned) who brings her new Maltese puppy in for their first photo session—photos she's hoping to sell to *People* or *Star* magazine, if that's, like, okay with me.

She walks in wearing twelve-inch heels and hair extensions—at least I think they're hair extensions, because last week's tabloids had her with a bob, and if they're not extensions I need to find out what vitamins she takes asap. She holds Maggie May (whose name is not connected to anyone she's related to or sleeping with, in case you were wondering) out awkwardly, not gingerly per se, more like she's just really uncomfortable holding the pup. Her detached demeanor shows she isn't used to genuine care.

"Doesn't Maggie have the funniest belly button?" she asks, as she pulls on Maggie May's tiny, hair-covered puppy penis. "I kiss her belly button every night."

The look that passes between Trish and me is one of shock and awe. It's this moment when we both realize that this poor dumb girl thinks her male puppy is a female. Hence the name Maggie May. How do you broach this subject with a tabloid wunderkind? How do you tell her that she's not nuzzling her girl puppy's tummy, she's fellating her boy dog?

Trish just walks out of the room. Leaving me alone to deal with this. Awesome.

As my mind searches for a delicate way to put it, the celebutante becomes aware of a long pause and the anguished look on my face as I stare at the little fellow.

"Is something wrong with my dog?" she asks.

"I'm sure the dog's fine," I say. "It's his *name* I'm not so sure about."

"Her name," she corrects me.

"Well, that's kind of an issue, too," I say.

I proceed to tell her about the slight mistake, and I assure her that the dog himself probably didn't notice or mind the error, so no harm done—although maybe she should find some other part of his body to kiss good night.

She's at first shocked, then extremely embarrassed, then almost instantly indignant. She storms out, her own handler trailing just behind as though he was on some leash of his own, and she seethes, "That breeder is *done* in this town." And I think to myself, that poor breeder is probably just the latest in a long line of people to whom the little brat hasn't listened.

Our third customer is a basset hound, and the photo shoot goes off without a hitch. Trish insists on setting him next to Lou in a contest of low-riders: whose ears are longer, whose belly is closer to the ground, which one looks more bored and depressed—in our human estimation, though, they're both clearly pampered and overfed.

And then it's time for dinner. I change into my clean, unstretched clothes and put my second shoe on as I hop to the door. I'm nervous and excited, and nervous, and ready, yet nervous and happy. Most of all happy.

Trish watches me hop around with a stupid smile on my face and gets this bemused look.

"Tonight's the night!" I yell, as I make my way out the door.

"Rod Stewart!" she calls back, thinking we're playing some sort of game.

# *trish*

Marriage kills love. I don't say that because I can't get married in most of the United States; I say it because a marriage contract puts conditions on love when love is supposed to be unconditional. That said, Layla and Brett have found a way to make it work, and I'm glad. Watching her rush off to sit across from my brother all moony-eyed, holding hands and talking about making smaller versions of each other, makes me almost long for that.

But then I think about the majority of my long-term relationships and the people I know in long-term relationships, and how most of them border on best pal/roommate situations—i.e., sexless and boring. And that's when things are going well. I don't mean to stereotype; in fact, that's one of my major pet peeves. News flash: All lesbians are not butch chicks or helpless femmes who date butch chicks. We are many and varied. To an extent. Apparently not *that* many and varied, because while some of *The L Word* can be a little unrealistic at times, the whole "sleeping with someone who has slept with an ex" thing is a truth. You kind of need to outsource if you want to avoid that.

I tend to consider myself an "iron femme." I'll wear a suit, but

I'll also sometimes wear killer heels and a super-hot dress. I love hair and makeup yet can write a brilliant business plan, cook a gourmet meal, change the oil in my car, get my nails done, and kick ass in soccer. I get things done, but I never compromise the fact that I am a woman. I don't need to chop all my hair off or be overly girly to satisfy or dodge stereotypes.

I'm currently between relationships and deciding between two girls. Both are exceptional, and each brings something completely different to the table. So rather than decide, I'm enjoying getting to know them both and just taking things as slow as I can—thus discrediting the popular joke: "Question: What does a lesbian bring to a second date? Answer: A moving van." I'm not about moving in five minutes after meeting someone. No, thanks.

"I'm back," Layla says, as she breezes back in. "Do I look like a mother?"

"You had the conversation, got busy, and you're already pregnant?" I look at my watch. "That is impressive."

"Not so much. I'm nervous. Am I ready? I'm totally ready."

"You just came back to have a conversation with yourself?"

"No," she says. "I came back because I forgot *this*."

Layla takes a stuffed owl off her desk and holds it up at me. I say "at" me and not "to" me because it's almost threatening. I hate that owl. Her mom made it for her, sewed it from scratch, apparently, and let's just say it hasn't held up through the years. It's green, for starters—I mean, owls are not green—and has one button eye, which is hanging from a thread, a dark stain on its stomach, and all in all it's just not an attractive entity. It's sat on her desk—I think because Brett banished it from their place when they moved in together—for the past I don't know how many years and I've always hated it, but she loves it and it's a remembrance of her mom, so I never say anything. Until now.

"What are you doing with him?" I ask.

"Who?" she asks.

"The decrepit owl in your hands," I answer, but before I finish I realize she was making a joke.

"*Hoo,* who," she says, mimicking an owl.

"Yeah, yeah, okay, I get it."

"I want to bring Mr. Owl to dinner."

"Why?"

"Because when Brett brings up kids and we toast the next phase of our life, I want to have Mr. Owl there. Because someday, maybe nine months from today, I will give Mr. Owl to my son or daughter."

"That's abuse," I say. "That thing is . . ."

I stop myself when I see her cocked eyebrow as she waits for me to desecrate one of the last possessions that ties her to her mother. I won't do it.

"It needs a bath, is all," I say softly. "And maybe another eye."

"I think he looks as handsome as ever," she says, puffed out and proud. And she shoves the thing into her purse and waves good-bye.

# *layla*

I'm seated across from Brett, and we've fallen into a conversational lull. Nothing on topic has been discussed yet, and he looks anxious but sweet. His eyes are darting around the restaurant, from the bread basket, to a waiter, to our neighboring tables, to a bizarre painting of a seductive-looking horse with a flower in its teeth, back to the bread basket, and after every few glances he lands back on me and smiles nervously.

I just want to hold him and tell him it's okay, it's all gonna be okay. I want to put him out of his misery and just blurt it out myself, but I know this is a big deal and I want him to bring it up in his own time.

"That sounds like quite a day," he says. "And I guess now we know that she really is a natural blonde."

"It was unreal. I was so embarrassed for her," I say.

"All that *and* you lost a cat."

"I wouldn't say lost as much as temporarily misplaced."

"Trish must have been beside herself."

"She was cool," I say. "Mostly. Until the woman blamed Lou."

"Ha!" Brett laughs. "And she *lived*?"

"Everyone got out alive," I remark, and smile reassuringly, as if to say, *Okay, babe, we don't need to have any more of this filler chitchat.* But we fall into another respite, which Brett uses as an opportunity to shove bread into his mouth.

Finally, I can't take it anymore. I reach across the table and take both of his hands in mine.

"Just say it," I urge, with a gentle squeeze.

Brett's eyes dart up and to the left, his brow furrowing. "Say *what*?"

"Just . . . say it." I repeat. "I know. And I'm ready, too."

He looks surprised. "You *are*?"

"Yes!" I insist. "It's time."

"Really?" he asks, suddenly sounding not so sure.

"I mean, *we* were practically kids when we met," I say.

"Exactly," he agrees. "We were kids."

"And now we're grown up."

"And we learn things about ourselves," he says, picking up where I left off. "And maybe who we were when we met, and what we wanted is different now. Because we're different now. In fact, a few of the guys were talking about a biochemistry class and they mentioned how every seven years cells completely regenerate—so by that logic, we actually *are* different people."

"Well," I counter, "I've known for a while this is where things should go with us."

"You did?"

"Of course. It kind of brings things full circle."

"Wow," he says, falling back in his chair and letting his shoulders drop away from his ears for the first time since we sat down. "So you'd say . . . you agree that we . . . we should maybe think about different options for moving forward?"

*Does he think I can't get pregnant? Does he forget that little thing we've been using called birth control? How about the weight gain I've suffered all these years from the hormones in that freakin' pill? We haven't even tried and already he wants to* adopt?

"I don't think we really need to go there yet, babe. We should at least *try* to do it ourselves first. Keep it simple. Plus, I hear the legal aspects and paperwork are a real bitch."

"Wow." His face is a mixture of unreadable emotions. "You are . . . you're really surprising me here, Layla. This is not how I thought this conversation was going to go. I mean . . . I . . . I guess I'm relieved, if surprised. So do you think we should set a time to really do this? Maybe pick a neutral spot?"

"You mean like a hotel?" I ask.

"We could use a hotel, I guess. I wasn't thinking of a specific place. I just thought . . . I don't know. So how do we proceed? Is it a temporary thing?"

"Temporary?" I ask.

"I mean, how far are we taking this?"

"You mean how many?"

"How many what?" he asks.

"Kids, you goose."

"Wait . . . what?"

"Are you asking me how many kids I'll want to have, ultimately? I don't know. I figured we'd just start with the one and take it from there."

# brett

*Holy shit. Is she pregnant? Are we in the same conversation? Am I in the twilight zone? I knew things were going way too smoothly.*

"A baby?" she says, which echoes in my head over and over again. "You look really confused."

And then it all starts to hit me in these fast-paced, montage-like flashes, punching me in the face, knocking into my pea-brain a terrifying scenario: the recent weirdness. *Bam.* Her mood swings. *Punch.* The amount of ice cream she's been sucking down. *Thump.* Her talk about taking up knitting. *Smack.* Layla moving furniture out of the extra room the other day. *Whack.* The ceiling-hanging mobile she bought—fuck, wasn't that a prop for a photo shoot? How could I have missed all those signals? But now she realizes that we're having difficulties and—

"Are you *pregnant*?" I blurt.

"Already?" she asks, like she's surprised by the question.

"Are you pregnant?" I repeat.

"No!" she says.

"Phew!" I let out a heavy sigh. "Thank God."

"I beg your pardon?" she says, seeming taken aback.

"Well, we wouldn't want to bring a child into the world just as we were . . ."

Layla's eyes widen. The relief I felt three seconds earlier gets replaced with panic again. Were we having two different conversations after all?

"What were we talking about?" I ask.

"You tell me, Brett," she says, and she doesn't look happy, so I decide to bite the bullet.

"I thought we were talking about us. About maybe taking a break."

"A *break*?" she repeats with disgust. "We're not Ross and fucking Rachel! We're married. Say what you mean, Brett."

"A separation?"

"Unbelievable," she says through gritted teeth. She's shaking her head, clearly shocked.

"I think we have a miscommunication here," I say, trying to backpedal or at least soften the situation.

"No, we *had* one. You just cleared it right up." Then she whips out that crazy stuffed owl she's had since I've known her. She shakes it at me. "And to think . . ."

But she doesn't finish her sentence.

"I'm sorry. I thought we were on the same page."

"We're not even in the same book," she says. "Not even in the same library!"

"No kidding. We aren't. Because I thought I got the book that had a happy ending. Not the one where my wife and I lose touch and she becomes such a part of my family that she may as well be my sister!" I snap.

"Hardly, because your sister doesn't like men. She's *smart*."

"So what does that make you?" I snap. "Because you . . . you *love* men. You've loved men since . . . how long exactly?"

"I'm not sure what you're asking me. How long have I loved *you*?"

"Yeah, I'm not sure what I'm asking you, either," I grunt. "How about this: Who's the first person you had sex with?"

## *layla*

So now you know. I lost it at fifteen. To say it was a rough patch in my young life would be understating things: It was like being dragged over a bed of nails in a nylon body stocking.

Why didn't it come out earlier? At first it was because I didn't want to blow things with my new boyfriend at the time—Brett—who just assumed that I was a virgin, too, and that we would lose our virginity together. For that reason I said nothing about my first and certainly only meaningless sexual encounter, which happened in the basement of Doug's house, drunk. It was our first time drinking, too, a silly experiment with Jim Beam that got way out of control. (It was as horrible as you might imagine, and worse—contrary to his confident assertions, his mom was upstairs folding laundry nearly the whole three and a half minutes.) I said nothing to Brett through high school and college because I feared the news would poison our blossoming relationship, even as I comforted myself with the rationalization that it wasn't a big deal. Funny thing about big deals: What looks like one to me doesn't always look like one to you, and vice versa. Better just to let the other person get a look and decide for himself.

Shame has a habit of snowballing, and by the time Brett and I were married, I was positively terrified of telling him, though doing so at any time before he stumbled on the truth by himself probably would have defused the whole situation. Instead, *kaboom*.

But I didn't take the vow " 'til death do us part" with the intention of dying before I turn thirty. And the vow was " 'til death do us part," not " 'til uncomfortable truths do us part." And since Brett and I are both alive and plan to be for some time, I am not parting with my husband.

Marriage is about commitment. And compromise. And if need be, change. If things aren't working the way they are—and clearly they are not—then I am willing to do the work necessary and/or make changes. But until I know what needs to be changed, I can't know how to work. So just before Brett and I get home, each not talking out of anger and sheepishness, I swear to him I'll make an emergency appointment for us with a marriage counselor for tomorrow night. Brett says he'll go, but he sleeps on the couch.

• • •

I walk into the office, and Brett is already there in the waiting room, seated by the window. There's an air conditioner jutting out of the wall, dripping condensation on a pile of month-old *New Yorker* magazines. What, are they trying to keep us awake by keeping it cold, or does the therapist just like to avoid seeing his patients sweat? Brett's nervously tapping his fingers on his lap.

"Hi," I say, trying to be civil—a grown-up. He'd already left the house when I woke up. It shocked me. I left a message on his cell phone telling him where to show up. "Thank you for agreeing to this."

"Of course," he answers distractedly, as a door opens in front of us.

"Mr. and Mrs. Foster," the therapist says, as he gestures toward the empty room behind him. "Please, come in."

The first half hour is awkward. I imagine the first half hour with any new therapist is awkward, but our therapist has an enormous flesh-colored mole just slightly to the left side of his nose, and for some reason I can't get past it. So while I make it seem like I'm making eye contact, I'm actually just trying not to stare at the mole. My eyes drift back and then dart away, and I put my hand on my chin and crinkle my eyes as if thinking, *You've got a really good point there,* but instead I'm thinking, *You've got a really big* mole *there*. How am I supposed to focus on fixing my relationship?

The fact that I have no idea what is going on with Brett makes everything even more confusing. I try to get Brett to tell me what needs to change, because obviously he's not happy, but he doesn't offer anything. I explain away my stupid *real* first time with bigmouth Doug, and aside from the one comment Brett barks out about our whole relationship being based on a lie—a bit of an exaggeration, given how truly unimportant to me the encounter with Doug was—he's not particularly combative. He just seems uninterested. At one point he actually asks the therapist, "You have a Chase branch next door. Do you know what time it closes?" Apparently, he's more interested in his savings account than saving our marriage.

Finally, when I bring up the whole seven-year-itch thing, he snaps. "This isn't about other women, Layla."

"Then what?" I plead. "What is it?"

"It's *you*! It's you . . . with my sister, you with my mom, you with my dad, you with my brother!"

The therapist's eyebrows rise.

"There's nothing going on with me and his brother," I say. Then I add, "Or his dad. And for the record, the Doug thing was more than fifteen years ago—before I even kissed Brett."

The therapist writes something down on his yellow legal pad. I'm not sure why he's taking notes, and I'm not sure how I feel about it, but I'm hyperaware of the beads of sweat forming above my brow. Guess the air-conditioner trick didn't work.

"You're not like a *wife,*" Brett blurts.

"What do you mean by that?" the therapist asks, and I'm all ears because I think I'm a pretty damned good wife.

"I mean that she's all over my family. She's very close with them. Too close. It's like they all come first. Her relationship with them takes priority over our marriage. She's partners with my sister, and shops with my mother, and plays card games with my father. I didn't get married to have another sister."

"I'm hearing you feel neglected," the therapist says.

"This is helpful," I add. "This at least lets me know what I'm dealing with. I know you don't want a divorce. I know you're frustrated, and I guess I understand. So okay, I'll make changes. Trish and I have a successful business, so that's not exactly going away, but I won't play any more Rock Band on the Xbox with your brother. And I'll cut down on the poker with your dad."

Brett just looks at his lap. One bead of sweat starts to make its way down my temple.

"Okay, fine. I won't spend so much time with your mom?"

Still he says nothing.

"Are you serious?" I ask. "Do you really want me to stop being partners with Trish?"

"I didn't say I want any of that," Brett says, still not looking at me. "You're not getting it."

"Tell her what you want," the therapist says. "Tell her what she isn't getting."

Finally, Brett looks at me. "I feel like you're my sister. Not my wife. And I do think we should get a divorce."

• • •

When you set out to live according to some grand master plan, you are essentially assuring yourself a lifetime of letdowns.

Expectation is planned disappointment, and I am nothing if not a planner. At twelve, I planned how I'd lose my virginity to the man I loved (I suppose the *how* is obvious, but I meant "how" as in: not in a car, not on prom night, and not to any current pop song that would one day be irrelevant and embarrassing), how I'd wear my hair at my wedding, and how old I'd be when I had my first child (calculating also how old I'd be when that child turned twenty-one).

Let's revisit those three things. We've just learned that I lost my virginity—no, not in a car, but alas to the scintillating soundtrack of Lisa Loeb's "Stay (I Missed You)" with a side order of Beck's "Loser." And to Doug. My wedding hair? On my wedding day my hair was still growing out from an Unfortunate Bangs Incident, so my updo was actually an up*don't*. And I'd planned to have my first child at the ripe old age of twenty-five, which would make me forty-six when the kid turned twenty-one. I am not only already four years late for that projection, but on the night I thought I was going to start the baby-making phase of my life, I learned instead that I'm quite possibly on my way to being single again. I'm also driving like a fugitive on the 405 to get home.

But not *my* home.

I need my family. So I'm driving straight to the only home the adult me has ever known: the Fosters'.

• • •

When I walk in I head straight to the basement and dig through five boxes until I strike gold—or rather gingerbread. I pull out the gingerbread-house kits and dust them off. I know that Ginny usually buys new ones each year, but there's always one or two tucked away in the basement, and I have a desperate need to decorate a gingerbread house.

I don't even go upstairs into the kitchen. I take off my jacket, turn on the AM radio, which barely gets reception, roll up my sleeves, and start decorating. A few moments later I hear Brett's dad calling down to me, although he doesn't know it's me who's down here.

"Hello?"

"Hi, Bill. It's just me."

"Layla-cakes!" he bellows, as he bounds down the stairs. "What are you doing down here?"

I wave my right arm before me to show off the beginnings of my house. "I am creating."

Bill cocks his head backward and bunches his mouth to one side. He reaches up to scratch his neck and looks to the stairs as if an explanation will be heading down—or at least maybe his wife. You see, there wouldn't be anything wrong with me helping myself to the basement and these gingerbread house kits, if it weren't October.

"Gin?" he calls out.

"Yeah, BillyBoo?" she answers, using one of her pet names for him.

"We're in the basement," he says. "Come join us."

"Who's we?" Ginny asks, as she makes her way down, in her cute gold slippers with the silver detail.

"LayLay!" she exclaims, overjoyed as always to see me. But her smile soon turns to a look of concern, and suddenly I know why Bill called Ginny downstairs. Although I hadn't decided at any point to start crying, apparently my eyes did and forgot to clue me in. The drip onto my house's gingerbread dog gives it away.

Ginny and Bill surround me, then sit on either side as Ginny rubs my back and Bill sighs heavily and looks down at his lap.

Finally, he speaks. "Do you want to talk about it?"

I open my mouth, but the words don't come out. I look at Ginny and remember our dinner and everything we talked about. It wasn't just me. She'd thought the same thing.

"Honey," Ginny says. "Whatever it is, we love you and we are here for you."

I look back and forth at them and open my mouth again to speak, but this time only a yowl comes out. I am sobbing like a baby.

"For gosh sake, whatever it is," Bill says, "it can't be that bad."

I sniff back a few tears and pick up a candy cane.

Bill takes the candy cane from my hand and a smirk spreads across his face. "Hey, what did Adam say on the day before Christmas?"

"What?" I ask.

"It's Christmas, Eve!"

"Oh, Bill," Ginny says, and I laugh at his silly joke, which turns into an even harder cry.

Sammy Davis Junior, always the intuitive beast, comes bounding down the stairs and jumps straight onto my lap.

"I love you guys," I say.

"And we love you," Bill says. "Dearly. Now, do you want to tell us why you've decided to start Christmas before it's even Halloween?"

"Not that we mind," Ginny adds. "I think it's brilliant to get a jump start on things."

"I just wanted to go to a happy time. I love our rituals. I love making these houses and cooking with you and going shopping and . . . and . . ."

And I'm sobbing again.

Ginny and Bill look at each other, both at a loss, and then Scott comes down to save the day.

"What's the hubbub, bub?" Scott says, directed at me. He's brought down a cup of Tropic of Strawberry, my favorite Celestial Seasonings tea. A tea that nobody else likes, yet they keep it in the cupboard just for me. I take the cup from him and sip. He must have heard me wailing from all the way upstairs, and he's on the second floor.

When I've had a few more sips of tea and finally stopped hyperventilating, I take a deep breath and tell the Fosters what happened at dinner, what happened in the therapist's office, and that Brett wants a divorce.

To say they side with me would be putting it mildly. To say they are furious with him would be an understatement. But to say that fifteen minutes later when Brett shows up, they tell him to go away—their own son—would be telling exactly what happened.

# *scott*

Hearing Layla cry makes me feel like throwing up. Literally. I hate my brother. How do you have someone like Layla and *not* want to have like fifteen kids with her? There are no other Laylas around. Believe me, I've looked.

Brett is a giant fucking asshole.

# *ginny*

*October 9*

*Dearest Ev,*

*I have set pen to paper—remarkable in this day and age, I know—because you once told me that if I ever felt like my heart couldn't take any more, I should contact you posthaste. Remember that? I never forgot it. I write you now with a heart so heavy I fear it may tear right out of me.*

*I don't exactly know how to say this, so I'm just going to go right ahead and tell you: Things here are suddenly about as serious as a heart attack, as Mother used to say. But I'm already getting ahead of myself. I fear I'm going to have a nervous breakdown, and then Bill will be proven right when he tells me I'm too dramatic and getting worse all the time, never letting things go, rehashing the bad over and over. He calls it "repetitive emotion disorder," which I don't think is funny one bit.*

*So tonight, well past the time Bill typically drifts off to sleep in front of the TV upstairs, our dear Layla charged into the house and began acting strangely. We asked where Brett was, and that made it worse. She cried and cried, so much so that we couldn't make out what she was saying, until Bill picked out the word "divorce," and naturally we both wanted to know who, and then when we found out, we were sorry we'd asked, because it turned out to be her and Brett. Our own Brett told this beautiful, precious girl whom we consider our very own—with all she's been through and her being an orphan, or as near as God made to it—that he doesn't want to be married to her anymore. And all the while, the poor dear told us, she was thinking that he was taking her out to dinner to talk about having children! To think.*

*Naturally, we thought at first it was the product of a bad argument, and we did our best to assure her that Brett must be either kidding or not in his right mind. But while I stayed with her, there was a knock on the door, and it was Brett. Evelyn, sure as I'm born, he wasn't even sorry, really. He kept insisting we listen to "his side of the story," and then he and Bill yelled at each other in the front hall. Bill came back looking somewhere between angry and downcast, and I knew. Brett and Layla had fought before—what couple hasn't, other than Bill and me, *wink*—but this was different. Brett said he was through. And you remember how impossibly determined he is, once he gets committed to an idea. His best quality and his worst quality all in one, just like his father.*

*Needless to say, I'm beside myself. It feels as though someone or something has died. I spent most of the night on the couch, clutching my Virgin Mary—the little plastic one you gave me with the painted flowers on her robe. Let me know if you think it would help for me to take out one of those Saint Jude ads in the paper.*

*I will tell no one, absolutely no one, that we talked, and I hope you'll do the same. Hard to say what they'd think if they knew I was reaching out to you again.*

*Ever your loving sister,*
*Ginny*

# *brett*

I just got the Heisman from my family. The Heisman is an award given each year to the most outstanding college football player. The actual trophy is a bronze statue depicting a player in action—arm thrust forward—stiff-arming some unfortunate would-be tackler who is unaware in that moment that he's being shoved aside by greatness. But I didn't get a trophy for being outstanding. Instead, I'm just *out*. I got the stiff arm when I tried to go see my parents—*my* parents—to tell them what went down with Layla.

She beat me to the punch. Probably got on the phone with them thirty seconds after we left that quack's office so she could start "spinning" like a presidential campaign manager. Great. Who knew I married Layla friggin' Stephanopoulos. And now they're all mad at me. So in the absence of a loving family, I decide to turn to my friends. First stop is Doug's house. He's only about a mile from my folks' place now, and we need to clear something up.

But Doug doesn't answer the door. Aimee does.

"Hey, Brett," she says, but she doesn't motion me in.

"Hi, Aimee. How are ya?"

"I'm good," she answers, and then closes her mouth, lips pursed.

There's a long, long awkward pause, and I'm reminded why I don't hang out at Doug's more often. Although, in Aimee's defense, this is bitchy even for her.

"Fantastic," I say. "Is Doug home?"

*"Doug!"* she screams, seemingly at me, since she's looking me square in the eyes, but she can't be mad at me because I just got here.

Finally, he appears behind her. "Hey, buddy," he says, as he steps outside to join me and closes the door behind him.

"Sorry, man. Didn't mean to just show up."

"No worries, man. You're always welcome."

"Was I interrupting something? Like a fight? Aimee seemed a little upset."

"Yeah, she is," Doug says, and looks down.

"Well, join the club, dude. I think you and I need to have a beer."

"Yeah . . . I can't go, man."

"She's already mad," I rationalize. "And you haven't even done anything yet. I say you double down on this thing. And you kind of owe me."

"No, man. She's mad at *you*."

"What'd I do?" I ask, but before I even finish my sentence I realize exactly what I did. News sure travels fast in these circles. "Oh, you guys heard?"

"Yeah, we did. Are you okay?"

I look at my watch. "That's gotta be, like, record time. I mean, it just happened. How the fuck did you hear?"

"Layla called Aimee. She wanted to arrange a time to return a mixing bowl that she borrowed. She was very emotional. About a stainless-steel half-quart mixing bowl. It . . . came out."

"Wow. Chicks."

Doug just nods. Then Aimee separates the blinds from the window and sticks her face through, bugging her eyes out at Doug. It's a cue for him to get his ass back inside.

"Go ahead, man," I say. "It's cool. I get it. We'll catch up soon."

"I am here for you, though, buddy. It's just a little raw right now. And since you seem okay, I'm going to calm Aimee down."

It's raw? For *Aimee*? She's not even that close to Layla. Maybe it's part of that female mutual defense pact. Or maybe Aimee is projecting, wondering if she'll get the dinner "talk" next. Whatever. She'd deserve it.

• • •

"You have got to be fucking kidding me," Jared says. It's the first thing that comes out of his mouth when I arrive at his front door.

"You heard, too, I see."

"Do you have any idea of the level of awesome that is your wife?"

"Well, awesome is relative." I picture Layla for a second, but the thought quickly transforms into a disturbing family portrait, with her at the center and me nowhere to be found. "And right now, awesome is not someone who turns all your relatives against you. I have a frickin' side in this, too."

"In all my years," Jared starts. "In all my years, I've met a lot of guys' girlfriends, and some of those guys got married to these girls, but not one of them was as cool as Layla. Layla is like the holy grail of wives. I mean, if you had *any* idea of what goes on in my innermost thoughts about *your* wife—"

"Dude," I cut him off. "There's a reason they're called your 'innermost' thoughts. Because they're mostly supposed to *stay* inner."

I let out some air in disgust, turn around, and walk back to my car. It's clear that I'm not getting any sympathy from the guys, who all are siding with my wife. They all want to sleep with her—*or have already slept with her,* I remind myself. Before even I did.

I'm driving aimlessly, stressing over heading home because

I'm not sure what the protocol is. Just when my stress is about to cross over into full-blown anxiety, I remember that my razor broke this morning, so I pull over at the convenience store to buy a disposable one.

Curious name, "convenience store," since the only thing that seems to be *conveniently* located there is liquor. So I grab my three-pack of razors, which is going to cost as much as a bottle of fine wine. As I walk to the counter, I notice Dustin Caldwell, one of my younger cornerbacks, haggling over the price of something he has no business purchasing: a liquor cabinet's worth of vodka, gin, whiskey, and some dreadful apple liquor. To top it off—as if it needs topping off—he smells as though he's already been sampling the goods.

Seeking to head off this budding scandal, and thanking God for the supreme coincidence that I'm there and not some administrator, I kindly intervene in favor of the law against selling alcohol to minors and insist on driving him home.

He is *adamant* that he walk. But I remind him it's nearly ten blocks, that he's obviously a little "under the weather," and that it's absolutely no trouble. Especially since I can use all the bonding I can get in these hard economic times.

Dustin pulls at the zipper on his hoodie and stares out the window for most of our ride, and then a block before we get to his frat house, he perks up. "You can just let me off here."

"Dusty, it's only one more block. We're not exactly going out of my way."

"Yeah," he says, and zips his sweatshirt up again for the sixtieth time.

Before we've even reached our destination I hear a cacophony of party sounds and music so loud I'm pretty sure I can feel the bass in my car.

"Oh, look at that!" Dusty says, as if he's surprised. "A couple friends must have popped over. I better be going now." He already has the car door open and one leg out.

"Not so fast, kiddo," I say. "What's going on in there?" As soon as the words slip out of my mouth I regret them. Bad enough that I have to play bad cop when I'm trying to bond a little with my team; I have to sound like an idiot on top of it? It's very clear what's going on. It's a party. They're all drinking. I'm pretty sure the legal drinking age is still twenty-one. And unless they've flunked a couple years, no one in that frat house is tall enough to get on that ride.

"Uh—" Dusty stammers.

"Tell you what," I cut him off. "How about I come inside and hang out with you guys a bit?"

"Like a chaperone?" he asks.

*Man, am I really this old?*

*Yes.* "No."

"We're not doing anything wrong," Dusty says, although his eyes have avoided mine pretty much since I bumped into him.

"I'm sure you're not. That said, I'm responsible for you guys. I'm here. I've found you guys doing things I can't technically allow. I'm not judging, but I have to be available and make sure nothing bad happens."

• • •

"Coach Foster!" I hear Kevin Bateman shout as I enter the house behind Dustin.

"Came to check out what you ladies call a good time," I say.

The party is your typical Friday-night let's-get-crazy gathering. Loud music. Plastic cups and beer bottles everywhere. Snack foods burrowed into the carpet. (Layla would have a fit.) Girls dancing like they're training for the Pussycat Dolls. Guys dancing halfheartedly, trying to balance the willingness to please the girl they're dancing with by dancing at all and the crippling fear that they might look uncool. And eyes. Hungry teenage and barely post-teen eyes darting around in search of that night's hookup.

Now they're all turning to see a football coach strolling in, certain that he's about to call the police and bust up the whole affair.

I sidle past a few students and try to ignore the creeped-out looks and "Oh my God, what's the coach doing here?" whispers.

But I power through and tell a few people that I won't bust the party as long as they keep the noise reasonable and the drinking doesn't get out of control. I ultimately manage to have a decent conversation with Ronnie Sidwell about watching *The Wizard of Oz* set to Pink Floyd's *The Dark Side of the Moon,* and then I destroy any and every opponent who dares to challenge me at Guitar Hero.

I'm walking out of the kitchen when Anya Hendrickson, an exceedingly well-built cheerleader, appears before me, blocking my path.

"Hey, Coach," she slurs.

"Hello, Anya," I say. I know her name because she's one of the newer (read: freshman, possibly not even eighteen) cheerleaders; she's one of the girls I hear the team talk about incessantly.

"Having a good time?" she asks, her head cocked sideways, her eyes trained on my lips, which start to feel dry, like the rest of my mouth.

"I am."

"I'm bored," she says.

"I'm sorry to hear that," I reply, as I dig my hands into my pockets and try to take a step to my right, edging ever so slightly forward, signaling that I'd like to pass. She doesn't budge.

But she does pull a small bottle of schnapps out of her pocket and takes a sip. "I hate beer. Jody got busted for selling her little brother's Adderall, and beer literally makes me yack. *Blegh!*" She mimics an aggressive vomit session and then recovers, coyly passing her hand through her hair as she holds up the bottle of schnapps like she's posing for an advertisement. "So it's this or nothing."

I think of those fake commercials they do on *Saturday Night Live* and picture Anya vomiting all over the place and then someone handing her a bottle of schnapps, which she takes and then smiles. The voice-over booms, "When your Adderall connection evaporates and beer just makes you blow chunks: schnapps. It's this or nothing."

"Want some?" she says, as she holds out her tiny bottle.

Schnapps is one step removed from NyQuil. I remember the last time I actually drank some. Seventh grade. I was on a ski trip and Skip Dougherty brought peppermint-flavored schnapps in his parka. We knocked it back on the lifts, and the mint liquor combining with the cold air made our throats feel like we were guzzling Freon.

"No, thanks," I say.

She shrugs and takes another swig. "College guys are so lame," she then announces with a roll of her eyes.

"It's part of their charm."

"It's not charming. It's pathetic. They're boys. Not men."

It's getting warm in the kitchen doorway. I'd like Anya to move so I can get the hell away from this potential train wreck.

"They'll be men soon enough," I promise, as I turn sideways and try to squeak through the space between her body and the entry. She doesn't move, and I inadvertently brush against her on my way past.

She grabs my arm. "Soon enough for who? Because it's not soon enough for me."

I look around the party and spot John Crooks. He's about six-four, built, one of my best players. "What about Johnny C. over there?"

"What about him?"

"I don't know." I shrug. "He's a good-looking guy. Tall. *Manly.*" *What am I saying?* I'm even creeping *myself* out.

"What about you?" she asks point-blank.

"I'm a hundred years old," I say.

"I bet you're not even thirty."

"I will be in December."

She leans close, and her hair falls on my shoulder. "I'd like to give you an early birthday present."

I instantly perform a snap cost-benefit analysis on the chalkboard in my head. On the plus side: She's hot and I haven't been with a woman other than Layla since . . . ever. On the minus side: My career would be ruined, my family would be disgraced, Layla would never speak to me again, I'd probably have to leave town after I got out of jail for statutory rape, and I'd never be able to teach or coach again.

It's a very close call.

Luckily, I'm saved by a quick vision of the headline in the local paper: *Condor Coaching Cad Caught Canoodling with Curious Coed.* I awkwardly turn Anya down with some line about seeing what's going on around the pool—though the house doesn't turn out to have one—and as I'm leaving the party I notice Dusty Caldwell and some kid I don't know snorting lines. I clap a hand on Dusty's shoulder to get his attention and he whips around looking guilty.

"Can we have a private convo for a minute, Scarface?"

His friend scurries off as Dusty begins to babble: "I hardly *ever* do that stuff, Coach. It's a party is all, and Nadia told me she gets all horny whenever she does coke and—"

"Shut up and listen for a minute," I say. "I'm gonna tell you about a teammate of mine back in college. He was a pretty straight shooter, but he also got caught up with a girl who wanted him to buy some blow so she could have crazy coke sex with him. Wanna know what happened to that very talented kid?"

Dusty hangs his head. "I don't know. He got kicked off the team?"

"No, he couldn't afford the coke. But she gave him crabs. He plays strong safety for Detroit now. Good guy." I pause for a moment and look meaningfully at him. "You see what I'm saying?"

"Not really, Coach," he replies, baffled.

"He was one of the lucky ones," I say pointedly. I'm done joking around. "I know at least a dozen guys—talented players—who lost every shot at their dreams by screwing around when they should have been focusing. Some of them dabbled with drugs, some of them drank themselves out of contention. If my old teammate had been able to afford coke for that skank, he probably would have been another casualty. Instead, he bought some of that crab shampoo, washed that girl right out of his balls, and got back to the business of being a focused ballplayer. And now he plays pro ball."

Dusty snickers. "In Detroit."

"Yeah, well, they may suck. But right now, on your best day, you wouldn't have a prayer of making their roster. Think on that, Cokie." Dusty starts to protest, but I cut him off. "Oh, you have plenty of talent, but your focus and discipline are half-assed. At best. And if *this* is any indication of where it's headed, there's no way you're gonna be able to compete in any championships. You have to trust in yourself and trust in your team. And you gotta kill yourself for both."

"I threw up on myself in Friday's game," Dusty mutters, without looking up. "I couldn't catch a cold."

I lean into him, serious as I've ever been. "Three things you need to get clear on, brother: One, you've got it in your head that championships are won based solely on what you do on the field. Wrong. Fifty percent of being a champion is about your behavior and composure during the one hundred and sixty hours a week when you're *not* on a football field. Second, I ever hear about you doing blow again, you'll be off this team quicker than you can say 'random drug testing.' Third, you've put me in a terrible position, and I'm gonna be taking a big risk by not reporting you this minute, so you owe me *big*, and I do not expect to be let down. You got that?"

Dusty nods as I turn to leave. But before I go, I offer him one more nugget. "Oh. And I've seen that girl you're with—and who else she's been with. Off the record, I think you'll be lucky if the only thing she gives you is crabs."

• • •

When I get back to my house, Layla has locked herself in the bedroom. I don't know if the door is actually locked, but it's closed, and I take that to mean "keep out." I'm not surprised. I spend the night tossing and turning on the living-room couch. Second night in a row.

To say our couch is not sleepworthy is a gross understatement. It's technically a love seat, and I honestly don't know how in the name of all things holy the thing earned that designation. Sure, you can cram two people onto it, but where is the love? You can't stretch out, you can't maneuver—there's barely enough room to move. Same goes for sleeping on it. I end up on my back with my legs bent over one edge and my head crooked up on the other, my chin mashed into my chest, giving me a scowl that looks like Winston Churchill's in that famous picture, though I don't know true pain until I try to lift my head the next morning.

• • •

Sun streams through the living-room windows, and I look around for Layla, half thinking she'll be making eggs and bacon and a thick fruit smoothie, humming happily to herself and telling me that whatever's in my tortured and compressed head was all a bad dream. But she's gone. And my suitcase has been set out—or, I should say, angrily chucked—near the door of our master bathroom.

It's in that moment that I realize I'm going to have to move out.

. . .

Noah Price, a guy in the UCCC math department, gives me a lead on a loft apartment. Four days later I'm moved in, though my new bachelor pad is not quite the swingin' place you'd imagine. I've got a plaid couch with one leg missing, lifted from the basement at my parents' (they didn't really speak to me when I picked it up); a recliner that reclined halfway one night and since then has declined to return upright; an inverted milk-crate table, inspired by countless campus residents before me; nothing on the walls (except about three-quarters of a coat of paint); a microwave with a door that won't stay closed (so I keep my distance); a good toaster (so I'll be eating a lot of toast); the last boom box in existence; and a box of condiments, from ketchup and mustard to rare chutneys and fish pastes that are rejects of my mother's fridge.

The plus side? I can leave dishes in the sink until 2012 and not hear one word about it. I can leave dirty clothes strewn about, and unless the piles start to smell or walk themselves, I don't have to pick up or wash them. The minus side? My place is a hole—and it'll get worse as I live there longer. Naturally, nobody'll want to come over. Even *I'm* going to be disgusted by it. But it's month-to-month. Like my situation. I would have gone day-to-day, but the landlord merely gave me a look when I asked, so I played it off as a joke.

None of my friends are going to want to hang out with me anyway, because my split has had a trickle-down effect on our friends' wives. They're all saying things to the guys like, "Oh, so is that what *you* want, too? You want to be a bachelor again now, *too*?" So the wives are pissed, and the guys are all pissed at me because I started it, so I have no one to hang out with.

I stop by Norm's Restaurant for a late-night snack, and I'm two bites into my tuna melt, sitting at the twenty-four-hour restaurant's counter, when I hear a semi-familiar voice. "Hey, Coach," it says, and I look up to see Heather.

"Hi," I answer, hoping she didn't see my attempt to talk to the woman sitting next to me five minutes earlier—which I swear was just me trying to be cordial. I mean, we *were* sitting next to each other. She wasn't even attractive.

"So your wife doesn't make a good tuna melt?" she probes.

"We're . . ." I think about how to word it. "Separated."

This seems to take Heather by surprise. "Wow. You okay?"

"Sure," I say. "Yeah. I'm okay."

"And already back on the horse," she says. "Struck out with that girl, huh?"

"I was just trying to be polite. Not hitting on her."

"Uh-huh," Heather says, with a wry smile.

"Fine." I exhale. "Think what you want."

"What I think," she says, as she takes the now-empty seat next to me, "is that for a coach, you've got no game."

"Please, have a seat," I say, too late, half kidding. "Are you here by yourself?"

"No," she says, as she motions to two women sitting at a booth. "I'm with those girls over there. The ones staring at us right now."

"Tell him you'd like to huddle!" one calls out.

"Shut up," she answers, and rolls her eyes. "Ignore them."

Then the other one chimes in. "Tell him he can go right up the middle. Tell him you're ready to go long."

"I apologize for them," she says. "Football humor."

"Yeah, I got that."

"I am sorry to hear about your separation," she says, and then smiles. "Not really. I mean, I'd be sorry if you seemed all bummed, but if you're okay with it—"

"I'm okay with it," I say.

Heather tells me she'll give me pointers on how to pick up women, which I politely decline, but she's adamant, so we start playacting like we've never met, and I have to try to pick her up. After a while the lines get blurred and we're definitely flirting. Her friends have left and we're there together, as if we'd planned it. And it's fun. It's actually nice to talk to a woman who doesn't know everything about you from the time you got your driver's permit.

When I finally say good night and head off home, I'm in a better mood than I've been for weeks.

# *layla*

John Lennon once said, "Rituals are important. Nowadays it's hip not to be married. I'm not interested in being hip." While I tend to agree with him on most things, I'm down on marriage at the moment, so we'll just focus on the first part: rituals. They *are* important. They create routine and stability—something I've always craved—and as such, I've always been the first to embrace family traditions wholeheartedly.

I love to cook the turkey every Thanksgiving with Ginny, each of us alternating basting duty throughout the day. I love making the Famous Foster Sweet Potato Soufflé: Ginny mostly steers that ship, but *I'm* the captain of marshmallow duty. When Christmas rolls around, there's nothing I like more than making gingerbread houses with the Fosters—although I got an early jump on my house this year. Traditionally, all of our gingerbread houses sit proudly displayed atop the mantel above the fireplace upon completion. Between then and Christmas, we all try to secretly eat doors and windows off someone else's house when nobody's looking. I love traditions, and on occasion even create them. My proudest creation? Movie Night.

Movie Night is a tradition I started with the Fosters long before Brett and I got married, and it's carried on ever since. It's the eight p.m. showing, every fourth Friday of the month at the Mann Village Theater. Whatever's playing. Since they show only one film, that last rule means nobody gets blamed for picking a bad movie, nobody fights over the genre, and nobody gets confused about where we're going or when. It's all predetermined. Life affords us so many choices—too many choices—so it's good that some are preplanned.

I show up at the Mann Village around seven forty-five and spot Ginny and Bill at the ticket booth. Ginny rushes over to greet me with a warm hug.

"I wasn't sure you'd show," she says, as she pulls back from the embrace and warmly moves a strand of hair that's attached itself to my lip gloss.

"Me? Miss Movie Night? Never!"

Bill hands me my ticket, and the three of us walk to the glass double doors. Then I hear someone clear his throat. I turn to see Brett, arms folded, head cocked back, chewing on something imaginary. Bill hands Brett *his* ticket, which he grabs without unfolding his arms.

"What are you doing here?" I ask. I didn't think he'd actually come.

"Me?" he says, a bit belligerently. "What am I doing here? What are *you* doing here?"

"It's Movie Night," I say, taking a few steps away from Bill and Ginny. "I started this tradition. There was no Movie Night before me."

"I'm no Roger Ebert, but I am relatively sure that movies existed before I met you."

"Yes, *movies* existed. But I started Movie Night," I repeat. "I started the Friday night tradition."

"With *my* family."

"And when we got married they became *my* family, too."

When he doesn't say anything to this, nor does he seem to be budging, I say, "I got here first, so I think you should leave."

"Seriously? That's your stance? Did you also call shotgun on my parents?"

"No, I just cultivated an actual relationship with them, as opposed to assuming I'm the golden boy simply because they hatched me. Your relation is just a birth accident."

"Yeah," he snarls, taking a step forward and pointing to Ginny's stomach, "Well, those stretch marks have *my* name on them. . . . Dear God, I wish I hadn't said that out loud."

"Really, Brett!" Ginny says.

"Sorry, Mom." He turns back to me and lowers his voice. "Did you really think I *wouldn't* be here?"

"I can actually think of several instances when you weren't," I say. "However, I have *never* missed a single Movie Night."

"You were *invited* then," he shoots back. "Now you're like that drunk uncle who won't leave after Christmas dinner."

"Charming," I say.

"I think you're making my parents uncomfortable," he suggests, but Bill and Ginny are in their own world. I wonder if they think this whole thing will blow over with us, even though Brett moved out a few days ago. Damn, that was fast.

Bill looks our way, smiles, and gives us a thumbs-up. "Let's go get seats, kids!" he chirrups. He's clearly trying not to take sides, though Ginny is obviously on Team Layla.

Just then Scott shows up, with Trish following close behind. Not wanting to make things worse, I walk into the theater and take a seat. Ginny sits next to me, and of course Brett insists that he sit on her other side. As we're settling down, Bill hands Ginny a big tub of popcorn and I notice Brett scowling at me.

"What is the problem?" I ask in a loud whisper. "You're showing up to *my* thing, yet you're giving me the stink-eye."

"Again, I fail to see how Movie Night with *my* family is *your* thing," he hisses. The lights dim and the previews start.

"Whatever," I say, as I dig my hand into the tub of popcorn on Ginny's lap.

"Exactly," he replies, digging his hand into the tub before I've gotten mine out. Each of us tries to forcefully remove the other's hand, which sends popcorn flying. All of this is happening atop Ginny's knees.

Other movie patrons are looking at us—deservedly, because we are behaving like a couple of children—so finally I stand up and announce that I am leaving.

"Don't leave," Ginny says.

"Yeah, Lay," Scott chimes in. *"Don't."*

"Please leave," someone a few rows behind us says, and a bunch of other patrons start to laugh, clap, and whistle.

I was already embarrassed, but this is too much. I kiss Ginny on the cheek and walk out. I hear Trish yell at Brett as I exit, but I keep going. I can only make out a couple of words: "asshole" and "dumbfuck." It's nice that Trish has my back, but it doesn't make it hurt any less.

# *trish*

One thing to know about Layla is that she is always punctual. Always. Which is why it's even more disturbing that the ever-precise Layla isn't here when Sandy Dobson, a gay-rights lawyer from northern California, arrives for her Monday-morning appointment with Marvin the wheaten terrier in tow. I wonder if the whole scene with Brett at the theater has stuck with her all weekend. I had a particularly good Saturday and Sunday with Kimmy, my new distraction, the blue-eyed stunner—so freakin' gorgeous I now finally get that whole moving-van joke—so Layla and I haven't been in touch since she stormed out. She called my cell late last night but didn't leave a message, and when I called hers this morning it went straight to voice mail.

I met Sandy at a benefit breakfast several months ago, and she's made a special trip down to Los Angeles specifically for this photo session. "Can I offer you something to drink?" I ask her, as I pour my own cup of coffee. Third of the day. "Coffee?"

"That would be great, thank you," she says, and I slowly, slowly pour the coffee into a mug, hoping that by the time I top it off Layla will be here. And by God it works.

"Sorry I'm late," Layla says, as she tosses off her coat but leaves her sunglasses on.

"Future's so bright you gotta wear shades?" I ask.

"Heh. Yeah. Something like that." She walks over to Marvin and plops onto the floor where he sits. "Hey, boy." Then she looks up at Sandy—I'm guessing she feels self-conscious, because she raises her sunglasses to the top of her head—and forces a smile. "I'm Layla."

"Hi, Layla. Sandy. And that's Marvin, which you gathered."

When Layla looks up at Sandy and I watch them interact, I see something I don't know that I've ever seen in Layla's face—and I know the many looks of Layla. Aside from the puffy eyes that tell me she's been crying, she looks hollow. Maybe that's not the right word, but I can't describe it any other way. Layla is so vibrant and engaging, yet there she is on the floor trying to connect with the dog, because that's safe but human contact is somehow dangerous. Even with me? Maybe this Brett thing is more serious than the stupid little spat I've been imagining. But how can it be? They've been together, like, *forever.*

We settle in to the photo shoot, and Layla is definitely not herself. I'm sure she's still getting great shots, but her heart's not in it and there's nothing I can say or do to fix it. I'm so pissed at my idiot brother I want to wring his neck.

Marvin rolls on his back to play dead. Layla snaps some shots as Sandy laughs and shakes her head.

"The irony!" Sandy says. "I swear I didn't teach him to do that. You know, his namesake was Marvin Mitchelson, the world's most aggressive divorce lawyer. He wouldn't roll over for anybody."

"Marvin Mitchelson?" asks Layla. "Never heard of him."

"He invented the concept of palimony: marriage with no rings attached. Some actor tried to screw his girlfriend—in every way, I might add—by living with her for years without marrying her and then dumping her without a cent, and Mitchelson convinced the court that she was entitled to half anyway. And this was in the seventies, when live-in girlfriends were considered tramps who deserved their bad fortune. I can't even imagine living back then.

"Anyway, Mitchelson was incredible," Sandy adds. "He could convince anyone of anything! He's kind of a forgotten hero to women, and a personal hero of mine—though I would never have needed his services." She gives both me and Layla a wink. "I figure he died forgotten and penniless, the least I could do is name my dog after him."

"Too bad he's dead," Layla says. "Think he could have convinced a jury to let me keep my husband's family even though the creep is divorcing me and trying to force me out?"

"What?" I practically shout. "I really don't get this tiff you and Brett are having." All I know is that I hate it.

" 'Tiff'? 'Tiff'? That's a quaint euphemism for divorce. Yep, Brett is tiffing the hell out of me," Layla snaps, and then turns back to Sandy. "Sorry, you don't need to hear this. And I was only kidding about keeping his family." But I can see the wheels turning in Layla's head as she looks hopefully back to our client. "Sort of."

"Sadly, you can't get legal custody of adults in a divorce proceeding," Sandy informs us.

I can almost hear Layla deflate.

"Not so long as we're mentally competent," I add, trying to lighten the mood. "You'd better not be suggesting that we're a few cards short of a full deck."

But Layla doesn't react. I'm not even sure she heard me. She's lost in her thoughts, and this clearly isn't just a half-baked joke anymore.

"You're serious?" I ask.

"I'm serious that I don't want to lose you guys if I'm losing my husband. I love you guys, and I know it's mutual—and it's by choice, not some dumb accident of birth, so why does Brett get to keep you while I get shoved out into the cold? This is a terrible time for Marvin Mitchelson to be dead. I need him!"

"Actually, this isn't exactly a legal matter," Sandy chimes in.

"Brett is not forcing you out of the family," I say. "Trust me. You're in this family. For better or worse. Clearly, right now is worse." And with that, I pull Layla in for a hug and feel her shoulders jerk upward a few times as she starts to cry.

This sucks beyond words. I'm really going to have to smack Brett.

# *layla*

The morning after hearing about Marvin Mitchelson, I start to call attorneys. I probably shouldn't have waited so long, but I didn't know when exactly Brett was going to start proceedings. Maybe I hoped he'd change his mind. *Of course* I hoped he'd change his mind.

I'm stunned to find that the first two shysters I call have already heard from Brett and therefore can't ethically or legally take my case; he and I are apparently drawn to the same advertisements. The third lawyer I call is just too damned expensive, and the fourth has *also* spoken to Brett.

Admittedly, a harsh rejection can put a person in an advanced state of stupid. Add to that being boxed out of all the decent lawyers you can find and/or afford, and you feel humiliated, inadequate, discarded, and alone—all lousy foundations for behavior in the average person. You start contemplating truly regrettable things, like eating saturated fat directly out of the carton of self-pity, dumping someone's entire DVD collection curbside, or leaving phone messages for an ex in this vein: "I'm sorry to call again but I don't know what else to do, because you won't answer your door, and if you'll just give this thing one more chance, I'll utterly debase myself to make you happy." I don't want to do any of these things—at least not yet.

Being a virtual orphan all these years has left me extremely sensitive to even the most minor slights and every pinprick of exclusion in any context: familial, social, professional—hell, even when I'm trying to buy a new shirt and the salespeople ignore me for ten minutes, it can feel like a spear being shoved down my throat. So as I arrive at the three-quarter mark in my box of Barbara's Shredded Oats cereal, I'm aware that the sound of my chomping is drowned out by my pulse pounding in my ears. The rejection effect is kicking in like a shot of Jägermeister.

Through this buzzing, a commercial catches my attention and I'm sucked in like I'm being hypnotized: "Have you been wronged? Feel as though nobody's on your side?" a man who slightly resembles Alec Baldwin says. "Then you need to call me *now,* toll-free. I'm on your side and I will *fight* for you. I will stop at nothing! And your initial consultation is absolutely *free*!"

I do need someone to fight for me! Someone with the young Muhammad Ali's gift of gab and Mike Tyson's eternal bloodlust. And as so often happens in life, at the precise moment when you need a sign, when you need a true bruiser on your side, you get . . . well, not exactly what you wished for, but rather Tommy Thames of Thames, Schlicter & Thames. And as the honorable Mr. Thames repeats the same stirring appeal in Spanish, I write down the number that comes up on the screen and resolve to call him.

• • •

I call Brooke from the car on my way to see this Tommy Thames, and she couldn't be less interested in hearing about my plight. In fact, she only perks up when she hears about my meeting with a divorce lawyer, since she sees the budding potential for her to have me as a wingwoman for her nights on the town.

"We are back in business, baby," she says. "Well, technically we were never in business, since you and Brett were together since you were like seven years old. Trust me: This is a good thing. We are gonna have so much fun."

"Fun, huh?" I say, not quite thinking that's what I'd call this.

"Oh my God, I went on the craziest date last night, I forgot to tell you. This guy picks me up for dinner, and proceeds to eat a bag of potato chips in the car on our way to the restaurant. Is that not crazy?"

"It's certainly odd," I admit. "Did he offer you a chip?"

"No!"

"Not very well mannered."

"Oh, it was disgusting. There were crumbs all over the car."

"How was the rest of the date?" I ask, hoping it gets better, if this is indicative of what's in store for me.

"Lame," she says. "Boring. He really didn't talk much. It was probably good that he crunched chips on the whole drive, because I didn't notice how freakin' dull he was."

"Yikes," I offer. "Sorry."

"Don't be. I fucked him. He wasn't that bad in bed. Kept his mouth shut, so that was good. Probably won't see him again."

I squint my eyes to read the passing addresses and realize I need to hang up and pay attention or I'm going to pass the office. That and the fact that this conversation is completely depressing me. I say good-bye, feeling worse than before I called, and pull in to the parking lot.

Inside the building, behind a door with a prominent No Smoking sign is a smallish lobby that positively reeks of smoke. The smell wafts from the upholstery, the carpet, the walls, and the *Men's Health* and *Woman's Day* magazines strewn across the faux-oak *(foak?)* end tables.

The receptionist's hair is a cumulus cloud of nicotine as she addresses me for the first time. "We're moving," she says, unprompted.

"Where are we going?" I want to say, but I let it drop.

"I know it's not what you'd expect, a . . ." And with this, she waves her hand at the lobby and her own crowded desk. But the sentence never gets an ending. So I wait mutely as she looks around in mild disgust.

Finally I say, "I'm here to see Tommy Thames. I'm Layla Foster. His ten o'clock?"

"Of course you are," she says. "Is it ten? I'll let him know. And since you appear curious, this is an Early American Colonial vintage law office."

Indeed, she is correct. If décor that resembles a patriotic seven-year-old's bedroom—complete with a bald-eagle wallpaper border and red-white-and-blue parade-drum table lamps—is a good indication of your attorney's total focus on legal matters, the place is a resounding endorsement.

"And the smoke stench. Oh, *awful*, I know. From Thames *senior*, God rest him. Never paid attention to the no-smoking thing. It's enough to make me think of quitting." She looks everywhere but at me, and clearly I am not the first audience for this commentary. "When you're leaving in another month, you try not to get too concerned with it."

She is obviously very concerned about the possibility that I might bolt at any second, but she overcomes her misgivings long enough to pick up the phone. "Ms. Foster is in the lobby." She hangs up. "Why don't you take a seat. He'll come for you in a moment. Can I get you anything?"

*You can get me out of here via the nearest window,* I think, but all I say is "No, thank you." I am extremely reluctant to comply with her seating request, but something about this woman tells me she's not to be messed with, despite her acknowledgment of the plight of anyone unfortunate enough to have to spend more than ten seconds in this ashtray of an office. So rather than obey my impulse to recast myself as a photocopier salesperson and get a quick dismissal, I sink with dread into a shabby side chair.

Then Tommy Thames calls to me. I see only half his body—he's leaning around a corner—but I note that the resemblance to Alec Baldwin isn't as redeeming as I'd hoped it might be. His face is fatter, ruddier, and coarser, and the hair, if possible, is slicked even farther back than it was in the ad. It's Alec Baldwin on a morning after an all-week bender.

In Thames's office is his chair; a desk with a phone, a closed notebook computer, one legal pad, and one plastic cup; a visitor's chair; a print of some stern old man in a judge's robe; and in one corner, a redwood forest of file folders that seems about to topple and kill us both at any second.

"We're moving," he says, as he sits down and motions for me to do the same, and I see for the first time a long stain running down his suit jacket. I wonder if he doesn't know it's there or he does know and doesn't care. I decide he's blissfully unaware, just to make myself feel better. "Remind me when the injury occurred," he asks, as he taps his pen on his long yellow pad.

"It's not a physical injury as much as an emotional injury," I answer. "This is sort of a matrimonial issue."

"Certainly these things call for some measure of respect and delicacy."

"Right now, I'm pretty upset."

"Oh, no—we'll definitely take the sick bastard for everything he's got. But we step lightly at first. Now, with all sympathies to the situation . . . any infidelity or physical abuse?"

"Never!" I say, as I laugh for the first time in days. Brett hitting me? Never. "It's not like that. It's sort of more about the relationship."

"Not exactly my forte. Been married three times, and the third one . . . let's say *that* one was the reason this move has been on hold so long."

Just what you want to hear from your prospective divorce attorney.

"Hear me out," I say. "My husband and I are, I think, getting a divorce. So that's easy."

He smiles. "I'm glad you think so. But you won't by the time we get done with this. No offense or anything."

I rub my forehead to clear the thought, close my eyes, then restart. "I mean, that's done. Sort of. Rather, I don't think the dispute will be complicated, because there are no kids and God knows not a whole hell of a lot to split between us. I'm not sure if he's filed the paperwork yet. I haven't heard." I open my eyes again. "Anyway, there's something trickier that I need your help with. This family that I married into: the Fosters. They're the only real family I've ever had. Between growing up with them when I was in high school and then my years of being married to their son, they really became *my* family. I love them. They are mine, too. Practically. Truly. *Legally.* And dammit if I'm not going to fight for what's mine."

"I'm not sure I'm getting what you're saying," Thames admits. "We can talk about distribution of real property, sure. They have some of your belongings in their house?"

"Yes. *Them,*" I say. "They are my family. If I am splitting up with my husband, then so be it. But I want his *family*."

"Well, you can't have that," Thames says.

"Why not?" I ask, and I mean it. *Why not?*

"Because custody is for minors. Maybe if the parents were incapacitated in some way—are they?" When he asks this, I can see he's probably thinking about how and why they got incapacitated, and if he can get a piece of *that* lawsuit.

"No, they're not. They are able-bodied and sound-minded."

"Then you're out of luck," he says.

"You said on your commercial that you would stop at nothing. Nothing means *nothing*. Which would include not being stopped by having no previous legal precedent."

He purses his lips and twists his mouth to the right side. I can tell I'm getting to him. And I know this guy. I saw his dream of being the next Johnnie Cochran when I spotted him on his commercial, so I'm not giving up.

"You seem like a high-profile guy," I say.

"I don't like to toot my own horn but . . . *toot*." He gives a smile that makes me slightly queasy.

"You wouldn't mind a headline, a little notoriety, some hate mail."

"Not sure what you're driving at," he admits.

"Well, this could potentially be a very high-profile case," I explain.

"*Hmm.* Keep driving."

"He wants a divorce? Well, I am going to file a countersuit—not just for divorce but for joint custody of his family!"

He taps his pen to his lips and shakes his head. Luckily, it's a thoughtful and not a dismissive shake.

"A lawsuit like this is unprecedented, if not impossible," he finally decides. "As I said, custody exists only for control of and responsibility for dependents."

"Isn't that the definition of the word? Things are *un*precedented only until they are *precedented*. And I don't care if that is an actual word any more than I care that a lawsuit like this has never been filed. I want to file anyway—if for nothing else than to make a statement."

"Statements are expensive," he says.

"I'm prepared to pay," I reply, not even knowing what I'm agreeing to, thinking I'll take out another loan if I have to. This is my destiny.

"Judges don't like them," he adds.

"Reporters do," I rebut. "And I don't think this will get ignored. A marriage certificate is a legal document. I am *legally* bound to that family. They are my in-laws. Imagine how groundbreaking this could be. The first case of its kind."

I'm calculating that he doesn't give a damn about breaking ground, except in that his firm is no well-oiled plaintiff's machine, throwing off private plane–level contingency fees, and a breakthrough is just what his reputation needs. Even something off the wall. I see the wheels turning in his head: the press conferences, the angry denunciations of justice denied on the courthouse steps, the movie deals. . . .

He smiles.

He's in.

# *brett*

Scott lost his virginity at seventeen to Carmelita, our Ecuadoran housekeeper, who wasn't exactly what you'd call attractive. To say that Carmelita had more of a mustache than Scott at the time they unmade the bed would be entirely accurate. I bring this up because I kept that secret, along with every other secret, as was my brotherly duty. Never once was the sentence uttered: "When you peed your pants before the third-grade Christmas pageant, who ran to Kmart to get you new underwear?" That was just a given.

Trish? I went to every single softball game she ever played. I will never ever get that time back. Plus, when she mangled her dirt bike trying to run Dwight Kozuchowsky over for calling her a "stupid lezzy," and accidentally hit and dented the Friedmans' Lexus, I fixed the bike and never told anyone about the hit-and-run. When she put one-fourth of a quaalude in my Cherry Coke to put me to sleep so I wouldn't bug her friends, I never said a word. Ditto for when I caught her raiding Dad's *Playboy*s. And the prizewinner of the non-uttered sentence department? "When you got gonorrhea from that Mormon chick, *who* drove to Tijuana to score you penicillin?"

The point is, I had their backs. Like brothers and sisters are supposed to. So why is it that now that I need them to have mine, they've gone totally AWOL? Same goes for my parents.

It's with this in mind that I head over to Casa Foster, ready at first to give them no more than a verbal slap on the wrists, but by the time I reach the front door, I'm hell-bent on busting it down and demanding that my family take me back as a full-fledged blood member. It's been more than a week since Layla and I announced our break, and they've had their time to make peace with it—or at least to soften and treat me better. This all just makes me angrier at Layla for having devoted the entire end of our marriage to stealing my family.

"Son," my dad says, as he bows his head slightly forward and nods. Not "Hey, champ!" or "Great to see ya, pal!" Just an acknowledgment that I am, for legal purposes, his son, and he's really not so sure how he feels about that.

I let this go and walk past him and up to Scott's room, where I find Scott glaring at me, his eyes squinted so small it almost looks like he's straining to see something just past me.

"Something in your eye?" I ask.

"Yeah," he says, and he blinks a few times and touches his eyelashes. "I think it's . . . disgust." He goes back to sketching demons.

"Good one. But maybe it's just eye boogers from all that crying yourself to sleep you've been doing."

"Dude, I can't believe you're doing this," Scott says. "You're so wrong. You're so *beyond* wrong."

"Am I?" I get in his face. "Well, I don't think so. And it's my life. And you know what? Right or wrong shouldn't matter. What if I *am* wrong? Shouldn't you still have my back?"

"Uh, no."

"Nice, bro," I say. "See if I have your back next time you get caught stealing mugs from IHOP."

"Whatever, dude." He shrugs. "I'm sorry, but I think it's really shitty what you're doing. It's unthinkable, actually. It's, like, apocalyptic. Layla and you? You're not supposed to break up. And the fact that you instigated it? I can't even wrap my head around it. Maybe I'd have your back if she dumped you and you were all miserable like you should be. But not this way."

I'm so pissed at the little bastard I don't know what to do with myself. There are less than a handful of people in the entire world that I feel like I can count on to take my side whatever comes. I know I've remarked that Scott loves Layla, but . . . this betrayal is staggering. I figured he'd eventually come around to my side.

I just stand there looking at him, my blood boiling, my jaw clenching and unclenching. Finally, I speak. "Let me ask you one question: Who turned you on to Motorhead?"

"What?" he asks.

"You heard me. Who turned you on to Motorhead?"

"Uh, you?"

"Yeah," I say, ready to break a stack of Motorhead CDs over his skull. "Me."

"Your point?"

"My point is: If it wasn't for me, you'd still be getting the shit beat out of you in a Nickelback T-shirt."

"Whatever, dude."

"Who gave you your first mullet? Wait, sorry."

"Exactly."

"No," I say. "Not 'exactly.' I have *always* had your back."

"And I've had yours," Scott returns. "Who snuck you water and candy for three days when you hid under the house after you got busted for faking your paper route?"

"And I thank you for that. And for the three cavities I got at my next dental visit. But—"

"Brett, *why are you doing this*?"

Scott stares at me, and I can see he's all busted up inside. That just makes me angrier. How do you say to your family that you feel your wife has been drifting away, taking you for granted, and before you even started going out with each other the witch was lying to you—and when you got angry about the whole thing, looking for some support . . . well, everyone seemed to support *her*! My parents even tried to mediate the day after we announced the split, asking me to be rational and not such a hothead.

"You're my fucking family, and you should support me, okay?" I growl.

"Brett, this is different. We're Layla's family, too. Who else has she got?"

"That's right," I hear my mom say as she enters the room. "Her father never came back for her. When Dad walked Layla down the aisle at your wedding, she became his legal daughter. That's what a daughter-in-law is. We all accepted her as family and love her like she's our own."

"But I *am* your own!" I shout, not wanting to hear any more about her.

"Yes, and so is she," my mom says, her lips pursed, left eyebrow cocked.

"Fine. Well, I hope none of you traitors ever need any blood. Because I'm O negative—the universal donor. But it looks like my universe is getting smaller. And for the record: Trish and Scotty are B!"

And with that I storm out—feeling like a total asshole.

. . .

In an effort to right my wrongs, or at least shore up alliances, a couple days later I go back to the 'rents place with my tail between my legs and a pot of mums for Mom. I hold the flowers in front of my face as Mom opens the door and say, "I'm sorry," in my best apologetic voice. "I've been a jerk."

"These are gorgeous," Mom says, as she takes them from me and motions to the backyard. "I'll plant them under Layla's tree."

I look toward the backyard, where a small army of landscapers is muscling a green monster into a hole the size of a moon crater. More precisely, it is a tree that Mom explains is a "gorgeous flowering crab apple" being planted courtesy of Layla, thus making my pathetic handful of mums look like a tricycle at a rally of Harley-Davidsons. How did my damn wife know I was going to bring flowers? Am I such a cliché? I guess I am.

So this is how she wants to play it? Because two can play at this game. And I'm pretty good at winning games, even if it takes me a couple of seasons. Starting to understand the gravity of this contest, I take my sad pot of flowers, tell Mom I forgot an errand I need to run, and get back in my car.

Dad loves cigars. Me, I never quite got as into them, but I do see the appeal. There's something relaxing about smoking a cigar. I guess it's because when you smoke you can't really do anything else, and I'm usually doing ten thousand things at once. For me to sit still is a rarity. On the odd occasion I smoke one, I usually find that I'm just sitting wherever I am, talking to whoever I'm with, enjoying the flavor. It's nice. So forty-five minutes later I find myself in Encino at Fat Stogies, buying my dad a humidor. I pass the cigar-store Indian on my way inside and ask Jack, the owner, why such a thing—probably never appropriate, but now definitely not PC—is at the entrance of every single cigar shop I've ever encountered.

"Because it's a cigar store," Jack informs me.

"Right. But *why* is what I'm asking," I counter.

Jack shrugs. There's a flat-screen TV on the wall and two guys smoking in the store, watching the L.A. Kings. One of them chimes in that if I Google it, there's a whole history. I make a note in my head not to do that later.

They've got autographed headshots lining the walls: John Goodman, Bill Cosby, Kevin James, Bobcat Goldthwait, David Hasselhoff, and some guy from *The Sopranos*. You go to any cigar shop—anywhere—and there's an autographed picture of a guy from *The Sopranos*. I lean in closer to see what the Hoff wrote on his picture. It says, "You guys are smokin'." I smile at the inscription and have Jack direct me to an impressive humidor, which I promptly purchase.

• • •

I can take the stupid tree in the Garden of Good and Layla. I can deal with her pathetic attempts to one-up me with my family, and it gives me no small amount of joy when Layla shows up the following week with a Cuban for my father and he proudly walks her to the Versailles humidor I bought him. But when I call for Sammy Davis Junior and he doesn't come because she's somehow hypnotized him into not leaving her side and wrapped him up with a dog-heart-thieving scheme, there's a line drawn in the kibble. Layla has crossed it. I remember one time when my parents were out of town and Layla and I were watching the dog. We jokingly fought over who he'd sit next to, who got to play fetch with him more, who he liked better. Sammy wound up sleeping *between* us every night that week so it didn't seem like he was choosing sides. Very intuitive dog. But this is *my* Sunday, since I *temporarily* agreed to her stupid plan about maybe alternating weekends. So what if I didn't call ahead and plan an outing like she suggested after Movie Night? That doesn't give her the right to be at the house. And Sammy is suddenly much less intuitive as he sits with his traitor head resting on her knee.

"You don't actually think that dog loves you more than me, do you?" I ask.

"Uh, I really hadn't given it much thought," she answers, without looking up. She's smiling at Sammy, who would appear to be smiling back.

"Well, he doesn't."

"Okay," she says.

"Just making sure you know," I reply.

"I understand that you think Sammy Davis Junior loves you more," she states.

*What's this doublespeak crap?* "No," I say. "I don't *think* Sammy loves me more. I know he does."

"Heh, right."

*Oh, no, she isn't going there.* "Yes. I know I'm right."

Then she laughs this annoying laugh that I've only heard eight thousand times before. It's that derisive laugh she'd give if we were watching some dumb show on TV, one of her nineteen bazillion dramas, and some guy made a romantic gesture toward the female lead on a day when I was in the doghouse. She'd give that laugh without looking away from the TV, but I'd know what she was thinking: *Wow. Must be nice to have a guy do something that sweet. I'm sure that guy on the TV would do those things for me if I wasn't married to this asshole.* Oh, and if it wasn't scripted by sappy dickwads who I swear write that shit just to make the rest of us shmucks look bad.

She gives that laugh. It makes my blood boil.

"Clearly you think I'm mistaken," I say.

"I'm just trying to play with Sammy. What's it to you?"

"That's my dog."

"No, he's not," she says. "He's a family dog, and technically he was Scotty's when we got him. 'We' as in: I was there, too, the day we brought him home."

"Home to *my* family's house."

"Whatever," she says. "Sammy and I know the truth. Don't we, baby?" And then she kisses Sammy on his snout. And if I didn't know better, I'd swear he nodded yes.

"The truth?" I say, raising my pitch a whole octave. "Why don't we put your truth to a test?"

"Um . . . okay?" She stares at me.

"Great. We'll have a duel."

She snorts. "A duel? When, Brett? At sundown? Give me a break."

"I'm serious," I tell her.

"Fine," she scoffs. "What's the duel?"

"We'll stand on opposite sides of the lawn and call Sammy. We'll see who he loves more."

"You can't be serious. This is the most juvenile thing I've heard you say in, well, minutes."

"Scared?"

"Yeah—not so much," she says.

"Great. Then you stay away from Sammy for the next hour or so, and when it's time we can have *my dad* bring Sammy to the lawn—the lawn that *I grew up on and you didn't*—place *my dog* in between us, and we'll just see."

"It's amazing our marriage didn't work out. You're the height of maturity," she mutters.

"You're the height of something else."

## *trish*

There are no words to describe the level of jackassery I am witnessing on the front lawn at Casa Foster. On one side we have Brett, who I love dearly but am also *obligated* to love by blood relation. And then we have Layla, whom I love and admire enough to have chosen as my lifelong business partner. Yet when I see the two of them, on opposite sides of the lawn, calling out to poor Sammy Davis Junior as he haplessly runs back and forth to the point of exhaustion, I want to kick them both in the vagina.

"Here, Sammy! C'mon, boy," Layla shouts. Sammy runs to her. "Good boy! Attaboy. Atta baby. C'mon, baby boy . . ."

"C'mon, boy, that's—no, Sammy! Here, buddy, c'mere," Brett hollers. And Sammy runs back in the other direction.

The intensity on Brett and Layla's faces suggests they're trying to telekinetically move Sammy toward them. Their mouths are magnets, perhaps, and the bigger they get, the greater the attraction. Back and forth Sammy goes, and I want to stop it—I want to put Sammy out of his misery and bitch-slap both upright-standing apes—yet I'm mesmerized. I watch like I would some poor assistant on a Starbucks run, carrying eleven lattes back to the office, one cup precariously perched atop the bunch, about to tumble over and spill everywhere. The cup will inevitably crash to the sidewalk, and I'll think to myself, *That was partially my fault—I'm guilty of not doing anything.*

"Sammy!" Brett calls. Back Sammy runs, although it's not so much a run as a confused trot. I watch this for a few more laps when suddenly I notice something curious. Sammy Davis Junior, like all dogs, is stomach-motivated. And upon closer inspection it's becoming apparent What Makes Sammy Run.

I walk over to Brett. "What's on your hand?" I ask.

"Nothing," Brett snaps. "Mind your own business. You're distracting him."

"Let me see your hand."

"Stop interrupting, Trish."

"What's on his hand?" Layla asks, as she starts to make her way across the lawn.

"Nothing is on my hand!" Brett shouts. "Go back to your mark. You're cheating."

"Funny choice of words, Brett," I say.

Layla has now made her way over, and she grabs his hand. She turns it over and then lifts it to her nose. "What is that . . . dog food?" she asks.

"No!" Brett snatches his hand back. "Like I'd put dog food on my hand." He rolls his eyes, exaggerating how offended he is at the very suggestion.

Layla grabs it back, leans in close to inspect. She sniffs again. "Liver paste?"

"What?" Brett says defensively. "I didn't wash my hands after lunch."

"You're cheating!" Layla says. "Disgust—"

But before she can get out the "ing," Brett notices something new on his hand and grabs at Layla's. "Hang on, Miss Perfect, what's on *your* hand?" he shouts.

"Nothing."

"What's this?" Brett inquires, as he points to what could be

Skippy creamy peanut butter if I were a betting gal, but I'm staying out of it now. "What is *that*?"

Now it's Layla hiding her hand behind her back. I feel like I'm refereeing children. Then I watch Brett grab Layla's hand and lick it.

"Peanut butter?" he says.

"What are you gonna say about it, Liver Paste?"

"I don't know what to say," he answers.

"I know what to say," I finally butt in. "Both of you—I'm saddened to think I associate with you. I just witnessed the most disgusting spectacle I've seen since Chevy Chase had his own TV show. You're trying to *buy* our parents, you're tormenting the poor dog, what's next?"

They're quiet for a moment. A single moment.

"Well, I was thinking about buying you a Vespa," Brett says to me. "But since you're so horrified to even know me, I'll just take that money and put it toward—"

"A life?" Layla interjects.

Then Layla and Brett resume shouting at each other, putting on quite a show—sniffing each other's hands, arms flailing, curse words flying—insisting that they start the battle over. ("No hands!") Sammy Davis Junior walks between the two of them, looks up at me, and barfs.

Brett turns to Layla. "So, you gonna clean up after 'your' dog?"

# *layla*

I like to think I add value to the Foster family. I wouldn't be so bold as to say that I am the glue that holds them all together, because that would be obnoxious and assuming—and we all know what happens when you assume.

That said, I am the one person who is closest to every member of the Fosters if you take each relationship as a stand-alone. Okay, well, maybe I'm not closer to Bill and Ginny than they are to each other, but I am pretty damned close to all of these people.

I'm the only one who plays poker with Bill and his gang of louts, and who's his first mate on the SS *Barbecue* whenever he wants a cookout: I pass out the plates and get more buns. Scott's more into art than sports, so he and Brett don't connect in every way. So it's usually me who bonds with him over his girlfriends, or lack thereof. He comes to me for advice nine times out of ten; we have our favorite TV shows that we watch. Ginny? We shop together, we have lunches at Il Pastaio on Canon every Saturday, and come holidays, we're the ones who cook and decorate to make the Foster home the institution that it has become. Although it's unfortunately now turning into a different kind of institution—or, rather, one or all of us are going to end up in an institution if we don't figure out how to manage this split.

Brett's being a total baby about his family siding with me. Which they're not. They're just not siding with him. They love us both, and they're treating the situation as they would if two of the other family members got in a massive fight. Which is making Brett feel like they're choosing me.

God, it's ugly. He gave his family an ultimatum yesterday: It's *me* or *her*. And he expected everyone to make a choice! This was right after he pitched a fit because I was helping organize a scavenger hunt that Bill and his friends are doing in two weeks, which he said I have no business getting involved in. Um, right. Except for the fact that the whole thing was my idea to get them to do something healthy that didn't involve poker chips.

I understand that Brett feels like I've somehow co-opted his family, but he was also the one who encouraged me to get close to them. He loved how close we all were, until he stopped loving me. Now it's inconvenient, so I have to stop?

I'm not letting go without a fight. Even then I'm not letting go. And so it's with this in mind that I show up at the mediation Brett insisted we immediately have, in order for us to decide how to deal with our separation and who should get quality time with his family. I have to admit he's been cool about the divorce, not pushing anything through yet or suggesting anything stupid regarding money matters. I'm glad to see there's one line he feels too sheepish to cross, because I'm not so sure how confident I am in my counsel.

Brett suggested getting this person he's heard about to mediate, and I agreed against my better judgment. (He was pretty convincing about not wanting either of us hit with frivolous lawsuit judgments, and I saw his point, considering how silly we've both been acting. But sometimes I just can't help it. He infuriates me!)

The whole family got instructions to show up at nine-fifteen a.m. at Happy Valley Family Therapy Center, which I guess doubles as a mediation site. Handy, when that whole therapy thing just doesn't work out. I wonder if it ever does.

I arrive with Tommy Thames at my side, wishing he'd pressed his suit. I kick myself for being shallow, but really, how hard is it to show up not looking like you've donned a shar-pei? He's been bugging me about filing actual legal claims for the divorce, and so far I've been putting him off.

Bill and Ginny are there when I walk in, as is Trish, who looks bored before we've even begun. I think she's still convinced this is just a fight and doesn't see why we have to get all dramatic. Brett is there with his lawyer, Tim Ning, the attorney I myself first called.

Tim sometimes works for UCCC, which is how Brett and I met him. He was negotiating the divorce of the college athletic director—and oddly, his subsequent retirement—after he got caught by his wife doing something similar to the doggy paddle in a steam room with a member of the women's swim team. He's something of a shark, and though he was kind of funny at that cocktail party, and Brett and he sort of chummed it up, now he just looks like an asshole. He reminds me of the character Ken Jeong played as the uptight gynecologist in *Knocked Up,* who scares the bejesus out of poor Katherine Heigl. No bedside manner. Ning smiles and actually winks at me when I walk in. I assume it's because he remembers that I also reached out to him when this began, but I hope he doesn't wink at all of the soon-to-be ex-spouses of his clients.

Scott walks in wearing a Warcraft T-shirt that I bought for him two Christmases ago and gives me a half-smile as he sits on the couch next to his mom. A short man enters next, wearing short sleeves with a too-short tie, and he's looking at us with what I swear is an apology. Everything about this man is apologetic, from the way he holds the folder in front of his chest to the way he leans toward us, though only from the neck up.

"I'm sorry," he says, "but it's time we begin. I'm Burt Hollander. And . . . Matt says hello, Brett."

*Matt?* Brett's moron friend from college? I don't know any other Matts that he knows. I dart a glance at Brett, and he looks kind of sheepish. Tim Ning smiles at me and shrugs. I feel my temperature start to rise. How is this going to be fair? How do Brett and Matt know this guy? No one else seems to be objecting, not even my counsel, Tommy Thames. I grind my teeth.

"You can call me B—"

"Mr. Hollander?" Scott breaks in.

"Or Mr. Hollander, yes. Yes?"

"Yes," Scott says. "I would like to say, on behalf of the Foster clan, if you will . . ." Scott draws a jagged circle with his right hand, but it's not exactly clear who is included.

"Scott!" Bill snaps. His son lowers his hand and says nothing more.

"Yes, well, good point," Burt says, as if to validate the circle. Each one of us nods in agreement, sensing that somehow this meek man is going to be deciding our fates, sitting in judgment of the whole circus. Excellent point all around.

Hollander is relieved. He smiles and speaks as though he's announcing what we've just won. "I've prepared a list of questions for Mr. and Ms. Foster," he says, looking around at all of us cautiously—then he realizes that we are all Mr. and Ms. Fosters. He seems very sorry.

The questions start innocently enough, and seem oddly like non sequiturs. I can't help but feel like I'm on a game show—the prize being other Misters and Misses Foster.

"Brett, what is your mother's favorite food?" Hollander asks.

"Uh . . . she likes angel-hair pasta a lot. And fish . . ." He trails off.

I throw my arm nearly out its socket, not unlike Horshack on *Welcome Back, Kotter*.

"Layla?" Hollander says, allowing me my turn.

"Ginny does like pasta, but not too often, as she shies away from carbs. When she has it, she prefers it to be cooked al dente and makes a delicious tomato-basil sauce so good there's almost no point in ever ordering pasta out in a restaurant, because it can only suffer by comparison."

"She's not just kissing ass here," Brett says. "She basically just gave my mom a rim j—"

"Brett!" Trish shrieks. "That's our mother!"

"Can we have us simply answer the questions asked so I don't lose my Cocoa Puffs?" Brett growls.

"If you keep talking like that," Trish says, "I'm gonna lose *my* breakfast."

"Nobody is losing their breakfast," Ginny commands. "And you shouldn't interrupt, Trish, dear."

I leap into the breach: "I'd like to add that while Brett simply mentioned fish, it's salmon Ginny likes to eat, because it's high in omega-3 fats and Ginny read Dr. Perricone's book and tries to live by his code."

Brett makes a face, and I make one back.

"Brett," Burt says, "when is Trish's birthday?"

"March," he says.

"March what?" Hollander asks.

Brett is quiet for a moment. It's March twelfth, but it's not my turn to answer.

"This is just trivia," Brett snaps. "Layla has a better memory for that stuff. Why don't we talk about less superficial things?"

"Right," I chime in. "Birthdays are totally superficial. You'd never care if everyone forgot your birthday. It's just trivia."

"My birthday's the twelfth," Trish says.

"I knew that," I say.

"I know," Trish responds.

"Great," Brett grumbles. "You guys can make out later."

Sensing the temperatures in the room rising, Hollander decides to take Brett up on his earlier suggestion. "Okay," he says, "we'll talk about less superficial things. What are your father's views on politics? Is he a Republican? Democrat?"

"He's a Democrat," Brett answers.

"Is he ultraliberal? Fiscally conservative?"

"Is that really any of your business?" Brett asks. "I mean, don't they say never to discuss politics?"

"Politics, religion, sex, and abortion, I believe," Trish agrees.

"I'm just trying to gauge how interested you are in the views of your family members," Hollander says. "How well you can answer these questions shows what kind of an interest you take in them."

"I'm plenty interested in my family. Just because I don't know what they like on their pizza doesn't mean I should have to share them with a nonfamily member."

"Layla is family," Bill says, and winks at me.

"Thank you, Bill," I reply.

Brett had picked up a pencil and now snaps it in half.

The rest of the mediation is more of the same. Hollander asks us each about Ginny's views on parenting. Trish's views on religion. Pizza gets left out of it, though I could have easily answered what everybody likes on their pie, whether they like thin-crust or deep-dish, and who likes it cold the next day. It doesn't matter. The whole thing is pretty much Brett with his mouth agape, then fuming, and me getting all the answers right.

Head in hands, he starts moaning at one point. "None of this matters. The only thing that really matters are my and Layla's feelings toward the family and vice versa!"

"Brett, you make an excellent point," Burt Hollander allows.

"So I have one final question, and it is for each member of the family, excluding Layla and Brett."

"Good," Brett says. "Let someone else be in the hot seat."

"Layla and Brett are both drowning and you can only save *one* of them. . . ."

# *brett*

It's total and complete bullshit. They can go on and on about how I was always a better swimmer, but I will never let them live this down.

So Layla wins her nonlegal, nonbinding declaration of joint custody of my family. It's basically a sort of reverse restraining order (she can't be prohibited by me from seeing them) or visitation rights on steroids. What a mistake I made, trying to be nice. Any real judge would not have just thrown her out of court but locked her in a loony bin.

This is what I get for listening to Matt, who swore up and down this was the way to go. I should never have called him after I couldn't hang with Doug and Jared, or taken his suggestion about using this Burt Hollander schmo, his cousin who's still finishing his social work degree and "occasionally does mediation work on weekends." ("It worked when Kristi and I ended it!") This is what you get for listening to a guy who lost fifty dollars and spent a weekend in the hospital after betting biologically produced methane, set afire, couldn't burn through cotton boxers. I was glad to win the fifty, and he'd better go stay with Corey's pal in Mexico, 'cause I'm going to find his ass and set fire to it again.

After leaving the therapy center, I take my mom out for lunch at La Scala, one of her favorite spots. I don't know if I'm buttering her up or if I just want to connect with her. Dad said he had something to do but that he might meet us there.

Mom gets excited because Larry King walks in just as our waiter is setting down my Coke and her iced tea. "I just love that he's bringing suspenders back," she says.

"He's not bringing them back," I tell her. "He's never *not* worn them, and nobody else is following suit—or suspender, as it were."

"Well, I love that he's got his own sense of style," she says, and then waves at Larry like she knows him. He politely waves back as the maître d' seats him at his table.

"That he does—and *please* don't do that, Mom." She does, though. She'll see a celebrity and wave or say hello or comment on something irrelevant. She doesn't get that just because she recognizes someone doesn't mean she knows them.

I get momentarily distracted from my embarrassment by a woman sitting alone at the next table reading a book called *Never Be Lied to Again*. The title is in all caps, and the cover looks as angry as the woman looks hurt. An alternative title flashes through my mind: *Never Be Laid Again.* But then it's gone.

"Sweetie," my mom says, "I know you're feeling angry with us, and I just want you to know that this isn't a contest. It never was."

"Yeah. I get that you think that, Mom. But can you see my side of it? Can you understand how frustrating it is for me to have you all side with her?"

"But we're not siding with her, Brett," she explains, as she touches my face and smiles, her crow's-feet reminding me of both her strength and her individuality. When she and her girlfriends first started getting wrinkles, they all made appointments for Botox and collagen and all of the other BS that I don't care to know about. But not my mom. She said she wanted to age gracefully. When her friends started shaving years off their age here and there, she'd reprimand them. She'd tell them that she'd earned each and every one of those years, and ditto for the wrinkles. Of course they joked and offered to give her theirs, but this remains one of the many reasons I love my mom. Which is why it's so hard to have her totally dog me right now.

"You *are,*" I argue. "You're my mom. How many times do we have to go over this?"

"As many as it takes for you to understand that our loving Layla isn't a threat to you. There's room in our hearts for both of you. Of course you're our baby. You're our flesh and blood. But Layla doesn't have anybody else. Do you want her to be all alone?"

"No." *Yes.*

"That's my boy," she says, and looks out the window. "What do you and Layla have planned for the weekend?"

"Huh?" I ask.

"Do you have any plans for the weekend?"

I ignore the fact that she's pretending that Layla and I are somehow seeing each other and emphasize the *I* in my response. "I plan to sleep, watch some football, and maybe sleep."

"How exciting."

My dad walks in and takes off his baseball cap. I see him before he sees us and wave him over.

"There they are," he bellows.

"Hey, look—it's Larry King!" My mom points. I gently nudge her finger back down.

"Hey, now!" my dad says. "Biggest ass-kisser next to James Lipton."

"Don't say that, Bill," my mom says.

"And Jeffrey Tambor on *The Larry Sanders Show,*" I suggest.

"He's a fluffer," my dad continues, razzing King. "He never gives anyone a hard time. He never questions anyone or digs deep. He just accepts their answers as they give them."

I laugh. Then, "Dad," I say. "Since I have both of you here . . . I was just trying to explain to Mom. It's almost like I see Layla more now than when I actually wanted to see her. We're separated. And I don't want her to be everywhere I turn. No matter what your personal feelings are on this breakup, you're my family, and you're supposed to stay loyal to me. Whether you agree with my decision or not."

"I understand," my dad says.

"Neither of us can move on with our lives with the situation as it is now," I explain, because I finally feel like I'm being heard. "Which is making me think that's what you want."

"I get it," my dad says.

"Thank you," I reply. I'm not sure he's going to amend his behavior, but at least I don't feel like everyone is either siding with Layla or denying that they're siding with her.

"Now, what's here for me?" he asks, as the waiter delivers what my mom and I both ordered—the Leon Chopped Salad. It's legendary.

"This was a mother-son lunch—you should have agreed to come right away if you wanted to horn in on the grub."

"That's rude, son. Though with the way your boys have been playing defense lately"—he picks up a fork—"I might just be able to sneak something up the middle." He reaches over and snags some of my salad.

I pretend I've just been stabbed in the heart, and my mom playfully nudges my dad for saying such a thing. I'm not sure if this has made us all closer, but I'm certain that I still want to throttle Layla.

• • •

Later, at home, I'm thinking very seriously of canceling cable. It took me so long to get it connected at my new place. And after all that work, there is *nothing* on. Not even a *Rockford Files* rerun or an old Steve McQueen or Charles Bronson movie that can be stomached. Nothing. Not one thing.

I'm staring at the on-screen guide, and what is half of the

stuff? "Paid programming." Well, I already paid for the programming, so where is it? And I think this infomercial guy is paying for his ad ("Learn Cooking by Hypnosis"?), and I'm not watching his shit . . . so one of us is getting screwed. Or both.

There's no good music on my iPod—none that doesn't make me think either of Layla and how angry I am at her or that I've already listened to it until I want to barf—and I have no good DVDs. Nothing in my refrigerator looks good. I leave the light off when I get ready in the bathroom, because I can't stand to look at myself.

Come to think of it, I'm thinking very seriously of canceling the electricity.

# *layla*

At work, the days are as easy as finding Birkenstocks in Portland—and as hard as finding a clock in a casino. It goes up, it goes down, in no particular order. Trish and I are still waiting to hear the details regarding the prototype we want to deliver to PETCO, and we haven't heard anything more about our loan.

Brooke and I meet at Quality, a favorite place of ours on Third Street, for an early breakfast before work and to catch up. She nonchalantly says to me, "You look good today," and it floors me. Feeling so much like purple ooze inside, how could I possibly look good?

"I'm so annoyed," Brooke announces next, as we sit down.

"Why?" I ask.

"I bought a brand-new dress for a job interview. It was on sale. What I didn't realize was that it was on sale because there was a hole in it. No returns. And I didn't get the job."

"Where was the hole?" I ask, knowing her interview technique. "A strategically placed hole could have helped you get the job."

"I was talking with a woman, and the hole was in my armpit."

"Oh, yeah, that sucks," I admit. "Are you sure you didn't get the job because of something you said?"

Brooke exhales and stares for a moment too long at the guy at the next table. His girlfriend and I both notice. Finally, she turns her attention back to me and answers, "I might have told her that her letterhead looked like it belonged to a little girl, her computer system was outdated, and that she should consider having the dark mole on her arm looked at for cancer."

"Oh my Christ."

"I was doing a good thing. What if it *was* cancer?"

I can't argue. Partly because she has a point, but mostly because the word *mole* reminds me of the flesh-colored mole the therapist had when Brett and I attempted our one session of couples counseling. When I thought we might actually be okay. When I still had hope.

The rest of our breakfast I'm like a zombie.

"Just cry," Brooke says, when she notices my chin twitching uncontrollably. "It's only me. I don't care. I mean, I care. But you know."

"Thanks." I sniffle as the tears stream down my face. "I'm sorry I'm such bad company lately."

"It's fine," she says. "Kinda makes me feel better about myself."

"You're not a very nice person." I grunt. But I smile for the first time in what feels like forever. She's at least consistent.

"Part of my charm," she replies.

I stretch our breakfast as long as I can, as I suddenly dread going to work. It's a mixed bag of the merely irritating and the suicide-inducing, as my anxiety and depression cause every pre-Thanksgiving Chihuahua-dressed-as-a-turkey photo shoot to make me want to pound a wide-angle lens into some dog owner's mouth—and a drumstick somewhere less pleasant.

In the week or so since the debacle with Matt's cousin-cum-therapist/mediator, not a word from Brett. All I know for sure is that his team is not doing very well. That I find out from the local paper. Not that I was expecting anything direct. But anything personal I now have to get secondhand. And the little news I can get is maddeningly sparse. It's *USA Today* condensed.

"It's hard, but he's soldiering on," Ginny said, when I asked.

"I think he's a lot stronger than we all gave him credit for," Bill says, with a knowing smile, but knowing what, I'm not sure.

"He's fine," Scott says. "Who cares?"

"The word that comes to mind is 'peachy,' " Trish adds.

Zilch. So naturally my mind sees him already remarried with a daughter and a house in Rancho Cucamonga.

# *brett*

Did you ever stop to consider what a lonely thing a bus stop is? All those people keeping a safe distance from one another, not making eye contact, walking to the curb to squint down the road every eight seconds, longing for the bus to come and liberate them from the excruciating awkwardness of standing there with other strangers who, like you, are too broke or too self-righteous or too close to their last DUI to drive a car? Hoping against hope that this isn't the time one of them turns out to be an escaped serial killer, doing thirty years to life for a mess of killings at lonely bus stops, using only the sharp edge of a fare card?

Or how lonely a streetlight is, helplessly resisting the dark?

Or a diner when you're eating alone?

I think I miss Layla.

Or maybe I don't.

I don't know.

# *trish*

It's becoming clear. Painfully. Brett is fucked in the head.

I visited him at his apartment, which is a fetid swamp far beyond the laziest college freshman's wildest aspirations, and I swear to God, when I got to the door, he was playing that Spandau Ballet song on the stereo. Loud. And he was *singing along*.

" 'Why do I find it hard to write the next line? Oh, I want the truth to be saaaid.' "

Well, I know *this* much is true: That boy needs to get laid. Too bad I'd have to beat his ass if he ever seriously touched another woman.

Of course it's frustrating. Much as I love Layla, and much as I consider her a better sister than he is a brother (most of the time), I have to admit to feeling some deep protectiveness about Brett. It hurts me to see him hurting. I think he's crazy for instigating the whole divorce thing, and stupid for being angry about that thing with Doug so long ago. God, how fragile is the male ego? (I think Shakespeare said that: "Oh, shall I compare the male ego to the shell of an unboiled egg? So fragile, and so easily crushed.") But Brett's the only one who can make peace with that.

Thank God I don't date men. They're all crazy.

# *ginny*

*November 3*

*Dearest Ev,*

*Something's wrong with Brett.*

*He never calls, and when he does, I cringe.* Cringe, *Evy—me, his own mother! I feel ashamed to say it, but sometimes when he calls, I see his number come up on the thing that shows the numbers of whoever's calling and I don't answer. Don't ever tell him! We're doing our best to keep it from Layla, to avoid seeming to meddle too much, but he's changed from my tough, lovable rascal into I don't know what. He sounded like that guy on public television who sells the books about discovering The You Inside. I can't remember, but you know what I'm talking about.*

*This afternoon, he dropped by after practice and walked past me into the kitchen without saying hello. He sat down, refused coffee and soda and Lorna Doones, and stared out the window for about six minutes. Maybe it wasn't six whole minutes, but it seemed like a good long time. Then he said, "Tell me something," and I said, "Okay," as if I have anything to tell. "Tell me," he says, "how you define happiness."*

*And then I was in for it. Because I was always so bad with abstract concepts. I can use the word in a sentence, but he wants philosophy, and you know that was never really my thing. But I do what he* really *wants—which is for me to ask him how* he *defines happiness. And then I'm* really *in for it. Twenty or thirty minutes of doom and gloom, all poured out with a rueful smile. "The promise of a dream that's inevitably crushed," or some such nonsense. The phone rang, but I couldn't answer it. He looked at it like it was objecting to his interpretation and he didn't care for the interruption so it could just shut up. And it did. I hope it wasn't you.*

*I couldn't even go to the bathroom. I kept looking for an opening, but he seemed so intent, and so out of sorts at the same time. So I listened and listened. I love him with all my soul, and it pains me so to see him like this—but I really had to go!*

*Of course it's an awful situation, and I get teary if I even let myself think about it. So I won't. I truly believe in my heart of hearts that much as I love him, he was at least partly the cause of this mess. But I feel he'll be okay again someday, someday soon. Of course I hope they'll stop behaving like stubborn children long enough to see that what they have is worth fixing. I never stop hoping.*

*Oh, I'm using this address for you because, when we were kids, I used to hear Dad ask Mom where you had gotten to, and Mom would always say "Heaven knows!" Now Bill has taken it up. I thought you'd get a kick out of that.*

*Love you always,*
*Gin (no tonic!)*

## *brett*

Now I understand why kids hate divorce so much: It often replaces the illusion of a cohesive, united pair of superheroes with the reality of two clueless, disoriented anger junkies who are not any more well adjusted than—shudder—the kids themselves are. I'll never forget the story Jared told me about when he was eight years old and his parents divorced. Apparently, they were screaming at each other at the top of their lungs in the very next room for three hours. The kids heard every heartbreaking syllable. When they finally came out, they sat Jared and his older brother down and calmly told them they were going to be separating. And that it would be "nice," because now they'd have two houses instead of one. Jared and his brother ran and locked themselves in the bathroom, holding each other and crying for the whole night. The parents couldn't even get the kids out of the bathroom to go to school the next day. It wasn't until four p.m. the following afternoon that hunger got the best of them and they were coaxed out by peanut-butter-and-jelly sandwiches on the other side of the door. That was the last peanut-butter sandwich he ever had. To this day Jared won't touch anything with peanut butter. A perfectly delicious food. Divorce fucks you up.

My family has taken to answering my calls like this: "Oh, it's *you*, Brett." Well, like it or not, they're going to have to deal with me. At least occasionally. Because a key stipulation of the agreement drafted by Burt—among about five things he worked up to make the whole absurd process and resulting nonbinding agreement seem official—was a continuation of Layla's "custody" scheme. Each of us gets the family on a designated weekend. I get them; she gets them; I get them; she gets them. This basically will keep Layla and me from running into each other accidentally, but it also has the effect of laying out ground rules for what was already becoming a grueling competition for the family's affections.

I take this very seriously, wanting to plan a get-together or special event. But I'm kind of stuck. Layla was always better at this sort of thing. I'm racking my brain, trying to dream up something that won't immediately be eclipsed, so I call my dad to see if I can trick him into coming up with a brilliant suggestion.

"No ideas?" he says, busting me about three minutes into the call. "Well, it's a tough situation, I know."

Then he says something that hits me like a fire hydrant in the crotch. I know he's joking—I *think* he's joking—but it still makes my blood boil.

"Maybe you should call Layla."

"What does that mean?" I snort.

"Nothing, nothing. We're just . . . The family has something special in our near future. When we go to the Sunday—"

"You made plans for this weekend," I challenge, "knowing that it's my turn?"

"For Pete's sake, it'll be on Layla's weekend!" he says. "But she's already arranged a doozy: Sunday at the spa for your mom and your sister, and Scott and I get a round of golf at LACC."

"Good for her," I say.

"Well, I'm just saying. If you two really are planning on buying our affections, you're falling behind good," he remarks with a laugh.

"LACC is private," I mutter, hardly hearing him. "How the hell did she swing that?"

"Some couple with a membership came in for photos, and apparently they loved the way Layla caught the moment where their dog's little tongue was just showing a bit—"

"*That* cheap trick?" I cut my dad off. "She gives them peanut butter, for crying out loud."

"Brett," my father says, suddenly serious. "Don't worry about it. It's not a big deal. This all just seems silly, and we don't expect you to match Layla's—"

"Fine. I won't," I toss out. And I hang up.

# *layla*

Through the grapevine, I hear a rumor that the family is free this Sunday. It's a Brett weekend, but without actually coming right out and saying it, Scott strongly hinted that the Fosters were being kicked to the curb.

Wasting no time, I hatch a plan to throw together a picnic lunch at the park. Nothing fancy. I'll prepare a few things, maybe watercress-and-cucumber sandwiches to start, grilled portobello mushrooms with roasted-pepper rémoulade, marinated corn salad, Southwestern-style chicken, a homemade forest-berry torte. Maybe there'll be some badminton or boccie. No big deal. And the whole thing will be a surprise; I'll tell them I'm picking up a bucket of KFC and a twelve-pack of Coke.

I call Ginny Thursday night and hash out plans. She's over-the-top agreeable.

"So, one o'clock, then," I say.

"That's fine," she says.

"Or would later be better? Would that give you more time?"

"Whatever you said before is fine."

"Because you and Bill and the guys don't have to do *anything*," I tell her. "I'll take care of everything." And then I think, here it comes: her pointless little insistence on doing something, contributing a dish, bringing a cooler, calling the city for a picnicking license.

"Okay," she says.

It's a first! For a moment, I can't believe my good fortune. There's no battle over whether I'm doing too much or going out of my way. But almost immediately my feeling changes. It's not relief but almost, *almost,* resentment. No pledge of Bill to get the grill going? No offer to throw together a dessert? Not even a store-bought Jell-O mold?

Still, I don't let my obvious hypocrisy get me down. I've got a date with the Fosters, and that always makes me feel better. Plus, Brett will be on the sidelines. Winning this round will be sweet.

# brett

God, I hate losing.

Saturday evening, after my Condors get clobbered by St. John's at an away game, I'm talking to Scott in my usual postgame state of nervous exhaustion, too tired to move and feeling very guilty that I'm not doing anything but lazing around playing video games. It's hell. We're playing Grand Theft Auto IV: the Lost and Damned because I got sick of Scott clobbering me at the new Madden. (WTF? Has he been practicing? He's making JaMarcus Russell look like Peyton Manning. Little bastard.) My senses are dulled, yet I'm irritable. Layla used to say I'd get PMS all game day, meaning I was "a little moody." Behind my back she'd say it, and my family and friends did a terrible job of keeping her secret. Privately, it made me laugh—every day except game day.

"Don't beat yourself up," Scott's saying. We're both doing our best to get past the fights we've been having; I came over to check out his newest painting—something mimicking some fantasy painter named Vallejo, and I have to say that I can appreciate the model's outfit—and he's talking about sports. "You knew this would be a tough year. You lost your entire front line and your best pass rushers. Everyone tells you that every week, but you still get down."

"Well . . ." I sigh. "Knowing we've got some holes and inexperience doesn't make losing any easier. I just wanted this year to be like the last few. I got used to winning, too," I say. "Maybe I even started taking it for granted."

"I know what would help," Scott says. Then he smirks. "It's too bad you're not invited."

"To what?"

"I shouldn't say," he says, practically guaranteeing that I'll find out, even if I have to beat it out of him.

"Right, you shouldn't," I agree. "But that's never stopped you before."

He pauses, maybe to give a quick nod to trustworthiness. Then: "Layla's doing a little picnic for us on Sunday. You bagged out, she stepped in." He pops Madden back in and gives me an amused, challenging look.

Now, I can't emphasize enough how dumb it is to put together a plan of action when you're beside yourself with rage. (I actually think that's what's behind a lot of blogging.) But I don't always listen to myself.

Trying to cover my ass, I say, "I didn't bag. I just . . . changed focus."

"What?"

"I know what I said to Dad on Thursday, but he didn't have to tell her—I wanted to *surprise* you. I know I come up a little short sometimes—"

"Sometimes?" Scott says.

"So I thought we'd switch it up and do a big breakfast thing."

"But you sleep until noon on Sundays," he challenges.

True. Not noon but definitely after breakfast. At least during the season and after game days. This little detail escaped me when I gave birth to this breakfast plan, which is turning out to be a preemie.

"That's part of the surprise," I suggest.

"Where are we going?" Scott asks.

Good question, and one in need of an answer. But right now I'm exhausted. "*Big* breakfast. Save room," is all I mutter. "Tell the others."

As he gives himself the Raiders again, and me the Steelers, I get up, toss down my controller, and head out of his room.

"Well, if nothing else, we're eating great on Sunday." Scott laughs.

# *layla*

The phone rings. It's Bill.

"What's up?" I ask.

"Just wanted to let you know we'll meet you at the park," he says.

"Okay, but I could pick you up. It's no trouble."

"It'll be easier. We'll all be over at our house when Brett drops us off—"

"Brett?" I interject, trying to keep from flipping my lid. "He's . . . I thought he wasn't doing anything with you guys."

"He's taking us to breakfast. But don't worry. We'll be done and back long before your little picnic."

*Little? Yeah, right. And the Pacific is my little ocean.* But I can't very well contradict Bill and risk sounding overly competitive. Which I'm not. So I keep my peace. "All right. No worries. See you at our little picnic!"

*Little, my ass.*

# *brett*

The problem with making a big deal out of breakfast is that it generally requires a reservation at a decent restaurant. When you oversleep on Sunday morning and wake up twenty minutes before you're supposed to pick up your dining companions, that's really a trick. It's all I can do to shower, shave, and tear out of my place to end up fifteen minutes late at the house. Trish is over, and the family's waiting.

"Everybody ready?" I say brightly.

"Almost everybody," Trish says, after looking me up and down.

And we're off—to nothing more spectacular than Duke's on Sunset Boulevard. It's a pleasant place, unremarkable except for the fact that it's been a Foster family breakfast hangout since I can remember. I'm hoping the lack-of-planning aspect will be overwhelmed by the nostalgia.

Indeed, it might have worked perfectly, but the forty-five-minute wait for the table undercuts my pitch somewhat. And when we're finally seated, there's some rock star at the table next to us and nobody can focus on the menu because they're all too busy trying to figure out if the person sitting with the rock star is a transvestite.

My mom thinks they're both women. Scott has to tell Mom that she washed a T-shirt with that guy's face on it probably a hundred times. The irony is that I used to make fun of this band solely based on the fact that this guy looked like such a chick—in his heyday, he was so androgynous it was almost uncomfortable watching his videos on MTV. And here he is sitting with another dude dressed up like a girl for completely different reasons.

Other than the sighting, breakfast is uneventful.

"That was good!" my mom says as we walk outside after we've eaten. "So *good*!" She's in that peacemaker mode, where she sets herself in the middle of the tension and splatters positivity everywhere, hoping to get a little on everyone.

"Good, yes," Scott allows. "Even excellent, maybe. But I'm not sure about big."

I shoot a few eye daggers at him and everyone piles into the car.

"Trish," Scott says, "you're familiar with the concept of 'big.' A big event, a big plan, a big breakfast—"

She interrupts, "Big head, big deal, big pain in the—"

"Right!" he interrupts back.

"Would you consider that breakfast big? Because Brett was telling me yesterday that this was going to be big, and since Layla—"

"Not the breakfast *only*," I say, with way too much energy for the moment. It's clear I'm inspired by something poisonous deep inside: jealousy, inadequacy, vindictiveness, competitiveness. The day's about to take a very dark turn. "That's just the beginning," I continue.

Right about now I've gotten myself halfway into the boat that'll take me to hell. One foot is still on the dock. But I can't do the splits. It's all aboard the dinghy to damnation. Straight to Hades we go, boys. Anchors aweigh.

I get on the highway and take off east.

"Uh," my dad says eventually, looking at his watch, holding it at a little bit of an angle, as if to allow me to see, too. "I don't mean to spoil the fun, but we're kind of committed to being someplace in about fifteen minutes."

"This isn't the way home, that's for sure," Scott says, peering out the window. "Unless we're doing the full circuit by way of China."

"What's up, Brett?" Trish says. "Where are we headed, seriously?"

"It's a surprise," I say.

"To who?" Trish rejoins.

"Cell phones off!" I snap, a little too maniacally. "My *ex's* rule!" And indeed, it is among the many amendments to the original Foster constitution, somehow devised by Layla, that cell phones are off on Sundays for the duration of any family outing. Mine will stay on, in case of emergencies, but no one else's. Not if they want to play by the family rules.

I see Trish in the rearview mirror, surreptitiously trying to make a call, and I growl at her, "No! Off!" She and the others look horrified as I hold out the baseball cap I've been wearing to collect all of their phones. I don't care if they think I'm nuts; this is *my* day. I set the hat full of phones down on the divider between the two front seats.

We're cruising due east along Interstate 10, approaching Pomona and San Bernardino but toward nothing I know. This is an unbelievably deficient plan, but then most plans conceived in haste and out of one hundred percent pure, fresh organic spite usually are.

In the backseat I hear a promising conversation between Scott and Trish.

"This is an adventure," my brother is musing. "Spontaneity is usually to Brett as tenderness is to you. But this is an adventure. It's out there. I don't know why you don't see it as some sort of unpredictable, fun, zany—"

"Adventure, yes," Trish says. "The word we're both allowing is *adventure*. But right now, my keen anticipation is directed toward a shiny and respectable Chevron station, or a McDonald's, or a Wendy's and its frequently cleaned toilet. Because I *really have to pee and Brett's not going to—*"

"Trish," Ginny says sharply.

"Yes, Mom?" Trish replies, and that's as far as it goes.

"I bet we're going to Knott's Berry Farm!" Scott shouts after another mile of silence. He's clearly excited.

And that's it! I can now reveal that the brilliant scamp has guessed my clever plan. I'm in the clear, and what's better, winning points on the cheap. Fill the fam up on ice cream and corn dogs, and the 'rents might even get a senior discount!

"But then why are we going east on Ten?" Trish asks. "Knott's would be south on I-five. Keep guessing."

*Gulp*. She's right. If he'd blurted out that proposal fifteen or twenty minutes ago, I'd be golden. Now I'm toast. I think in a panicked moment that I'll take an exit ramp and turn around, claiming I was taking extra precautions against blowing the surprise too early. Or I could triangulate south on . . . what? The 605?

"He could be taking the Six-oh-five south to throw us off the trail," Scott suggests, holding fast to his dream.

"We passed that ten minutes ago," Trish scoffs, and suddenly I want to jam a GPS down her throat.

When Scott's phone rings, the jolt is like high voltage shot through the car. He lurches forward, grabs the phone from my hat, and smiles devilishly. "Hello?" he says, answering. "Yeah, sorry. He collected everybody's cell." Then he holds the phone out to me. "It's Layla. She wants to talk to you."

"Way to turn it off when I asked you," I tell him. I take the phone and brace myself.

"Hello?" I say.

I can't tell whether we're in a bad cell area or the person on the other end is in a *really* bad state, or both, but it's hard to make out what she's saying. Still, I'm getting the general drift. F this, f that, where do I get the f'ing nerve—that sort of thing.

"Look," I say, "it's my Sunday with the family, and just because you feel a need to wedge yourself in between me and them every bloody chance you get doesn't mean I have to allow it. We both agreed to live by that mediation, and that's what I'm doing. Even if it's bullshit, me having to fight for my own family."

A few choice words back at me, then my turn again.

"Well, it's *my* Sunday, so we're all going for a little . . . to get . . . to spend some time together. I don't ask you for reports on *your* weekends."

She's saying more things I don't care to hear (much of it accurate and richly deserved, but damn me if I'll surrender now), so I give the phone back to Scott.

"What?" he shouts into the phone, plugging one ear against the road noise.

"Don't tell her where we're going, Scott," I warn.

"I'd tell you where we're going," he says into the phone, "but I don't know."

"And don't give her our location."

"Hadn't thought of that," he says. "We're going east on Ten toward . . . like, Ontario. If we didn't have Mom and Dad aboard, I'd say maybe we're Vegas-bound."

"I *like* Vegas," my mom says. "The dealers are very nice, don't you think, Bill?"

My dad looks out the window. "If we're going to Vegas, I'm going to need to stop and get underwear and a toothbrush. And I'll need to borrow about a grand."

Scott hangs up, and the car is agonizingly silent for a minute—or a year, I'm not sure which. Then it happens: I see my salvation. Green Hills U-Pick Orchard. Pomona. About ten or fifteen minutes ahead.

"You see? Apple picking! And berries. Surprised?"

"I think berry season is over, darling," Mom says helpfully.

"Well, then, we'll stick to apples," I say impatiently. "But that's what we're doing. We're going to this farm and picking our own fruit."

"I wonder if I could pick myself another family," Scott mutters, and I am astounded at how perfectly he reminds me of a despondent nine-year-old. I guess he really wanted Knott's Berry Farm.

"Look, this is going to be *fun*!" I tell them.

"This is going to make for a hell of a story when I get back," Trish allows. "Assuming we get back."

Miraculously, as we pull up to the place, I see it's a fairly authentic family scene: perfect sunny morning, fall in the air. I may accidentally have hit the jackpot.

But then . . . disaster.

"Looks like apples are out of season," says my dad.

Thinking fast, I glance around and leap at the first opportunity I see. "No, no, I didn't mean *apple* picking. That was just a ruse. The true surprise is that *we're picking walnuts*! See? They grow those here, too."

"I've never heard of that," Trish says, staring at me.

"Me, either," says Scott.

"Well, then, that's why this will be so much fun" is my reply. "Who doesn't like to try something new?"

Trish looks around, then sets off ahead for the main barn and the swarm of families apparently here either for the walnuts or for refrigerated cider and fresh donuts.

"Where are you going?" my dad calls out.

"Look for a gift shop," she says dryly. "If I'm going to be with Brett all day, I'm going to need one of those *I'm with Stupid* T-shirts."

## *layla*

I am out-of-my-head pissed. My teeth lock together and my whole face tightens; I can feel it from my jaw through my ponytail. I'm mad as hell, and I'm not going to take it . . . well, I'm not going to take as much of it as I've been taking.

I sit in the car for a second, speculating on where they've gone. Let's see. They're headed east on 10? Brett's in charge. Now, going on the evidence of the past five years, when it comes to devising interesting places for excursions, his imagination doesn't extend much beyond the multiplex.

As I drive, I wear an expression that frightens even me when I see it in the rearview mirror. I cut off a guy in a pickup truck, and he guns it to get even with me and glare or flip me off or something. But as he draws even, he sees the face I'm wearing. He then pretends he's just looking around, minding his own business, and is suddenly intensely interested in a billboard advertising *The Valley's Leading Lady for Real Estate!*

*Damn straight, buddy.*

Then I remember something beautiful. Scott signed me up on a website that lets people follow where he is, using the GPS on his phone. I told him it was totally obnoxious and a little unsettling:

Why would anyone want people to be able to follow their every move on the Web? I imagined tech-savvy high-school kids telling their skeptical parents this would be a great way to make sure they were keeping out of trouble on a Saturday night, then linking the tracking site to a little GPS they'd leave in a friend's bedroom while they went party-hopping. But at this second, I've become a big believer. I just hope he's logged in and active.

*C'mon, please.*

*Bingo!*

# brett

The best things in life are free, they say. Though this day actually wasn't—if we do the picking, why are the damn nuts so friggin' expensive?—miracle of miracles, the next few hours are nice. Odd, yes, but very nice. I'd even go so far as to say *fun,* despite the jokes. ("We don't need any more nuts in this family," my brother keeps saying, cracking himself up.) My mother loved the experience, my father liked it, Trish tolerated it and had some laughs, and Scott came away a happy young man, especially after stuffing himself with fresh, warm donuts and drinking himself stupid with cider.

Heading home, we're driving along, looking like a flashback to a Chevy ad from the fifties. We're feeling the breeze from the open windows on our faces, hair blown back, smiles all around, when out of nowhere, the Grim Foster appears. It's Layla—or at least her car—and she's closing in fast. I roll up all the windows.

If you haven't seen *The Ring,* I won't spoil it for you. But she's like that goony girl in the nightshirt, coming up at supernatural speed in the rearview mirror. I mean *creepy* fast. I blink, and she's transported closer. I look ahead, then to the mirror, then back to the road, and in the three or so seconds it takes, she's jumped forward as if carried along in time-lapse photography.

Now she's alongside our car. And she's motioning for us to pull over.

Mom waves at her.

"Look!" she says. "It's Layla. Isn't that a nice coincidence?"

# *layla*

*Pull over, Brett. You can't run. It's time for a good old-fashioned ass-kicking.*

# brett

I can't hear her, but I can see her. Layla's hysterical, going off like a howler monkey in the cage of her Jeep's passenger compartment. It's mayhem in my car as my dad and Trish demand that we stop the car and talk to her, if only to prevent a rollover.

We take an exit and pull in to the parking lot of a gas station, parking way in back. Layla is close behind.

As I pull to a stop, the scene in my car is practically a coordinated attempt at a prison break. Scott is doubled over and moaning. Trish is telling me to "Open the door, quick, I think Scott's ill." My mom is saying I'd better follow Trish's advice. And then Layla's there, standing stiff, knocking on my window.

"You need . . ." my mom tells Scott. "Oh, what's that thing you take when you need to go to the bathroom?"

"An emetic is for throwing up. I think it's a diuretic," my dad suggests.

"Hell, no, that's for taking a leak," I snap.

"I think it's called an enchilladic," Trish offers.

"That's not even a word," I scoff.

Dad shakes his head at me, then pops out of the car. "Layla! We're rescued!" he says.

*"Rescued"?* And at this moment things get appreciably worse. Somehow we've invited a police presence. Two troopers have stopped filling up their cruiser with gas and are now watching our exchange. This is always a cause for some scrotum tightening, and I'm worried that this incident will soon escalate to a gun battle, given Layla's howls.

"How dare you spirit them away like a thief, even after I made a whole plan with your mom!" she screams, throwing her arm out in my mother's direction but getting only a frightened look in return. This is the scariest any of us has seen her—and for me, that's saying something. "I did a rémoulade! I had boccie balls!"

"That's nuts!" I shout back, then glance around, hoping no one will make a joke about our afternoon excursion. No one does. When I look back at Layla, I start wondering whether she's carrying any of the boccie balls in her purse, and I keep a good distance just in any case.

"You were grabbing a bucket of KFC. It was no big deal," Trish interjects, looking apologetic.

"So I lied," Layla hisses. "It was a *huge* deal. Two kinds of chardonnay, chilled! Cloth napkins! Napkin rings!"

"Well, Mom and Dad could have spoken up and—"

"Of course they didn't," Layla says in disgust. "They moved right through fear into the Stockholm syndrome. Otherwise, they'd have ratted you out to those cops by now for parent-napping."

The two troopers are still a distance away, watching. I'm sure they were hoping for something tidy, for everyone to apologize and go home. I was hoping for the same thing. There's a guy cop with short brown hair and a caterpillar mustache—a giant of a man you'd think twice before crossing in any circumstance—and a lady cop who's really quite pretty, projecting smirking authority with her sex-fantasy-tight uniform and dirty-blond hair tucked up into her hat.

The guy—Officer Paul Kramer, I see from his name placard—steps up to my car, watching Layla and me dubiously. It's almost dusk, and he shines a flashlight into the backseat to see my mom, Scott, and Trish. They stare back at him with a mix of disbelief and amusement. The female cop approaches next. Both troopers then stare at me, looking as though their patience is waning.

"Officer," I say, "this is a huge misunderstanding. These are my parents, my brother, my sister . . . my family. This was a family outing."

"True," Trish says. "Breakfast was nice. The kidnapping didn't enter the picture until afterward. That's when things got really *nutty*."

I shake my head and glower at her, and she smiles.

Kramer is clearly an old hand at family conflict, so he knows enough to look past the verbal shoving match between children, whatever their ages. "He's your son—and him, too? And she's your daughter?" he asks my mom and dad, shining his light around at each of us, the true Fosters.

My dad speaks up. "Sorry at this moment to say it, Officer, but yes, they're mine. Ours."

"This is . . . not usual," my mom says, looking horrified, which drives my humiliation further home. "They're usually so much better behaved."

Scott groans. He tumbles over Trish, flings the back door open, and tears off toward a row of bushes with his hand pressed tight over his mouth.

"We've got a runner," Kramer barks to his partner, and he stumbles backward a little and fumbles for his nightstick before giving chase.

"He's not a runner," Trish shouts helpfully. "He's just got diarrhea or something."

Sure enough, Scott manages to just barely make it to where the bushes begin before he bends at an inhuman angle and throws up, hard. His arms are raised like airplane wings, steadying him, and again he lets loose. After a few coughs and spits, the worst is over. He wipes his mouth with his sleeve, looks at the sleeve in disgust, then turns to Officer Kramer, who has his nightstick in hand.

"Don't shoot!" he says, waving his hands wildly. Then, after spitting one more time, he leans over, spent. "I just had too much cider."

Kramer holsters the nightstick. "No crime in that," he admits, wincing at the smell.

*Agreed.* But a crime has taken place here, and my ex is responsible.

## *layla*

"I'd like to report a kidnapping," I say to Officer Kramer, who's returning from watching Scott leave the contents of his stomach in a row of bushes.

"Who was kidnapped?" he asks.

"Them," I say, pointing to Brett's car, where Ginny, Bill, and Trish are staring at us. "And him," I add, pointing to Scott.

"Good news," he replies. "Case solved. There they are. Looks like they're fine."

"No, you don't *understand,*" I say. "The older lady, she's my *mother*. Well, not literally. Technically, they're all in-laws, but it feels much closer than that."

The cop is staring at me, waiting for a punch line. He sighs and then begins speaking into the little radio mic on his shoulder.

"Female, approximately . . ."

"Twenty-seven," I suggest helpfully.

"Twenty-nine!" Brett interjects. "Twenty-freakin'-nine and not one second younger!"

"Female, approximately . . . twenty-eight, initially reporting a two-oh-seven—"

"Is that kidnapping?" I interject. "Because this was *definitely* a two-oh-seven. He'll say he was just going for a nice drive with the family, but this is a two-oh-seven all the way, and don't waste money on a trial, because he's guilty!"

"For God's sake, Layla, we were on the way home!" Brett shouts. "You didn't have to go all O.J. on us!"

"You *stole* them!" I scream, then wheel toward the cop. "What's the code for human trafficking?" I lean toward his shoulder mic so the dispatcher can hear. "It's a two-oh-seven in progress—and the suspect is a complete friggin' jerk!"

The trooper shoots me an angry glare and lets go of the talk button on the mic. "Ma'am, I'm the one who gets to talk into the radio. Do that again and I'll tell them I've got a three-ninety, possibly a fifty-one-fifty, and I'm bringing her in."

I look questioningly to the lady cop, and she kindly tells me, "Drunk, possible mental case." She leans closer. "Don't worry, he knows you're a ten-ninety F-one."

I give her the same bewildered look.

"Domestic dispute, no violence alleged."

# *trish*

Watching the two-ring (Brett and Layla) circus unfold and collapse before my eyes is hardly fun anymore. Though I love them both dearly, I pride myself on detachment. For instance: Right now I'd like to detach each of their heads from their bodies and kick them out onto the freeway.

I mean, *honestly*. Sure, they got married young. Sure, they had sizable differences that only revealed themselves well into their time together. Sure, Layla became too dependent on us as a surrogate family and forgot that a traditional marriage is still one man and one woman, or something like that, but certainly not one woman, a guy, his brother and sister, and his borderline-elderly parents. Sure, Brett glommed on to someone who worshipped him, who basically bought all his shit, and then practically loaned him the capital to go replenish his inventory. Sure, all of those things. But at the end of the day, they're both *killer* people—two smart, attractive, accomplished professionals, both reduced to trying to get each other arrested.

To tell the truth, I'm slightly cold, tired as a six-year-old after one of those birthday parties where parents rent an inflatable moon jumper, and sick to my stomach from watching Scott hurl up the afternoon's festivities (also like a kid coming off a moon jumper). Plus, I'm disgusted by this spectacle of watching two people try to overcome loving each other, two people who I think probably still do. Though you can't tell from their foaming mouths and glistening fangs.

# *layla*

"A ten-ninety F-one. No violence." The lady cop looks at me sideways, then at Brett. "And you're going to keep it that way, right?"

"I'm letting him off easy, that's for sure," I reply.

Brett is staring with disgust at Scott, who continues to stick his tongue out and spit into the dirt near the bushes. "Ugh, tell you what," he suggests to me. "Take this one off my hands, and I'll pay *you* the ransom."

With the help of the officers, who apparently feel obligated to see this silliness resolved, we hash out a plan. Scott and Bill will go home with Brett, and I'll take Ginny and Trish. The women all seem so tired that they'd just as willingly go to jail to get some rest.

A little chatter comes across the police radio. Something more pressing has come up, and I feel particularly embarrassed about wasting the cops' time. They get back in their car, but not before the lady trooper turns to me. "I feel a little jealous of people like you," she says. "It takes a really big love to make anyone that crazy. Or a lot of crystal meth."

And with that, they're gone.

# *brett*

Singlehood (or is it singledom?) is actually kind of sweet. When I first moved out, some of the benefits of living alone occurred to me. One was that I hadn't slept alone for the better part of ten years, other than occasional angry layovers on the living-room couch or that horrible mattress in the guest bedroom. (What can I say? We didn't get many guests, and they were usually just my unwelcome friends sleeping one off.) That first Sunday I woke up not because someone's knee banged into my ass or a hand lazily covered my mouth and nose and stopped my breathing but because my body had gotten enough sleep, and I could watch football in my underwear until midafternoon without someone ragging on me to "at least put on some pants or a T-shirt." Jesus, could I now live my life free, as the Founding Fathers intended? Damn straight. And just about now I was beginning to hit my stride. Any minute.

At UCCC, as you might guess, we don't cast a very wide recruiting net. Not when we can't offer football scholarships to entice people. Mainly, we stick to recruits within the surrounding region, a car ride away. Rarely, there's an overnight. And when that's not happening, when Coach Wells and I aren't visiting high schools and eating casseroles with kids and their parents, and when the team's not practicing or playing or reviewing film, I've got all the time in the world. Now that the wife and all related running around has been eliminated from the picture, suddenly the world is my oyster. I can catch up on all the *Entourage* and *Two and a Half Men* I can shake a stick at. Better yet, I can stop putting off my brilliant idea for body-tight athletic apparel that regular people can actually afford.

Or, rather than trying to lose myself in work, I can quit trying to give myself a guilt trip and just wind down from a fairly momentous event in my life. I can call over a buddy—whichever one of my supposed lifelong friends isn't caged at home for the night by his wife in a way that's surely not nearly as interesting as it sounds.

Significant others. Wives and husbands. How people change when they become a unit. What a person did when they were single just doesn't happen afterward. A guy or girl just can't do all the stuff they used to. They go without. They *sacrifice*. When I think about how I was when I was independent, self-sufficient... Come to think of it, was I ever alone, independent, self-sufficient? From as early as I had a driver's license, I was with Layla.

Well, no more. I'm back to being something I never was: on my own. And you know what? It's a little slow-paced sometimes, but it's nice. It's really an opportunity more than anything. Now's my time to shine. Not glow—not like one of those green necklaces kids wear at fireworks fairs. I'm going to *explode in glory,* like the fireworks themselves.

I explain this to Jared, who's over watching a Monday-night game. He didn't react much to the stuff I told him about the walnut picking and the "kidnapping," but now he says, "You go, man. Don't let anybody piss on your flame. More important . . . you got anything to eat in this house? Watching football makes me hungry. I'm like Pablo's dog."

"Pavlov's dog?" I correct him. I remember at least this from Psychology 101.

"Him, too," he says. Then he starts talking about the mudballs Layla used to make. They were some sort of Rice Krispies, chocolate morsel, butterscotch, peanut, and marshmallow combination. Neither of us wants to go into superlatives, because it'll make us both miss them more, but we're on the same wavelength: They were unbefrickinglievable. They even overcome my annoyance at her.

He sighs.

"Don't say it," I say.

"I'm not," he replies. "Any mention of the mudball would just bring us both down." He sighs again. "But . . ."

"Now you're going off all John Wayne Bobbitt on me."

"What?" he asked.

"Half-cocked," I explain—but it's already too late, because the idea is already planted in both our minds.

My rush to the kitchen yields a bag of pretzels—or what was a bag of pretzels but now is mostly salt. Being the good host, I offer it to Jared first.

"You know, when these go empty, you can just recycle them," he remarks.

We sit in silence until the next commercial. It's a life insurance ad.

"I'll make the fuckin' mudballs," I cave at last. So I get up and run to the front door before he can talk me out of going to the supermarket.

In fact, he's thinking just the opposite. "And don't waste time chatting with some floozy," he says.

"Well," I say, not missing even a beat, "if I see your girlfriend there, I've gotta at least say hi. And can she check for my socks in her sock drawer?"

The door slams on some reply beginning with "F—"

# *layla*

There's an old episode of *The Twilight Zone* where a man with a hideously deformed face lives as an outcast until he boards a spaceship and gets sent to a planet where everyone is like him. Even though Rod Serling, that weird music, the black-and-white pictures, and the bongos always creeped me out, this moment always made me cry. The pain and dislocation of a solitary soul wandering the world, looking out through a hideously deformed face . . . It's vividly real, particularly now.

How to describe my oppressive feeling of dejection, rejection, and swollen-eyed reflection? It's like walking through a steady drizzle, but it's a drizzle that's not cleansing like water . . . more like tree sap. It seeps into my ears, and I can't hear what people are saying. They speak to me, but it doesn't register. I'm literally moving more slowly. I'm being careful not to cross streets if Don't Walk is even flashing, because I'll never make it in time.

Naturally, little things take a backseat at a time like this: opening mail, getting a good night's sleep, eating. Of course, the refrigerator is practically empty—especially after I wasted so much on that picnic yesterday. Who wants to go grocery shopping again after that? Still, I'm not at the point of voluntary starvation, so I shove this emotional weight the size of Nebraska off my back for a moment and drive to Ralphs.

Sure enough, going inside is surreal. People surround me, each living in a little world I know deep down is perfect and untroubled. *Bastards.* I grab a cart and push it in front of me. I need the support.

Fruit first. I pick up an apple, and as I rotate it, looking for spots, I catch sight of the little sticker with the product number. Back in the day, which I guess means up until about a month ago, I made it a point to peel those stickers off every piece of fruit in the house. Maybe it was partly obsessive-compulsive, but as I did this, I thought about him, the man I loved, and it seemed like a nice thing to do. Just a little thing but thoughtful.

So here is the sticker, staring up at me. I pull it off.

I start to cry. I'm standing in a supermarket, holding a now-naked apple, stripped of its identity, an offering to a once-vibrant love now rotted away to nothing, and it all seems so sad. At some distance, a few people glance over, but as soon as I look their way they pretend not to notice and uncomfortably go back to sorting through bananas and bagged salads and feta cheese. I can't blame them. It's weird when people cry in public. When I see people crying in public—at least pairs—I usually assume it's because they're breaking up. When you see two people together and one is crying and the other is cocking his or her head and leaning in and *not* crying, odds are they're done.

"Are you all right?" asks a stock boy.

"I have food allergies," I say, lacking a better explanation. He turns away, satisfied with this reason and probably not interested anyway.

I sniff, get myself together a little bit, then try to soldier on, pulling single-serving boxes of popcorn and rice and ready-made pasta meals into the cart. I must look horrendous. I did nothing to my hair—not with a comb, not with a brush, no clips, ties, or bands. I can only imagine what my eyes look like, but I'm putting on a brave face. A brave face hideously deformed by the thought that I'm now alone, a stranger in a strange lane at Ralphs.

Thank *God* I'm still part of something good, is all I can say. Thank God I'm still a Foster.

# *brett*

The mudballs are in jeopardy.

What's the problem? It's one of those sightings that begin with promise and end in embarrassment: Hey, there's a hot girl in the produce section, a hippie chick with wavy hair and sandals and jeans and a nice ass and . . . it's Layla.

I get this crazy idea that I should go up and say, "Hey, Layla, I didn't think I'd find *you* behind those melons." After the cops left yesterday, after I'd had time to simmer down, I almost wanted to give her a hug, she looked so distraught. I'm always getting stupid ideas. Thankfully, I don't always follow through. After a few seconds of rational consideration, I'm certain I want to avoid her at all costs. Why eff up this day of all days with a Rock 'Em Sock 'Em Robots routine?

She's hovering around the cereal aisle, I think, as I duck behind displays and make my way to the ingredients I need. But now I've lost her. *Shit.* Even if I score everything I need, I'm bound to get stuck behind someone chatty in line, and then she'll walk up right behind me. And then we're sunk.

I'm going to wait for the right moment and then just make a run for it.

# *layla*

This is bad. I'm so fucked in the head that I swear I see Brett through the front window, running across the parking lot with his jacket up around his ears. It's clearly time to just abandon my cart and go home. My ability to play at normalcy must have a limit, so I'll come back tomorrow.

Absolutely sure that every eye in the entire place is fixed on miserable me, I sleepwalk out of there and drive away, grocery-less.

# *brett*

Back at the ranch.

After a quick detour to a liquor store, it's a humiliating return that I cover for by being hostile: "Here," I say, shoving a beer and a bag of chips at Jared, "and don't say a fucking word about the mudballs."

He looks at the bottle. "If this were some cheap shit, I'd be tempted," he replies. "But since you knew not to insult me, you have bought my silence."

Apparently, about ten seconds' worth.

"Dumbass," he says.

I could have used a mudball, too.

• • •

Life is unfair. That's just a fact. My sister reminds me of this Thursday, after barging into my apartment and treating the place like a hazardous waste site, which it isn't—not yet. I mean, it could still get worse. After I list all the bad stuff that has happened to me recently, Layla and the state of my team, she says, "Life's unfair," and I consider it a point proven and a job well done. God bless her, shitty people skills and all.

She starts in on me then. She doesn't bring up Layla, but I get all manner of finger-wagging about checking out, my losing team, how I'm probably not giving my players the commitment they deserve, and about adopting the diet of a twelve-year-old trapped overnight in a 7-Eleven. She has other concerns, too.

I'm tough enough to listen to about half of it, not bothering to give any defense, then I basically kick her out of the apartment. What does she know? She doesn't know anything about my job; she's only going by the recent losses, the burrito wrappers, and the empty Mountain Dew and Miller bottles. And the smell. There is admittedly a mild odor about the place, but I've called the landlord.

I'm kind of surprised things have gotten as bad as they have. I'm usually excellent at putting on a front. Out in public, I can always appear to be my commanding self. At least I could until some point during this week. I was coming home at night and just getting into bed to stare at the ceiling, true, but up until that moment I was on the field screaming until my throat bled about lapses on special teams, mental mistakes, lazy footwork, you name it. But at some point Wednesday, or maybe Tuesday, I must have been feeling particularly empty, must have gotten a little too close to choking up over a mistake—maybe my voice even cracked when I said, "Crawford, if Williams makes one more catch today, I'm going to staple you to him!"

Anyway, he looked at me carefully and said, "Sorry, Coach. I'll try harder."

Deron Crawford never says "Sorry" or "I'll try harder."

And I said, "Thank you." I *never* say "Thank you."

I didn't say another word for about a half hour. Then I went home.

Frankly, the novelty of the bachelor pad wears off pretty quickly when you're not doing anything to really enjoy being a bachelor. Being pissed off, sad, and miserable gets you so far. There are only so many times you can eat day-old (okay, I don't know exactly how old) pizza, only so many sports highlight reels you can watch, only so many days you can not shave, go without bathing, basically live in filth, before the mere sight of yourself is repulsive.

For that reason, today I've woken up. I mean, I've been awake technically, but truly I've been sleepwalking. I've done okay with the team for the most part, but when you're only eighty or ninety percent there, and the job requires about double that level of involvement—triple when you have a team of mostly newbies like mine—you're shortchanging them. I missed the last coaches' meeting, claiming the flu, but the truth was I was sitting home with the shades drawn, drinking Miller High Life. Trish pointed out that I've been listening to a little too much weepy chick music lately, and she's right.

I have a job. I have a life. And now, although I've actually been conscious and wide-eyed since about four a.m., wallowing in self-pity—which really should be self-hate, because I brought this on myself—I can respect the notion that sometimes the world needs you more than you need it.

It's with this fact in mind that I pick myself up and actually take a shower, which is a good thing, because as I walk to the UCCC administration building at about ten a.m. on Friday morning, I bump into Heather. And when she starts flirting with me again—we've been jokingly flirty since the night at Norms, at least I think she's been joking—suddenly something comes to me: Spending time with another woman is no longer cheating. Which is kind of interesting. Especially since in addition to the ten thousand other "traditions" that Layla introduced to our family, we have the corn-maze fiasco coming up, and I've been dreading it.

I'm torn, because I don't want to see Layla and yet I don't want to abandon the family right now—especially not when she's looking like the good kid to my bad one. Maybe if I bring a date, not only will it make the night more enjoyable, it will show Layla that she's being ridiculous. That it's time for her to move on as well.

"What are your thoughts on corn?" I ask Heather.

"Corn?" she repeats with a funny smile—probably due to my out-of-left-field question. "I love corn. I like it on the cob, off the cob, buttered, with Lawry's Seasoned Salt, white, yellow, creamed, popped. . . . I love corn."

"That is a much more enthusiastic answer than I expected," I admit.

"What can I say? I'm a fan. Of corn."

"That is very good news," I reply, and she cocks an eyebrow. "Because my family does this corn-maze thing, and it's happening this weekend, and I thought maybe you'd like to join us."

"Are you asking me on a date?"

"Kind of," I admit. "Yes."

"A first date?"

"Yes?"

"With your family?"

"Er, weird?" I ask, realizing her point.

"Yes," she says.

"Well, the corn maze is Sunday," I point out. "We could have a first date tonight, so the corn extravaganza wouldn't be it. Hell, we could even have a second date tomorrow. But that would make the corn maze our third date, and . . ."

I stop talking, but it's too late.

"And technically, that's the date where I'm supposed to put out."

"No," I say incredulously. "Well, yes. Technically, I believe the rule is three—five if she's hot."

"Charming," she replies.

I go for broke: "So as long as you wouldn't mind having sex for the first time in front of my family, in a corn maze . . ."

"No, I wouldn't mind that at all," she says. "Tell you what. I will take you up on a date between now and then. Tonight or Saturday, you decide. Worse comes to worst, we can always go out for burgers after your game tomorrow." She winks. "I will subsequently decide if there will be a second date. We can take it from there."

"Fair enough," I say.

"There's one other thing I like about corn," she says. "Those little things that you stick on the ends of a cob. Bonus if they look like miniature corn."

"I could like you," I say. Then, "That was out loud, wasn't it?"

She nods and smiles.

Well, mystery has definitely never been my strong suit.

# *layla*

The first of what became our annual corn-maze event—or, as I named it, the Foster Family Maize Maze—started about six years ago. Living in L.A., you tend to get jaded. You're so caught up in all things Los Angeles that you can miss out on some incredible traditions practiced across America. I'd only read about corn mazes, but it sounded like a fun thing that we could do as a family.

That day, I called everyone and said I had a big surprise for them. I told them to be at Casa Foster at eight a.m., to wear comfortable shoes they didn't mind getting dirty, and to be prepared to do some walking.

We all got to the house and hopped into the SUV. The whole way there, everyone kept asking where we were going and where I was taking them, but I wouldn't tell. I just turned the radio up louder and sang.

When we pulled up to the maze, Trish was the first to speak up.

"Are you fucking kidding me? A corn maze?" she said.

"Have you ever been to one?" I asked.

"No, I haven't," she replied. "By choice."

"What the hell is a corn maze?" Brett asked.

"She kept it from you, too?" Bill said. "Good going, Lay-lay!"

"Can someone clue me in?" Scott asked.

"*I* knew about it," Ginny said. "I, for one, am excited. Layla told me the idea, and I thought it was wonderful."

"Typical," Brett said.

"Like some sick joke on the whole family," Trish remarked.

"Cornholed," suggested Scott, never one to let a chance slip by to be inappropriate.

"Really?" I said. "Is this that awful? Can't you wait until we've at least gotten out of the car before you cry like a bunch of babies? This is supposed to be a fun day."

"I still don't even know what everyone's talking about," Scott said.

"It's a corn maze," I repeated, and then explained it was exactly what it sounded like. A labyrinth. A maze made up in a field of corn. It's a game—a puzzle, really—and we're the pieces. We're given maps and clues, but as simple as it seems, people always end up getting lost. It's a way for farmers to supplement their income, by hosting families as they run around like rats trying to find their way out.

"And this is supposed to be fun?" Scott said. "This is what I gave up my Sunday for?"

"Like you had other plans." Trish laughed.

Once they settled down, we split into two groups so we wouldn't all get lost alone and ran into the maze. There were different stations we had to find, and when we got to each post the people running the maze would give us a ticket to prove that we'd found that base and could move to the next. They gave us flags to hold, and there were tall lifeguard stations so if we got lost we could wave our flags and they would come get us. We ran around all day to the point of exhaustion. Bill, Trish, and Brett didn't finish because it got dark, so Team Layla, Ginny, and Scott won.

We went back the next year so Bill, Trish, and Brett could try to dethrone us. They didn't. By year three it became a tradition.

Now here we are, six years later.

Since I started the tradition, I certainly wasn't backing out. I actually thought Brett would skip it, since he always complained about how silly it was. You can imagine my surprise when Brett not only shows up but brings a date.

"This is Heather, everyone," he says, as he presents the woman I saw on his football field—the woman I may or may not have felt threatened by, but I told myself, *Don't be silly, Layla. Your husband loves you. He's not interested in other women. Especially not younger blond women. With great bodies. Bodies that I could never have even if I went to the gym seven days a week. For twelve hours a day.* Yet here she stands before me. At my event.

"Hello, Heather," says Bill.

Brett's watching me to gauge my reaction, but I won't look his way. His eyes are burning a hole in my forehead, but I keep this frightening fake smile on my face and look everywhere but at him. So of course he has the nerve to rub it in.

"You remember Heather, right?" he asks me.

"I do," I say. "Nice to see you again. And what a surprise."

"Heather loves corn," he replies.

"Don't we all," Bill adds.

Heather looks between us and gives a nervous laugh. "I forgot another corn thing I love," she says to Brett. We're all waiting with bated breath. "Corn Pops!"

*Tee-hee! She loves Corn Pops! What the fuck is going on?* Am I really standing here with my husband, his family, and his date? What am I supposed to do, grab the nearest scarecrow and pretend that he's *my* date? Laugh with him and whisper jokes while running my hands through his straw hair?

The maize maze is definitively my stomping ground. I rack my brain to think if there could be anything more disrespectful than what Brett is doing at this very moment. I contemplate setting the whole place on fire, right then and there, and wonder if it would explode in a rain of popcorn. But then I realize that a) this isn't a cartoon—this is my life, and b) in this life, I'm not an arsonist.

"I think we're going to be uneven," Scott says, as Heather's presence makes us a group of seven. I'm already feeling uneven.

Then Trish walks up with Kimmy, a girl she's been seeing but has yet to bring around the family. It's a big move for Trish—and not because she's afraid of what we'll think of her. It's because Trish is super-picky, and doesn't just bring anyone around. This must mean she really likes her.

Kimmy's a pretty girl with wavy, light brown hair, which has been fashioned with two skinny front braids tied back to make a sort-of headband. The result is a sweet hippie hairstyle that suits her. She has crystal-blue eyes and a slightly crooked smile that looks like she's permanently in on the joke.

"Trish brought a friend, too," Ginny points out.

"Hey, everyone, this is Kimmy," Trish says. "Try not to be too embarrassing."

"Same goes for me," Brett suggests.

"Yes, the same goes for you, Brett," Trish says. "It was mostly *directed at you*. Try not to be a complete bonehead."

"No, I meant the same goes for me in terms of everyone else," Brett says.

"I know what you meant, douche," Trish says, and I imagine a high five with Trish but don't actually go for it.

"This is Heather," Brett says.

Trish offers up a hello, but then there's silence. Bill senses the general awkwardness and tension, so he claps his hands together and rubs like he's warming them over a fire.

"So how should we divide teams?" he asks.

"I'll swap with Mom, and Kimmy can be on our team," Trish says. "Obviously."

We divide up and head out.

I don't know what pisses me off more: the fact that this seems to be the first time Brett is enjoying himself at the corn maze in years, or the fact that I am so miserable. Either way, the day sucks. My senses are heightened, and everything I see, taste, hear, touch, or smell is tainted by Heather. I see a sign for the maze that says *Where getting lost means finding fun,* and I wish that Brett and his date had gotten lost on the way here, because their mere presence has hidden fun completely.

I end up "getting lost" myself, sneaking out of the maze and into the petting zoo, where I feed the goats and llamas and cry for about forty-five minutes. I thought being around the animals would make me feel better, but every goat I look in the eye seems to know my pain. They look sad, and I feel sad and somehow exposed. I pass a desolate pumpkin patch on my way back and think I catch Brett and Heather out of the corner of my eye but can't bring myself to check. Have they snuck out, too? Are they in this pumpkin patch sharing a romantic moment?

I'm ill. This day is making me physically ill. I pass a scarecrow and consider stripping it of its clothing so I can put it on and spy. This is when I know it's time to leave. When things turn farcical, I draw the line. I look around, trying to find someone to let them know I'm leaving so the family won't think I'm lost, at least in the literal sense.

The first person I happen upon is Bill—who seems flustered in his own right.

"Well, I can't find Ginny," he says.

"Way to keep track of your team," I tease, but when I realize he's actually concerned, I tell him I'll help find her.

We spend the next hour looking for his wife, and as time goes on, Bill gets more and more upset—though I'm not sure what he's so frightened of. Finally, we find Ginny taking a tour of the grounds with Girl Scout troop 64. I notice a sadness in Bill's eyes as he reunites with her, a sense of relief yet still soaked in angst.

"Good-bye, Daisy!" she says, as she waves to her new friends. "Nice talking with you, Maddie!"

That situation resolved, I tell Bill and Ginny to say good-bye to everyone else for me. Then I take off, but I'm momentarily distracted from my own misery by whatever is going on with Bill and Ginny.

To say the day didn't go as planned would be a gross understatement. All I *can* say is that I don't ever want to eat corn, see corn, or hear about corn again for as long as I live.

And Brett is an asshole.

• • •

The next day at work I'm still seething. Is this how it's going to be? Is he actually dating *already*? Is Tee-hee Heather the Corn Popper the reason he wanted to leave? I have a million questions, and I go from being angry to sad to furious to bitter, back to sad, to miserable, and then pretty much stay at miserable.

"I don't know what he was thinking bringing her, but he's obviously acting out," Trish suggests. "He was looking for a reaction, and I think under the circumstances you handled yourself well."

We're waiting for Leo, a shar-pei that we've photographed before. Leo gets his portrait done every three months to update his profile on Dogbook. For the uninitiated, Dogbook is like Facebook, but for dogs. It's an online community where dogs can post pictures, have friends, and let their friends know what's going on in their lives. Leo has a doggie parent with *way* too much free time on her hands, if you couldn't guess, but we at TLC don't look a gift horse in the mouth. Unless he's posing for a horse dentistry ad.

The doorbell rings, and in walk Leo and Donna Solowitz, a New York transplant who at thirty-four is fresh off her second divorce and likes to announce that all she took was four million dollars, the Maserati, and Leo. Apparently she was married to a man of excessive wealth, since she deems that a bargain.

"Hi, girls," she clucks. "Leo had steak tartare on the patio at

Clafoutis, so could ya just check his teeth to make sure he doesn't have bits of meat in them? Thanks."

I look at Trish and give her a knowing smile. Trish doesn't like it when someone asks you to do something and then thanks you in advance before you've accepted.

"C'mere, Leo," I say. "Let me see those choppers."

I pull Leo's skin away from his teeth and marvel at how much of it there is. He has the cutest rows of saggy skin—they make you want to pull and stretch them, not to the point of pain but just enough to see how much there really is. Leo has regular dental cleanings, so his teeth are in fine order, and when I take a peek inside his mouth there's no tartare—or even tartar—to be found.

Donna plops herself on the couch and lets out a sigh. "You would not believe the men I'm dating," she says. "Trish, you're better off with women. Layla, don't ever get divorced."

"I'm separated," I say, although I wish I didn't.

"Oh, honey, I'm sorry," she says. "But really—what was your husband? A teacher or accountant or something?"

"A football coach," I say. "College. Division Three."

"Exactly," she says. "There's no cha-ching goin' on there. He's doin' you a favor. Now you can find a guy who's got some substance."

I might not have loved football, but I liked that Brett was a coach. I loved it. I loved watching him connect with the team and knowing that he was doing what he loved. And why am I thinking of him in past tense, like he's dead? He's still a coach.

I hate this. And I don't want to continue this conversation with Donna Solowitz at all, so I change the subject. "What would you like for Leo's photo today?"

"I'll tell ya—and you're not gonna believe it," Donna replies.

"We will," Trish answers.

"Leo is in love with a Maltese named Princess Madison," she explains. "They met on Dogbook and they are in love, love, *love*."

"Have they met in person?" I ask, as I try not to wince picturing the size discrepancy between a shar-pei and a Maltese, and hoping they haven't.

"No," Donna says. "Not yet. But they will. Princess Maddie Boo lives in Chicago, so we're going to take a trip soon."

"Wow," I let slip.

"Her mom and I exchanged phone numbers, and we talk on the phone all the time," Donna goes on. "We became instant best friends. We're thinking of starting a line of couture dog collars together called Leo Loves Madison. Leo, of course, gets first billing."

"Of course," I say.

"I'm sorry," Trish says, and I suck in breath, because here it comes. "I want to get this straight. You didn't know this woman at all. You both made online profiles for your dogs. They became 'friends'—"

"They fell in love," Donna interrupts.

"Right," Trish says. "They fell in love. Over the Internet. And now you are flying to Chicago to let them meet in person."

"And to talk about our company," Donna reminds her.

"Got it," Trish says. "Just wanted to make sure I was understanding the situation fully."

"What can I say?" Donna shrugs. "It's love."

"That is just fantastic," Trish says. "Now, does Leo prefer the mouse, or is he more into using the keyboard?"

Donna, not picking up on the joke, launches into her plan. Then my cell phone rings. I see Brooke's name on the caller ID and excuse myself to answer.

She opens with, "I've figured out what my problem is."

"I'm intrigued," I say.

"I've been interviewing with women. Women are jealous bitches. All of them."

"That does indeed sound like a problem."

"Well, problem solved. I interviewed with a dude today. A hot dude. And guess what?"

"You got the job?" I ask.

"No, I got laid."

"And then you got the job?"

"Nice," she says. Then, "Yes, I got the job."

"That's great," I tell her. "Congrats!"

"I didn't get laid," she tosses out. "I was kidding about that part. But I will. I could see him undressing me with his eyes. And I wasn't wearing any underwear."

"Well, I'm very happy for you. And him. But I'm at work right now, and I do need to get back to it."

"Fine." Brooke sighs. "Abandon me. It's only fair. I'm abandoning you."

"What do you mean?"

"The job's in Vancouver," she says casually.

"What?"

"I know. Crazy, right? He's a producer, and he's about to do a movie in some rural town in Vancouver and he needs an on-set assistant. How freakin' fun!"

"Wow," I say, a bit stunned, separation anxiety kicking in. "That sounds incredible. But how long are you gone for?"

"Months! Until the movie wraps," she says. "Oh my God, that was so fun to say. I've always wanted to say my album 'dropped,' but a movie wrapping is a close second. I am so cool. You now have a very cool friend."

"Lucky me," I say. "But seriously, I have to go. I'll call you later, Captain Hollywood."

"You won't be hearing from me for a bit. Seriously, Layla," Brooke warns. "I hear cell phone service is really spotty where I'm going. Isn't that exciting?"

I conjure up the image of her tromping in her Prada shoes through Hicksville, British Columbia, someplace with one Motel

6, where Mom's Greasy Spoon is the best dining option open nightly until seven p.m., and fight back a snort. I'm sure I'll hear from her two seconds after she gets off the plane, and she'll be screaming bloody murder.

We hang up and I go back to Donna and Trish. Donna is talking. Trish does not look at all amused.

"So I was wondering if you have a green screen. Princess Madison just changed her profile picture, and she's holding up a sign that says *I love Leo*. Well, she's sitting next to it. It's placed in front of her, or to the side, somewhere you can see—you get it. Anyway, if you had a green screen we could CGI a street sign that reads *Madison Avenue*—you know, from New York, my old home and Maddie's actual namesake. We'll have Leo holding up a sign that says *I love . . .* and pointing up at the sign."

"Wow," Trish says.

*"Hmm,"* I add. "We don't have a green screen, but you could probably do that in Photoshop. I'm just thinking of the best way to get Leo to look like he's pointing."

"You're so good," Trish whispers, as she walks past me and over to the kitchen. "You have the patience of Job."

"I don't have Photoshop, and anyway, I don't know how to do all that stuff," Donna whines. "If I pay you extra, will you do it?"

I look at Trish. She isn't smiling.

I smile at Donna. What else do I have to do these days?

• • •

Actually, I do have something on my plate.

I don't consider myself a builder, per se. Per anything, really. So when Trish tells me that PETCO finally called and gave us the specs for the prototype we need to build for them, as well as how much we'll need to invest to get the TLC Paw Prints pet photo booth up and running, I'm a little leery, to say the least. Not because I'm not willing to try, but because situations like these often find me trying my hardest, messing up majorly, then calling in a professional. I'm just not that handy. So my hesitation at the project is not me being lazy or unwilling, it's the fact that a) I don't want to push all the work off onto Trish, and b) I see myself eventually going on eBay and buying an existing photo booth.

Sounds dramatic, I know, but there was the time I tried to build a doghouse for Sammy Davis Junior. I won't go into details, but let's just say that while the Fosters praised me incessantly for the final result, they wound up using it for firewood. When I was in grade school, I couldn't even make that stupid thing out of tinfoil, cardboard, and duct tape—or its simpler cousin, the slit in the paper plate—to watch the eclipse. *I am not handy.* This is all I'm saying.

But Trish swears that "This is where memories are made," and "This is the exciting part," and something else about me "sucking it up," so I go online to do a little research on building your own photo booth. Granted, the listed examples I find are not photo booths in which you'd take pictures of pets, but there is a surprising abundance of how-to articles on the matter, including one step-by-step instructional from an undergrad at Carnegie Mellon. I also check eBay for photo booths just in case, and I am horrified to find that they start at $5,750.00 with a buy-it-now option at $7,900.00. Not an option. Not unless this PETCO deal was written in stone.

At three o'clock, Trish calls and tells me to meet her at Home Depot so we can buy the wood for the three exterior walls. When I arrive, I'm momentarily stunned by the hordes of Hispanic men standing around the entrance, looking to pick up labor gigs. It bothers me to think we live in this great country, yet people still have to stand around and practically beg to do menial labor every day. Not even a whole sixty seconds later, a lightbulb pops up over my head suggesting Trish and I hire one of these able-bodied gentlemen to do the job for us.

"No, we can't hire a Mexican guy," I hear from over my shoulder. I turn to see Trish wearing a smirk.

"I didn't say anything about hiring anyone illegal."

"But you thought it," she replies.

"Did not."

"Come on," she says, and she tugs at the sleeve of my hoodie and drags me inside.

The place is huge. *Who can find anything here?* To the do-it-yourself-ignorant, it's like Walmart, Costco, and Sam's Club, but with much less fun to be had and no people in hairnets and plastic gloves handing out snacks. Note to management: People get hungry, especially when the Coffee Bean & Tea Leaf next door is out of their favorite muffins.

As we pass through one of the aisles—I believe it was Doorknobs—and alongside the portable fans and fluorescent lighting, I happen upon a rack of black-and-orange Home Depot baseball caps. I promptly take one and put it on my head.

"I can see your plumber butt taking shape already." Trish laughs.

She whips out the list, and I'm even more terrified of the project. We apparently need six one-fourth-inch sheets of plywood cut four feet by six feet. Had it been up to me, I'd have thought we needed only three. We need wood screws, a screwdriver, molding, a jigsaw—which makes me realize that at some dark point in human history, jigsaw puzzles were actually cut out by hand—a computer, an interface/controller, an LCD monitor, a photo printer, a shelf, hinges, a swivel eye hasp (What the hell is a hasp?), a padlock (Really? In case someone tries to run off with our six-foot booth?), a bench, a curtain, and of course a curtain rod, and a software program that Trish apparently already has. For our prototype, we won't include some of the hardest parts—like a coin-and-cash acceptor.

"That would be so *cool,* though," I plead, a bit unrealistically. "And one that takes credit cards."

"Right. And sensors to tell whether the owner is uglier than the dog and adjust the lighting accordingly."

For a second I'm thinking that would actually be a very cool feature, but then I see she's gone deadpan on me.

"A lot of stuff would be nice," she says, "but we have to remember something: We're semi-broke. Unless you have money to throw in? I imagine with the whole Brett scenario you're less liquid. . . ."

"I didn't plan on my marriage being wrecked," I remark.

"No, I'm not blaming anyone. We just don't need a money acceptor right now. PETCO can take what's owed at the counter. For now." She sighs, then adds, "I really believe in this. It could be so big for us. For now, we hold our noses and give it our best shot with what we've got."

She hugs me, and I'm certain her sniffle is fighting back tears of stress.

I ponder the sticky situation. According to the PETCO people, the first prototype is due asap, even though they were the ones who delayed on the specs. (Corporations!) We have to simply go forward and hope our first attempt isn't considered a flaming bag of dog crap on their porch, so to speak.

As we exit, I look longingly at the dozens of willing-and-able men offering their services. Trish knocks my hat off my head and asks, "Did you pay for that?"

"I assume so," I say. "They saw it on my head when they rang us up."

"You just stole that hat."

"I did no such thing," I argue. "It was right there on my head. If the cashier didn't ring it up, that's her fault."

"Check the receipt," Trish demands.

"Seriously?"

"Do I look like I'm kidding?"

"No, you look like Ms. Murphy, my mean second-grade teacher who hit my hand with a ruler." To say Ms. Murphy was a kind woman would be like calling Victoria Beckham fat.

I pull out the receipt and do not see the hat listed anywhere. I put it back in my pocket. "There, I checked the receipt, just like you asked. Can we go now?"

"What are you, twelve?"

"I suddenly feel like it," I admit. "Am I in trouble?"

"Go back in and pay for the hat," she commands. "I can't have your shoplifting fantasies bringing our project bad karma."

"Okay," I say, "but a) I did not shoplift. I honestly didn't even think about the hat when we were checking out. And b) I don't like your attitude."

But I walk back into the store and tell the cashier that she forgot to charge me.

"You can have it," the cashier says. "It's okay."

"I'd really rather pay for it," I say.

"Why?" she asks, perplexed.

"Because my partner is outside, and she's crazy and will seriously go loony tunes if I don't produce a receipt. So can you just ring me up, please?"

The cashier looks at me like *I'm* the one who's one beak short of Daffy, but she takes my $9.99.

• • •

The building of the booth takes a shorter time than I'd imagine, and Trish and I get into only two fights, which is kind of amazing, considering the magnitude of the task. I had us slotted for at least four. All in all, we put the thing together in about two days—the casualties being my thumb and her sanity. (Is it my fault that I like to listen to greatest-hits CDs? I don't think that's a crime. And p.s., listening to any whole album just for the rare gem of a song you might like doesn't make up for the time spent listening to sucky stuff for the other seventy minutes. To which she'll say, "Don't listen to sucky artists," to which I'll say, "Show me one band besides Radiohead that continuously puts out a solid entire record.") (Or Wilco.)

When it comes time to test the booth, we bring Sammy Davis

Junior over and sit him on the bench. And our first photos are . . . blank. We open the curtain to make sure he is indeed still sitting there like a good boy, which he is, and it takes two more tries before we come to the realization that either Sammy Davis Junior is a vampire who does not show up in photographs or we didn't take into consideration the height of the animals versus the specs of the people booth. This probably needs to be addressed.

What we subsequently realize is that animals come in many heights and sizes, so we'll need an adjustable bench or removable ledges that will work to prop the pets up within view, support owners who want to make it a "family" portrait, and at the same time not be an eyesore. This takes an additional day's work. But after about one hundred or so fits and starts—overexposures, underexposures, the back of my head appearing as the camera goes off late, blank sheets pouring out of the printer in pairs and triplets—we finally witness a miracle: With about two sheets of photo paper left in the printer tray, we see an undeniably cute trio of snapshots of Trish forcing a smile for the hundredth time, Sammy proudly, if nervously, perched on her lap.

The TLC Paw Prints photo booth is born. Or whelped.

# *ginny*

*November 18*

*Dearest Ev,*

*I wish you lived closer so you could have joined us at the corn maze, or as Layla calls it, the maize maze. Isn't she clever? She brought a friend, a girl named Heather, and we had such a nice time.*

*I had the worst nightmare last night and I can't tell Bill because I fear it would frighten him, so you're the only person I can talk to about it. Last night I dreamed that Bill died. It was the most terrifying dream I've ever had. He went to bed before me but only by about fifteen minutes. I was washing up and doing the ten thousand things we do before bed—why is it so much easier for men, Ev? I swear we got the short end of the stick on so many levels.*

*Anyway, I finished up my before-sleep routine and crawled into bed next to Bill. I leaned over to kiss him and he didn't respond. I thought for sure he was teasing me, because for all the times he falls asleep watching TV, he never falls asleep before we kiss good night. So I climbed over him and bit his nose—not hard, just teasing him back, since I thought he was trying to pull a fast one. Then as my eyes adjusted to the light in the room, I thought I noticed that his eyes were slightly open. So I shook him. And he didn't wake up. I jumped over him and turned on the light, and, Evelyn, it was the most frightening thing I'd ever seen. Bill's skin was all purple or brown or blue—dark and dreadful. And I screamed. I screamed so loud in my dream that thankfully I woke myself up.*

*I tell you, for all the times I've been angry and said* I could just kill him, *I take them back. Of course we say silly things like that when we get angry, and you and I both know that Bill—for a time—made me very, very angry, but the thought of my Bill not alive on this earth is unbearable. Enough to make it crystal clear to me that I want to be the first to go. I don't mean tomorrow, mind you, so don't hop on a plane and euthanize me, ha, ha.*

*Won't you come for Thanksgiving? I know the kids would love to see you, and it's only a few days away. I know it's last-minute, but how wonderful it would be for us all to be together.*

*And between you and me, I think Brett and Layla are trying to have a baby! I don't know for sure, but last I heard they were talking about it, and I couldn't be more pleased and proud. Am I really old enough to be a grandmother? Careful how you answer, Ev—you are still the older sister! Remember how when we were young and I was jealous that you were older? I used to always tell you that someday I would be older than you and you would just laugh and laugh. Oh, to be that innocent.*

*Do consider spending the holiday with us. I miss you so very much.*

*Your always-will-be-younger sister,*<br>*Ginny*

# brett

Holy shit, does dating suck.

Such pressure! Seriously. If you look at my relationship with Layla, it started in high school and never stopped. We first kissed after a basketball game in tenth grade, and other than going out for pizzas, or to movies with our friends, or renting movies and watching them with my family, we never dated—not like adults, at least. We never had a real first date. I can't believe I actually almost brought Heather out with my family for *our* first date.

When I tell my friends—those friends I actually still consider worthwhile, who aren't hog-tied with their own penises—they laugh and tell me I need to take Heather out properly. They say that taking her out for burgers after the UCCC game versus Occidental last Saturday was an idiotic move, especially after choosing the same restaurant as the rest of the guys, and that they're surprised she came to the corn maze the next day. I suppose they're right. And she wasn't exactly thrilled to see that my ex was at the maize maze.

So a proper date. Which is what, exactly? The truth is, I have no idea. So I ask around.

First I ask Scott, because he answers when I call the house for my dad.

"Dude, what's a good first-date activity?"

"Fuck you. I'm not helping you. Jackass."

"Put Dad on the phone," I say. "And by the way, you still live at home. Dick."

My dad gets on the line and I toss the same question at him.

"Buddy," he says, "it depends on the person you're taking out. Is it Heather? I only met Heather at the corn maze, and with all our running around, I didn't really get to know her."

"I know," I say. "But some general ideas would be helpful."

"Well, in my day things were a little different, but here goes," he begins. "Don't go to a show or movie on the first five or ten dates. You can't talk, and the entire point of dating is getting to know each other."

"Ten dates?" I gasp. "You can't seriously expect me not to see a movie for ten dates! That's Crazytown."

"There are plenty of fantastic things to do on a date. You could take her to a museum."

"Yawn."

"Maybe she likes museums," he replies. "This is my point. Maybe it's not 'yawn' for her. You need to get to know her and find out what she likes."

"We can't talk at a museum, either, really, can we? Why do I feel like I'd get in trouble and get shushed every time I spoke?"

"Probably because the last time you were in a museum was on a class field trip and you were goofing off."

"True enough," I admit. "But I'm still not taking her to a museum. This is a first date. Well, second, actually." Come to think of it, I don't know if it counts as a third. I'm half wondering that. Even more pressure.

"The key to a great first or second date is to leave you both wanting more," my dad continues. "Always better to err on the side of caution. Better a date be too short than have her watching a clock, wondering, *When the hell is this thing going to be over?*"

"Thanks for the vote of confidence, Dad."

He surrenders. "Just take her to a nice restaurant and go from there."

I suppose I can't choose burgers with the guys again.

• • •

Trying to figure out my options, I ask Coach Wells when I see him on the field the next day.

"I hear tapas is a good first-date option," Coach Wells remarks. "The wife always wants to go out for tapas. I don't know when tapas became such a big deal. It's like sushi needed a rival for overpriced bullshit food. But she goes on and on about how it's a collaborative effort, which creates conversation, sharing, eating with your hands, feeding each other. . . ."

"Easy with the feeding each other," I say. "You know I'm kind of a germaphobe. I don't know where her hands have been."

"Sounds like you really like her," he observes.

"I'm kidding!" I say. Even though I really don't like the idea of eating with our hands. Not at all. Instead, I say, "Isn't tapas tiny food? I wouldn't be surprised if the word actually means 'tiny' in Spanish. All I know is every time I've had it, I've always made a pit stop at Damiano's for a slice before I got home."

"Okay, so no tapas." Coach Wells grunts. "You have a ton of other possibilities. Just think about what you want to say about who you are, and take the usual restaurant parameters into consideration: the vibe of the place, the location, the type of food. You might want to try a cozy, candlelit place—somewhere intimate where you can soak each other in and get to know each other. Or you could go the hip-and-trendy route. Ask one of the guys on the team to tell you someplace that will impress her and make you look like you have a life."

"Which I don't?" I ask.

"Just don't take her anyplace where you might run into Layla," he replies.

"Like the corn maze."

"Yeah, you're definitely not one for overthinking things," he mutters. "We should have had this conversation before that happened."

"Hindsight," I say. "The only perfect science."

Still, I'm left with no real suggestion. I just want someone to say, "Go here," and then I'll do that. Is that so much to ask?

• • •

I ask Doug for his input, and all he offers is "I'm so laughing at you right now."

Surprisingly, it's Jared who saves the day. "Take her to the Santa Monica Pier," he suggests. "There's tons of stuff to do there. You can win her stuffed animals. You can fish. . . ."

"Fish?" I echo.

"You won't fish. But you can ride roller coasters, eat fun food, look through the coin-operated telescope. . . ."

"You're a huge dork," I say.

"I love a telescope," he says. "Don't hate. I could have been an astronomer."

"I'm not hating, dude," I allow. "Honestly, you're the only one who's given me a solid suggestion that I can just take and not have to think about it."

"It's what I'm here for," he says.

I pick Heather up at her apartment and tell her we're going to dinner and then we're gonna have some fun. She cocks an eyebrow, but I assure her that it will be incredible.

Before I got Heather I scoped the area, and it seems that the most efficient date plan leaves us with two restaurant choices: Bubba Gump Shrimp Co., which is actually on the pier, or The Lobster, which is just south of the pier on the southern side of Ocean Ave. The two restaurants couldn't be more different.

The Lobster is a historical landmark that's been around for as long as I've been alive, and I'm sure longer. It's a top-notch seafood restaurant in such a prime location that no matter where you sit you will have an amazing one-hundred-eighty-degree view of the Pacific Ocean. If you go around sunset, you've got a breathtaking lookout and a very happy dinner companion. I've been there once. With Layla. And she got sick the next day, and we never knew if it was food poisoning from the mussels or if she got sun poisoning, because Layla was always very fair-skinned and we'd uncharacteristically spent the day lying out like a couple of beach bums. Okay, enough about that.

Bubba Gump is a casual, family-type place. I'm pretty sure it's popped up only in the last fifteen years, and if memory serves it is a by-product of the movie *Forrest Gump*. Top five reasons why I'm leaning toward *not* taking Heather there: 1) It's a chain. 2) It's a tourist trap. 3) I imagine there are several tables at all times with screaming kids. 4) It has Bubba in its name. 5) I don't eat shrimp.

Oh, and 6) *Forrest Gump.* Stupid movie.

I have only two problems with The Lobster: 1) Layla and I went there. It's probably not ideal to take a date to a place I've been with my wife . . . but at the same time, I've been with Layla for a thousand years, and that knocks off a whole lot of options. 2) Layla may or may not have gotten violently ill from it. That seems like a strong argument in the *against* column, but a) it could have been sun poisoning, b) it wasn't me who got sick, and c) I'll just steer Heather away from the mussels. What are the odds that she's gonna want mussels? And d) Layla literally shudders when we drive past the place, so I know there's no chance of running into her there. Yes, The Lobster is the better choice. It's certainly the classier choice.

The maître d' at The Lobster seats us at our table and hands us our menus.

"I love mussels," Heather says, and I wince. Tiny beads of

sweat start to form on my upper lip, and I sit there and hope she doesn't notice.

"Mussels . . ." I say. "They look good piled high on a plate, but really, not a lot of food in those shells. And the texture?" I shudder.

"Really?" she says. "Maybe you just haven't had the right mussels."

"Oh, I've had the right mussels," I say. I don't even know what that means.

"Have you, now . . ." she says, and it somehow sounds like we're talking dirty, and I don't know what she thinks I was insinuating, but I want to get off the subject of mussels yet still put the kibosh on her ordering them.

"There's sand in them," I say, as I point to the beach just in case she doesn't know what sand is. "They're dirty. If we were taking a vote, I'd vote no mussels. But we're not voting. If you love them, you should order them. Order whatever you want. Get the mussels."

"I think I will not get the mussels tonight," she says, with a long look at the menu, now almost certainly taunting me. "Clearly you have issues with mussels, and I don't want to send you to therapy."

"My mother ran off with a door-to-door mussel salesman when I was five."

"Well, you've grown up remarkably well, considering," she says. "Anyway, in honor of my favorite writer, may he rest in peace, I may just *Consider the Lobster*."

"Good idea," I say. " 'Cause I have had mussels in this part of town and that's *A Supposedly Fun Thing I'll Never Do Again*."

Heather winks at me for playing off her reference, we share a quiet toast for David Foster Wallace, and from that moment forward, dinner goes off without a hitch. When we're finished we walk to the pier. The sun is almost setting, and it's a really phenomenal view. I think about Layla and how much she loves sunsets. We used to argue about clouds. She'd say that it was the clouds that made sunsets beautiful, so when people would say, "It's a beautiful day—not a cloud in the sky," she'd think they were idiots.

The top of the pier is where they shot one of the openings for *Three's Company*, so I mention this to Heather and then have the misfortune of getting the theme song stuck in my head for the rest of the night. We walk past the stand where you can get a grain of rice with your name on it, and Heather says she doesn't understand why anyone would want a grain of rice with their name on it. I agree.

First, we walk through Playland, the arcade, and aside from the Skee-Ball, there's nothing too exciting in there. What I do notice is that everything there is so much smaller than I remember it. I suppose it's because every time I ever went to the actual pier I was a kid. I came with Layla when we were in high school a handful of times, and even then I remember it being bigger.

We exit Playland and start walking toward the rides. I'm surprised to see a Taco Bell on the pier, which I'm pretty sure wasn't always there, and the Coffee Bean is definitely a new addition.

We get to the part of the park that has the roller coaster, the Ferris wheel, and the bumper cars. What throws me is that when I was a kid, I thought of the people who worked there and took our tickets and let us on the rides as adults. Now that I'm an adult, I'm stunned to realize that all of the people running the rides are teenagers in a permanent state of mild disinterest. And I wonder what my parents were thinking when they turned me over to these careless clods. Which then makes me feel very old.

"So," Heather says, as she looks around at all of the carnival-type games. "What are you going to win me?"

Pressure. I look around. There's a reason carnies have such an impeccable reputation for honesty and fairness. You've got your ring toss—the carnival midway equivalent of going after the

Triple Crown on the back of a three-toed sloth—tiny rings that you throw at a bottle neck that's definitely wider than the rings. There's the Whac-a-Mole, which I'm pretty sure is rigged. And the beanbag toss, where you have to knock three milk bottles off a barrel (hint: a howitzer couldn't knock those lead bottles down). None of it looks winnable.

"We'll just have to see," I say.

"We won't be leaving until you win me something," she remarks, and although she's smiling, I can tell she means it. I suddenly feel parched.

"You look around and pick a game for me, and I'm gonna go buy a Coke," I stall. "You want something?"

"No, thanks," she says. She looks around, focused.

I walk toward the vending machine. No Coke. Only Pepsi. I walk to the other end of the amusement park area and again, Pepsi. The whole place only has Pepsi machines. Which I find offensive and oppressive. I like Coke. And this is America, and I like to have a choice. I don't want my soft drink dictated to me. It's not right.

I walk back empty-handed and see Heather with a giant blue stuffed gorilla—I kid you not, the thing is three-quarters the size of her—and she's got this shit-eating grin on her face.

"I won!" she screams. "I won the ring toss! Nobody wins the ring toss. I got it on my second try!"

"How many attempts do they give you?"

"Twenty-five! They give you that many because it's so impossible!"

"Yet apparently not," I say, looking back and forth between Heather and the gorilla, knowing unfortunately that she's just made it even clearer that I have to win her something and that I'm going to have to carry this fucking thing around for the rest of the night. I'll be that guy everyone looks at and says, "Poor sucker."

She hands Magilla to me, as expected, and then just stares, wide-eyed and waiting.

"I think I want that dog," she finally says, and points to a stuffed beagle at the Whac-a-Mole.

I roll up my sleeves and hand the woman running the game three dollars. Yes, it costs three dollars for one attempt. I look to my right and my left to scope out the competition. There's a cop (shouldn't he be catching bad guys and not whacking moles?), a boy who looks to be about eight years old, his dad, and a sixteen-year-old couple side by side. I figure that the eight-year-old is my most serious competition. Probably a mole-shark. Looking all cute and innocent, but with the eyes of a killer . . .

The bell rings and we all start pounding the moles. It's pretty easy. I'm fast, I'm accurate, I'm enjoying the game. I'm certain it's a shoo-in. The eight-year-old wins. *Prick.*

I hand another three dollars to the woman and take a stance: the best, most comfortable position for me to whack those fucking moles. Now I'm pissed and I can see this may not be as easy as I thought.

The bell rings . . . I whack, I lose. Again. I hand over another three dollars. I play once more, this time pounding harder than I have thus far—not that it makes a difference but because I'm pissed off and taking my anger out on the moles. And one hour, twelve minutes, and sixty-three dollars later I have won Heather the small stuffed dog she requested. Totally worth it.

As the evening winds down, we eventually find ourselves standing at the pier. It is here that Heather turns to me and point-blanks it: "So when are you going to kiss me?"

I hadn't actually done this on either of our other dates. Please don't ask me why.

"Who said I was going to kiss you?" I tease.

She just looks at me expectantly. For a second I think about Layla, the only person I've kissed since high school. This is why I didn't kiss Heather after the corn maze; for some reason, pulling the trigger on a kiss still feels like infidelity. But I realize I need to push Layla out of my head, and the best way to do it would be to kiss this girl. This beautiful girl who is asking me to kiss her.

What the fuck am I waiting for, anyway? I go for it. I lean in and stop short just before our lips touch. Heather smiles, and I can feel her breath as she exhales a small laugh. I close my eyes, and the next thing I know I'm kissing a gorgeous girl on the Santa Monica Pier—but either she has freakishly long arms or there's a very small person tugging at my jeans.

I break away from the kiss to look down, and there's a small boy holding my leg.

"Hi," I say to him.

Heather laughs and leans down. "Hi, there," she says. "What's your name?"

Before he can answer, his mother storms over and smacks him on the ass. She says something in Spanish and guides him away. She doesn't acknowledge us (though I don't know what I'd expect her to say), but the odd moment seems an omen that perhaps this date should come to a close. It was a very nice date, and that's enough for now. For that reason, I tell Heather I've had a nice time and I start to walk us back to my car.

Oddly, I don't even wrestle with whether or not I should go inside her apartment when she asks me. I simply tell her that "I'm not that easy," and send her off with another kiss and the promise of a phone call.

Dating. Not sure how I feel about it. I guess it depends on your end goal.

Right now I still don't know what mine is.

• • •

It's Thanksgiving week, and UCCC has had more losses than I expected this year. I blame myself. We're way out of any conference title contention. I haven't been all there, giving it my usual two hundred percent, and I feel I'm doing the team a disservice. I tell

Coach Wells I'm thinking about quitting, because he and the guys need a better effort even for the last few weeks of the season.

"Son, I know you've been going through some things," Coach Wells says. "But you gotta remember: Never get too high with the highs or too low with the lows."

"I know," I say.

"That goes for everything. Just take it one play at a time."

"I just feel bad. I hope my lack of focus hasn't caused—"

"Nonsense," he interrupts. "You haven't caused anything. And even if you did—you know we're a family. We don't kick anyone out for a few stumbles. You've got to do a lot more than that to lose privileges here. But we're your *second* family. You go take care of your real family. Go stuff yourself with turkey. Next season we'll start over, and in January we'll hit the road again, see if we can't drum up some new recruits. And I don't mean drum majors."

I truly love that man.

Still, the recent dip in the Condors' performance reminds me that I should focus myself, too. I really need to look into getting one of those things I've heard about called "a life." Knowing that they don't just happen upon you between trips to the refrigerator to see if something that wasn't there twenty minutes ago (like a pastrami-and-Swiss-cheese sandwich) has magically appeared (it hasn't). Monday I decide to finally get the proverbial ball rolling on Wonder Armour. I make a few calls and talk to one of my players, whose dad has a clothing business. He tells me the best place in downtown L.A. to get clothing samples made, and makes me swear on the success of the Cowboys never to tell anyone else.

The following day I make an appointment, and hours later I'm driving down an alley, past a faded billboard with an impossibly long and lean blond woman lying sideways, touting some sort of brandy I don't recognize: "So Smooth You Won't Know It's Gone . . . Until It's Too Late." Recipient of *Advertising Age*'s 1987 Double Entendre of the Year Award, I guess.

I pull up to a windowless gray door at what appears to be a large abandoned warehouse in the middle of a nondescript L.A. commercial district. It's the right address: "The number is twenty-seventeen, but the two is missing," the fast-talking proprietress said on the phone in an almost impenetrable Chinese accent, and sure enough, there's no two. And there is a button, which I press, which summons someone inside.

"Who there?" comes a voice across the intercom.

"Brett Foster, about the . . . having samples made?"

There's a very long pause. I'm not sure my explanation has proved convincing, and I'll need to slump down on the doorstep and cry, Dorothy-like, before they'll let me in. But then the door opens and I'm being given the once-over by Katie Hu, the owner of this fine establishment. Katie's about four-eleven, with the voice of a screech owl and bright blue eye shadow to match. Her hair is tied in a ponytail, and she purses her lips and pushes out her nose, making her face seem a little like it's pointing accusingly at me. But most remarkable is her body—not the shape of it, which is fairly typical, but the way it's encased from head to toe in a single sleeve of brilliantly neon-green fabric, so that she looks a little like an irradiated pea pod.

"Like it?" she asks, smiling slyly.

My cover is blown, I'm thinking, but no, I've made a very strong effort not to stare at the lime bodysuit. Instead, I think she simply starts all conversations with strangers like me by using a reference to her attire.

"Lycra," she says proudly, pinching it away from her body to demonstrate its springiness as I follow her to a freight elevator. "I design it all myself."

The gate slams down and we're slowly rising toward a deafening din, a chorus of industrial sewing machines presided over by a sea of seamstresses.

"I could never have made it as a designer," she says, a smile tossed away like junk mail.

"That goes without saying," I reply. Then, catching her glare, I immediately throw out, "Well, it's such a cutthroat, *artificial* business. It's so refreshing that someone of your talents would actually choose to apply herself *this* way, as opposed to the mere popularity contest of the fashion business." I don't know what I'm saying.

"Exactly," she says, and she leans in closer, squinting at me a bit. "But if I ever see these designs anywhere, I'll know who stole my idea."

"For a while there I thought about going pro as a seamstress, but I blew out a thumb while thumb-wrestling," I say, attempting humor. The joke disappears into the cultural chasm between us, never to be heard from again.

I go on, trying to put her at ease. "Don't you worry. My dream is to bring my value-priced, lightweight, breathable underapparel to the sports-loving masses."

She stares back blankly, apparently having heard a lot of half-baked dreams in her day.

She walks quickly through the maze of the production floor, which is amazingly clean but smells of burned toast for some reason. Maybe it's the blizzard of sheer effort. Her Lycra hisses with each step, and she motions for me to follow.

"They call this place Little Shanghai," she says, waving an arm overhead, indicating who knows how much real estate. "Work fast, not so much money. Like China. But not as many people. Good here for the prototype, not so good for the big volume."

"Too small," I say, but she shakes her head without looking at me.

"Too expensive. I pay in one hour what they pay in one week. Even Shanghai is getting too expensive for manufacturing. Too many iPod and Mercedes. But Shanghai is easy to pronounce, so we stay Little Shanghai."

We reach her office, which is a forest of fabric, buttons, sample books, and other oddities of the apparel trade.

"I'm famous, you know," she says.

"I didn't," I reply.

"Look at my wall. What do you see?"

I look at the wall and see what looks like a large yet virtually cupless woman's bra encased in glass. I'm not sure if that is what she's referring to so proudly.

"That?" I ask.

"Yes!" she exclaims. "I was the designer of the Manziere."

Unsure of what she's referring to and not wanting to offend her, I smile politely and nod.

"The Bro?" she asks. "*Seinfeld*? This was real deal. But I get no credit."

And then it starts to come back to me. She's talking about the *Seinfeld* episode when George's father wants to create a bra for men, and he and Kramer invent one but argue over whether to call it the Bro or the Manziere. I'm not sure which won.

"You made that?" I ask.

"Hollywood calls me all the time," she brags, as if Hollywood is a fat man in a suit, chomping a cigar, pinning its hopes for the next blockbuster on her fertile imagination. I wonder briefly whether he is.

"Then I came to the right place," I reply, not sure how to move off topic and back to my Wonder Armour. I decide the best way is just to change the subject, which I do. I lay it out, explain my product, show the designs I've worked up and the ones I've commissioned from the graphic designer I met on Craigslist, and then wait as she sits and fondles her chin for an uncomfortably long time. Finally she responds.

"So," she says, as she rubs her hands together like she's trying to start a fire, "if I give you a discount on the prototype, you want to go fifty-fifty with me?" I guess the true mark of a good idea is someone wanting to steal it or join forces.

I politely decline her offer, and we arrange to meet again in a week's time when she'll have my prototypes ready, in several variations. As we walk back through the factory, I have a strong feeling that I'm onto something, and I'm elated. The sun streams in through the high glass windows, and I feel as though it's shining specifically on me. At last, a dream of mine is on its way toward becoming the real deal.

# *layla*

When I was a little girl, my favorite thing to eat was tuna-noodle casserole. I used to make it with my mom, and I loved putting it together nearly as much as eating the final product. There are more ways to make a tuna casserole than you'd think, and the several variables can make or break the dish. The standard method is to top the thing with bread crumbs. Some people use cornflakes *(blegh),* but we used crushed Lay's Classic potato chips, which added a special kick. It was just us two in the house, and the dish was huge—I suppose we *could* have halved the recipe—so there was plenty to save for later.

Whenever we made it, I'd snack on the leftovers for a week. I'd stand at the refrigerator with a fork, pull back the tinfoil, and eat it cold, right out of the casserole dish. My mom would sometimes catch me in the kitchen and I'd think she was going to reprimand me and tell me to get a plate, heat some up, and sit down to eat it, but she'd always grab her own fork, nudge me aside, and take a bite herself.

I say that we made it together, but the truth is that she was the one doing all of the work. She'd cook the noodles and mix the soup in with the tuna and add everything else and stir it and pour it into the baking dish, and then I'd proudly cover the top of the casserole with the potato chips. My part wasn't terribly difficult or important, but my mom would act like the art of topping the dish with potato chips was the most critical part of the endeavor. I can't even hear the words "tuna-noodle casserole" without thinking of my mom, and it always makes me smile. Cooking was love.

Maybe that's why Thanksgiving has always been one of my favorite holidays. It was extra-hard the first Thanksgiving after my mom died, but the Fosters were already treating me like a family member, so it was a no-brainer that I'd share the holiday with them. And Ginny—sensing my loss and displacement—somehow knew the exact right thing to do: She asked me to help her with the cooking.

She was making her sweet-potato soufflé, and she had two bags of marshmallows sitting atop the counter. I wasn't feeling particularly useful up to that point, but then she turned to me and said, "Layla, I always put marshmallows on top of the soufflé. It's the most important part of the dish. Would you be so kind as to help me out and put the marshmallows on for me?"

Not only did it remind me of making the tuna-noodle casserole with my mom, it made me feel useful, like I was part of something. Ever since that first year, the responsibility of the marshmallow topping always falls on my shoulders, and I proudly and lovingly place each marshmallow in its proper position. She treats it like art, and I feel every bit the artist.

As I've grown up with the Foster rituals and advanced my cooking skills from absolute hazard to mere liability—I'm kidding; I'm actually an excellent cook—I also have my own dishes that I've added to the feast. Ginny and I now almost equally share the Thanksgiving cooking duties.

Ginny asks me to show up at seven-thirty a.m. to begin prep work for the day, so we can make sure we have the turkey in the oven by eight a.m. sharp. Ginny says the reason our turkey is always moist and flavorful is that we cook it with love. And by "love," she means it's a bigger pain in the ass than a thirsty two-year-old. We take turns basting it every twenty minutes for the seven or eight hours the thing cooks.

"Can I just skip the basting this one time?" I asked her once in the early years.

"Go right ahead, love," she replied sweetly. "When they ask why the bird is a little drier this year, I'll just let them know you thought you'd try something different."

My request never surfaced again.

So, that's twenty-four times of opening and shutting the oven, ladling meat juices, broth, orange juice, and whatever else we are using over the turkey. Two times slightly cooking my right arm. Three others, I'll convince myself I've seriously roasted my flesh to a fine golden brown.

Having just been through the corn-maze fiasco, I'm concerned about whether Brett is planning to bring back *that girl,* but I put it out of my mind and show up as requested. Brett does surprise me once again—but this time with not a girl but an apron. As I walk into the Foster kitchen, Brett is there already, fully caffeinated, game face on, wearing an apron that says *Is it hot in here or is it just me?* Ginny is nowhere to be found.

"It's just you," I'm tempted to say, but instead I force out a pleasant hello, trying to be mature, wishing I could secretly replace his apron with one that says, *Candied yams for brains.*

"Good morning," he answers. I think about whether I should have said good morning instead of hello and search for his hidden subtext. Why is it such a good morning to him? Did he have an extra-special night last night? Did they go for round two first thing this a.m. so she could send him off with a smile?

Luckily, Ginny materializes and takes the focus off us and onto the task at hand.

"Morning, kids," she says. I love the fact that she still refers to us as kids. Granted, we do sometimes deserve the description.

"Morning, Mom," Brett says, and kisses Ginny on the side of her head.

"Morning, Gin," I say. "What's the plan of attack?"

"Brett can get the gizzard and do all of that unpleasant stuff while you and I chop the celery and carrots for the stuffing," she suggests. "Then, once we get the bird in the oven, we'll split up dishes and see who wants to do what."

"Sounds great," Brett says.

"Yeah," I add. "Peachy." And I say it so kindly that the sourness is lost on both of them. Well, on Ginny, anyway.

"Where did the yams go?" Ginny says, panicked.

"The yams?" I ask.

"The sweet potatoes," she snaps. "For the soufflé."

"I thought I saw . . ." I open the refrigerator and see that the soufflé is there—already made, and waiting to be baked in the oven. "It's done, Ginny. See?"

"Oh, right, right," she says.

For the next two hours, Brett and I take turns outcooking each other. Let's be clear that Brett—in all my years as his girlfriend and then wife—has never spent a single Thanksgiving in the kitchen. I don't think he's ever even made it to the kitchen by way of clearing a plate. Thanksgiving is and always has been about the football game, so this is way out of character.

Further, it's confusing to me, because I can't tell if he's doing it to be near me or to gain points with his mom. Is he just trying to make sure I don't get any closer to his family, so that he can gain some ground with them again? Because he's not being an overt jerk, it's unclear.

It's really a food fight in the most literal sense. It becomes so serious I can only think of our anthropological need for survival; food playing into this theory turns it up about twelve notches and makes our cook-off stressful and harried. I find myself sacrificing ingredients and my tried-and-true methods through discomfort. I'm so panicked that when my zucchini bread is burned to a crisp I can't even point fingers, although I know in my heart I did *not* turn the oven to "broil."

Halfway through the day, I start feeling hollow. I like being there and love the ritual, but suddenly I'm in a contest against the person I thought I was going to grow old with, and it doesn't feel right. Also, part of the joy of cooking Thanksgiving dinner for the Fosters was that I was helping Ginny prepare this meal for my husband.

When we get to the actual meal, and Ginny suggests that before we begin we all talk about something we are grateful for, I start to get choked up and feel even more out of place—for the first time in as long as I can remember.

"I'm grateful for this wonderful and crazy family," Bill says. "I love that no matter what is going on, we always come together on this day. And, of course, I love the grub, which is evidenced by my ever-growing gut."

"Oh, Bill," Ginny says. "What gut?"

"And that, ladies and germs, is why I keep her around," he jokes, and she wrinkles her nose at him, and for a moment I watch them and it's like they're the only two people in the world, still so in love after all these years. I feel a stabbing pain in my chest, which is a longing for what they have. I had it. I *thought* I had it. And yet, as I sit here across from my would-have-been one and only, I start to resent him for taking that away from me. It washes over me in a new wave of sadness that's masquerading as anger. So when it comes to my turn, all I can say is, "I'm grateful that my husband opted not to bring a date."

But that's not the worst of it. In all our racing to outcook each other, I had my hands in this bowl of cranberries, that platter of garlic mashed potatoes, and ultimately deep inside the private parts of our bird as I thrust the stuffing into every crevice. And just as Bill is about to carve the aforementioned turkey, I notice a conspicuous absence on my ring finger.

"Stop!" I shriek at the top of my lungs. My heart starts racing and I start sweating and circling the table. I grab a large spoon and begin to dig into every dish on the table, messing up the beautifully plated meal. There are peas and carrots flying, confused looks going back and forth, and tears streaming down my face though I don't even know it.

"What is it, honey?" Ginny asks.

"She's losing it," Trish says. "And who can blame her?"

"I'm not losing it. I lost it," I say.

"Told ya." Brett smirks.

"It's gone!" I cry, as I look to each confused face before me—searching—hoping someone will help. Then I resume vandalizing the meal, cutting into the turkey, dragging out the stuffing I'd so forcefully shoved in earlier.

"What's gone, Lay?" Ginny asks, and she stands and walks toward me, placing her hands on my shoulders to steady me as I shake. She gently takes the serving spoon I'm using to desecrate our feast from my hand and moves my hair out of my face. My eyes dart back and forth, staring into hers.

"My ring!" I say. "My wedding ring! It's somewhere in this meal."

"Holy symbolism, Batman," Scott mutters.

"No kidding," Trish adds.

"It's kinda coming off anyway, right?" Scott says, and I glare at him.

"Engagement or wedding?" Brett asks. "Because one is a much more expensive digestive."

"Good band name," Trish says. "Expensive Digestive."

"The band," I clarify. "The symbol of our marriage."

I realize I'm falling apart, but I can't stop it. I've totally lost control of myself, my relationship, my life. All I can do is maniacally dig through food.

"Honey," Trish says. "Step away from the soufflé."

"It will all still be edible," I say, unable to stop. Trish sees the gravity of the situation, takes my hand, and guides me into the kitchen to calm me down. At which point I start bawling uncontrollably. Even harder when I spot my ring on the floor.

# *scott*

To hell with it. To hell and back, then back again to hell, with a stop in Vegas for a magic show.

I used to write songs about Brett in my head. They reflect my long-held belief that he's a dumbass in most respects. They were stupid, and they made no sense. But I see now it was more than sibling rivalry—mainly because he'd never consider me his rival at *anything*. (Well, maybe Madden, since I started kicking his ass. I practiced good and hard to do that.)

Anyway, I love him—yeah, yeah. And maybe there's been some envy of his genetic advantages, and his luck with Layla, and his charm, and his athletic ability, and his Fisher-Price plastic lawn mower he wouldn't let me borrow (I'm going back a while on that one, but I can hold a grudge) . . . but there is a limit. So I took the whole situation as inspiration.

"Every Little Thing He Does Is Spastic." "Black Hole Scum." "Sweet Child O' Moron." "He Ain't Heavy (He's My Butthole)."

That last one I sang to him. He called me a jealous little man, I called him shit-for-brains, and we agreed to disagree. Just before he punched me so hard in the shoulder I had to wear a sling for a week.

But now it's reached a climax. I've watched my brother destroy a perfectly good thing. I didn't ever—not once—get involved in their relationship in any way except to hang out as the dutiful little tagalong.

But you know what? If he doesn't appreciate her, it's his loss. And I don't see why it can't be my gain. I'm not stepping in when they're having some stupid fight. He brought a freakin' date to the corn maze. Which I won't even go into. But really? If he can date, then so can she. And I'm a grown person and she's a grown person. He gave her up. It's not his business who she dates. Or who I date.

And maybe it's just me imagining or exaggerating something, but I think the table is at least partially set, as they say. For instance, she's always saying things to me like, "Sweetie, can you get me some paper towels?" or, "Sweetie, we're out of paper towels—can you go get some?" or, "Sweetie, can you run an errand for me if you're not doing anything?"

Not like anyone's lusting after anyone. I'm not saying that. That would be crazy talk.

## *layla*

So, Saturday Scott calls me and tells me he ran into his ex-girlfriend.

"I could really use a talk," he says. "Could you meet me at the Apple Pan?"

"Of course," I say, and I throw on my Adidas.

The truth is, the Apple Pan is a bittersweet choice of restaurant. Brett loves it, and we'd go there at least once a week. He'd wax poetic about their burgers with as much enthusiasm as he'd describe the most amazing eleventh-hour football miracle he'd ever seen. If you ask him why he loves the place so much, he'll say it's "because it doesn't change." Or his favorite expression, every time he walks in the front door, just after he's taken an inhale deep enough to suck all of the air out of the place: "It's like coming home."

I suppose it makes sense that since they grew up together going there, Scott would love it as much as Brett, but when he asks me to meet him there, although I say yes without hesitation, I feel a stabbing in my heart.

I walk in, and Scott's sitting at the counter with a seat saved next to him. He waves me over and smiles awkwardly. I feel bad for the kid and wonder which ex he ran into. None of them stick out in my memory, because none have lasted all that long, so this is actually somewhat surprising—this sudden need for a chat about a girl.

"How's the burgeoning artiste?" I ask.

"Not burgeoning so much," he says, with a shrug.

"Why not?" I prompt. Scott's really talented, and yet he sits on his ass in college, waiting for someone to discover him but never putting his stuff out there. He needs to enter shows and really push himself—or maybe start on a comic book, which is one of his real dreams.

"I need a partner" is his excuse. "Without Neil Gaiman, Dave McKean was just . . . Dave McKean. Together they made *The Sandman*. Without the story, I just draw pictures. I need someone to make it all make sense."

"Well, until you find that person you should keep drawing," I tell him. "You're too good not to be exercising that muscle."

He laughs. "You said 'exercising that muscle.' "

"Ugh." I groan. "Why do I try?"

We make small talk from the time I sit down until our burgers arrive. Rather, his hickory burger and my grilled cheese sandwich. Scott peels back the paper his comes in and starts in on a Brett-like seminar.

"You only peel back as much as you need," he says. "They wrap the burgers in this paper for a reason, and if you unwrap the whole thing and try to eat it, it falls apart. I love watching rookies come in and take the whole thing out."

He snickers as he nods toward a guy three seats down doing what Scott just warned against. It's a sloppy burger, that's for sure. Better, the guy is hunching his shoulders to try to conceal the damage, so it looks as though he's praying over it.

"There's never an off day in this place," Scott marvels, as he opens his mouth extra-wide to take a bite. "The burger is homemade, yet it tastes exactly the same every time. But not in a fast-food, McDonald's way."

"I get it," I interrupt. "You love it here. You love the place, you love the burgers, you love the waiters, you love the institution."

# *scott*

I love *you*.

## *layla*

"You love the familiarity," I go on. And before I can say, "Oh my God, this must be a sign of the apocalypse," Scott puts cash on the table, under the bill, and covers it up with a salt shaker.

"Wait a minute," I say. "What's going on? You just bought my sandwich."

"It's five bucks." Scott shrugs and looks away. "No big deal."

But it's a very big deal. "You never pay for anything," I say. "What's up? What's going on?"

"Okay, fine," Scott says. "She didn't break up with me. I broke up with her."

"Oh, we're finally talking about the girl?" I tease. "So okay, you broke up with her and . . . what? You regret it? You saw her and she looked great and you realize you made a mistake? You want her back? You can get her back. You weren't wearing that shirt when you ran into her, were you?"

"No, I don't want her back," he says, almost seeming disgusted by the thought.

*But isn't that why we're here?* I wonder.

It's almost as if he reads my mind. "Wanna know why I asked you here?" he says, ripping his burger wrapper into little itty-bitty pieces. "Because I saw that girl and it reminded me of why I broke up with her. I broke up with her because she was nothing like you. Because I wanted a girl like you."

"That's sweet, Scotty," I say. "I'm sure you'll find the right girl one of these days."

"There's only one right girl," he says, now looking right at me. "And now that you and Brett are over—"

"Whoa, buddy!" I interrupt, and suddenly I'm tasting spoiled mayonnaise in my mouth and my eyes are stinging like I've just bitten into a lemon-crusted jalapeño sandwich. "Let's not get crazy here."

"I'm not getting crazy," he says. "I'm getting honest. You get one life. One shot at happiness."

"I think you probably get more than one shot at happiness. But yeah. Only one life."

"I've been in love with you since Brett brought you home in tenth grade. You were wearing a Skid Row T-shirt with a tiny hole in the neck. It said *Youth Gone Wild* on it and had a picture of a dude who looked like a chick, and I asked you about it and you said Sebastian Bach was the only guy you'd ever kiss besides my brother if given the chance, and I wished I was Sebastian Bach. And I fuckin' hated that band. And then that song 'I Remember You' came out and I couldn't escape them. It seemed almost ironic. I'd have daymares—"

" 'Daymares'?" I ask.

"Nightmares during the day when you're awake," he explains. "I'd be in love with my brother's girlfriend and I'd become this sad Bukowski-like drunk, and I'd wind up on skid row and it would all come full circle."

"A lot of that was exaggerated for artistic effect," I say. "But to the issue at hand, Scotty, I'm kinda feelin' a little like Dorothy on this one—meaning totally flipping blown away. I don't want to be insensitive, but I'm not one hundred percent sure you're not fucking with me. Because this is so out of left field."

"Are you blind?" he says, and his voice goes up about two octaves. "Have you really been oblivion this whole time?"

"*Oblivious,* and yes, I guess I have," I say, wanting to shift time forward to a month from now.

"Well, now you know, then," he says, and takes his snow-cone cup out of its holder, pours the last bit of Coke he has left into it, which is not even a sip's worth, and drinks.

"You don't want *me,*" I say. "I'm the path of least resistance. You think you want me because I'm nonthreatening. I'm around all the time. I'm familiar. Like this restaurant. But the truth is the food here may not be as awesome as you think. You're just conditioned to think so because your dad and brother took you here as a kid and hyped it up. It's this landmark institution, and people come here and are willing to wait, Lord knows why, to sit at the counter and eat burgers that I'm not sure are better than In-N-Out's but cost twice as much. You follow?"

"You insult my favorite restaurant *and* my taste in women?"

"C'mon, Scott," I say. "You know you don't mean this."

"Okay, if you say so," he says, oddly letting go of the notion of our relationship like a dirty napkin. I'm trying to be sensitive to him but also not blow this up into an awkward mess.

"I do say so," I say.

"Fine," he allows, and then cracks a smile. "You're not that hot, anyway. I was just seeing if I could get sloppy seconds and hold it over Brett's fat head for the next ten years."

"Please," I tease back. "You were five minutes away from pulling out a mix tape."

Scott laughs. "Yeah, that would have been *really* embarrassing."

## *scott*

And as she gets up to hit the ladies' room, I slip a perfectly good CD onto a passing busboy's tray.

# *layla*

I wonder if it was Thanksgiving that did it. That, or Heather at the corn maze. Either way, it's not every day you have your mother-in-law suggesting she fix you up with potential dates, so I'm certainly not taking her seriously, nor am I prepared when I answer my cell phone to find Eric Ehrlich—a would-be suitor—on the other end.

"Didn't mean to catch you off guard," he says, after the very long pause from my end. "Did Mrs. Foster mention that I'd be calling?" he asks.

"You know, she did, but I didn't think it would actually transpire," I reply.

"Hard luck with the gents lately?"

"No," I say. "I mean, yes, I suppose, but not the way that sounded. It's not like I can't get a date or anything. I just haven't been trying. I've been . . . not dating for a while. I only just recently got separated."

"Sometimes you just gotta get back on the horse," he says, and I can't help but visualize all the many images this unfortunately conjures up.

"Right."

"So when do I get to meet you?"

"I don't know," I say, and start to think about it. This is going to be the first date I've been on since . . . high school? The thought of this sends me into a conversational tailspin. "This is weird. Is this weird? I don't know. I just haven't dated in a really long time, and now that this is becoming a reality, I'm just thinking that maybe—no offense—but maybe my first date shouldn't be blind."

"Well, that's good news for both of us because I have twenty-twenty vision," he says, completely undeterred by my mini-meltdown. Which I'll admit is slightly promising. Or slightly frightening. He's either patient and understanding or desperate and ugly.

"That *is* good news," I say.

"Good. We both feel better, then. How's Friday?"

"Friday? As in *this* Friday?" I echo stupidly.

"Yes," he says. "Friday, this Friday."

"Um, yeah," I finally spit out. "I think I can do Friday."

After all, none of the shows I watch are on Friday. Then again, all of my shows are readily available on DVR, and I have enough shows right now to keep me busy for the whole weekend. But I suppose a few hours with Eric on Friday couldn't be too painful.

"Great," he says. "Do you like Greek?"

"Food?" I ask, and immediately regret it. What do I think he means, the language? Did I just make a very unfortunate sexual remark to a guy I just met? Of course he means food.

"Yes. Greek food."

"I do like Greek food," I say.

"You hate Greek food," Trish says from behind me, and I wonder how long she's been listening. I wave her off and turn to give her a dirty look.

"Greek sounds great," I reiterate.

"Perfect," he says. "I'll touch base on Friday and we'll arrange to meet."

"Sounds good," I say. "Thanks for . . . calling."

I hang up. Big sigh. My mother-in-law is pimping me, and I'm sure she thinks it's for my own good.

I spin back around to Trish. "Do you *mind*?"

"Do *you*?" she asks. "You don't like Greek food."

"So what?" I say. "I was on the phone. That was a conversation between me and not you."

"Greeks like to butt-fuck," she says.

"Lovely," I respond, but I cringe at the thought of the Greek-related sexual innuendo that transpired sixty seconds earlier. I forgo the riposte of a lesbian joke, knowing Trish's sometime sensitivity.

"I'm just sayin'. So who were you lying to?"

"Eric?" I say, as if I'm asking a question rather than answering one.

"Eric Ehrlich?" Trish asks.

"Yeah, I think that's what he said."

"Why were you talking to Eric Ehrlich about Greek food? Oh my God . . ."

"Oh my God *what*?" I ask, as Trish bursts into a laughing fit. "Your mom gave him my number. She's fixing me up. Which is totally awkward. When Ginny said she had someone she wanted me to meet, I didn't really think she was being serious."

Trish won't stop laughing.

"Why is that so funny?" I ask.

"Because Eric is not your type. He's not anybody's type. Well, I suppose that's not fair and he's gotta be *someone's* type, but he's certainly not my type, and Mom tried to fix me up with him when I first started dating women."

"Wow. Didn't you start dating women freshman year of college?"

"Yup."

"And he's apparently still single."

"Yup." She laughs. "And he took me for Greek food, too!"

"Terrific," I say. "So back up a bit. Why is he 'not anybody's type'?"

"He's pear-shaped," she says.

"Come on."

"Seriously. He's pear-shaped. We know how unfortunate it is when a woman is pear-shaped, but it's far more devastating when it's a man. If anything, that date pushed me even further to the other side."

"Okay, *how* pear-shaped?" I ask.

"Like a big, giant, humongous, gargantuan pear."

"That's very pear-y."

"Very pear-y indeed, my friend."

Our doorbell buzzes, and I'm glad to be excused from the conversation. I walk to the front door and see a midforties blond woman in a navy pantsuit barking into her cell phone. "I'm here, I gotta go, I gotta go!" she says, and then hangs up. "Hi, I'm Debbie."

"Hi there, Debbie," I say, and can't help but look expectant because she seems to be missing the one thing we need for our photo shoot. "Come in."

Debbie walks in and answers her phone as she does. "I told you I had to go," she hollers into the phone. "What?"

I look at Trish, who shrugs, and we both stand there and wait for Debbie to finish her call.

"No, I'm at the photo place!" she screams. "I'll call you later." She hangs up and looks at us blankly for a long moment. Neither of us knows what to say, because we're both uncomfortable about this woman yelling at whoever keeps calling her, and we don't see a *pet* to photograph, so we're kind of at a loss.

"I'm Layla," I say. "This is Trish."

"I'm so sorry," Debbie says. "It's been one of those days."

"We all have 'em," Trish says.

"I forgot Charlie," Debbie realizes. "My dog."

"That's new," Trish says, and looks at me.

"Dammit!" Debbie yells, and then looks apologetically at us. "Don't worry, I'm not mad at you. I'm mad at myself."

"*And* whoever was on that call," Trish jokes, but Debbie doesn't find it funny.

I clear my throat. "I'm sure we can fit Charlie in later if you want to go home and get him. We can wait a little while for Charlie if you want to—"

But Debbie flips open her phone and calls, I'm assuming, whomever she was just on the phone with. "Do you know that you got me so upset that I left without Charlie?" she seethes. "I'm here at the place to have my dog photographed and I'm without a dog. Without a dog!" There's a pause when I think the poor person on the other end is answering, which is quickly interrupted. "Yes it *is* your fault. Yes it *is*."

"Do you notice anything about this crazy person in our midst?" Trish asks me under her breath.

"Besides the fact that she's insane?"

"Yes."

"No, I don't notice anything else. It's hard to notice anything else."

Trish laughs and leans in closer. "She's pear-shaped."

"Go fuck yourself," I say to Trish, because she knows I'm going to start laughing and there's no good reason for me to be laughing, and of course we both start laughing uncontrollably.

"And now they're laughing at me," she bellows.

"No, we're not laughing at you," I say, and motion to Trish. "I was laughing at something *she* said. We're not laughing at you. This is . . . this happens all the time. So you forgot the dog. It's no big deal."

Debbie squints her eyes at me and then at Trish, then she turns on her heels and leaves. We can still hear her making the person on her phone call miserable for a solid thirty seconds after the door closes behind her.

"I'm going to guess that she's not coming back," I say.

"We kind of *were* laughing at her," Trish corrects.

"No, I was laughing at *you*. For commenting on her shape. And pear-shaped is kind of funny."

"Fine, *I* was laughing at her."

"You're an idiot."

"Beware the pear. That's all I'm sayin'."

• • •

When Eric calls me that Friday I tell him I'll meet him at the restaurant. He picks The Great Greek, which is actually a pretty good restaurant and would have been okay if it didn't involve me driving to the Valley. For Greek food. With a pear-shaped person. But honestly, it's been years since Trish has seen him. He could have grown out of that shape and into something else. And who cares if he *is* pear-shaped.

I spot him from behind as soon as I walk in. He said he'd be wearing a purple shirt, and that he is. But it's not a purple shirt as much as an eggplant-colored shirt. And he's not just a pear. He's an eggplant-sized pear. I curse Trish for saying anything. Maybe I wouldn't have noticed. Now all I can think about are fruits and vegetables. I walk over and tap him on the shoulder.

"Eric?" I ask.

"Layla," he says. "Great to meet you."

"You, too," I say.

"Can I offer you something to drink? Do you like beer? Wine? Mixed? Something fruity?"

I choke on my own spit and start to cough. "Water," I say through wheezes, then add, "Please."

Once we're seated at the table, I ask him how long he's known Ginny and almost confess to knowing someone else she fixed him up with but think better of it.

"I'm her podiatrist," he replies.

"A doctor," I say.

"Indeed." He nods proudly. He's a foot doctor. Of course we need them in the world, but I can't help but think it's a kind of odd choice for a profession. I immediately feel guilty and decide not to judge.

"What made you . . . How did you get into that? Did you always know you wanted to do that?"

"I love feet."

I start to judge again.

"Well, then, I guess it's a good fit," I say.

"I knew I wanted to be a doctor—and a specialized one at that—and I didn't want to spend seventy years in school, so I explored a bunch of avenues, and when it came down to it, it was just a no-brainer. Feet really spoke to me."

"That's . . . Wow," I say, thinking I really don't want to talk about feet any more than I want to talk about fruit. "It's great that you love your job."

"I do. Feet are so amazing. When you think of it, they carry your whole weight. What would you do without feet? You couldn't *walk*."

"No, you sure couldn't," I admit, as I check my watch only three minutes into my date. I start counting how many times he says "feet," and it almost becomes like he's speaking another language. Feet language. And "feet" stops sounding like a real word.

"There are seven thousand, eight hundred nerves in our feet."

"So tell me something else," I say, begging to change the subject. "Do you play any sports? Watch any sports?" Why am I asking about sports? All I've lived and breathed with Brett for our entire life is sports. Enough sports.

"I don't play sports, or watch them, really, but funny story: I've treated some famous athletes, and believe me when I tell you that they have the worst feet you've ever seen."

"I believe it," I say, trying to head him off at the pass.

No such luck. "The wear and tear from all of the vigorous

activity does quite a number on their feet. Once I treated Michael Jordan."

"Sports injury?"

"Plantar wart. Routine, really," he replies.

"Isn't that something," I say.

And finally our waiter comes to our table, and I've never been happier to see someone in my life.

"Are you ready to order?" he asks.

"We've been so busy gabbing away that we haven't even looked," Eric says. "Give us a few minutes."

"I think I can wing it," I say, my eyes darting around the menu, desperate to find something to order and move this evening closer to its end.

"Nonsense," Eric says. "We're in no rush. Give us some time."

I smile miserably at the waiter and watch him walk away like I'm twelve years old and seeing my best friend in the world leave for summer camp. It's dramatic and heartbreaking.

• • •

The next day, as I'm recounting each unfortunate moment from the previous evening—every second of my life that I will never get back—I'm constantly interrupted by *me too*s, nods of recognition, and uncontrollable laughter from Trish.

"How is it that you let me go out with him?" I ask.

"Don't even go there. I warned you."

"You kind of did," I admit.

"Thank you," she gloats.

"I can't do this," I say, head in hands. "I don't want to date a bunch of random men. I thought I'd dodged that bullet. I was *married*. To someone great. At least he *was* great."

Trish sighs. "You can always come out with me tonight. I guarantee no men will hit on you where I'm going."

"Because no men will be there? That sounds refreshing." Better than sitting at home watching the DVR, at any rate. Or waiting for the damn bank to call about our possible loans for the PETCO project, which is simply waiting for that final step to move forward.

"Though I will warn you," Trish continues, "your drunk lesbian can rival an aggressive frat boy any day of the week."

"I can handle that," I say, and I look forward to a girls' night. Me and Trish. A bunch of lesbians. And no stress.

• • •

We get to The Abbey and it's decorated for Christmas, since it's the first week of December. There are both men and women there, but the men are gay, so they have no interest in me, which is just what the doctor ordered.

Maybe it's the alcohol, or maybe it's the setting, but after Trish and I have two drinks each and her hand grazes mine, I start to get this awkward, panicky feeling that maybe she's hitting on me. Which would be ultra-surreal and bizarre. Then her hand seems to accidentally graze mine *again*. Scott was one thing, but *this*? Is Bill next? I don't know how to react. Was it an accident? Am I supposed to ignore it? Am I being crazy? Do I say something?

I decide to just let it go. That lasts about forty-five seconds.

"Um . . ." I say.

"Yeah?"

"This is awkward."

"Being in a gay bar?" Trish asks, surprised.

"No," I say.

"What?"

"I'm just gonna say this because I don't know how to react here, and maybe I'm misinterpreting but . . ." I drift off, not sure how to just say what I said I was going to.

"Dude. What?"

"Were you just . . . ? Are you . . . ?" I manage to get out.

"Am I what?" Trish asks, getting annoyed.

"Hitting on me?"

Trish literally does a spit-take. Beer everywhere.

"Tell me you're kidding," she says.

"I'm kidding?" I say with a raised pitch, sounding much more like a question.

"Oh my God, you're serious?"

"I was . . . sort of . . . But now I'm not . . . I guess?" I say, somewhat relieved.

"I love you, dude. But not like that. Seeing you more than the ten hours a day I already do would scare me straight."

"Fair enough," I say, totally embarrassed by my accusation. "Let's just forget this happened and blame it on the venue. And the drinks. And my mental state. And you know . . . global warming. Whatever."

"Forget this happened? I am going to make you eat shit about this every day for a very long time."

"Yeah, I pretty much figured."

I do love being single again.

# brett

Christmas cards. I never got the point. Awkward, insincere small talk printed on overpriced greeting cards. I wouldn't say these things to you in person. I wouldn't write them to you in a letter. I therefore don't want someone else writing them for me in four-line stanzas illustrating heartfelt prefab musings on your importance to me. And don't get me started on the "family newsletter."

Layla and I always made a mockery of Christmas cards—or at least we played around with the tradition. We'd go to Wal-Mart or Sears or the closest mall and take one of those cheesy portraits and make cards out of the photo, but we'd create a new bullshit backstory every year and dress for the occasion. The DeBonis from New Jersey, moving to Cali after turning state's evidence. The Hurleys from Dubuque. The Avgambishis from New Delhi. It was silly but fun, our friends always enjoyed them, and we had a good time in the process. (I can't imagine Heather wanting to do that—although we've had a couple more dates that I've rather enjoyed. She's a cool woman, and I'm working myself up to the point where we'll consummate the third-date rule. I'm running behind schedule, but I don't mind her thinking I'm in no rush. It sort of adds to my charm.)

I'm just finishing up some plans for the Condors' season-end banquet when my dad calls to tell me the family's headed to Sears for a family portrait. I think he's kidding. When he tells me that Layla is the one behind it, I think I want to hurl.

"Dad, we're broken up," I say. "Almost divorced. We never even did a family portrait when we were together, and p.s., *we're not her family*."

"Brett," he says in his sternest voice. "She's looking for a solid mooring point in the storm of confusion that is your marriage."

"Our marriage is over," I remind him. How many times do I have to?

"She wants something tangible to hold on to."

"Buy her a teddy bear. Better yet, remind her about that stuffed owl her mom gave her. This is ridiculous."

And yet somehow, four days later I find myself at Sears with my mom, dad, sister, and soon-to-be ex-wife.

"Smile, little brother," Trish says, when she sees the scowl on my face.

"Fuck off," I say.

"There's the holiday cheer I'm looking for." She shows her own pearly whites and turns back to talk to Layla.

There's a two-year-old named Monica tossing unwanted props and screaming at the top of her lungs. "Nice, Monica," her mother says. "Nice . . ."

"What's nice?" I ask nobody in particular. "The fact that she's crying hysterically or the fact that her diapers smell like they haven't been changed since last Tuesday?"

"Oh, Brett," my mom says, shaking her head.

"I'm April. Is everybody here?" the gum-snapping, nineteen-year-old manning the camera says once she finishes with Monica. I want to ask if we can spray the place down with Lysol, but I refrain.

"We're missing one," Layla points out, referring to Scott, who's not here yet.

"You are a beautiful family," the girl says.

"Thank you, thank you very much," Scott says, as he enters, doing a lame Elvis impression.

The girl laughs. She notices the book he's carrying. "Tad Williams, eh? Nice. I liked his *Memory, Sorrow, and Thorn* trilogy more than *Otherland,* though."

*Nice. Nerds of a feather.*

Scott's about to reply when my mom smiles and thanks April, too. Then she looks Trish up and down. "Is that what you're wearing?"

"No," Trish says. "You're imagining this. I'm actually wearing a ball gown right now."

"I'm not complaining, honey," Mom says—but "Is that what you're wearing?" doesn't generally come off as a compliment. I can see the raised hairs on the back of Trish's neck.

"Can you explain the question, then?" Trish implores. "Because clearly this is what I'm wearing. I didn't bring a suitcase full of options."

"I was . . . Oh, honey, I'm sorry. That came out wrong," Mom says.

"Speaking of coming out wrong," Scott speaks up.

"What does *that* mean?" Trish asks.

"It wasn't about you, spaz," Scott says. "I was going to tell a funny story. But never mind."

"No, tell us," Trish demands, calling his bluff. She's clearly counting on his story to fall flat on its face.

It occurs to me in this moment how far apart Scott and Trish are. Never mind emotionally or developmentally or age-wise—I mean how physically far apart the two of them are whenever the family is together. They always seem to find a way to make sure something or someone is between them. Right now, it's three other Fosters, a faux Foster (Layla), and a wingback chair.

"Trish, what are you trying to prove?" my dad says sternly. "We accept you. No matter who you love or what you wear."

I don't know whether it's the stress of the impending holiday season or Mom's (no doubt semi-unintentional) slight about what she's wearing, or the lighting in the store, but Trish is suddenly locked and loaded for bear.

"And we're supposed to accept you no matter whom *you* love?" Trish hisses. Which in itself is bad, because she never uses "whom." It's formal, and that can only mean it's *on*.

"Trish!" my mom says, and I'm confused. Scott doesn't seem to know what's going on, either, from the look on his face, but Layla looks down and won't look up.

"I'll pay someone to translate," Scott throws out. "Who does Dad not love?"

"That's a great question, Dad," Trish says, looking straight forward at the camera, still a boiling-yet-covered pot. "Tell us exactly whom you love and whom you don't. I'm dying to know the answer to that question."

"What's she talking about, Dad?" I ask, but my father ignores me, his eyes trained on Trish.

"This is highly inappropriate," he says.

"Why? Because your secret is out?" Trish replies, eyes ahead, stony smile on her lips.

"Speaking of coming out wrong," Scott reprises, trying to lighten the mood. None of us are having it.

"Whoa," I say, but before I can turn on the filter and come up with the right euphemisms or consider the circumstances, there among the twinkly lights, satin bows, Santa and Mrs. Claus figurines, and posters blaring about the *Holly-Days Sale—Savings Throughout the Store!* I ask point-blank, "Did you cheat on Mom?"

"This is not the time, Brett," my father says. "And no."

"Yes," Trish says, not nearly as quietly, staring forward. "He did."

The nineteen-year-old photographer has been fiddling with her camera, and she becomes even more intent on her lens, trying hard to pretend she's not hearing any of this. Scott shrugs at her, and she smiles understandingly when their eyes meet.

"You guys," Layla says. "Let's not argue."

"Why are you even here?" I snap, embarrassed that my family is falling apart in front of her.

"You cheated on Mom?" Scott asks my dad. He's clearly processed it for a moment and now has been struck. Something of an eternal kid, this simpering smartass who revels in people's head-shaking disapproval has changed a bit in the shock of this awful possibility, and the smartass is gone. "Tell me if this is true."

"No!" my dad yells. "It's one hundred percent false. And I just told your brother, this isn't the time! Do you see your mother complaining?"

"Can we not do this in front of strangers and Layla?" I say.

"Layla is not a stranger," Scott snaps.

"I said 'Layla *and strangers,*' which would imply that she is separate from the strangers. How could she possibly be a stranger? She's with us every fucking moment of her spare time, like it or not!"

"Well, better get used to seeing even more of her," Trish says, *still* looking straight forward. She's smiling maniacally as she adds, "Because it seems we're both going to have a lot of spare time."

"What do you mean?" Layla asks.

"The bank called. They just rejected our loan, so Paw Prints photo booths are likely dead in the proverbial water dish."

"What?" Layla blurts. "They said it was almost a done deal. They wait until we're this far along and PETCO's ready to go forward? When did they tell us, and why didn't you tell me? Why did this happen?"

"About an hour ago, to answer the first question, and I did just now. And remember that lady with Rex the cat? Um, turns out she's a bank manager."

"Dad cheated on Mom," Scott mutters slowly and quietly, still stunned.

"I did not, Scott," Dad says. "We can talk later."

The confused and horrified April finally speaks up. "Are you all where you'd like to be for this photo? I have some other people coming and—"

"We're perfect right where we are," Trish says.

"Okay. On three, then, everyone say 'Holly-Days'!" April exhorts. This wipes the smile off even Trish's face. We stare at our teenage photographer as one seething mob. "They make us say that," she explains sheepishly. "One . . . two . . ."

"Wait—where are Mom and Pop?" my mom asks suddenly and frantically, for some reason using the names by which her own parents went. All of us turn our attention to her.

"Three!" *Click*.

Not exactly a keepsake portrait.

"Is that an existential question?" Trish asks. But the way our mom is looking around isn't lost on any of us. This wasn't a charming attempt to lighten the mood, break the tension, or change the subject. She was serious. She's looking for her parents, my grandparents. But they're not coming. They've been dead for ten years.

"If we've come all the way downtown for a portrait, we really should wait for Mom and Pop," she says anxiously.

My dad just puts his arm around her and walks her outside.

# *layla*

After that, um, *atypical* photography session I wasn't sure what was going on with the Fosters, but later that night, when no one else is home, Bill calls me to come over. He has me follow him upstairs to what has become an office of sorts, full of boxes and magazines in stacks, papers piled neatly around a desk.

Behind the tallest pile he finds a box with metal edge protectors. He sits me down, pops the top, then pulls out a stack of letters.

I thumb through them, not getting it at first but then noticing they all have *Return to Sender* stamps. And the addressee? Brett's Aunt Evelyn, Ginny's sister.

"Check the postmarks," Bill says. A year ago, nine months, six months, a few weeks. "Go ahead and read one," he suggests.

I pull out the top letter. It's an invitation to Thanksgiving.

That'd have been a hell of a stretch for Aunt Ev. She's been dead for eight years.

# *brett*

I had to run a few errands, but I call Dad as soon as I get home, and it keeps going to voice mail—meaning he's probably avoiding the whole thing for a while. Or maybe he's on the phone with someone else who wants to know what the hell is going on but doesn't want to hold a group discussion. That'd definitely be *my* style.

I finally reach him after an hour. "Alzheimer's?" I ask after a very long pause.

"I don't know," he replies. "The woman in question, whom your sister mistakenly believed I was having an affair with, is June, a college friend of mine—a married woman whose sister-in-law is suffering from Alzheimer's. She agreed to meet me for coffee, to talk me through some of Mom's symptoms and see if it all added up. Trish saw her giving me a supportive hug and made all the wrong assumptions. You know Trish. She can get a little overprotective, and she jumps to conclusions. I didn't want to say anything to you kids about the Alzheimer's until I knew more, so I just put up with your sister's nonsense while I sorted it out. I made an appointment for Mom to see our doctor later this week, but she seems to be worsening, so I've pushed it up to tomorrow. You can come if you want."

The rest of what he says sounds like Charlie Brown's teacher to me, that *waa-waa* language that's undecipherable. I hear my dad say things like "forgetful" and "disoriented," and they hit me like a Mack truck. You hear statistics—"fourteen percent, one in seven, 1.7 million"—and it seems remote. Like tsunamis hitting faraway islands. As if you're somehow immune. It's like they say: Nothing really happens in the world until it happens to you. He's talking, but none of it makes sense. And strangely, the person I avoided throughout the entire Sears photo shoot is the only person I really want to talk to right now. Not Heather, not Doug. Layla.

After hanging up with my dad, I stare at my broken toaster for about five minutes then lift the phone to call. I hang up before I even dial. I hold the phone in my hand and just stare at it while it gurgles out a new dial tone. How is it, I ask myself, in my moment of greatest need, that my go-to person is her? And how did I lose that?

I know how, and it's my own doing. Worse—I'm not sure if I want to reach out to her because she's the only one I'm used to confiding in or because I really miss her. I've been having these pangs lately, but I just don't know what the right move is. Do I call her? Is that totally selfish? She's going through this, too, though. My mom is just as much a mom to her as she is to me, minus the first fourteen years. And Layla's already lost one mom. Not that my mom's going anywhere. If she was going somewhere, she'd never know how to get there. *Fuck*.

"So this totally wack-a-doo family walks into a Sears . . ." I say, when I hear Layla answer the call.

"Is this a joke?" she says.

"I wish it was," I admit. "How are you?"

"Shitty. How are you?"

"Same."

We both hold the phone in silence. Somehow I feel comforted knowing that she's on the other end, but somehow I don't think she feels the same.

"What do you want, Brett?" she asks.

"I just wanted to talk to you."

"About?" she asks.

"Everything."

"Everything 'us'? Or everything 'your mom'?"

I think for a minute, because I want to be honest, and in probably half that time she knows the answer. She probably knew the answer before she asked the question.

"My mom," I say.

"Yeah," she says. "That's what I thought."

"I'm sorry," I say.

"Me, too." And we sit in silence for another long while. She finally breaks it. "Nothing's for sure. Your dad will take her in for tests, so before we get all of the information, let's not think the worst."

"Always the optimist," I say.

Layla is. Always has been. When I was young and thought I was some brooding Jack Kerouac type, she'd call me on my pessimism. She'd say, "Always the pessimist," and I'd correct her and say, "I'm a realist, man," and she'd laugh at me because she recognized that I wasn't nearly as cool as I thought I was but would never dare tell me.

More silence sets in. Naturally, the first thing that comes to mind never should have left my mouth: "Well, at least Dad's temporarily in the clear on the whole affair thing."

"Huh," is all she says.

*Huh.*

I feel so confused by this new information about my mom. I probably shouldn't be reaching out to Layla, but I don't know any better. I don't know any different. She's always been there. And in a true testament to her character, she hasn't hung up on me yet. Which I damn well know I deserve. She's not talking, though. She's letting me lead the conversation. And I don't know what to say.

I hear her sigh, and I press the phone closer to my ear. Then the reason behind the sigh sinks in and I step outside my self-centeredness and speak up. "I should let you go."

"Okay," she says, and that hurts worse than I thought. Did I want her to say, "No, I'm here, we can stay on the phone"? Probably. But she doesn't owe me that. I've totally destroyed her reality, and here I am trying to lean on her when she's got no one to lean on herself.

"Okay," I say. "Thanks for . . . Just thanks," I say, and I hang up.

# *layla*

I'm not sure what he expects from me. When I saw his name on my phone's caller ID, I desperately wanted to ignore it yet couldn't answer fast enough. And then I couldn't get off the call fast enough.

I don't know my place in the family anymore, but they've been my whole world for so many years that it doesn't seem like now, in this time of possible crisis, that I should back off. At the same time, I can't watch another mother disintegrate. Ginny stepped up and for all intents and purposes has been a mother to me since I lost my own, and the thought of losing Ginny to another horrendous disease is too much to bear.

I know it's the natural order of things to lose one's parents eventually. They always say what a tragedy it is for a parent to outlive their child—but what about the child who is still a child? *That* doesn't feel natural. And certainly not in this lightning-strikes-twice scenario. Not that Ginny is dying, but the mere thought of her being sick or in pain in any way ties me in knots. I find my eyes tearing up at regular intervals for irregular reasons. Like when I'm looking at an inscription on the side of a Starbucks coffee cup. Or when I'm catching up on news stories. Or when I'm breathing.

There's no acceptable reason for this. The fact that this news is happening around the holidays makes it that much more difficult.

# brett

On the way to the doctor's office with my dad and mom, I look out the window at the restaurants, dry cleaners, tire stores, banks, and juice places. For a moment, it seems to me that they are all different now. I'm not sure how, but the world has tilted.

And because of it, I feel that no one should be going about life as though nothing's happened. Maybe the stores should all close so I don't see content, disinterested people wandering about. It's a self-centered thought, that they all should be as bewildered and anxious as we are, somehow. But they're not. It's a strange scene to my mind, which now wants time to stop for a while—and perhaps start going backward. But that's not going to happen, obviously.

I said I wanted to tag along, and as hard as it will be to hear whatever the doctor has to say, it would be even harder not to be there.

Scott and Trish are already waiting when we arrive. The room is tiny. We all cram in, which makes the situation that much more uncomfortable.

"I'm sorry, honey," my mom says to me.

"What? Don't be. This is nothing to be sorry about. It's not your fault."

"I'm just sorry you have to go through this," she says. "I know you're frightened."

"Don't worry about me, Mom," I say. "I'm fine."

I'm not fine. I'm anything but fine. I wish Layla was here right now.

The doctor walks in and introduces himself. Dr. Frankel. He asks us all to take a seat and says that he'll go over everything, but if we have any questions while he's explaining how the testing will go, we should feel free to ask.

"The first thing we're going to do is a CT scan and an MRI," Dr. Frankel says. "We'll do this to rule out tumors, hemorrhages—maybe she had a mild stroke and nobody knew—and hydrocephalus, which can masquerade as Alzheimer's disease."

There. He said it. The dreaded A-word. I heard my mom catch her breath when he said it, which made it that much worse.

He goes on. "These scans can also show the loss of brain mass associated with Alzheimer's disease and other dementias. In Alzheimer's, the region of the brain known as the hippocampus may be disproportionately atrophied. If we see this, then it's pretty straightforward."

"Okay," my mother says.

"We'll do an EEG to detect abnormal brain-wave activity. Typically, an EEG is normal in people with mild Alzheimer's disease. The EEG is, again, meant to rule out other types and causes of dementia, Creutzfeldt-Jakob disease, for instance."

"Okay," she says again.

"Your symptoms do match up with early-onset Alzheimer's. I'll know better when we've examined your scans and administered some tests." He goes on to explain the neuropsychological tests they'll do both as interviews and as paper-and-pencil tests. He tells us these tests will take several hours, and they might agitate my mom. He warns us that she may get frustrated having to answer what seem like obvious questions but that we should reassure her and help keep her calm if anything should arise. These tests are used to determine which areas of cognitive function are impaired and which areas are still intact. They assess memory, reasoning, writing, vision-motor coordination, comprehension, and her ability to express ideas.

There's one thing I notice throughout the visit. It's that my mother says "okay" to everything. That's not who she is. Before now she'd have asked for a second, a third, a seventeenth opinion, called the doctor a fine young man (but a little goofy), and told him the carpet was fine and not at all the problem—but the window treatments were another matter. But she's just accepting of everything the doctor tells her. This is what kills me. Because for every "okay" she utters, the look on her face says otherwise.

For some reason my mom doesn't grasp the severity of the situation. It becomes very apparent to me that until this moment she thought there was another option. That maybe she could just take a bunch of ginkgo and she'd be okay. And yet once she hears everything the doctor says, she's just so resigned.

I feel helpless. I feel scared for her. I'm never comfortable in doctors' offices to begin with, but when I see my mom this vulnerable, it's just too much to take. I notice my dad keeps looking at me to make sure I'm okay, when really the only person we should be concerned about is Mom.

When all is said and done the doctor asks if we have any questions. The only question I can think to ask is *Why?* But I don't ask.

• • •

The tests come back positive. Which sounds so misleading. *Positive.* She has Alzheimer's. The doctor explains the different medicines. He tells us the one he's leaning toward doesn't cure it—nothing does—but it will improve her thinking, memory, attention span, and ability to do simple tasks.

We're all crowded into the same tiny room again as we listen to the doctor give us the results of her memory screening and diagnostic workup. He tells us about her orientation, attention, cognitive skills, and recall. He tells us again that her test results are all consistent with Alzheimer's. Every time he says it I flinch. They can't stop the disease, but they can slow the progression in some people. He tells us of the emotional, physical, and financial challenges of caring for someone with Alzheimer's, and mentions that caregivers are subject to high levels of stress and that we should all do as much research on the subject as possible, which will not only help my mom but will also help us understand and cope.

Then he starts talking about her diet. Says he'd also like her to take vitamin E and vitamin C twice a day, and tells us that a diet rich in omega-3 fatty acids could positively impact cognitive decline. I notice that everything he says is directed at us. Not her. It dawns on me that my mom can no longer take care of herself. And I want to cry.

Instead I storm out. Then I cry.

# *layla*

Trish tells me that Ginny has Alzheimer's, and I sob. I sob for Ginny, for Trish, for Brett, for Scott, for Bill, for me. Trish and I cancel all our appointments that day and cry together. Then we resolve not to be a couple of sad sacks . . . and then cry some more.

# *brett*

Christmas shopping. I fuckin' hate it. It's the one time of year when people bug me, stores with people in them bug me, and parking lots bug me. (Okay, parking's a year-round pain in the ass, but the holidays make it even more fun.) I do feel that people are a little friendlier around Christmastime, but the trade-off isn't worth it. Where do these people hide for the rest of the year, and can they please go back there? And do they really need to bring their screaming kids shopping with them?

I have to buy presents for the family, of course, but a new conundrum has reared its ugly head: What about Heather? Are she and I at Christmas-gift-giving-level seriousness? And if so, wouldn't any gift further emphasize how serious we are? I've heard friends talk about it, and now I can see why they hate when a birthday or gift-giving holiday comes at the beginning stage of a relationship. There's so much pressure. Well, I guess it depends. It can be cool if you're really into the person and want to show how much you dig them. But what if you're tentative? At your own peril, it's wise to avoid at all costs the gift that screams, "I'm feeling really tentative about this!"

And what about Layla? I know under normal circumstances a divorcing couple wouldn't buy gifts for each other, but these aren't normal circumstances, and Layla is positively not normal. I know she's going to be at our house. She's at pretty much every event we have, holiday or otherwise. So do I get her a present? Coal? Do I not bring Heather around? Or do I bring her along to give Layla a strong hint: *You should get one of these, too—and while you're at it, get your own family.*

It's in this throwaway notion—the idea of her finding her own family—that I get a sort of twisted inspiration to go out and do just that. She *does* have a family. I mean, she has a dad out there. Somewhere. Who's to say that if I track her father down and bring him to her it won't be a tearful reunion—the stuff *Oprah* episodes are made of? It'll be a bonus for me if he takes her off my hands. I mean, deep down I know she'd like to have a relationship with the guy. Who wouldn't want a relationship with their father?

Somehow I have it in my mind that this is going to be an epic search, tracking down this long-lost father. But it turns out that pride was the only thing ever really in the way of finding the guy. After a little Internet-aided detective work, and some guesswork about what you'd call yourself if your stage name was Nicky Foxx, I find Nicholas Foxx still living in the area: Hollywood Blvd., Apt. 4G, Hollywood, CA 90028. It angers me when I find this listing. How do you spend your whole life—or at least the last twenty-seven years of it—living twelve minutes from your only daughter and not ever attempt a reconciliation? Sure, Layla didn't hunt him down, either, but one of them was supposed to be the adult. It's probably hard for an already-rejected daughter to imagine anything has changed and to retain that kind of hope.

The phone number isn't listed, but I think a proper visit is in order anyway. I get in my car, marvel at the fact that it still smells like last night's fries—there are no fries like McDonald's fries (though I preferred them when they still were made with beef fat)—and head to Hollywood. I don't even consider what I'm going to say. It's only when I reach his apartment and actually get out of my car that I stop to gather my thoughts. My first thought is that the place is a dump. He's gotta be pushing fifty by now, and this is the best he could do? So much for those rock-star dreams.

There's no possible way I can formulate some momentous, moving introduction in the amount of time I have, so I decide just to wing it.

"Yeah?" someone says through the intercom, and I'm momentarily speechless.

"Uh . . . um . . ."

"I think you got the wrong apartment," he says.

"No, wait!" I shout. "Nicky?" I ask.

"Who wants to know?" he says.

"I'm married to Layla," I say. "I mean . . . yeah. Your daughter, Layla. She's your daughter. I'm her husband. Technically. Still."

Seconds feel like days as I stand there and he doesn't say anything back. Then I hear a loud buzz, so I push the door open and walk in.

It's even dumpier inside than out. There's no elevator, so I walk up four flights of stairs and find the father formerly known as Nick Brennan, currently masquerading as Nicky Foxx, shockingly resembling the face I've spent more time looking at than anything else in my whole life, staring back at me.

"Is she okay?" he asks. He doesn't motion me in.

"Yeah," I say. "She's okay."

He looks me up and down. I imagine he's summing me up—deciding if I'm good enough for his daughter—and I think to myself this guy has a lot of nerve giving me the once-over. I do the same, though. He has her chin—or I guess she has his. And his nose. And his teeth. She always said she never had to wear braces, and I guess he's proof of good dental genetics. His dark brown hair is short and neat, a few streaks of gray at the ends. His mouth hangs slightly open, in either amazement or lifelong exhaustion; I haven't been around him long enough to know which. He wears dark slacks and a plaid shirt unbuttoned over a T-shirt with the faded logo of some diner on it. I'm kind of blown away looking at him.

I only met her mom a few times before she passed away, and that was so long ago, but I remember thinking that Layla had her mother's eyes, that they crinkled at the sides when she smiled and laughed. I thought someday she'd get lines there and be pissed but I'd always think they were beautiful. Like her.

"I'm Brett," I say. "Brett Foster."

"Right," he says. "I knew her last name became Foster. Come on in."

"Thanks," I say, and I follow him to the couch.

"Can I offer you something to drink?" he asks. "I've got whiskey, beer, and maybe some Tropicana, but I'm not sure on the OJ."

"No, thanks," I say. "I'm okay."

"You're a coach, huh?" he asks. "I read something about you taking your team to a few championships."

"Yeah," I say. "But that's not all I do. I mean, it's all I've done. But I've been recently inspired to do something I should have done a long time ago." *Oh, crap. I'm running off at the mouth again. Oh, well.*

"What's that?" he asks.

"Oh, just this business venture. It's a great idea, but I didn't have the bucks to start it for a long time. Finally I just said fuck it and at least got started on making a sample or six so I'd have something to show someone who could actually get me the capital—"

"We should talk," he says. "I always know people with too much money looking for promising ground floors to get in on."

*Huh,* I think. I look around, taking everything in. The place is dark and dusty. Nick has posters of old rock bands—Van Halen, Black Sabbath, Led Zeppelin—all over his walls. There's another of Eric Clapton, and a tapestry hanging from the ceiling. This isn't the home of a fifty-year-old man. Or it shouldn't be. I'm not convinced he can get me the money to make my Wonder Armour. Not that I even came here for that in the first place. I get myself back on track.

"So how's your life?" I ask, hoping he'll say, "Empty. I miss my daughter. I hate myself."

"It's pretty good." So much for that. He goes on, "You probably think I'm an asshole for leaving Layla and her mom."

"No, that's not, *not,* my business," I say. Then, deciding it's absolutely my business, I ask, "Why did you?"

"I had dreams. I had dreams of making it big. I wanted to be out on the road doing gigs, or in the studio every night writing songs with my band, or rehearsing. I couldn't come home every night and take care of a wife and baby. I couldn't do it. I couldn't do both things. So yeah, I was selfish. But the truth is I didn't think I was leaving forever. I thought I was gonna make it. I thought I'd come back with lots of money—I'm talkin' life-altering money—and they'd be pissed, sure, but they'd get over it. And the cars and the clothes would make it that much easier. I wanted to be Eddie Van Halen, you know?"

"Okay," I say, allowing him his side.

"But that didn't happen. And there are so many reasons. One, because there already *was* an Eddie Van Halen. Two, because everybody *else* at that time was also trying to become Eddie Van Halen. Everybody was trying to look like him and play like him and sound like him . . . and nobody did it as good as he did. Then it was like everybody kept trying to one-up Eddie. Playing faster and louder and longer . . . it became too much. Eddie was the perfect blend of everything a guitar player should be. He was technical, yet he played from the heart. It was natural. But all these guys kept getting so technical. Does that make sense?"

"I guess." I shrug, not sure what Eddie Van Halen has to do with his abandoning his wife and two-year-old.

"It's like, let's say you get a scoop of vanilla ice cream and you love it. It's the best thing you've ever had. So the next day you want it again. But this time you put hot fudge on it. And that's great, too—it's even better than the plain vanilla. So then you add strawberries to it, and then peanuts or cereal or fuckin' M&M's. Before you know it you've got this crap in your bowl, everything's overpowering the one good thing you started with, and all you want is a fuckin' bowl of vanilla ice cream."

"Right," I say. He does have a point.

"So I tried inventing my own thing. But by the time I realized that I needed to do that, music had changed. MTV had its stranglehold. The music business changed forever. For record companies it was great. But from the point of view of a musician, it was the worst thing that ever happened to the business. It took an auditory art and made it visual. When you walk into an art gallery and you look around at the walls, you're checking out a visual art. When you buy a record—we had records back then—and you listen to it, that's what you call an auditory art. That's what music was supposed to be: something that stimulated your auditory senses. But MTV took music and made it a visual art, and it became more important to the audience what you looked like than what they were listening to. I wasn't about that. I was about good music. Quality music. Not a three-minute movie. It got to the point where artists were writing songs with the visual of the video in mind, not thinking, *Is this a good song?* Music isn't supposed to appeal to your eyes or your nose or your sense of touch. It's supposed to appeal to your ears."

"Right," I say. I'm not sure if I should cut him off.

"So one night I was playing in a Night Ranger tribute band, and one of the managers at the club knew I was getting burned out. He knew I needed cash and offered me a job a couple nights a week doing sound, and I took it. And I've been doing that now for almost twenty years."

I listen to him go on and on about this stuff, and in a way it makes me hate him less, knowing that, at the very least, the thing he left Layla and her mom for was something he lived, ate, and breathed. He didn't just pick up and start another family somewhere, like some people's parents I know. He had a dream. It just didn't work out.

"Probably more than you wanted to know," he says, a bit embarrassed. He lights his third cigarette since I've been here. "I always say, *don't get me started on music*."

"It's interesting. But it's not why I'm here," I admit.

"For the record: Honestly, I thought I'd make it. I thought I'd make it and make them proud and come back and spoil them rotten." He taps his lip with his thumb, and I can swear he's breathing more heavily. "But that didn't happen. And of course when you're trying to live the rock-star dream, you get mixed up in some bad shit. I was doing drugs back then. A lot of drugs. So was everyone I knew. And I had friends who were divorced and saw their kids, and they'd get high before they picked them up for visitations. I knew I didn't want to be *that* guy. The last thing I wanted to do was be hangin' with my kid and have to sneak off to do a line in some bathroom. And then, God forbid, get in a car with her and drive her home. I couldn't risk that. So I stayed away.

"Yeah, I got clean, but so much time had passed by then. I was ashamed. I felt like a loser. And I don't feel like a loser in *any* other area of my life. So I guess it's partially pride, but it's also because . . . you know . . . I've kept tabs on her. From a distance. I know she's okay. I may be an asshole, but I feel like she's probably better off without me. I've been watching. I know she has a new life. Your life. Your family."

"Well, Nick, or Mr. Foxx . . . if you don't mind me saying so, you're right," I tell him. He brightens a little. "You're an asshole."

He squints at me as if he's winding up to say something, then just chews his lower lip and nods.

"But in life, we sometimes get second chances," I go on. "And where Layla is concerned, it may just be time to get the band back together. . . ."

# *layla*

Christmas Eve. Probably my favorite day of the year. Usually. At the Fosters', we've always had a tradition of opening up one present each on Christmas Eve and saving the rest for Christmas morning. Granted, this is a childish ritual done mostly for the benefit of impatient kids, but Brett, Trish, Scott, and I were all just big kids anyway, so we never discarded it. I love the warmth, the smells, the food, the excitement, the house full of people—everything. It's the perfect day. And as it only comes once a year, I always try to wake up at the crack of dawn to make it last that much longer, to get the full experience, to milk the day for every last second.

I don't know how it's going to go this year, things being as they are, but I walk into the Fosters' house determined this time to maintain my dignity, what with my little meltdown at Thanksgiving. I've had a few months now to get used to the separation, and I'm dealing with it a little better. I feel pretty confident that Heather won't be there, since she wasn't at Thanksgiving and now Brett's dealing with his sick mother. I also like to think he'd leave that line uncrossed. Bringing a date to the corn maze was one thing, but holidays are sacred. And this being my most favorite holiday . . . well, I just feel relieved knowing it's for family only.

Of course the first thing I see when I walk in is Heather. So much for Brett having a conscience. Or class. Or any regard for my feelings, my heart, or my favorite day of the year.

"Hello, everybody," I say. "And Heather."

There is a chorus of hellos back to me, but the only one I can hear is Heather. Maybe because the devil is speaking through her.

"Hello, Layla. Nice to see you again."

*Vermin. Scum. Home wrecker.* That's what I want to say back to her. I say nothing, though. I try to smile and accidentally bite my lip, which I know will turn into a canker sore in two days, and I hate her even more. *Whore.*

Dinner is awkward and painful, and I don't know my place. I'm watching Heather be included in things she has no business being included in, and nothing tastes good. I can barely get the food down, and I fake smiles and hardly speak through the whole meal.

"Layla," Ginny says, as she clears her plate. "Come."

I take my plate and follow Ginny into the kitchen, and although no words are spoken, there's plenty being said. We immediately get into a rhythm with the dessert prep, and I feel like I can breathe again. We always bake fresh gingerbread cookies right after dinner, so they're hot off the press when we open our one gift. Then Scott always launches one of his ritualistic lines: "Check it out, Dad," he'll say, "you always wanted us to get ahead in the world," and he'll bite the head off the gingerbread man. Every one of us shakes his or her head, but it still makes me feel good.

Ginny pushes two bowls toward me: one in which she's already mixed the flour, salt, baking soda, and spices; the other is empty, but she knows I'll pick up where she's left off. The second bowl will be for creaming butter, sugar, eggs, and light molasses.

While I'm going to town on the wet ingredients with the electric mixer, Ginny is lightly flouring the surface for me to roll the dough once it's ready. It's somehow calming—the rolling and the flattening—even if I am imagining that the rolling pin is a Mack truck and the dough is Heather's face.

I roll the pin harder and faster until Ginny notices and starts to laugh. "What are you doing to that poor gingerbread?" she asks, playfully touching my nose with a flour-coated finger.

"I'm . . . What?"

"It's supposed to be a quarter-inch thick when you cut the men out," she says. "Not paper-thin."

"I hope you're making gingerbread women, too," I hear Trish say from behind me. I turn and give her a hug.

"Do we have women, Gin?" I ask.

Ginny just looks blankly at me.

"I'm gonna take that as a no," I say.

"Sexist pigs," Trish mutters, and she swipes her finger in the bowl, samples some of the leftover gingerbread dough, and prances out.

I look at the flattened dough and realize that it would be impossible to cut cookies out of it, so I scrape it all up—it really is quite thin—and make a new ball to roll, this time being careful not to take out any aggression.

Once I've rolled and cut the cookies, I get to my favorite part: decorating them. I put M&M's on for eyes—which I suppose are technically larger than gingerbread people's eyes, but if they have a thyroid condition, they could potentially have big buggy eyes like that, or at least that's what I tell myself. I look up at Ginny as I place the last set, and pop a handful of leftover candies into my mouth. I feel a calm just being there with her.

Until *she* walks in.

"Can I help with anything?" Heather asks.

"No, I think we've got it," I say.

"Okay," she says, and scampers out like the rat she is.

I follow her outside about a minute later, and I find everyone seated in the living room.

"When are we doing presents?" Scott says, and turns to me. "I wanna open my present from Layla."

"Who says I got you anything, twerp?" I tease.

"You don't fool me," Scott says. "You always get me the best gifts."

It's true. I do pride myself on my gift-giving—which, if we got psychological, could say something about me, although I have no idea what. I always go out of my way to get great gifts for people. I like getting people nice things but, more important, well-thought-out things. Like, Ginny loves scented soaps and lotions, so I will get her those as a stocking stuffer. But I truly believe soap along with candles is a cop-out gift. The gift that says: I didn't want to think really hard about this, so here is a candle/bath set/whatever. Nice enough, especially if the person goes through them like Ginny, but I'd never give that as a main present. Who among us doesn't want to feel at least a little like people went out of their way for us?

"Okay, it's true," I say. "I brought gifts." I look to Heather. "I didn't get you anything. I'm sorry."

"That's okay," she replies. "I didn't get you anything, either."

"I got you *both* something," Brett says. And he hands Heather a wrapped package that I know he didn't handle himself because he has the wrapping skills of Edward Scissorhands.

"Should I open this now?" she asks.

"Sure," Brett says, and I want to hurl. I seriously feel the bile creeping up.

"It's so nicely wrapped!" Heather coos, and I bite my tongue and watch as she tries to open the gift without tearing the paper.

Just rip the paper. *Rip the fucking paper!* I want to scream. But then I have to laugh.

"Bath products!" Heather squeals. "And a candle!"

He got her bath products. *Ha!* I look to Trish, and we share a knowing smile. Then Brett slides a gift in front of me. It's an almost identical-looking package. Did he get us both the same thing? Am I on equal footing with Heather? Is she on equal footing with me? Did he get me fucking bath products? And a candle? He couldn't. He wouldn't.

He did.

There. Are. No. Words.

"I got you something else," he says, checking his watch.

*Thank God. Thank the Lord. Thank Jesus and Moses and Oprah.* I knew I meant more to him than that. Than *her*.

Brett gets up and walks out of the room. Odd. Must be a big gift, I think. Then he walks out of the house. Did he buy me a new car? Is he standing, James Bond–like, in the driveway, staring back at the house with a self-satisfied smirk on his face, his finger poised above the button on a remote-control device for the explosives he's secreted away in the fruitcake?

The discomfort level in the room, already about a seven on a one-to-ten scale because of the still extremely awkward situation among Brett, Heather, and me, is steadily rising through the midteens toward twenty. Why did he get me anything at all? We're through, and in this uneasy truce we've negotiated for sharing the earth's most precious resource—my adopted family—I know I'm accepted and yet the natural first one to be let go. Last in, first out: the option and not the necessity. If he really understood the power he possesses to push me aside, he could just start getting closer to them—

Aha! That's it. This is his new strategy: appear decent, show kindness to Layla, quit alienating the blood relatives, and the bloodless one will be easier to let go. It's brilliant, coming as it does during the holidays, when most people's emotions are spinning just a bit out of their normal orbit and meltdowns are peering around every corner like kids trying to catch a glimpse of Santa Claus.

A minute later, Brett walks in with a strange look on his face. It's a look I don't recognize, and I feel like I'm pretty well versed in the many expressions of Brett. He stands in the doorway and stares at me.

"Layla?" he says. "I got you something extra-special. Something I know you weren't expecting, yet something I think you'll appreciate."

"Wow," I say. "Quite a preamble."

"Well, it's quite a gift," he says.

"Way to blow up her expectations." Scott laughs. "This thing better be pretty freakin' good."

Brett steps out of our line of sight and then reappears a few seconds later with that same look on his face. "Layla," he says, "I know how important family is to you, so I present to you . . . your father."

Everything feels like it's moving in slow motion. I feel my heartbeat, and I think I can even hear it. I wonder if anyone else can. *Is this really happening?* I see Brett stepping aside, but is my father going to materialize in his place? My *father*? Whom I haven't seen in more than twenty-five years?

Sure enough, in walks a man who I guess is my father. I haven't seen him since God knows when. I don't have any memories of a relationship with him, and can only recognize him from pictures my mom had. He's aged but not too terribly. He's older for sure. I look at his face, the wrinkles, his lips, his eyes. I look to see if I see myself in this strange person who was once my dad, but I can't look too long. I don't want to look too long. He doesn't deserve that long a look. He doesn't deserve anything. I think a million things and feel even more. The conflicting emotions are short-circuiting my brain.

"Layla?" the man says.

I can't say a thing. I'm speechless. I'm angry. At him. At Brett. At Christmas. I look at Ginny and Bill. I look at Trish and Scott. I can't look at Brett, and I'm loath to look at Heather—how dare he allow her to be in the mix when he thrusts my long-lost father before me? I turn to my father to sneak one last look, then run out the back door and drive away.

• • •

I spend Christmas Day in bed, ignoring all phone calls from the Fosters. The holiday has been ruined forever.

I got Brett a signed Troy Aikman football jersey. His hero. Number eight. I hate myself for going above and beyond and getting kicked in the gut in return. Why did I feel the need to still get him something so nice? If I wasn't at my wits' end when I ran out of there, I'd have grabbed the gift bag and taken it back. And then donated it to some charity. Maybe he didn't open it.

Though I wouldn't have admitted it before—in fact, I'd have sworn the opposite, that it was meant to shame him with my goodness—I put a lot of thought, and dare I say love, into that gift. That's evaporated like snow on Santa Monica Boulevard. I hate Brett Foster.

*Wow.* I've never felt that before. Maybe that was what I needed to get past this, to get past him. Maybe he did me a favor? If the inspiration to stay inside for the better part of a week and gain four pounds in the process is a favor.

New Year's Eve I stay home. Brooke, who's back six weeks early from Vancouver, due to some complications on set that apparently involved a megaphone, Mountain Dew, and the director, tries to get me to go out with her, but there's no way I'm going out to ring in the New Year (curious as I am to hear what fresh hell she'd gotten into). This is the first time I haven't spent New Year's Eve with Brett since I was sixteen. I watch a bunch of bad television, and also *Forrest Gump,* which always makes me cry. Brett hates the movie, and so it seems fitting that it's on and I'm enjoying it.

Ginny calls my cell phone at 12:01. I look at her name on my caller ID and almost don't answer. But I can't ignore her calls anymore. We haven't even spoken since Christmas.

"Hi, honey," she says. "Happy New Year!"

"What's so happy about it?" I reply.

"Oh, come on now. Where are you?"

"I'm home, Ginny," I say.

"Oh, dear . . ."

"What?"

"I'm used to catching you out having fun with Brett in some loud place."

"Well," I answer, "I'm sure there's a good possibility that Brett *is* out having fun in some loud place. Just not with me."

"This isn't right," Ginny says. "It's just not . . . Bill?"

I hear her shuffling, and the phone sounds like she's covering it with her hand.

"Hello?" I say.

"Honey, do you want me to come over?" she asks.

"No, no, I think it's time I separate."

"What do you mean?" she asks.

"I just think . . ." I pause to gather my thoughts. I haven't really thought it through at all; it's just sort of coming to me as I say it, but it feels right. "I think it's time I move on. Tomorrow is the first day of a new year. And I think it's time I actually . . . well . . . change out of the pajamas I've been wearing for three days, but also, you know. I think you know."

"I do," she says. "And I don't like it one bit."

"I don't, either, Ginny," I say. "But after what he did—"

"Would you believe I think he meant well?"

"I would believe that you believe it, but I don't believe that he did."

We sit in silence on the phone for a long while.

"I love you, Ginny," I say, and I start to cry because it feels like I'm ending more than the phone call.

"I love you, too, Angel," she says. "I'm here for you always."

"I know," I say. And I hang up. I don't say the word *good-bye*. I can't.

# brett

New Year's Eve. Amateur night. The pressure is unbearable. I've never liked being around idiot drunk people under any circumstances, and it just so happens that about seventy percent of the populace is idiot drunk people on New Year's Eve, making beer-goggled bad decisions before resolving to stop making bad decisions in the following year.

You're trying way too hard to have fun, spending absurd amounts of money to get into places you otherwise would never want to go, drinking far more than you would on any other night, pretending that Ryan Seacrest is entertaining—and if that wasn't depressing enough, you have to listen to drunken, slurred renditions of "Auld Lang Syne" and "Good Riddance (Time of Your Life)."

If you're married, you have to spend a fortune on the night so that you and your wife can swear that next year you're staying home. Just like you swore you'd do last year. If you're single, you run the very real risk of waking up in a bed with a person of the opposite sex who may or may not have been a first or even fifteenth choice, had you not been drunk, a person of the same sex who may have jump-started your experimentation phase—one that you'd never even considered before and now unfortunately can't remember, or a person of indeterminate sex, which, well, that's just not good news for anyone. (I won't tell you which of my friends has passed along these stories of single New Year's Eves. Because Jared would hate me for that.) Anyway, New Year's Eve is a bad, bad night.

When I was a kid I loved it, of course. It was an excuse to party. Then the good times were far outweighed by the bad. Like the year my hangover lasted two full days, during which time I was unable to get out of bed except to clamber to the bathroom, eyes still shut, hoping my aim was decent, begging to be shot in the head. Or the time I lost my car in Tijuana. Or of course the time Scotty had the bright idea to mix Jägermeister and Goldschläger, a combination that inspired the "wet T-shirt contests are sexist" wet T-shirt contest that involved Scott, his friends, my friends, and myself (all male) climbing up onto a bar for an impromptu wet T-shirt contest, resulting in not one but two people slipping off the bar, onto the floor, and breaking limbs—an arm for young Scotty and a leg for Duane Gustovsen, who coincidentally never hung out with us again.

But now I couldn't give a shit. Now it's just another day of the week. Yet this one reminds me that another year is ending, I've gotten a year older, and I've accomplished much less than I wanted to.

But of course Heather asks me what we're doing, so the pressure is on. Fucking New Year's. Which brings up another point. I wonder if she's expecting that our big "third-date" night will happen then.

"What do *you* want to do?" I ask, trying to put it back on her.

"Go out," she says. "Have fun . . . drink way too much . . ."

I search her face for a hint of irony, hoping against hope that she's kidding and she'll say so any second. Nope. Nothing.

"Cool," I say. "Have you heard about anything fun happening?

Anywhere specific you'd like to go?" Where I can spend hundreds of dollars on mediocre food and, even worse, give my credit card in advance so they can fuck me starting rightthissecond?

"I have some friends who are going to the Viceroy," she says. "That sounds fun."

"We haven't really commingled the friends yet," I say, half kidding. "Are you sure New Year's is the best time to do this?"

"Why not?"

And that's how I find myself at the Viceroy, having spent one hundred ninety-five dollars per person to get in, fifteen dollars on parking, and then to my astonishment learn that none of this includes the dinner that we apparently signed up for: a two-hundred-fifty-dollar-per-person four-course dinner that includes a champagne toast and entrance to the New Year's Eve celebration at nine-thirty p.m. Turns out what I paid for in advance was the "celebration," which is nonrefundable and would have been included in the dinner package. But now I'm out nine hundred five dollars.

This alone starts the evening off on the wrong foot, because of course I can't complain—I'm not an asshole, nor am trying to be one—but this is a predicament Layla and I would never have found ourselves in. Layla hates things like this. And the idea of spending that kind of money for one meal and the privilege to celebrate somewhere would make her as sick as it makes me.

But Heather isn't Layla.

"This is Krista," Heather says, as she introduces me to one of her girlfriends.

"Hi, Krista," I say.

"And this is Kelly and Stacia," she says, with regard to the two other girls who are with us.

What Heather didn't tell me was that I would essentially be attending girls' night out with her and her three friends, who would talk incessantly about bad dates, online sample sales, and weight gain. Did these girls scare off all their boyfriends? How are all of them single? Why are all of them single? Were they hoping I'd help them attract other men?

I sit and force smiles through all four courses, checking my watch constantly, praying for time to move faster. Heather doesn't include me in much of the conversation, or if she does, it's to explain who this person is in this story that they are telling—a person I will never meet and a story that can't end fast enough.

I sit next to Heather and really take her in. I'm usually so involved in the time we spend together, be it in conversation or activity, that I haven't had a lot of time to sit back and assess all that is Heather. She's pretty. She's very pretty. And she has a fairly good sense of humor. Most of the time. But her laugh kind of bothers me. It's not totally annoying, it's just not Layla's laugh. And she doesn't laugh at my dad's jokes the way Layla does. And it used to bug the shit out of me when Layla would humor my dad, because I felt like it encouraged him, but when Heather didn't laugh at my dad's jokes it really bummed me out.

"What do you get when you put together a brown chicken and a brown cow?" her friend Stacia asks when the ladies have clearly had a lot to drink.

"I don't know," they all say.

"You get a brownchickenbrowncow," Stacia says, but she says it in the onomatopoeic imitation of the generic porn riff: *bown-chicka-wow-wow.*

I admit I have told this joke before, and I do get a kick out of it, but for the rest of the night I'm surrounded by four drunk women who think it is just high-larious to yell *brownchickenbrowncow* over and over. And over and over. It's no longer funny. Or cute. And unless it's going to lead to a fivesome upstairs in one of the hotel rooms, it is seriously working my last nerve.

The "celebration" part of the evening consists of me watching Heather dance with her friends, me losing Heather for the good part of an hour, and Krista drunk-dialing her ex-boyfriend. When he refuses to meet her there, she melts down, resulting in Heather deciding that she should go home with Krista to be a good friend. And I should go home alone.

On my way home, some drunk idiot bumps into my car at a red light. Of course he does.

"I thought it was turning green," he says.

"They all do eventually," I reply, lacking the energy to throttle him.

After all is said and done I get home at three a.m. And I'm pretty clear in my head that I don't want to go out with Heather again. I wrestle with whether or not to call her and end things tonight or wait until tomorrow to do it. Which is less assholeish? Ruining her New Year's Eve? I mean, this way she can really bond with poor Krista. Or New Year's Day? That seems worse somehow: It starts her year off on a bad note. I pick up the phone to call her.

"Heather?" I say.

"Hey, you . . ." she slurs.

"How's Krista?"

"She's okay," she says. "You know, men are jerks."

*Funny you should mention that,* I think, but out loud I say, "That they are."

"But not you." She giggles.

"No, I'm one, too," I correct.

"No, you're not, you sillysilly," she says.

Layla never would have called me a sillysilly. I feel even more strongly about what I need to do.

"Oh, but I am," I say. "I can prove it."

"How?" she asks.

"Well," I say, "I think that maybe it's too soon for me to be dating. And you're such a great girl, you don't want to be a rebound. You deserve better."

"Oh my God, are you breaking up with me? On New Year's Eve?"

"I did debate whether to do it tonight or tomorrow. I thought this was the lesser of two evils."

"There's only one evil on this phone call, and it's you!" Heather shouts.

"Good one!" Krista screams in the background.

"Well," I say, "okay, I'll take that."

"I can't believe you, Brett," she says. "I can't believe you're doing this."

"I'm sorry," I say. I already feel guilty enough about Layla. This is the last thing I need. I don't say this to her, of course.

"Whatever," she says, and hangs up. And I think it's over. But then she and Krista prank-call me until six a.m. Which would have been much more effective if they'd been sober enough to use the code that blocks caller ID.

I'm woken by another call at seven a.m. on New Year's Day. I'm certain it won't be the Drunk-Dialing Duo, because the lull in calls for the past hour leads me to believe that they've finally passed out, so I answer.

"Top o' the year to ya," a chipper, unfamiliar male voice says.

"And to you?" I reply, my pitch raised to suggest I have no idea who I'm talking to.

"It's Nick," he clarifies. "Foxx. Layla's—"

"Hi," I cut him off. "Happy New Year."

"Yes, it will be," he says. "Listen—you got a business plan for that idea of yours?"

"Not a *plan* plan," I say. "Not in writing or anything."

"Get one," he says. "And have it ready in a week for a meeting with a buddy of mine."

"Okay," I say, and we hang up.

I'm not sure why he's taken such an interest in me and my idea, and if he wants a piece of it or if he's really just trying to help his friend out. I do need something, anyway, some sort of business plan. I just hadn't gotten that far. I make a mental note to put a call in to a buddy when it's not seven a.m. to enlist his help in rushing together a design package and a little market analysis, and to also get some basic financials from Katie Hu—Ms. Manziere—so it sounds like I actually know what I'm talking about.

• • •

Twenty minutes later there's a pounding on my front door. I'm convinced that I was wrong about them having passed out and it's going to be Heather and Krista, unable to sleep, still drunk, and pissed off. I open the door and to my surprise find Layla, with two cups of coffee in her hands and a bag from Western Bagels.

Western Bagels are an L.A. staple. There are actually eleven Western Bagel stores in L.A. but only one is open twenty-four hours. You can go there anytime, day or night, and their bagels are fresh out of the oven. I'd say at least once or twice a month we'd have bagels and a shmear from Western.

"This is a nice surprise," I say.

Layla hands me the bag and one of the coffees.

"You want to come in?" I ask.

"No," she says. "I'm sure you have company, and I don't want to . . . I just wanted to say something to you, and I wanted to do it in person."

"I don't have company," I say.

"I still don't want to come in."

"Okay."

"Happy New Year," she says.

"You, too," I answer.

Layla looks past me into my apartment and then back at me.

"I want a divorce," she says.

"Yeah," I say, confused. "We're getting one."

"No, I mean, I want it now. I want the divorce. From you, your family . . . everything."

I feel like I just got the wind knocked out of me.

"Okay," I manage to utter.

"You're moving on," she says. "I get it."

"Well, actually—" I start to say, but she plows right through my sentence.

"I'll agree to a no-fault divorce. We can forget everything I ever did. Forget my stupid case. My *custody,*" she says, with a derisive tone, as if she's suddenly disgusted by herself.

"Well," I say, "I'm sure you'll still spend time with my family."

"No," she says with resolve. "I'm giving your family back to its rightful owner. You can have them back. They're all yours."

"They're yours, too," I say, so surprised I can't pull together a coherent counterpoint. Suddenly, all I want is for her to still want my family.

"No," she says. "They're yours. You found mine for me, remember? So you win. I'm gone." And with that she turns and walks away.

I stand there holding the bag of bagels and the coffee, wondering what just happened. Wondering if all this time I never realized that there was some reality where Layla wouldn't be firmly entrenched in my life. Some awful unthinkable reality.

*What the fuck just happened?*

# *layla*

There was something so freeing about giving Brett his family back that for the first time I feel like I can breathe. I feel almost dizzy with freedom. Who was I kidding? They were never really mine to begin with.

I call Brooke and tell her to meet me at Runyon Canyon for a hike. It's a new year. I can start it off healthfully, let go of the past, breathe in the fresh air, take in the beauty of the mountains. It all feels natural and cleansing, like I'm exactly where I'm supposed to be. Except the altitude mixed with the cardio makes me feel a little light-headed once we get halfway to the top. I used to hike Runyon all the time. Am I this out of shape? Have I let myself go in marriage? *Gah!* I swore I'd never be that person. Well, not anymore. I stop and take a drink from my water bottle, and we keep going.

"Where are all the hot single guys?" Brooke asks, as she steps over a pile of something brown and gooey. "And has every dog in Los Angeles come here to take a shit? Seriously. I've seen more piles of crap than trees!"

"I don't know," I say.

"It's disgusting."

"I guess I'm used to it, being around animals all the time."

"I see no hot men." She sighs. "This is a total waste."

"We're here to get exercise. To start the year off positively."

Brooke looks at me like I'm possessed. "I was just near Vancouver, remember? Outdoorsy. Women, Lord help them, wear skirts and tennis shoes. I had plenty of positive healthiness. Wait a minute—are you on antidepressants?"

"No, you jerk," I answer. "I'm just trying to start the new year off on the right foot."

"Well, your right foot just stepped in dog shit."

• • •

When I part ways with Brooke, I drive to Ralphs supermarket and seek out black-eyed peas and donuts. The black-eyed peas because of my Southern college roommate. She'd say, "Remember, eating black-eyed peas on New Year's Day brings good luck for the entire year!" It's apparently an American tradition down there. And me, being a sucker for traditions, always went along with it. But somewhere along the way I stopped. Now, feeling like it's high time my luck changes, I'm all for it.

The donuts are because I once read somewhere that the Dutch believed that eating donuts on New Year's Day would bring good fortune. The ring of the donut symbolizes "coming full circle," completing a year's cycle. I suppose by that logic I could have just taken one of the bagels that I brought Brett, but this feels better. I can say good-bye to last year—the last many years—by giving my past the bagel, and by giving myself the donut. Plus, who are we kidding? Donuts taste better.

I want to start this year with a clean slate. So it's with that in mind that I decide to call my father. Ginny called me after I ran out of the house and left his information on my voice mail, "in case I changed my mind." I'm not sure I have, but I am sure that I didn't handle that situation at all well, and if he has something to say to me, I suppose I can listen.

"Yello," he says, when he answers his phone.

"Hello, Nick?" I say.

"This is."

"Hi," I say. "It's Layla."

There's a pause. I wonder if my crazy reaction pissed him off, if now he doesn't want to talk to me. I probably wouldn't want to talk to me, either.

"I'm really glad to hear from you," he says.

"Okay," I say.

And we arrange for him to come to my house.

• • •

It's so odd to call this man my father. This man who's looking around my house, picking up photographs—pictures from events that he damn well should have attended—and smiling at them. I watch him check the place out, and as he does this I check *him* out: his face, his posture, his wrinkles from not wearing sunblock.

He turns, holding a wedding photo of Brett and me.

"You look beautiful," he says. "Was it a nice wedding?"

"It was everything I wanted." *With the exception of having a father to walk me down the aisle,* I think to myself. But Bill did it, and the day was still every bit as perfect. There's nothing to be gained from getting digs in.

"I'm glad," he says, and he reaches into his pocket and pulls out a newspaper clipping. He holds it out to me and I see that it's my wedding announcement.

"Hey, I remember that," I say. I look at it, yellowed and torn. *He's carried this with him all these years?*

"As feeble as it sounds, I always loved you," he says wistfully. "You were always my little girl."

"Not so much a little girl anymore," I say, and I walk to the kitchen, where my black-eyed peas are simmering.

"Not anymore," he echoes. "It makes me feel old."

I stir the peas. I don't know what to say to that. I don't know what to say to him. I don't know if there's something he wants to say to me, or if Brett simply badgered him into coming around so I'd get the hell away from the Fosters. I walk back out and see him holding another photograph, and it looks like he wipes a tear away from his right eye, but I could be wrong.

"I keep your wedding announcement in my wallet," he says, "as a reminder that you turned out well, that you had a good life, but also as a reminder of my failure, so I don't forget how I abandoned you."

"Well," I say. "Yeah."

"I'm ashamed of myself. What I did."

"You should be."

"It was shitty," he says. "It was selfish. And I'm sorry."

I take this in. I don't know what to say back. It's okay? It *wasn't* okay. It wasn't okay for him to leave us. It wasn't okay for me to lose my only other parent and have to deal with it on my own, when my father was potentially in the same zip code.

"You don't have to forgive me," he says. "I don't forgive me, either."

"I don't see a point in holding on to anger," I say. "Really, it's been so long. I mean . . ."

"I know," he says quietly. "But I'd like you to tell me how you feel. How you felt. I'd like you to have the opportunity to express what you feel."

"I feel like it's been twenty-five years," I say, not wanting to get into anything heavy.

"It has, but I think I have twenty-five more in me," he says. "Maybe we can start from here. I'm not saying I'm going to win any father-of-the-year awards, but I'd like to try to be in your life. If you'll have me."

How do you start a relationship with your father as a grown, married, soon-to-be-divorced woman? What does that even look like? Do you go through scrapbooks and catch each other up on everything you missed? Do you start as if this is the first day of your life and pretend the past doesn't exist?

"I'm making black-eyed peas," I say. Completely off topic, but I just don't know how to respond. Of course I want a dad. But I don't know this man. This man is a stranger.

"And you don't have to decide right now," he says. "I just want you to know that if you have any interest in having a relationship with me, I would love that. That it would mean the world to me. And I know you don't owe me anything—I know that."

I start to feel nauseated. I don't know if it's the donuts I ate for good luck turning out not to be such good luck or if it's the stress of this situation, but it comes on suddenly, and I feel nauseated and clammy and almost like I'm going to faint. Or throw up. Or both.

And I do. I run to the bathroom and throw up.

"Hey, are you okay?" my father says. *Nick* says. I don't know what to call him.

"I am," I say, as I wash my face and brush my teeth. I come out and shrug at him. "I ate three donuts today. For good luck. For the new year. It's a Dutch tradition."

"Is your husband Dutch?"

"No," I say. "I just thought I needed some good luck this year."

He smiles at this. Cocks his head. "You remind me of your mother," he says.

I burst into tears. I've had nobody say this to me . . . ever. I have no relatives who knew her, and it's the biggest compliment and probably the most comforting thing I've ever heard. I remind him of my mother. The most amazing woman in the world.

He walks to me and hugs me. It feels nice. But I feel ill. Too many emotions. Sensory overload. I hear an odd ringing in my ears and everything starts to dim.

And the next thing I know I'm on the floor, my head propped in Nick's lap, while he has a cell phone in his hand and is frantically talking to a nine-one-one operator.

. . .

I lie on the bed in the freezing-cold room they took me to and wonder if this is it for me, if I inherited a weak system from my mother, if I'm going to die. I'm afraid and antsy and frustrated at how long it's taking the doctor to come in, and angry at my father for suddenly being here and seeing me in this vulnerable position.

"I feel like this is my punishment for leaving you all those years ago," he says, genuine tears in his eyes.

"Well, I'd say between the two of us, I'm getting the worst of the punishment about right now."

"Does she have any allergies?" the nurse asks. Nick looks at me, pained and clueless.

"My dad sees the role of father as more of an emeritus/figurehead/sperm donor position," I reply.

The nurse looks at us blankly.

"I don't have any allergies," I answer.

"I'm sorry," he says.

"Stop saying that," I grouse.

"Okay."

He walks to the window. We remain in silence for a long while.

"Do you want me to leave?" he finally asks. "I don't want to, but I will if you want."

"No," I say. "I don't have anyone else."

He walks to me and gently touches my head. He starts running his fingers softly through my hair, moving it away from my face. I close my eyes. It feels nice. Then a doctor pulls back the curtain and steps in.

"I'm Dr. Trevino," he says, and smiles widely at us. "I've just looked over all of the preliminary test results. You're fine. Everything's fine. And I have wonderful news. You two are going to be parents."

"Oh, *God,* no," my father says, laughing very nervously. "I lost my parenting license a long time ago. I got fixed during Reagan's first term."

"TMI," I say.

"This is my daughter," Nick clarifies. "I got snipped right after she was born."

"No offense taken," I say, clearly offended.

"Then you're about to become a grandfather," Dr. Trevino announces. "Congratulations."

I look at my father in shock. He's beaming with pride. I'm stunned. Speechless. How can this be happening? I knew I'd missed a couple periods, but that's happened in the past during times of shock, and with everything going on with Brett and the Fosters, I just . . . I don't know what to say. I have no words. Except: "Did you shut off the stove before we left?" I ask my father. "The black-eyed peas."

• • •

The phone rings when I get home, and it's Bill. I wrestle with answering. Here I have my real dad in my house and my surrogate dad calling me.

I answer. "Hey, Bill," I say, trying my best not to sound pregnant.

"Hi, baby," he says. "Do you have some time?"

"Sure," I say. "Of course."

"It's Ginny," he says. And it sounds like he's crying.

"What is it? Did something happen?"

"No. It's just . . . I'm losing her," he says. "She canceled her bridge club. You know how much she loves her bridge club. But she kept forgetting little things last time and was embarrassed. It's breaking my heart."

"I know," I say. "I'm so sorry."

"Me, too," he says.

I have news that might brighten his spirits. He's going to be a grandfather. But I just don't feel like I can tell him. I've only known for a few hours myself, and I need time to process it all.

We hang up, and my father looks at me.

"You didn't tell him," he says.

"I know."

"This is good news, isn't it?" he asks.

Yes. It's good news. All I ever wanted was a family of my own. A real family. My flesh and blood. I always dreamed of the day when Brett and I would get pregnant and bring a life into the world. A little piece of each of us. Forever blended together. Forever bonding us that much more.

But now? How am I supposed to feel? I have so many mixed emotions. Yes, I'm thrilled to have a baby. But I'm going to be a single parent? That's what I land on. And that's what I tell my father.

"It's great news in theory," I say. "It's all I've ever wanted."

"Then I'm thrilled for you," he says.

"But this isn't how it was supposed to be," I go on. "I was supposed to be happily married. I was supposed to do this with a partner. I know what it's like to be raised in a single-parent household. I know the stress it put on my mom, and I know how it felt for me."

"I get it," he says. "You didn't have a father. But that baby sure as hell is going to have the world's best grandfather." He almost seems happy.

For me, it's a look into a future hell of chasing babysitters, missing recitals, trading weekends with Brett, the man who's cast me into this pit. But for Nick, it's a glimpse of redemption. He's *definitely* happy.

Despite the queasy feeling bubbling inside me, the happiness is contagious.

# brett

Nick and I arrange to meet at his investor friend's office. He's some current or former player at a record label—I can't tell which by the lobby—and I wonder if this is Nick's desperate way of trying to salvage a career in music and seeking favor by hooking this guy up with me. I also feel awkward about it, since Layla and I aren't even speaking, and I can't help but wonder if he has inside information about her and this is all just a ploy to either divulge it to me or get info for her about me.

Turns out it's neither. This is a business meeting through and through. His friend, Wayne Stanhope, is short and pudgy, with shifty eyes that dodge around the room and a receding hairline. I wonder if the tightly pulled ponytail he wears isn't receding it even farther.

"This is Wayne," Nick says. "Wayne, this is my son-in-law."

"Son-in-law?" Wayne says, with profound surprise. "You've been busy."

"Nice to meet you, Wayne," I say, momentarily stunned by the way I was introduced. Prior to now I've never been anyone's son-in-law. Technically I was, but I didn't know the guy, so the wording never came into play. It's kind of cool, the way he's adopted me. And I feel more than a pang of guilt over Layla and the situation with my family. I've been thinking about her a lot during the past few days.

We go over the proposal, and then Nick takes it upon himself to try the prototype. I didn't know he was planning to do this—he just takes one of the sample garments and exits, reappearing moments later with his unbuttoned and untucked shirt, the Wonder Armour sucking him in. His mushy, unshapely body actually seems to benefit from being stuffed into the compression garment. He's not fat by any means, but he's clearly not been doing any sit-ups. If he showed up at a few of my practices I could certainly whip him into shape. I refrain from telling him this. I don't know too many rock stars (or rock-star wannabes, in Nick's case) who live at the gym. Except maybe George Lynch or Henry Rollins, but they're the exception to the rule. Man, are those guys huge.

"Hey, this isn't bad," Nick says.

"I might like to try one on myself," Wayne says, and proceeds to unbutton his shirt and disrobe right there in the office.

Not wanting to give the impression I'm not a team player, I awkwardly hoist off my sweater and start to unbutton my shirt. Soon after, all three of us are dressed in Wonder Armour and stretching about the office. I don't have to imagine what a bizarre scene it is, because Wayne's assistant walks in and stops short when she sees us all standing and maneuvering our bodies to test the fit, and the look on her face says it all.

"What do you think?" Wayne asks.

She looks to each of us for a beat and then deadpans, "If Cirque du Soleil calls, I'll put them right through."

• • •

Nick and I leave together, and we're not three feet out the front door when Nick's cell phone rings. It's Wayne asking him not to show the prototype to anyone else. He's sold. He wants to be an angel investor. I'm stunned by the quick turn of events and ask Nick what *he* wants out of the deal.

"I just want you and Layla to have a good future," he says.

"You know we're separated, right?" I ask. "Headed for divorce?"

"Yep," he says, seemingly undeterred.

"Okay," I say, confused by his generosity but not wanting to seem ungrateful.

# *trish*

Brett shows up at the studio, which is currently housing yours truly and April (of the Foster family holiday picture debacle), who I found and hired in a terrible hurry once Layla said she needed an extended leave of absence after we called and told PETCO our funding fell through. I can't say that I'm happy to see my brother. He looks around at the pictures on the wall. Pictures of Sammy Davis Junior. Pictures of Lou. Various random pictures of other customer pets that were favorites.

He stares for a moment at April. I think he must be trying to figure out where he knows her from, but he can't place it. Lou runs over to greet him, but I stay where I am.

"You know, she really has talent for this," Brett says. He looks at me. "Don't get up, really."

"I won't, limpdick," I reply.

"Limpdick," he repeats. "Charming."

"What are you doing here?" I ask.

"Can't a brother come visit his sister merely to say hello?"

"He can," I say. "But *you* never have, so obviously there's a reason you're here. What is it?"

He shifts his weight from one foot to the other, tries to look past me to see if Layla's here. As if I can't tell what he's doing.

He holds up a mug. I recognize it. He and Layla went to Color Me Mine a long time ago, and she made what is the ugliest mug in the history of all painted pottery.

"I found this," he says, "and I thought Layla might be here. I haven't seen her in a while, and I thought she'd get a kick out of seeing it."

"After seeing you, the only kick she'd get out of it would be throwing it at your head."

"I thought it would make her laugh. And I thought it would be nice to see her."

"Really?" I ask. "Are you seriously going to pull this shit now?"

"What shit?"

"Leave her alone," I say.

"Look, bridge troll," he replies. "I'm not in the mood to answer your three questions to gain passage. Is she here?"

"No, Brett," I say. "She's not. Take your ugly mug and go."

"Okay," he says. "Clearly you're having a bad day. So I'm just gonna ignore that. Do you have any idea when she'll be back?"

"I wish I did," I say.

"What does that mean?" Brett asks.

"She's been gone for almost two weeks," I inform him. "She's working freelance gigs, and I have a stand-in." I toss my head toward the rear, where April is arranging cat toys for the sixth time today.

April's not terrible, but she's not Layla. Although she did manage to behave in a politic, Layla-like way during an episode earlier this week. That celebutante who'd mistakenly been blowing her bowser came back to have her newest pet's photo snapped. She was particularly pleased with her new Norwegian blue. It was a funny little thing, she admitted, but she'd bought the ferret off a *different* dealer than her Maltese, and the dealer had sold her on it after going on and on about its beautiful plumage, which supposedly appears in late fall. (She planned on coming back for more shots then. I didn't discourage her.) April managed to say nothing throughout. She simply gave the "ferret" a few pieces of cheese, got a couple of great shots, and suggested the woman name it Mickey.

She seems to enjoy the work, and she's particularly good with felines.

"That's not possible," Brett says. "You and Layla are partners. She works here."

"No, Brett," I say pointedly. "It's entirely possible. She's totally distanced herself from me, our business, and our family. None of us has seen her, and it's your fault."

Surprisingly, this seems like news to him. "Oh, really?"

Normally I'd say, "No, *O'Reilly,*" as I've done for years, to keep things light. But we've grown far enough apart, Brett and I, that the usual niceties all taste sour. So I don't put them in my mouth anymore. "Yes, Brett," I say. "Really."

"Huh," Brett says, and sits down, clutching the hideous mug for dear life.

"If you ask me, I think she's started seeing someone," I say. I don't think for a minute that it's true, but I'm trying to dig the knife in a little deeper. Because I'm of the strong opinion that he deserves it.

"What?" he asks. "Who?"

"How should I know?" I say. "But maybe she's happy. I hope she is; she deserves it."

"Yeah, she does," he says, seeming unsure.

"Leave her alone, Brett," I say.

"What am I gonna do?" he asks. "Bang on her door and demand that she stop seeing this mystery man? It's not my business."

"Damn straight it's not," I agree.

"Right," he says. "Like you know about straight."

"There's the door," I say. "So you can leave now."

## *brett*

Trish was a jerk, but she was right. I owed it to Layla to leave her alone. So twenty minutes later I find myself banging on Layla's door. I'm not proud of it, but there I am. It starts as a knock, but when I press my ear against the door and hear her laughing, along with someone else—it's a man's laugh—my knock turns to a full-fledged bang.

After what seems like five hours but is probably less than a minute, Layla opens the door. A crack. And peers out.

"Yes?" she says.

"May I come in?" I ask.

"No," she says.

"That's funny."

"I'm not kidding."

"Do you have a guy in there?" I ask.

"I might," she says. "What business is it of yours?"

"It's my house," I say, suddenly indignant.

"Wrong," she replies. "It *was* your house."

"Fine, Layla," I say. "Have fun with your mystery man."

"I will," she says. "Thank you."

And she shuts the door. And I walk around the back of *my* house to let myself in the back door.

"Are you kidding me?" she says, when she spots me tiptoeing in the kitchen.

"No," I say. "I'm not kidding. I have a right to know who is in my house with my wife."

"Unreal," she says. "News flash. It's not your house anymore, and I'm not your wife anymore."

"That's not official yet," I say.

"Well, it can't happen soon enough."

"Do you mean that?" I ask.

"Yes," she says, chin jutted outward, which is a telltale sign that she doesn't mean it. So whoever this clown is, he can't mean that much.

"Who is he?" I ask, and then walk past her into our living room, where I see her father.

"Hello, Brett," he says. "Nice to see you again."

"You, too, Mr. Foxx," I say sheepishly. Then I turn to Layla. "It's your father."

"I'm aware," she replies.

"I didn't know you were in touch."

"We have been for a few weeks now," she admits. "Thanks to you. So now that your curiosity is satisfied, feel free to go."

"Can I speak to you?" I ask. "Alone?"

She just stares at me, expressionless.

"Outside?" I urge.

Layla sighs and leads me into our tiny backyard, where she then turns and waits for me to say whatever I want to say. She's got her arms crossed defensively and looks like I'm inconveniencing her terribly.

"Does it have to be like that?" I ask, trying my best to be charming. And apparently failing.

"Yes," she says. "What do you want?"

What do I want? Jesus, what *do* I want? What did I do this

whole thing for, get started down this whole damn path? I was feeling so taken for granted, and our life had gotten so routine, and then I was so mad about her and Doug, and that "lie" upon which we'd based our marriage—and God, that seems so stupid right now. Like I care what happened so long ago. I was acting like a fucking child, feeling like Layla got to have her cake and eat it, too. I was looking for my own cake. I was seeing temptation around every corner, girls like Heather who are sweet but—not to be mean or anything—really can't compare to Layla and are destined for someone *else* to make them happy. I was wondering what the hell I was doing with my life, wondering why Layla seemed to care about me less, watching us slowly distancing ourselves. I was complaining how she wasn't fighting for me anymore, coming to my games, dressing herself in sexy outfits . . . but what was wonderful about our relationship was that we didn't *have* to do those things out of obligation. Of course she liked it when we were winning, but it got boring after a while, and maybe she felt less needed so she left a game or two early, or even skipped one now and again. Who cares? If we were losing our fiftieth game in a row, and there was no one else in the stands, and it was ten degrees below zero (okay, that never happens in California, but you get the idea) then, in *that* situation, a thirty-ton Mack truck couldn't have dragged her away from the game. And why wasn't *I* supporting *her*? We wanted the same things for the longest time—and still do, I'll swear it. Of course, I just spent three months rebuffing her attempts at fighting to keep me in her life. In fact, I even brought back into her life the very man who caused her the most pain—partly out of spite. Mostly out of spite. Initially. But . . .

"What do I want? *You,*" I say. Why not just get right to the point?

"That's funny," she snaps.

"I'm not kidding," I say. "I want you back."

"Too bad," she says. "I'm dating now."

"Fine—add me to your dance card."

"That's a laugh," she says. "You never dated me to begin with. You wouldn't know how to court a woman if your life depended on it."

"That's such crap," I say, futilely denying the truth. "We dated. I dated you. We did. We . . . dated." Why isn't my brain working?

"We never dated, Brett," she says. And that's all.

Well, okay, she's right that we never dated. Not really. But almost anything can be fixed. Almost. "Fine," I say. "Let's start now."

"Dating?" she asks. "Really?"

"Yes. Really."

"I don't think so," she says.

"You won't go on *one* date with me?" I urge.

"I don't see the point."

"That's okay," I push. "*I* see the point. You don't think I courted you, right? So let me court you."

"This is ridiculous," she says.

"One date," I beg. "That's all I ask."

"If I say yes, will you leave?"

"Yes."

"Then yes," she says.

"Good answer," I reply. "You won't regret it."

"I already do," she says over her shoulder.

## *layla*

Brett picks me up right on time. He brings me daisies: the only flower I've ever really liked. But, while it's a sweet thought, this all seems slightly silly—like we're playing dress-up or acting out some sort of play. Still, I take them and put them in water, and together we walk to the car like we've done a million times before, only now everything's completely different.

"So," he says, as he opens the passenger-side car door to let me in. "I thought we'd hit Katsuya for lunch and then a surprise."

Flowers, opening the car door, sushi—he's rewriting the Brett Foster dating manual cover to cover. (Not that he ever had enough material to write a manual.) Katsuya is my favorite sushi place. He's trying to pick one of *our* places. The only problem is I'm pretty sure I'm not supposed to be eating sushi. Not too big an issue, because half the stuff I love on the menu is cooked. The baked crab roll, for instance. If I could marry a food, I would marry that roll. It's perfection. But how do I navigate around the stuff we usually order that I can no longer eat? Because I'm not telling him the truth about my condition. Not yet. I'm glad I'm not showing.

"Sounds great," I say, as I sit and reflexively open the glove box. I always do. There's never anything new there, yet I always feel compelled to open it.

"So, did I tell you I took a little excursion to Chinatown?" he asks.

"If this story involves a 'happy ending,' I'm gonna advise you not to—"

He cuts me off. "Nice, Layla."

"I try."

"Not *that* Chinatown. A manufacturing district called Little Shanghai."

"Yes?" I prompt.

"I got a prototype made," he says. "Wonder Armour."

I'm floored. "Really?"

"Really!"

"I don't believe you," I say. Because I don't. I'd figured he'd been spending all his time with Corn Pop Girl. I wonder what happened to her.

"I swear," he says. "I'd disrobe right now to show you if I wasn't driving."

I laugh. "You're wearing it right now? Now I *really* don't believe you."

"O ye of little faith," he says, and then changes the subject.

At one point in the car ride, Brett reaches over and grabs my hand. We'd always held hands when we drove together. For some reason this action chokes me up, and I look out the window so he doesn't see. I'm probably just feeling emotional. Hormones. How weird is it that I'm pregnant and Brett doesn't know? I say this in my mind over and over so loud that I wonder if he can hear me. *I'm pregnant.* I can barely wrap my head around that alone, then add in the fact that Brett doesn't know . . . Oh, and we're in the middle of an ugly divorce, yet we're kind of on a first date. It's just all Bizarro World.

When we're seated at Katsuya, Brett starts to unbutton his shirt.

"What are you doing?" I ask.

"I told you!" he says. And he pulls back his shirt to reveal his prototype for Wonder Armour. A sleek black second skin. I'm truly blown away.

"You did it," I say.

"You seem so surprised," he says.

"I am," I admit. "I'm kind of stunned."

"Well," he says. "You said it yourself. It was time for me to get off my ass and actually do something about it instead of just talking. The thing wasn't just going to create itself."

"I'm really proud of you," I say, and I mean it.

"Thanks," he replies. "I even found a source for the funding last week. A hundred grand! Unbelievable luck, interesting story for some other time. But it's all happening."

Suddenly, I'm angry. I'm feeling all of these different emotions, but anger is at the top of the list. Why now? Why is he *now* getting his shit together? Only after we separated. Why couldn't he have done it when we were together? Don't get me wrong, I love that Brett does what he does for a living. But if he has another ambition, and an idea, why did it take my absence to get him to act on it? Why couldn't he get motivated to grow up and do this for us, for our future, for our baby, three years ago? Or three months ago? Why now?

I let it go. I have to. I need to put my feelings aside and take this evidence that he's motivated as a positive sign for the baby's future. He or she will maybe actually have a responsible father, even if the parents aren't together. Brett even—shocker—asks me for help, admitting he can't do his Wonder Armour plan alone. And for a while I eagerly talk about marketing plans with him. There's an excitement in the air as we imagine both of our respective businesses taking off—though his has now skipped over mine in all likelihood, what with the loss of our loan and me pulling out of TLC—and I'm happy for him and he's happy for me, but everything is tinged with regret. And of course there's a sadness about Ginny.

He opens up to me about how frightened he is, and how difficult it is for him to see his mother not be the woman he's always known. To have her ask the same questions he just answered an hour earlier and get irritated if this is brought to her attention. It's a fine line they have to walk with her, and it's not easy. I feel for him and I feel for her, and I feel sheepish for abandoning everyone just as things were getting tough. I offer to be there in any way I can without stepping over any boundaries.

Lunch goes fine. He doesn't even notice that I didn't order a spicy tuna roll. Or any raw fish. On our way out of the restaurant he tells me to use the restroom if I need to, which is slightly odd, but once we get into the car I find out it's because we have a long drive ahead of us.

It's a beautiful drive up the Pacific Coast Highway, where we spend long stretches not speaking at all, just taking in the scenery. This is something we always said we'd do—drive up the coast—yet in all our years together, we never did it.

Turns out we're going to Santa Barbara. This is the surprise. And what he plans to do there is an even bigger surprise.

"There are eight wineries and tasting rooms in warehouses within walking distance of one another downtown," he explains excitedly. "One of them is even in an old tire warehouse."

"We're going wine tasting?" I ask.

"Sure are!" he says.

This is really not good. This is beyond not good. This is awful. The sushi I could navigate around, but wine? I'm not going to drink wine. And how am I going to tell him I'm not going to drink it when I bugged him forever to go wine tasting with me and now he's finally gone and set it all up?

I suppose I can spit. That's what you do, right? You spit. You taste and spit? Swirl, sniff, sip, spit? Isn't that how it goes? But he knows I like a glass of wine. *Oh, this is bad.*

We pull up to the winery, and it's charming and picturesque. I try to separate my anxiety from the beautiful day that he's planned, because he really has gone out of his way to make a nice day for me, but my apprehension keeps creeping back up. I start to panic. I can't do this. I don't even think I should sip and spit. I'm freaking out.

"I don't drink," I blurt out. So much for subtlety.

"What?" Brett says, as he looks at me quizzically. "You drink me, Scott, and my dad under the table."

"Well, you don't know me anymore," I say. "I've changed."

"Really?" he says, with a bemused look on his face. "You've changed."

"That's right," I say. "I'm a whole new woman. A woman who doesn't drink."

"That's odd," he says. "But fine. You don't have to swallow."

We both laugh, as it's our custom to race each other to the punch line: "That's what *he* said."

But then when he hands me a wineglass, I get serious again. And nauseated.

"I really don't think—" I start to say, but the nausea takes over, and it must show all over my face.

"Are you okay?" Brett asks, concerned.

"No," I say. "I told you I quit drinking. The very smell of the wine is making me—"

I can't take it anymore. I grab a spit bucket, turn away, and throw up. A nattily dressed man walking by comments, "I didn't care for the merlot, either." I want to knock his glasses off.

"I'm so sorry, Lay," Brett says, rubbing my back.

"I told you I quit drinking," I say defensively, hoping that my throwing up won't give anything away.

"I didn't really think you were serious."

"Well, I was," I say.

"What can I do, Layla? I just wanted us to have a nice time. To reconnect. How can I make things better?"

"You can't," I say. My emotions are all over the place. "Unless you can invent a time machine and go back in time to undo your leaving me, there's *nothing* you can do."

This just hangs there in the air. Brett looks down at his left sneaker. I stare out the window. We gather our things and drive home without speaking.

The date? Total *fail*.

# *brett*

Dads are supposed to know all about navigating relationships. So I go over to my parents' place to talk to my dad about Layla, what's going on, and how I tried to have a nice date with her but my mere presence made her physically ill.

"If you're going to fix things, you have to first figure out what was broken," he says.

"I know what was broken," I say. I think about my childish focus on myself and yet can't bring myself to say that. Instead I remark, "Everywhere I looked, there was Layla. She'd become so tightly integrated into the family, it's like I almost started to view her more like a sister than a wife." Because she seemed more focused on them than on me.

"Well, she was your wife, not your sister," my dad remarks.

"I know," I snap. "I made a mistake."

"We all knew you were making a mistake."

"Saying 'I told you so' doesn't help. Maybe I should just go talk to Mom. She won't even remember what an asshole I am."

The look on my dad's face tells me I've overstepped. That and the fact that he walks out of the room.

I call Coach Wells and ask him to meet me at our spot: Baby

Blues Barbecue in Venice. I know he won't let me down. And even if he does, I'll still have the ribs.

"Sounds like you missed the signal," Coach Wells says. "You decided to drop back to pass and she was thinking it was a running play. You need to figure out a way to get on the same page with the rest of your team."

"I'm not talking about my team," I say.

"Yes you *are,* moron. That relationship with Layla is the most important team you are ever gonna be on."

He's right. I know that.

He goes on. "So *now* you wanna play in the national championship? You gotta earn your trip. You can't just decide you suddenly want to play in the title game. You don't just waltz into the Super Bowl if and when you feel like it. You gotta go through the play-offs. You gotta *earn* it. You gotta keep fighting."

I shake my head, feeling like earning it is the last thing I can do.

Coach Wells knows me. He puts his arm around me and says, "You know, kiddo, I meant to talk to you about something at the end of the season. Dusty Caldwell came to me. He said he saw how—let me get this straight—'whack' you were looking, and he wondered what was going on. He wanted to assure me that you're one of the best coaches he ever had, and wanted to tell me you stopped him from doing something pretty stupid earlier this year. He didn't elaborate. He also said that he didn't care what our record was this season, next year he's going to break every interception record in the books. And do you know, I think that kid could do it. So do you know what I'm saying?"

I do. I really do. And it's perked me up.

"One more thing," Coach Wells adds. "He says he's done visiting the Crab Shack. I have no idea what that means, and I don't think I want to."

• • •

It's a confusing day when you go to your lesbian sister for relationship advice and tips on how to get a girl back. Not to mention humbling.

"Ouch," I say, as she smacks me upside the head.

"Hold still," she says, and reaches her arm out to do it a second time.

"Are you kidding me?" I say. "Quit!"

"It's too fun," she says. "And deserved."

"Fine, but that's it. No more."

"Idiot."

"I know, okay? I know."

Kimmy walks out of the kitchen and smiles at me. "Trish always said this day would come."

"Really?" I say. "I'm gonna get *I told you so*'s from my sister *and* her girlfriend? Have you even been her girlfriend long enough to have those privileges?"

I smile, so she knows I'm kidding. She smacks me upside the head like Trish did. It catches me off guard.

"Hey!" I shout.

"Yes," Kimmy says, "I qualify. And I'll be sticking around, so get used to it." She shows me an engagement ring around her finger.

Trish beams and wraps her arms around Kimmy's waist from behind. "She's not going anywhere."

It's sweet to see Trish this happy. And rare. If I wasn't so desperate for help—and if I wasn't so sensitive about mistakes and marriage—I'd rub her nose in how in love she is. Because that's what we do.

"Who's gonna be the best woman?" is all I manage. Weak, I know.

"You're gonna have to do something major," Kimmy muses, as we get back to my dilemma.

"What she said," Trish agrees.

"I know." I sigh. "But what? I have no idea where to start."

"What have you tried?" Kimmy asks.

"Lunch," I offer meekly. "At one of our spots. And wine tasting—something she always wanted to do—a beautiful drive up the coast, and then she yaks."

"Pardon?" Trish asks.

"She threw up," I confirm. "Apparently, she quit drinking and—"

"Wait," Trish interrupts. "Who are we talking about here?"

"Layla," I answer, annoyed. It's not like she didn't hear me. Making me repeat it for comic effect is not my idea of a good time.

"I'm gonna let you two talk this one over," Kimmy says. "But I suggest you show Layla what she means to you in an unexpected way. Show her that she comes first, above all else."

Kimmy walks off, leaving Trish and me staring at each other.

"You fucked up, brother," she says. "I don't know what to tell you."

"What can I do?" I ask. "What does she need?"

"A bunch of money would be nice. Oh, and a husband who's not a total idiot," she says.

We sit quietly as this resonates, and suddenly it's crystal clear what I'm going to do.

"You're a genius," I tell Trish.

"I know," she says. "But why are you pointing this out?"

I don't take the time to explain.

# *layla*

Do people always want what they can't have? Is the grass always greener? Am I suddenly on the other side? I don't know, but for more than a week Brett has done at least three things a day—every day—to show me that he's changed, that he's grown up, that he wants me back.

Today it was: a) a song medley that he sang into my voice mail ("It's Been Awhile" by Staind, "We Built This City" by Starship, and "Tonight, You Belong to Me," the odd yet sweet song sung by Steve Martin to Bernadette Peters accompanied by ukulele in *The Jerk*); b) the case of my favorite brand of split pea soup (Andersen's, no bacon) that was delivered to my door—I'm talking thirty-six cans of soup, more soup than I know what to do with—accompanied by a note that read "*Soup*pose we get back together"; and c) a five-line e-mail inspired by the letters of my name:

L – Let's pretend I wasn't such an asshole.
A – Anytime you're ready I'm here. (And I love you.)
Y – You know we belong together.
L – Lucky for me you're a forgiving kind of girl.
A – Although you have two L's and two A's in your name, you only

have one Y. I'll bet nobody has ever pointed this out to you. I see the fact that I was the one to do so as an excellent reason to get back together with me.

He's been relentless. Maybe if he was so enamored with me when we were together we never would have broken up. So every time I start to swoon over his little gestures, I remind myself that he wasn't. That he grew tired of me. That he broke my heart. That he's . . . at my front door?

I hear the knock and see through the window that it's him. He shrugs as if to say, "Yup, it's me."

I open the door and gesture for him to come in.

"We can't be over," he says.

"You did this," I reply.

"I take it back."

"There are no take-backs in divorce."

"Really?" he says, all kinds of cocky. "What about Pam Anderson and Tommy Lee?"

"What about them?"

"They got back together. A bunch of times."

"Are they together now?" I ask.

"Depends on what time it is," he replies with a smile. "Okay, seriously, what about Melanie Griffith and Don Johnson?"

"They divorced."

"Woody Allen and Mia Farrow?"

"They did not get back together, you sicko. He hooked up with her daughter."

"Eminem and Kim."

"Really?" I ask. "He wrote songs about wanting to kill her. Brutal, violent, maiming and killing. The mother of his kid."

"But love prevailed, did it not?"

"Actually, I think not. I don't know. They fall into the Pam-and-Tommy category. Boy, you're really making a strong case here."

"Fair enough," he says. "But we can make it. We need to give it another shot. Things weren't even bad. I was just an idiot."

"I just don't get why now?" I ask. "You had me. I wasn't going anywhere. Why now that I'm suddenly out of your reach am I so interesting to you?"

"It's not because you're out of reach," he says. "It's because . . . I don't know. I know it sounds trite, but it took losing you to realize what I had. What I wanted. What my future was supposed to be. That's *you,* by the way."

"I'm your future?" I ask.

"Pretty much," he suggests. "So if you don't come around, I'm kinda fucked. My life will be like that empty fortune cookie."

I laugh and remember the time several years ago when we were eating Chinese food and after our meals we opened up our fortune cookies to read them aloud to each other, but his was empty. When he asked what it meant if there was no fortune in your fortune cookie, I told him it meant he had no future.

"Remember that?" he asks. "We cracked up."

"I remember."

"I miss you," he says. "I miss us."

"I miss us, too," I say. "But the us I miss was in my mind. Because the you I thought was half of us would never have done what you did."

"It was a mistake, Layla."

"I'll say," I reply. "And if I take you back, when will the next mistake happen? Next month? Next year? Next time the school hires a new SID?"

I find I'm getting angry again. He softens me up, but then I remember how hurt I am and I just want to scream.

"I didn't even . . ." he starts to say. "I mean, we didn't . . . Look, it's not going to happen again. You're my life, Layla. You're my family. And I want us to make a real family. I want kids. With you."

"Well"—the words come out before I can stop them—"you get half your wish."

"Huh?"

"I'm pregnant," I spit out. "Why do you think I'm wearing all this loose clothing these days? Do you really think I stopped drinking wine by choice? So now you *really* won't have to compete with me for your family, because I'll have my own."

Tears well up in his eyes, but I'm not falling for them. I can't. I'm too hurt.

"That's great!" he exclaims, all pride and smiles.

"Yeah," I say. "It is. For me. But you left me. This is *my* baby."

"Our baby," he corrects.

"My belly, my baby," I say.

"You're serious?" he balks.

"As a sonogram."

"That's my baby."

"Wrong," I say.

"Our baby?" he corrects.

"Nope," I counter.

He stiffens.

Just stands there. Silent.

Then he squints his eyes at me. "You want joint custody?" he spouts. "I'll show you joint custody. That baby is half mine!"

"Get out," I say.

"Already on my way," he hisses.

He walks to the door and stops. He turns to look at me. I feel myself jut my chin out and steady myself for whatever he's got, but he changes his mind and walks out—not even closing the door behind him.

I find myself hysterical and oddly wanting to call Nick, whom I still can't bring myself to call my father even though that's what he is. I do call him, and he's at my door within twenty minutes.

"Oh, sweetheart," he says when he sees my ruddy face streaked with mascara and tears. He's making an effort, trying to be there for me. Maybe because I'm pregnant and he sees a second chance. Maybe I'm willing to give him one.

I fall into his arms even though I'm still undecided.

"What happened?" he asks.

"Brett . . ." I say, but I can't get any more words out. I just sob uncontrollably.

About five minutes later, when I've regained some composure and we've relocated to the couch, I tell Nick that I told Brett about the baby and how excited he was. How I saw the elation in his face—not a touch of trepidation—everything I'd have wanted if we were still together. But I lashed out to hurt him like he hurt me. I crushed his spirit right then and there, and hated myself for doing it in the split second that I did.

"He loves you so much," Nick says.

"Well," I say, and again the filter between my brain and mouth seems to be missing, "your version of loving your wife isn't exactly what I was hoping for."

"I deserve that," he says. "But Brett's not me."

"No, he cut and ran *before* we had the kids. As far as he knew."

"Do you know what he said to me when he came to my place?" he asks.

"I have no idea," I say. "I can only imagine. 'Please take this girl off our hands. She's yours. We've had our fill.' "

"No," Nick says firmly. "He respectfully listened to me blather on and on about myself. Excuse after excuse. But then when I shut up long enough to let him get a word in edgewise, I tell ya, his eyes lit up when he talked about you."

"The excitement of getting rid of me, maybe."

"Brett may have acted like he was throwing me in your face as an act of aggression, but that's not what it was. That's not the kid who came to see me. Sure, he couched the presentation in pride and anger and childishness. What was under all that was love."

"Ha," I say.

"You weren't there," he goes on. "He said I was an idiot who'd missed out on watching an amazing girl grow up. A girl who deserved a family. He said, 'Here's this beautiful, brilliant girl that you haven't even bothered to get to know. Meet her. Get to know her. I dare you not to fall in love with her.' "

I feel like my heart is in my throat. Why is everything so freakin' hard?

"That's very sweet," I admit.

"Brett's a good guy," he says. "He messed up. Royally. But at least he's coming around months later instead of years."

"Or never," I add pointedly.

"See?" he smiles, ignoring my barb. "They say girls with daddy issues have broken pickers: They pick the wrong men or, worse, men like their fathers. Good to know your picker wasn't broken."

• • •

With a renewed sense of optimism I stop by the university to surprise Brett and see if he wants to have lunch. Instead of Brett, I find Heather.

"Hi, Layla," she says, all chipper.

I'd never asked Brett what happened with Heather, why they ended things. *If* they ended things, I suppose. I'd like to think they did.

"Hi, Heather," I say back. "Awkward question: Is Brett around?"

"I haven't seen him recently," she says.

*"Recently" meaning what?* I wonder. *Recently, like, a week? An hour?*

"Oh, sorry," I say, not knowing if I should be sorry, not knowing what went down with them, and not wanting to ask, yet desperately wanting to know.

"Don't be," she says. "You had the right idea. Cutting off contact completely. I broke up with him on New Year's and he took it so hard—poor thing. He won't stop calling me, texting me. I mean, have some self-respect, right?"

"Right," I say, suddenly feeling queasy.

"Men," she says, and smiles and shakes her head as if we're both in on the joke.

"Okay," I manage to utter. "Well, sorry to have bothered you."

"Oh, don't be," she says. "Honestly, it's fun to have someone to compare notes with. Although you could have warned me what a loser he was. Girls are supposed to stick together."

Normally, I'd jump down her throat. I'd tell her Brett's not a loser. That he's the best guy I know. But I can't.

He's been calling her? Texting her? Has he been writing her letters spelling out her name?

H – How could I have been so dumb?

E – Every time I think I know what to do about Brett, I'm wrong.

A – Any man who couldn't see right through her whole "Forever 21" thing isn't worth the trouble.

T – They've got some nice stuff there, don't get me wrong. But those awful patent-leather belts in baby blue and lime green, with the braided-rope bracelets and jean jackets with the torn cuffs? C'mon, even the store's *buyer* wasn't serious about *that* trash.

H – Hate is a strong word, yet I think I hate this woman. And Brett, for that matter.

E – Evil. As in: She is evil. And you get a double if you use "extremely evil."

R – Running her over with a car sounds appealing.

## *brett*

My mom doesn't laugh anymore. Or smile, really. At least she doesn't when nobody's looking. I used to catch her smiling as she cooked or made a bed or fed the dog or took out the trash. My mom was a happy person. Now she only smiles if someone's there and she's expected to. And it looks fake and forced. Almost like she's in pain. I'm afraid that she is.

They say it's not a physically painful disease, but it is a disease. And in its base form—the word *disease* splits into *dis* and *ease,* meaning she's not at ease. How can that be comfortable? How can that not be painful? Emotionally, at the very least. So my mom doesn't laugh anymore. As a result, no one feels like saying or doing anything funny anymore.

I want to talk to her about Layla, but I can't. I don't want to burden her with my bullshit or, actually, *try* to burden her with it only to learn eventually that she has no idea what I'm talking about and maybe isn't sure who Layla is, or who I am, for that matter. She's not quite at that point, but it's coming and it's dreadful.

The shocking thing is, Scott is stepping up. He's no longer wallowing in self-pity, and has taken to going on walks with Mom every day. And when she asked recently if they were going to go for a walk just half an hour after they returned, Dad says Scott smiled, told her yes, and put his sneakers back on. So he's becoming less selfish, and both of them are getting their cardio. He's also been spending time with April. Turns out that in addition to being a bit of a photographer, her real talents lie in her imagination—or, rather, her dream of one day writing sci-fi and fantasy fiction. She's got all these ideas that mesh perfectly with Scott's flair for illustrating the fantastical, and the two of them are conceiving a comic book. If it's autobiographical, it's guaranteed to be good for some laughs. *DorkBoy and the Shutterbug.* He swears the sex is phenomenal, but I hope they don't put that in.

I've never felt so helpless in my life. Or so desperate. I wish I could make Mom promise me she'll get better. Promise me she'll live at least another thirty years. Promise me she'll know her grandkids and remember them from day to day. I'm about to give her a grandkid and I can't even tell her. I don't feel right about having good news when everything feels bad. And I don't even know if it *is* good news. Layla's saying it's *her* baby. Like I had nothing to do with it.

I call Tommy Thames, the lawyer Layla brought to that screwy mediation thing, to see what she's really thinking—and because Tim Ning isn't calling me back these days. We set an appointment for the next day, and when I walk in I nearly choke on the smell of smoke in the office. It's like everyone in the world who ever smoked came to this office to exhale.

About fifteen minutes after I complete reading the year-old *People* magazine in the waiting area (amazing how fast celebrity gossip gets stale), Thames pokes his head out and waves me toward him, almost like nobody else is supposed to see him there. "We're moving," he says. "It just got put off."

It's odd, being in his office. But he's odd, from what I recall of my brief dealings with him. I tell him the whole story. Well, I tell him the story from the point where the little mediation left off. I tell him how the whole joint-custody thing didn't work so well and yet how, after all is said and done, I'm desperate to get Layla back—how I'm actively trying to win her back. I tell him how she dropped the baby bomb on me and how not for a second did I think it was bad news. How I thought it felt right. That it was perfect. That it was time. That it was exactly the reason for us to quit the crap and start picking out colors for the baby's room. And how she basically told me to fuck off. That because I screwed up, she was trying to keep me as far away from her womb as possible, and the future taking shape inside it. And then I told Tommy how he fit in. Again.

"Huh," Thames says. "I played along with that mediation—and the rest. Those phone calls from Layla during the whole thing, they sounded more like calls from my kids when they were five and seven and used to fight over who got to drink out of the backyard hose first. I am through," he adds, "with the two of you and your back-and-forth. It's clear you don't hate each other, and neither one of you wants to take the other to the cleaners, so there's really no money in it for me."

"Obviously I don't hate her. I love her," I say. "I'm trying to get her back."

"You two are ridiculous," he says. "And she is my client. Not you. I'm crossing a serious ethical line just talking to you."

"No argument from me. Layla and I are ridiculous. And you are unethical, but back to the business at hand. That baby is half mine. And I have every right to be in its life."

"She wanted joint custody of your family," he says. "You want joint custody of her fetus. . . . What's next? She seeks joint custody of your football team and you want joint custody of her hair appointment?" He sighs and picks up a paperweight shaped like blind justice—though I can see in this version that she's peeking out from under the blindfold. *Clever.*

"Look," Thames continues, "you definitely have legal rights to any child you helped conceive. So does she. You also have the right to sue the supermarket when milk goes bad. But that doesn't mean every damn dispute should land in court. I'm saying this not only because neither of you has money—although mainly for that reason—but also because in this case it's true."

I see his point, but the fact remains that this situation is out of hand and I need his help. So I tell him as much. But he just shakes his head.

"Let's not lose sight of what you really want," he says. "You were trying to win her back before you knew about the baby."

"Right," I say.

"So why are you here?" he asks. "Do you want half of her uterus or half of her heart?"

I stare at this walking anachronism, with his wild hair and wrinkled, stained shirt, sitting among the chaos of his professional life. And it seems to me appearances can sometimes be very dishonest, telling us lies about who really gives a damn about us. It seems to me this man has stopped chasing ambulances for at least a few minutes to actually give a damn about Layla and me, and that makes me grateful, and it makes me listen very carefully to what he's saying.

"If it's the former, you've got a case, but I can't ethically represent you, and I'd rather not get disbarred, so I'll have to refer you to my cousin, who's an exceptional attorney, judging from his grades in law school last year.

"If it's the latter," he says, "you'll have to make the case on your own."

He stands, sending a strong hint that it's time for me to go, but he stops me at the door, puts a hand on my shoulder, and smiles. "My advice? Whenever I faced a hostile judge and jury—and I'm afraid that's what you've got here—I always tell my clients to be as honest and genuine as possible on the witness stand. To show their humanity. If that doesn't work, I start showing up for closing arguments in a chicken costume and try to get my client a mistrial."

The door closes behind me, and I'm half tempted to ask his disinterested secretary if I can borrow the chicken costume.

# ginny

*February 5*

*Dearest Ev,*

*I don't know quite how to get to this so I'll just come out and say it. I'm sick. And it's not a cold or the flu or the chicken pox. Remember when we had the chicken pox? You had them first, and I slept next to you in the top bunk to make sure I got them, too. This is a sickness I wouldn't share with you. I wouldn't wish it on my dear sister—on* anyone. *They have me on medicine. It's called Aricept, and I think it helps, but I'm not the best judge of myself lately. I do notice a difference if I miss a dose, so that says something.*

*I have good days and bad days. We've been through a lot as a family, but Bill has shown me that he truly meant it when he said "forever."*

*The kids are really being wonderful, but I'm still brokenhearted over Brett and Layla, who haven't quite found their way back to each other yet. I'm hoping they do. But now I'm afraid you'll never hear about it if or when it happens, and that's made it all that much harder. Because as much as it pains me, it's time I stop writing you. I'll always miss you, but I'll need all my strength and focus to wage this fight, and where I'm going I don't think you can help me. Bill and my doctors agree. In fact, Bill is insisting I stop writing these letters to you and I don't have it in me to argue right now.*

*You know I've always loved you and looked up to you, and you've helped me get through a lot—more than you could ever imagine. For the next stage of my life, I've got my family.*

*See you in heaven. (I hope not too soon.)*
*Ginny*

# *layla*

Macaroni and cheese. I didn't eat it much as a kid, so it's not like I'm regressing or reaching out to a comforting time. Yet it's all I want. In various forms. Sure, Kraft straight out of the box, cooked as indicated, is the gold standard. But since all I have any interest in is mac and cheese, I have taken to spending countless hours researching new recipes. (I myself have invented at least three, and mac and Jack is currently my favorite—possibly because I just like saying the words. And that's Jack as in cheese, not as in Daniel's.) Anyhow, there's an entire website dedicated to the foodstuff, http://macaroniandcheese.net, where I've found at least a dozen new versions, some of which include: four-cheese macaroni (A+), seven-cheese macaroni casserole (a little busy for my tastes, C–), Mexican mac and cheese (Olé A), spicy mac and cheese (F, spicy isn't fun when you're pregnant), beef and mac (C), chili cheese and mac (A+)—I mean, I could go on and on, but the bottom line is that all I want to do is eat macaroni and cheese, and when I'm not eating it, all I want to do is research new and exciting ways to eat it next. This is possibly a coping mechanism.

I haven't seen Brett since he stormed out of my house. After I told him to leave. After Heather and her breasts told me that she dumped him and that he's been trying to win her back. Why do we say and do the exact opposite of what we want? Because we want to test people? Because we think they're mind readers? Because there's a corkscrew turn somewhere in the connection between our brains and mouths that takes perfectly civil, sensible thoughts and spins them around backward before they come out? Or because we really just love macaroni and cheese?

It sucks. I'm lonely and hormonal and I miss Trish and I don't know how to balance our business with my distancing myself from the family. And my heart aches for Ginny.

And I truly, deep down, want Brett to be a part of this baby's life.

I can't say that to him, though, because I have too much pride. My cupboards are filled with pride, and I am considering building a shed out back where I can store the surplus, because every time I consider opening up to him and the family about what I'm going through, I immediately dump the thought in the trash, ashamed of how foolish and vulnerable I'd look. I'm tired of looking stupid and desperate and vulnerable.

I keep having strange dreams. Once I was swimming in an upside-down pool. I dove in, and the water disappeared and I fell out onto the concrete deck. I tried to get out, but I kept going deeper, sinking into the concrete. Another time, Brett had become a successful investment banker and lived in a luxurious blimp that flew nonstop around the world, hosting dazzling parties. And in another that I've suffered through about eleven times now, I'm screaming and nothing comes out. I wake up trying to scream, and there's a persistent wail but it's only the alarm clock. I'm conscious but completely fogged in.

This time, instead of the alarm clock filling in for my scream and causing further confusion, I hear knocking. I'm disoriented for a second, because I can't place the sound, but then I realize it's not part of the dream at all: There's a strange person at my house.

I peer through the storm door and see a figure I don't know, who may or may not be strange.

"Layla Foster?" the man asks.

Instantly I feel panic. Someone showing up at your door, asking if you're you, is never a good thing—at least from what I've seen on TV and movies, unless there's a big Publishers Clearing House van nearby and the person knocking has a camera crew, balloons, and an oversized check. This person has none of the above. I look for the van anyway. Nothing.

"Yes," I answer.

"This is for you," the person says, and when I open the door, he hands me a piece of paper.

I open it to find it's from my lawyer—or at least a person with the same last name as *my* lawyer—and it's a notice to appear at a new mediation, which I can only imagine is regarding the custody of my unborn child.

*Is. He. Fucking. Kidding?*

I don't know who I want to strangle more, my husband or my ex-lawyer. Is that even ethical? Can his relative even take this case? If it *is* actually allowed, can the Thames family be so unprincipled as to throw their own client under the bus?

The depression that sets in is a new low. It feels almost like the first time I saw Brett with Heather after we split up. I'd known we were technically split up, but I hadn't anticipated him ever actually dating. This feels like that times a hundred. How can he do this?

I call Trish and she doesn't answer. I leave a weepy message that I regret the second I hang up. I call back to leave a second message telling her to disregard the message, and then a third telling her that I stand by everything I said but am sorry for the whining. I consider calling a fourth time just to apologize for being annoying, but I don't want to be a parody of that guy in *Swingers,* and I worry that she'll get a restraining order against me if I make one more call.

She doesn't call back.

Four days later, she still hasn't called back. Trish has never not returned a phone call from me. Trish and I have never even gone four days without talking. Sure, things were stilted after I decided to take a break from our business to let Brett have his family back, but I've never ignored a phone call from her.

I feel ill. As if it wasn't bad enough to lose the only family I had, now I'm potentially losing my baby to a hostile takeover. Isn't there some sort of Gloria Steinem–type nouveau-feminist icon who wants to fight for the rights of me and my unborn child? But do I even want to fight? I'm so tired of it all.

My heart is broken into so many microscopic pieces that it would be impossible for even an experienced and extremely anal paleontologist to put it back together. I'm so dazed and confused, and not in a Richard Linklater, fun indie hit, Ben-Affleck-before-he-was-famous kind of way. No, I'm "dazed," as in not knowing which way is up, and "confused," as in not knowing what I'm going to do next. I get it together long enough to call Tommy Thames to give him a piece of my mind, but he won't come to the phone. The only info I can get from his oddball secretary is that he is planning to attend the mediation with me and that I should "remain calm and not worry so much."

She says those exact words to me, and I feel like there may be some double-dealing going on. If Thames's brother or cousin or whatever is suddenly Brett's lawyer, why is Tommy Thames going to accompany me to the mediation? I have a million questions and feel like I have nobody to ask.

I spend the next eighteen hours in bed. I bring new meaning to the word *wallow*. But then I get past the sad and enter the mad. Furious is more like it. And it's with this new resolve and the anger of a lion protecting her cub that I answer my door to receive Tommy Thames on the morning of the mediation.

"You're wearing that?" he asks, which I find odd, not to mention off-putting and insulting.

"I was planning to," I say, looking down at myself.

It's true. I've looked better. I could have more carefully planned my outfit or put something on that could actually be considered an outfit . . . or showered, for that matter. But I'm too angry to care. The baseball cap will have to do. And I tell Thames as much.

"I'd reconsider," he says.

"Why?" I ask. "Because *he's* going to be there?"

I can't even bring myself to say his name. He's become a pronoun. One said with permanent italics.

"Well, yes," Thames says.

"I don't need to impress him," I say.

"No," he replies. "You don't. But you do want to appear qualified for parenthood."

"What does that mean?" I ask.

"It means you haven't even washed your hair," he replies, unapologetic.

I open my mouth to say something about wrinkled suits, stained shirts, and shar-peis, but nothing comes out. Which is fine, because he's not done talking.

"I'm going to go down the street to the diner and give you a half hour to clean up and make yourself look presentable," he says. And then he turns around and closes the door behind him.

When Thames returns, I have showered and changed into a pretty A-line dress and knee-high boots, and I've pulled my wet hair back into a neat ponytail.

"That's more like it," he says, with a smile. But then a look of concern grows out of his grin. "Are you sure about the ponytail?"

"What is going on?" I snap. "Are you my lawyer or my stylist? And who the hell is representing Brett, and why does he have your last name?"

"Let's go," he says, with a sigh.

In the car, when he's not looking, I take my hair down out of the ponytail and let it air-dry into loose waves.

. . .

When we pull up at the address, I'm confused to realize we're at the Beverly Hilton Hotel.

"What are we doing here?" I ask.

"The mediation is in a hotel conference room," he tells me. "Oftentimes, law offices create an environment of hostility, and the purpose of this mediation is to step outside of the traditional realm and encourage open lines of communication so both parties can come to a mutually agreeable arrangement without litigation."

"We didn't meet at a Hilton last time," I say, but that's silly, because the last time was kind of a joke anyway, and he's tired of my questions and doesn't say anything in response.

I follow Thames to the conference room and stop outside the entrance to take a breath. *Brett is probably behind those doors,* I think, *and I want to be strong.*

"Whenever you're ready," Thames says.

"We could be here awhile," I say. I'm hesitating to enter, and he thinks it's nervousness, and it probably is, partly. But mainly I'm preparing my preemptive strike. If on top of everything else he's done, Brett wants to make a bone of contention out of my baby, he's at least going to know what I think of the whole idea, and the complete disgrace of a human being who hatched the idea. Complete, utter, and total disgrace. This phrase inspires me, I take it as a battle cry, and in the ten seconds or so that I stand there working myself up into a terrible fury, I seize on this assessment of the situation as the right and proper one and commit wholeheartedly to bursting in on him with both barrels blazing.

As I shove the door open I sing out in full voice: "You are a complete, utter, and total dis—!"

I never get it all out, because I'm not prepared for what's on the other side. Brett. Ginny. Bill. Streamers. Trish. Scott. The photographer from Sears. Nick. Brooke. Balloons. Friends from high school. Friends from college. Presents. Smiles. And . . . it's a *baby shower*?

I turn around to say something to Tommy Thames, but he's not there anymore. He's vanished back to wherever such odd angels of smoke and kindness reside.

Brett steps forward. "Surprise," he says, with a soft smile.

Tears start to blur my eyes.

"I'm an idiot," he goes on.

"He is," Scott says.

"Complete, utter, and total," Trish agrees, punching Brett hard on the shoulder.

"Ow," he says.

"But he planned this whole thing," Trish continues, "so we're giving him another shot." She squeezes her brother's shoulder and smiles at him sweetly.

My guard is still slightly up. "What about Heather?" I ask.

"A mistake. It didn't even go very far. I know you probably don't care, but she and I never . . . you know. I couldn't. She wasn't you. No one is. No one ever will be. Anyway, I ended things on New Year's Eve."

"I hear that's a popular night for it," I say without thinking. "*You* ended it, or she ended it?" I kind of have to ask.

"I ended it," he says. "Me. And then she proceeded to prank-call me for the next five hours. I'm not kidding. And now she's talking trash about me around school. Which I don't even mind, because it's just karma coming back to kick me in the ass."

"Well." I sniff. "I'd say something about your terrible taste in women, but—"

"Listen," he says. "I'm going to say one last thing about Heather, and then I promise not to mention her again."

"What?" I ask.

"She was great."

"What? Boy, you are—"

"Listen," Brett cuts me off. "Before I dumped her and she became a bunny-boiler, she was great. Funny. Attractive. Nice. Smart . . ."

"Keep it up," I practically snarl.

"But I still didn't want to be with her. Didn't want to be having dinner with her when I knew I'd rather be having dinner with you. Didn't want to kiss her, and definitely didn't want to sleep with her, even though she was undeniably hot—"

"Okay, I get it," I say.

"The point is that it wasn't Heather. It was me. Or, rather, you and me."

I start to soften again.

*"I love you,"* he says, like it's a confession and he hasn't been to church in a few decades. "I love you, and I love that baby."

Tears are streaming down my face now. I can't stop them.

"I know it's probably early for a baby shower, but we wanted to get a jump on things," he goes on, clearly nervous. "And I'm not assuming anything about us here. I just wanted to do this for you. We did. Your family."

"You didn't call me back," I accuse Trish, taking a napkin discreetly from a table.

"I was protecting us both, because I wouldn't have been able to keep this a secret," she says, with a shrug. "Besides, I knew you'd forgive me. And by the way, Brett here got our loan back on track."

"What, did he go and whack Rex's mother?" I ask.

"No," she replies. "Brett and your father had some angel investor for his underwear."

"Wonder Armour," Brett corrects.

"And they showed him *our* business plan and redirected the funds to Paw Prints," Trish says. "So if and when you're ready to do this, we have the funding to launch the pilot."

I'm kind of amazed. This is a bit of sensory overload. I look around at all of our friends, at Bill and Ginny. At Trish and

Kimmy, who I've desperately wanted to get to know better but haven't been able to with the situation as it's been. Is that an engagement ring on Kimmy's finger? Oh, the Fosters. I've missed them so much. It hasn't even been that long and it feels like an eternity. I look over at Scott, who has his arm around . . . April? The photographer from Sears? What the hell have I missed?

"She makes it all make sense," Scott says to me, and then winks and adds, "She's twisted in all the right ways."

"Layla," Brett says, and he holds out what looks like a contract. For a moment, I recoil. Is he trying to trick me with a shower into giving him joint custody of my baby?

"You've been a member of the family for years," he says. "This just makes it official."

I look down at what he's presenting me and see that the papers have nothing to do with the baby. They're adoption papers? For *me*?

"All you have to do is sign," Brett says.

I'm stunned enough now that the tears stop. It's so overwhelming that I just open my mouth, hoping something intelligible will fall out. But nothing does. I'm stone-cold *stunned*.

"Of course, if you sign those papers," he goes on, "we will officially be brother and sister. And we can't be married or have a romantic relationship again. And that's okay with me if that's what you really want, because all I want to do right now is make you happy. But if you might consider the *other* way you can rejoin our family . . ."

I take a step forward, and he meets me the rest of the way. We connect at the lips and I can feel everyone staring at us, sort of holding their breath, until Trish says, "Ugh, I HATE it when straight couples make out in public," and the whole place erupts in laughter and applause. Tension gone.

"I'm so sorry," Brett says.

"I know," I say.

"I love you," he adds. "We can fix this."

"I want to," I reply.

"We're having a baby," he says, with a smile.

"I know," I say.

"So I'll stop acting like one."

"Promise?"

He kisses me again and I take that to mean *Yes*.

"We love you," I hear Ginny say, and I finally take a moment to look around at everyone there. Ginny and Bill, and just behind them, smiling, too, is my father.

"Nick and I have agreed to joint custody of *you,*" Bill says, and Ginny nudges him.

"I didn't sign those papers," I tease.

"Can I steal you away for a minute?" Brett asks.

Of course the answer is yes.

He takes my hand and walks me outside by the pool to a small garden in the back of the hotel. He points to a large rock that seems to be wedged into the soil, standing up. "Remember when I took you to that graveyard?" he asks.

"You mean with my dad?" I ask. "Of course." My heart is beating a million miles an hour.

"I'm thinking kind of the same thing here. That's my headstone right there. The old me. The stupid me."

I shake my head in disbelief. "Brett—"

"No. Let me finish. What I did . . . it's inexcusable. I made a terrible mistake, and now I realize this me is me without you. The me I never want to know again. I was scared to be a grown-up," he says. "I'm not scared anymore." He kicks some dirt onto the rock and kisses me.

We kiss again and then reenter the party, where I take everyone in. This messed-up, mixed-up collection of misfits and miscreants is my family. They're the most insufferable, maddening, unpredictable, irreplaceable, glorious bunch of yahoos I've ever known. God help me if I ever come close to losing any of them again.

I'm truly happy, and though that's no great accomplishment, you can't believe how strange and lovely it feels. It's been . . . I can't even remember when I last felt weightless, without envy and spite and anger and the whole messy stew of emotions that bubble up inside when you're losing something important to you.

I'll tell you just how happy I am. I actually catch myself singing quietly aloud as my dad picks up his guitar and begins to play "Layla." Brett kisses me and joins in. It's a great song, even though its backstory, about Clapton stealing Pattie Boyd from George Harrison and all, is a little seedy. But was it all Clapton's fault? I mean, a lot of people still think, and a court found, that Harrison stole "My Sweet Lord" from the Chiffons' song "He's So Fine," so maybe he had it coming.

## *brett*

The buzz around campus is that there's a new graduate assistant in the English department and she's smokin' hot. . . .

Okay, kidding. But I just hate happy endings.

## ABOUT THE AUTHOR

CAPRICE CRANE is the author of the novels *Stupid and Contagious* and *Forget About It*—both winners of *Romantic Times* awards. She has written for film and television, including the first season of *90210*, and is currently writing for the television show *Melrose Place*. She divides her time between Los Angeles and New York City and is at work on her fourth novel.

www.capricecrane.com